The DARKEST PARTS of ME

For my boys.

Austin—you are the love of my life. Forever and always.

To my son—I wrote this book so you would know your mama followed her dreams to show you that you can follow yours too.

Authors Note

Trigger warnings: Discussions of suicide and death of a parent.

Contents

PROLOGUE

*H*ome.

Home is all he can think of as he slides on his pressurized helmet. It's been months since he's put it on, and while the fit remains unchanged, he can't say the same for his space suit, which hangs loosely on his limbs, reminding him he's lost more than a few pounds since he last wore it. What once allowed for effortless movement is now more of a hazard than anything.

Powering up the pod, he checks the systems with steady hands. The escape capsule is still fully operational, despite the state of the rest of the ship. A vessel this size is meant to be operated by a crew of at least six. Alone, he has been keeping it functioning to the best of his abilities. A task that has become more difficult with each passing day.

He deemed many systems throughout the ship "not critical," saving only those that will keep him alive for at least a few more weeks. One of those more critical items is the maintenance of the escape pod. The capsule was designed to survive an assortment of disasters, but nothing is ever a guarantee, and he wanted to ensure it was in the best condition should he need it.

This pod can hold two people if needed, but even with the extra space, he still feels claustrophobic as he climbs inside and seals the hatch, hissing as it closes.

The air inside is stale, the thick metal walls are cold and dull, but as he slides into the pilot seat, an overwhelming sense of calm washes over him.

Perhaps that should be credited to his years of training and experience. After spending half his life preparing for all kinds of scenarios, sitting in a pilot seat is second nature for him, but a year on the run has taken a toll, draining him, not only physically, but mentally, too. Trying to remain hopeful, a once simple task, now wears him down piece by piece.

He knows he can never go back to the way things were or who he once was. He's tried to accept his fate—one he hates to think about. He often finds himself mourning the people he'll never see again and the luxuries he took for granted back when he thought he was serving a purpose for the good of all mankind.

It all seems like a lifetime ago.

When his thoughts wander into those dark moments, he wishes he could still be blissfully unaware of the things he now knows, especially because, as things become more bleak, he has accepted he will not survive the vastness of space much longer. Either by starvation or capture, the reality facing him is, soon, he will be dead. And he would rather die by his own hand than at the hand of those traitors who have already murdered millions.

He escaped them once, but there's no way they would let it happen again. If captured, before being put to death, he knows there would be torture—used first as a punishment, and second to gain the information they so desperately want. He would never tell them though, withholding would be the only way he could atone for what he did.

In those first few weeks on the run, he was certain he'd find another survivor, or at least a place to lie low for a while. And yet, he's still running—well, technically, floating, as he shut off the autopilot a couple of weeks ago to keep the ship pressurized and the oxygen flowing. He tries not to think about the fact that he's drifting through an endless abyss with no direction or idea of where he's going.

Asleep in the control room, he's startled awake by an insistent pinging. Blinking away the dreariness, his gaze lands on something he thought he'd never see again.

A planet.

An inhabitable one, he notices from the stats on the screen before him.

He observes the shades of greens and blues making up the surface with peaks, valleys, and oceans. It's similar to his home planet and the inhabited worlds he came across during his exploration of this galaxy. He can only assume he must be somewhere along the outer rim in an unknown solar system. But since he shut off navigation two weeks ago, he can't be sure.

Now, staring at what could be a haven, he prays this will be where he finally finds peace. A place where he can once again feel solid ground beneath his feet, breathe fresh, clean air, and not worry every day may be his last. He dreams of beginning again—finding somewhere to build a new life, and trying to amend all the mistakes he made, perhaps even fixing everything so it won't feel as though it had all been for nothing.

He secures his safety harness, then runs through a well-practiced series of buttons and switches, ensuring the pod will be guided into the gravitational pull of this world that is calling to him like a beacon of hope. Laying his head against the seat, he takes a deep breath, repeating the one word that has given him solace on the days when he had none.

Home.

He's going *home*. With a grin, he presses the pod's release button to venture into the expanse of the unknown, once again.

CHAPTER ONE

Renn

FIVE YEARS LATER

I can still see every single one of their faces. The pure panic flashing in their eyes, the sound of explosions, and the eerie creaking of bending metal. It was complete destruction.

The nightmares make it all too real, and it isn't until the droning sound of my alarm pulls me from sleep that I remember I'm in the comfort of my bed, and those events happened a long time ago, somewhere far, far away from here.

I can't remember the last time I truly slept through the night without dreaming of that horrific day. Some nights are better than others, but it always happens.

Rubbing my eyes, I try to move my legs, but they're trapped under the weight of the forty-pound shepherd dog lying on top of them.

She doesn't move an inch.

One way or another, Shy always finds her way onto my bed sometime in the night, but her presence is more of a comfort than an annoyance. I reach down to pet her fluffy, pointy ears, and she reluctantly stretches her legs then bounds off the bed.

My room is in the cabin's loft with the kitchen, bathroom, and living area on the main floor. It's an open space with windows and large skylights above allowing ample daylight—and moonlight—in.

It's not much, which is the way I like it.

Simple.

I follow Shy down the steps and flick on a few lights to illuminate the darkness, as it's still pitch black outside. She patiently waits by her bowl, her tail wagging wildly as the clanging sound of the food falls into it. I leave her to enjoy breakfast before heading to the back door. Sliding on my boots and grabbing a jacket, I brave the chilly yet comfortable morning air.

I begin every day the same, waking before the sun peeks over the mountain tops, and watching the night sky full of scattered stars slowly fade away as the sunlight gradually takes over the darkness. The back porch of the house is the perfect place to see the sky before the day begins, as there are fewer trees on this side of the house to block the view. It has become a habit to take this time to remind myself how fortunate I am to be here, standing on solid ground, surrounded by clean, unfiltered air, and not forever wandering through the cosmos, or worse, dead.

The last five years have been an adventure, to say the least.

When I took my first step onto this planet's surface, my survival training kicked in without much effort or thought—just one of the many areas I was trained in during my years at the academy's extensive space program. I was merely a child when I was accepted into the academy, but by the time I was twenty-five, I had reached the peak of my career in the space exploration field.

At the time, I never would have thought that six years later, I'd be living as I am—in the quiet and ease of a small town. My previous life was the opposite in almost every way imaginable. My days used to be filled with the unknown in my exploration of the great expanse of this galaxy, but now, my days are routine and unsurprising, something I find myself enjoying.

Here's the thing about space: it has no rules. Space doesn't care what you want to do or where you want to go. It will always find a way to remind you that *it* is in control, and because of that, you have to prepare for anything and everything. Including, but not limited to:

- *How to survive a crash landing.*

- *How to survive if you become abducted.*

- *How to survive if you become stranded.*

Now, I would add one more to the list of these scenarios:

- *How to survive in a world that is not your own.*

While this world is familiar in many ways, it was still foreign, which meant I had the extraordinary task of learning to blend in—and fast. The academy never intended for us to be living long-term on a planet, so this was uncharted territory. While I wasn't trained for a scenario exactly like this one, my skills and tech made it possible. According to my planetary scanner, this world was inhabited by the species commonly known as humans, which wasn't a surprise, and being human myself, it made the endeavor to survive much more achievable.

These are all well-known facts from where I come from, but more than a millennium ago, the simple question of, "Are we alone in the universe?" morphed into a new idea of, "How many of us are out there?"

As people from my planet ventured off into the galaxy, it didn't take long to discover other civilizations existed on numerous planets, and as the discovery of these worlds continued, it made that question harder to answer. Space is endless—infinite—-but it's still in our nature, no matter what planet a person originates from, to be curious and search for answers.

In my personal experience, I'm always astonished at just how similar human beings are to each other, even when separated by billions of miles. Humans *always* carry the same characteristics, and it goes far beyond genetic make-up; it's also behaviors, desires, and needs. All human beings experience the same spectrum of emotions like love, hate, ambition, perseverance, curiosity, desperation.

The only aspect that differed in my encounters with other beings was that my world is far more advanced in technology and knowledge. We are the alphas in this galaxy, so to speak, and because of this, we're the most capable—calling the shots. The problem is, as history tells the story of all humankind, power, more often than not, is wielded for control—something my world learned to abuse tremendously. Humans of my world were not willing to give up that control, and it turned into something menacing, which was partly how I ended up here.

And so the most challenging and personal mission of my life began.

In those first few months, my translator was something I valued more than anything. If I could communicate with humans, I could make everything else work. The translator is a small device that I would place behind my ear, making it almost invisible unless someone knew it was there. Its function was to allow me to interpret whatever languages were spoken in this world and learn them quicker. The more the translator took in the language, the faster it understood.

The plan was simple: I set up a base camp, then went out on short recon trips around my area and gathered what information I could about the culture. In no time, I was able to understand the structure of society, and soon, started making direct contact. Although stressful, high-stakes situations are something I'm familiar with.

Besides, I didn't have a choice. It was either adapt or die.

Once I was comfortable, I sought means to earn money. Then, day by day, month by month, my appearance, the way I spoke and acted, transformed. It wasn't long before I had no need for the translator, as I learned to play the part of a "local" easily.

I established a permanent residence not far from my crash site in a town called Solitude Ridge, nestled in a breathtaking mountain range. In about a year, I went from "the new guy" to an accepted member of the community.

I suppose my training taught me how to do this, too. How to blend in. Study people. I just hadn't realized it until it actually worked.

While I have fully assimilated on this planet, I wish I could say I feel a sense of accomplishment in doing so. I'm a new form of human, but at the end of the day, the fact is, I'm an intruder—a trespasser—and they have no idea, no suspicion, that an otherworldly being, who looks and speaks like they do, is living among them. I'm merely pretending to be a man living his life like any other person on this planet.

I find it strangely coincidental that the name of this town means "to be alone." I've learned everyone has their own reason to yearn for solitude. Some people live busy, stressful lives and want to take time to escape the everyday routine, while others crave the feeling of the wilderness and want to get lost in the beauty of nature.

For me, it's a bit of both. It's why my home is secluded near the woods—a place both in solitude and close to nature.

The jingle of Shy's collar breaks me from my thoughts as she makes her way out onto the deck and sits beside me, waiting for the signal that we can go on our regular morning walk. She's the only living creature on this planet who truly knows me, and unfortunately for her, because she can't talk back, I tend to tell her everything. But she doesn't seem to mind being my personal sounding board.

"We've got a busy day today, girl. I need to go to the auto shop, then head over to Grant's to help him clear some things in his yard," I say, bending to rub her head. "Sound good to you?" Her golden brown eyes blink at me, and I take that as my answer. I rub my hands over her dark fur for a few more seconds. "Let's go." She immediately reacts to my words and happily jumps down the steps of the porch as I follow.

There's a trail that starts from the back of the property and leads to the surrounding woods. It's a few miles long, but we venture down the familiar path as the sky becomes brighter. Warm rays streak through the branches over the trail, and as I peer into the distance, the sun emerges, appearing over the peaks.

The beauty of this place never gets old to me. Maybe it's because I haven't been here long in retrospect, but it's my own personal solitude, allowing me to remember the people who should be where I'm standing now—alive and well.

But they won't ever be, because of me.

I'm here in this wondrous, peaceful corner of the universe, but I don't deserve it. Not one bit.

It isn't fair.

Shy and I walk on for another mile before turning around to go back home.

Home.

The word that guided me here is always in the forefront of my mind. And as much as this place has become a home in every sense of the word, it doesn't change the fact that there will come a day when this life comes to an end.

A day when I will answer for the crimes I've committed.

CHAPTER TWO

Maven

Welcome to Solitude Ridge:

"Where solitude inspires the soul."

The large, wooden sign, which boasts carved mountains followed by the town's motto, welcomes me like an old friend.

I can't believe I'm back.

There was a time when I wasn't sure if I would ever return, not to mention if I *could.*

At first glance, everything looks exactly the same. The same small shops and businesses line Main Street, and the wooden boardwalk that trims the road is still as worn as I remembered. The structures hold the same moody color scheme of navy blues and dark greens from when I last saw them. It's clear that they are well-loved and maintained.

That's something I always loved about the Solitude Ridge locals: their dedication to the town, its appearance, and its people. I've missed them over the years of my absence.

In Solitude Ridge, the people are not just part of the town, they *are* the town.

I slow to a stop at a red light, watching a parade of people cross the road, bags in their hands as they rush from shop to shop—most likely hoping to get a souvenir to commemorate their trip, or gear for camping, hiking, or whatever outdoor activity they came here to do.

Solitude Ridge hosts tourists year round, but the warmer months are the most popular, as it's known for its picturesque hikes leading to insane views. My eyes scan the trees—still full and green, but I spot hints of gold and yellow doting the leaves at this higher elevation. The forest is doing its best to conceal the change of season that will be here before we know it.

My family and I have been coming to Solitude Ridge for as long as I can remember. My parents purchased the land where they built our family's cabin before I was born, and over the years, during breaks from school or on weekends, you could always find us here in our second home.

We come to Solitude Ridge every chance we can.

Or at least we used to.

As the light turns, I urge my car forward, praising my luck that despite the curves and slopes of the mountain roads, the small trailer is still attached to my car. I look to my left and notice that the bike shop has been replaced by what appears to be a coffee shop—which I'm definitely *not* complaining about. The road from here is a series of twists and turns, but I know this road well, having traveled it countless times over the years.

In a way, it feels like only yesterday that I was last here, but in another, it feels as though I haven't *ever* been here.

Five years.

I can't believe it's been *five years*.

I shake my head, trying to remove the thought.

Keep it together, Maven.

I repeat the mantra over and over, refusing to fall apart, especially while driving. What good would that do? We've only been here a couple of minutes, and if I break down now, living here won't be plausible.

I check my rearview mirror, making sure no boxes have fallen out of the flatbed trailer my car is pulling, and to be sure Mom is still following me. She smiles warmly, peering through her windshield. I'm sure she's having the same mix of emotions and thoughts I am—returning to a place we love, excitement about seeing our friends again, but also, the bittersweet memories that remind us of a time when things were different.

Memories that are remnants of a full, but past, life.

So many places in this town hold so many minor, insignificant moments with my dad, but now that he's no longer here, they are possibly the most valuable things I have left of him.

We drive through the outskirts of town, passing neighborhoods and resorts until we start to encounter miles upon miles of private land. The trees are taller and closer together, and the more distance we travel makes it feel as though we've stepped into another world.

I always loved this feeling—the sensation of escaping and entering a world made just for us.

No matter the phase of life I was in, Solitude Ridge was always exactly what I needed it to be. Sometimes, the woods were a place of adventure, and other times, a sanctuary. It was our family's oasis—a place far from the hustle and bustle of life.

After ten miles of nothing but trees and brush, the familiar street sign comes into view: Spruce Road.

I've driven down this dirt road numerous times, but after the last few years, seeing it only in my dreams and memories, the real-life beauty is overwhelming. Large branches hang over the narrow lane like a canopy, almost completely blocking out the sunlight all the way down the long stretch of road.

And then I see it, the gravel stone driveway.

I pull up the drive, my tires crunching against the small rocks, before a break in the thick, evergreen foliage reveals a cabin. A wave of nostalgia washes over me, fast and powerful, and I feel a combination of relief and heartache as I take in the cabin for the first time in years—for the first time since my dad was still alive.

My mom pulls up next to me in the driveway, and I step out of my car gingerly, my legs stiff from the long drive. She exits her car, and without taking our eyes off the cabin, we walk until we both face the front of it, standing side by side. She grabs my hand and squeezes it, but we remain silent for a few minutes, absorbing it all.

The dark blue siding fits the ambiance well, and the immense windows on the front of the A-frame structure seem to be in great shape, while the bright, sunshine-yellow front door is as welcoming as I remembered. The massive spruce trees surround the cabin as if creating a cocoon, providing shelter from the unforgiving sun. Sitting on the expansive front deck are the same whitewashed rocking chairs—as if they've been waiting for us to return.

"Well, here we are," my mom says with a sigh, breaking the silence.

"Here we are," I reply, still observing the cabin that has frequented my dreams.

She tilts her head to me. "Are you sure you're ready for this?"

I honestly don't know, but standing in this spot, looking at years of history, makes me feel like I'm honoring my father in a way.

The cabin itself is an homage to my dad's work as an architect—he designed and built this place himself.

His hands touched every slab of wood.

He hammered every nail.

He designed a place for his family to create happy memories together.

I doubt he ever thought of the grief it would cause his wife and daughter someday.

He etched himself into every corner, leaving us with a constant reminder he was here but he's not really *here* anymore.

But despite all of that, it was time for me to come back, to come to terms with life at Solitude Ridge without my dad in it. Even with him gone, I still love this part of the world. Yes, he's everywhere I look, but this place holds more for me than just memories of him. It holds part of who I used to be, too.

"I shouldn't have waited this long to come back—it's way overdue," I finally reply.

"I know, but . . . everyone heals in their own way."

I turn to face my mom, grabbing her other hand in mine. "I'm ready. I promise."

She smiles, but I see the sadness and worry in her eyes as she tucks a strand of my long, dark hair behind my ear, scanning my round face.

"Are you okay, Mom?"

She turns back to the cabin and smiles wider. "Yeah, I think your dad would be happy that we're here."

I squeeze her hand tighter as I look toward the cabin. "I think you're right."

Hand-in-hand, we walk up the creaky steps to the front door. Mom withdraws her key ring and fishes through it to find the one that hasn't been used in years. It still glides in easily as she turns the lock, the worn handle twisting, and then she softly pushes the door open. Muggy air meets us with the familiar smell of a dark nuttiness that has always lingered in the walls.

The furniture was removed, leaving it bare save for the appliances in the kitchen. The vaulted ceilings are as tall as I remember and are met with natural, dark wood walls and floors.

A set of stairs at the back of the cabin leads to the loft, which was where I slept if I wasn't camped out in front of the fireplace. Continuing our perusal of the main floor, we approach the bedroom in one corner and the bathroom in the other. Like the main area, both are bare but clean. I reach for the light switch near the door and flip it on, but nothing happens.

"Ah, I forgot I asked Grant to shut the power off when they packed everything up," my mom says.

It was too emotionally daunting for either of us to come back here those months following the accident, and I *physically* couldn't—as I was bedridden for so long. My mom didn't dare leave my side, but the cabin couldn't stay as it was forever. After a year of sitting untouched, our friends in town, who are more like family, packed up the cabin and ensured it was secure and cared for until we returned.

"I'll go around back to flip the power on," my mom continues, jutting a thumb over her shoulder. "Mina said some more boxes and furniture are in the storage shed."

I spin on my heel and head through the front door. "Let's get the trailer unloaded. We can go through the shed later," I say flatly.

"Sounds good."

I prop the front door open so we can easily carry things inside, then remove the tarp laid out over the boxes on the trailer while my mom goes to find the power box. The rustling sound of the tarp echoes off the trees, reminding me how truly quiet it is out here.

It's weird how I missed the sound of silence.

Stacking a few of the smaller boxes on top of each other for my first load, I begin the route inside, unload, and head back to grab another. My mom was hesitant at first to let me lift that much weight when we loaded everything onto the trailer back home, but I assured her I would be fine. My back and knees have never been the same since the accident, but I was cleared to go back to normal movements and routines by my doctors a long time ago.

We make quick work of unloading the trailer, and when the last box is placed inside, I sit on the floor, wiping sweat from my forehead as my mom leans against a stack of boxes.

"I say we unpack the rest of the boxes later. Want to go into town?" she asks, giving me a knowing look.

I smile wide. "I was hoping you would say that."

She laughs, reaching out her hands to help me to my feet. We rummage through our bags to find something to change into as our shirts are damp with sweat. I find a pair of denim shorts and a black top, then quickly brush out my hair before twisting it back into a bun on top of my head. My mom changes into a floral blouse and a flowy skirt, leaving her wavy, strawberry-blonde hair loose around her shoulders. We look like complete opposites, which we are in many ways—appearance and personality wise. My mom is bright and upbeat, and I am moody and skeptical.

As we make our way to the car, I can't contain my giddiness. "I can't wait to see everyone!" I say louder than I mean to, but seeing our friends again was a big reason for wanting to return at all. If we didn't have close relationships here, I'm not sure I ever would've even considered it.

"Me too, sweetheart," she says, smiling and turning the engine over. "So, to the bookshop first?"

I give her a bemused look. "Of course! They're expecting us!" I exclaim.

She laughs again, backing out of the driveway. Both of us are beaming, and I realize I can't remember the last time either one of us smiled this way—grinning like we're actually looking forward to something.

If this is the only thing we gain by coming back here, then I say it was worth it.

CHAPTER THREE

Maven

I roll my window down, the fresh mountain air blowing in my face with a comforting crispness that I dearly missed. As the bookshop comes into view, my heart expands, and a smile spreads across my face. The red sign hanging above the door is so worn that it's hard to distinguish what it says, but I know the name well.

Tall Tales Bookshop

Before my mom can put the car into park, I reach for the handle on the door.

"Maven! You're a grown woman, for crying out loud! At least wait for the car to stop moving before you decide to jump out of it!"

Ignoring her pleas, I quickly walk up to the shop, a warm light shining through the old windows, which were probably at one time crystal clear but are now foggy with age. I catch a glimpse of the rows of bookshelves inside and pull open the heavy, wooden door, the bell above the entrance chiming a welcoming tone as the strong, wonderful scent of paper crashes into me. A young woman with beautiful, brown skin, dark hair, and warm, hazel eyes appears from behind a stack of books.

"MAVE! You're back!" she says, throwing her arms wide. She probably calls me "Mave" more than anyone, and I have her labeled as "Tash" in my phone. Simple nicknames, but ones that have always stuck.

"I'm back!" I run toward her and fall into her arms.

"Oh my goodness, Maven! I've missed you so much. I've been waiting all day for you to finally come by. I almost called, but I didn't want to rush you." Tasha gives me a comforting squeeze, and I return the sentiment with all my heart because I've missed her too.

Tasha has been my best friend since I was six years old, but I haven't seen her in person for a couple of years. She came to see me in the hospital—though I wasn't awake to remember—and once I started recovering, we texted and video chatted almost every day, and she came to visit me a few times. Seeing her face-to-face comforts my soul—this visit is long overdue.

"You're here, like *here* here!" Tasha exclaims.

"I know! It's kind of insane—it feels like it's been forever, but it also feels like I was just here, you know?" I reply with a deep exhale, but before I can say more, the charming sound of the bell rings again as my mom enters the shop. In the time it takes me to look back to where Tasha has been standing, she has already run past me to wrap her arms around my mom.

"Tasha! You sweet girl, how are you?"

"I'm great, Tova, even better now that my favorite people are back in town."

"We're happy to be back. Right, Mave?"

They both look at me, waiting for my response. I know they mean well, and this is probably just their way of gauging how I'm doing, but I'm not entirely sure how I feel. Luckily, I've had years of faking my way through these attempts at inquiring about my mental state. Although, it's been a process uncovering how many questions have underlying intentions.

When people ask me, *"How are you?"* they really mean, *"How have you been since the accident?"*

Or, *"What have you been up to?"* means they want to know how well I've adjusted.

Most of the time, I let it roll off me without a second thought, but there are some occurrences when the true answers to those inquiries linger in my mind. I wish people would let me handle it in my own time instead of trying to pry answers out of me like my feelings are in a locked box that has no key.

I wish I could say that *now*, but I think better of it. I don't want to add on to this already emotional day.

"Very," I say with a smile.

And it's true, I am happy, but that word seems so basic compared to all the feelings flowing through me now. Because honestly, I'm feeling a lot more than simply joy, but labeling it as happiness is enough.

I wasn't expecting everything to magically fall into place. I want to take it one day at a time, and right now, my best friend and I are standing side by side, and that is all that matters to me.

There's a sound from the set of stairs toward the back, and I already know who's making their way down the creaky steps from the apartment above the shop. The distinct sound is something I have heard countless times over the years. Tasha's mom, Mina, rarely had anything but a bright, sunny smile on her face, and as she comes into view, it looks like that hasn't changed an iota as my mom and I meet her at the bottom of the stairs. Tasha is my best friend, and Mina is my mom's.

"I thought I heard you two. Come here!" Mina pulls us into a tight hug, squishing the three of us together. As we break apart, she asks, "Have you two already been up to the cabin?"

I look to my mom to answer. "We have. We actually just came from there. Thank you again for taking care of everything, Mina. It's made everything manageable."

Mina smiles warmly, taking hold of my mom's arm. "Of course! Happy to help, but it wasn't just me; a lot of us pitched in, so it was no trouble at all."

The four of us chat for a few minutes about trivial things, like how the weather was on the drive up, but I can tell Tasha is as anxious as I am to go out to dinner like we've been planning for weeks.

Unable to wait any longer, Tasha interrupts. "I say we let you two catch up. Maven and I have other plans." Tasha winks at me.

"You mean you don't want to sit and talk with two middle-aged women all night?" Mina replies with a smirk.

"No offense, Mom, but yeah."

"Oh, Tash!" she says, swatting at her as we make our way to the door, laughing.

"I'll see you later, Mom," I say over my shoulder.

"Have fun! See you later. Remember not to stay out too late, we have a lot to do tomorrow." Her light, sing-song voice carries through the store as we exit the shop, and when I look through the window as we pass, my mom and Mina are already in a deep conversation, both of them smiling and giddy. I hear my mom laugh before the door completely closes, and I'm comforted that my mom is relishing the time with her best friend just as much as I am.

I haven't seen her smile as much as she has today in a very long time.

Tasha and I are linked arm in arm as we make our way through town.

"Does The Blue Bird sound okay?" Tash asks, squeezing my forearm.

"Is that even a question? I've been thinking about their scones all day. I've missed them so much," I say, beaming. Just talking about them makes my mouth water.

As we make the short trek from the bookshop to The Blue Bird, we weave in and out of people on the sidewalk—a couple of them I recognize, but most are tourists. Unfortunately, the ones I make eye contact with notice me too, and they quickly turn a grave face into a smile, offering a sad nod—a look of pity flashing across their faces.

I'm prepared for these reactions.

Sort of.

One of the downsides of Solitude Ridge being a small town—and there are few—is that it means everyone knows the details about your life that most neighbors in large areas or cities normally wouldn't. I'm not surprised that people remember the accident because it was significant for our community, and I watch the recollection on their faces as if it were yesterday.

But for me, it feels like a lifetime ago.

I try to push aside the grief of recalling the countless trips here over the years, and try my best to focus on the fact that they were good times as we step inside The Blue Bird, the warm, bright-blue lights imitating the restaurant's sign. The interior hasn't changed a bit, with its cozy style—but I don't recognize the people working. While the staff has always been mostly made up of the local teenagers, I look for familiar faces, but see none. Or maybe I do know them but they've changed so much in the last five years I don't recognize them.

We take our seats in the familiar, bright-blue laminate, upholstered booths, and a young girl wearing the staple blue-and-white striped button-up shirt and white apron takes our orders.

The Blue Bird is known for good food, but the scones are the main pull. Each is perfectly baked to create a rich, buttery texture—crisp on the outside and soft in the middle—covered in powdered sugar, and served with a side of sweet icing to drip over the top. Tasha always dumps her entire cup of icing over her scone, while I like a little drizzle. Not too sweet; just the perfect amount to balance the flavors.

"So, tell me everything! Please don't leave anything out," I say once our food arrives.

"Hmm, where do I even begin?" she asks, folding her arms in front of herself and resting them on the table. "Well, Kaden and Trista broke up about twenty times since you were last here, but they got married about a year ago, if you can believe it."

"I *don't* believe it, actually," I say with a chuckle. They were the last couple I'd ever thought would settle down together. "Tell me more!" I urge, loving how Tasha's personality shines when spilling gossip. I've missed her bright positivity and enthusiasm.

For the next hour, Tasha fills me in on all the town drama as we indulge ourselves with the deliciousness of the battered and fried perfection. I spend most of the time laughing, as Tasha's highly entertaining exuberance fuses into everything she says.

"Oh! And we have a legit coffee shop now with *fancy* drinks, desserts, and everything," she goes on eagerly.

"I saw that when we pulled in. I love it!"

Baked goods and coffee are my weaknesses.

"Yeah, a retired couple bought the space about a year ago, and it's been a big hit with the town and tourists."

"That's great!"

Tash stops for a moment, pursing her lips and giving me a knowing look. "So . . ."

"So . . ." I mimic.

"How are you *really* feeling about being back?"

Tasha might be the only person in my life who gives it to me straight and asks me to do the same. She doesn't dance around tough subjects, and it's refreshing most of the time, but definitely not now.

"Honestly," I say, pausing for a few more seconds, "I don't know yet."

She studies my face. "Was it hard seeing the cabin again?"

I nod. "But it also made me happy. It's all just weird."

Tasha hums in agreement. "I have to say, seeing you walk into the shop today was like witnessing a miracle." Her eyes appear glassy, like she might cry, but she keeps it in. I coyly smile, not ready to go there—not even with her.

"Yeah, I guess in a way it was."

"And what about work?"

"Everything went smoothly, actually. As soon as I made the request, it was just some paperwork to fill out and I was good to go. Turns out, taking a sabbatical was a lot easier than I thought."

Tasha nods along. "That's amazing."

I shrug. "It's my dad's company, so I doubt they could have said no."

Tasha looks a little lost on what to say next. Instead, she takes my hand from across the table. "I'm proud of you, Maven, and in case it wasn't already obvious enough, I'm so happy you are back."

With both my hands now holding hers, I say, "Me too, and thank you." We hold on to each other for a little longer until I change the subject.

"Anyway. What do you have going on tomorrow?"

Tasha huffs dramatically. "Inventory day."

"What does that entail, exactly?" I wonder, picking up the last bit of scone left on my plate.

"It's terrible! We have to go through every single book in the shop to check it for damage, clean off the shelves, and scan them into the new system to catalog. All the books we don't keep, we're donating." She releases a long breath.

I don't admit it, but I'm dreading my day tomorrow too. My mom and I agreed to go through everything that had been packed away, but so much of it was my dad's . . .

"What if I come and help you?" I ask, hoping to put off the anguish for a bit longer.

Tasha perks up. "You want to help at the shop? Don't you have a bunch of unpacking to do?"

She's right, but I don't want to think about it. Not yet. It was enough for me just to see the cabin again, and I have no motivation to dive into the past all at once. I have time. It isn't going anywhere.

"Truthfully, I think it might be good for my mom to look over my dad's things alone first. I'm sure there are more items she'll want to keep than I will, so it might be good to give her some space."

Tasha contemplates my answer for a moment, but she looks convinced. "Okay. I mean, it would be amazing if you did. It could actually be fun if it was the two of us."

"Well then, count me in!" I say enthusiastically.

"Okay, but fair warning, we need to start early to get as much done as we can before the weekend."

I shake my head. "I don't mind. Like you said, it will be fun."

Tash looks pleased, and I'm glad she doesn't push further on the fact that I'm clearly avoiding going through my dad's stuff.

"In that case, we better head back so we can get up bright and early," she says, scooting out of the booth, and I follow.

"Sounds perfect."

The mountain air kisses us in a cool, crisp breeze as we return to the bookshop. Strings of lights adorn every lamppost, creating a tapestry of a dream-like ambiance through the streets.

I've always loved the way the town feels in the evenings. The low sunset rays behind the tall evergreen trees shadow them in black as they are silhouetted against the twilight sky. The bookshop is closed for customers, but there's still light streaming from the windows as we walk inside. My mom and Mina must have moved their conversation to the upstairs apartment where Tasha and her mother live. We're quiet as we make our way up, but before we reach the door leading to the apartment, I pause when I hear my mother's voice drifting toward us on the other side. The door is slightly ajar, and Tasha reaches for the handle, but I softly grab her hand before she touches it. My mom is speaking in a low, serious tone, but I can hear her words clearly.

"I was shocked when she suggested it. Visiting is one thing, *living* here is another. I'm trying to be supportive, but . . ."

"But what?" Mina asks in the same low tenor, like they are unconsciously trying to whisper.

"She *still* never talks about it. She's been so focused on getting well and her career that she hasn't made room in her mind to mourn him. Not really."

Tasha shoots me a concerned look, but I ignore it, leaning closer to the door.

"Maybe living here will help her do that. With so many memories of him, living in the cabin, how could she not?" Mina asks.

There's silence for a few seconds, and I think about opening the door, but then my mom speaks again.

"I thought so too at first. She loves this place so much, but I worry she will focus on everything else—like making trips to the bookshop, the coffee shop, anything to distract her—so she can ignore everything that reminds her of Marc. She's still running away from that day, and I fear it will only lead her to face more down the road. I'm not sure if she's ready for it."

I knock on the door, pushing it open abruptly. "We're back!"

Both women are sitting at the island in the small kitchen, and they jump as I barrel in.

"Hey, girls!" my mom says a little too loudly, and I pretend Tasha and I weren't just eavesdropping on their conversation.

"Did you guys have a good time catching up?" I quickly ask.

"Of course we did," Mina replies, grabbing my mom's hand.

Tasha keeps giving me side glances, and I shoot her a "we'll talk about it later" look.

"So, Mave, were the scones just as good as you remembered?" Mina asks.

"Oh, absolutely! There's nothing like them anywhere," I say.

"Did you tell her about the coffee shop?" Mina asks Tasha.

"Of course I did. They will be pleased to know their best customer has now arrived," she says, blowing her lips.

"I'm already planning on getting a coffee there tomorrow," I add, not attempting to refute that comment because she's probably right.

"Speaking of tomorrow, we better get going. Still lots to do at the cabin," my mom says, standing, and I catch the worried glance Mina gives her before we head for the door.

On our drive back, my mom asks about Tasha and our night. I share some of the gossip, and then I ask her, "What did you and Mina talk about?" I try to sound as subtle as possible, wondering if she will actually tell me what I overheard, but I'm not at all surprised when she says, "Oh, just mom talk," shaking her head like it was nothing major, and I leave it at that, knowing better than to pry further.

We remain silent the rest of the way home, but my mind is anything but quiet. I knew my mom had reservations about me coming back to Solitude Ridge. I mean, who wouldn't after what happened here? But I didn't know her concerns for me ran so deep that she doubted my capability to *succeed* here. But the biggest problem isn't if I believe her, it's that she knows me better than anyone, and I hate that she's worried. It makes me think maybe I haven't been playing it off as well as I thought. Her words keep echoing over and over in my mind.

"She's still running away from that day, and I fear it will only lead her to face more down the road. I'm not sure if she's ready for it."

The truth is, she's right. I am running away.

And I fear that maybe the thing I'm running away from is something that, no matter what I do or where I go, I will never escape.

CHAPTER FOUR

Renn

Shy and I leave Grant's house and head back into town to run a couple of errands. I worked all day, then went straight to Grants, and I stayed longer than I'd planned, but I don't mind. With Grant getting on in years, small tasks that need to get done around the house add up. So, in addition to clearing some fallen tree branches in his yard, I also changed a few burnt-out lights and cleaned up a little around his house.

Grant was one of the first people I met in town, and he hired me for small jobs like repairing siding, roofs, painting, pretty much anything he could think of, which helped me get a foothold here. So I do all I can to return the favor when I check in as often as I'm able to.

"We need a few things from the grocery store," I say to Shy. She has her head hanging out the window, tongue dangling out of the side of her mouth. "I promise we'll go on a walk before it gets dark." There are still a few hours until sundown.

The drive into town is something I do almost every day—either for work at the local auto repair shop, to help the townspeople with odd jobs, or to find something else to keep me busy. It makes me chuckle because, originally, I tried keeping a low profile. I stayed away from other people and only went into town when I needed something, but the completely isolated life didn't pan out. A year in deep space with only myself in the darkness and stillness had changed me, and I couldn't live like that again. When I was alone, it was easy for those deep, dark thoughts in my mind to slowly creep in—I wasn't sure I'd be able to survive it if I had to do it again.

After a few months of working odd jobs around town, I purchased my cabin from an elderly couple who moved to be closer to the city, and things worked out better than I could have ever hoped. Solitude Ridge gives me the balance that I need. I enjoy staying busy, and even though my day-to-day is wildly different with the association, I try to fill my life with purpose, while still having time at the end of the day to remove myself from the world.

It's been years, but every time I pull up to The Peak Pantry—"The Peak" to locals—my stomach gets a nervous jolt, remembering the first time I stepped into the store and made real contact with a human here. It didn't take a lot of investigating to figure out where to get food, and I needed sustenance desperately. The added bonus was that it was the perfect place to observe the humans on this planet. The Peak is the only grocery store in town, making it a focal point for the locals, so I can always count on spending a few extra minutes talking to a neighbor or two whenever I stop in.

I hop out of my truck, keeping the window rolled down for Shy. She lazily leans her head out the window to watch me, and as soon as I enter the store, I hear, "Renn! I was hoping you would stop by today!" as a middle-aged woman with bright red hair waves me over.

"What's up, Val?"

She beams in response. Valery and her husband, Drew, have owned the store for over twenty years. I don't think she cares much about selling goods, but rather, the gossip going around town. She is the town's unofficial news source, I've learned, and if you want to know something, or need word to spread fast, just tell Valery, and she'll make it happen.

"Do you have any plans tomorrow?"

"Well, that depends," I say with a smirk, leaning on the counter she stands behind. "Who's asking?" She smiles wider—Valery is feisty, so I like giving her a hard time.

"Mina is doing some cleanup at the bookstore. She mentioned she might need some help getting rid of a few boxes of old books."

I nod. "I see." I pretend to think about it for a second or two, but she and I already know my answer. "I'll stop by tomorrow and see what I can do," I say, winking.

Val gives an amused chuckle. "That's what I thought you'd say. You're a good one, you know," she says, patting my arm. She makes this comment almost every time I speak with her, and every time I hear it, I can't help but think, *If you only knew who I really was—what I really was—I doubt you would still feel that way.*

I spent so much time believing I was "the good guy" and that I was accomplishing an agenda for the greater good, when it had been a lie all along. However, my life now is as much of a lie as it was six years ago, the only difference being, now, I have control of it. It's just me—my choices, my actions, and whatever consequences have yet to be revealed to me. In a way, I think that's what motivates me to help those around me in the way I do. It's not for attention or praise, but proof that my pure intentions are actually bringing about good. This way, I can see all possible outcomes of my actions before me, and I can try every day to move on from my past transgressions—try to throw away the evidence of a false life. But there will always be those memories engraved in my mind. I hate returning to that past life every day like I do, but my training taught me vital abilities that make me useful to the community here. Mending things, medical aid, problem-solving . . . to name a few of the myriad of skills I was conditioned to perfect and carry out on command. In the end, I hope whatever I leave behind from my invasion of this planet will be something worth remembering.

"I try to be," I say, stopping my thoughts from wandering too far. Val pats my arm again. "I just need a couple of things, then I'll be on my way," I add.

As I turn toward the aisles, she calls out, "And handsome, too. Have I ever mentioned how handsome you are?" Her face turns smug, waiting for my response, because I already have a smart remark for Val.

"Well, I don't have to try in that area, but thanks for mentioning it," I say, disappearing down an aisle, but not before I give her another wink.

As promised, Shy and I went on a quick walk when we got home. On days when we have more time, we hike up to my crash site. It's about a six-mile journey from my cabin, so it takes us most of the day. Escape pods are programmed to "land" in remote areas so that they go unnoticed by unsuspecting inhabitants. And while I lived at that site for several months, there's now no evidence anything extraterrestrial happened at that spot deep in the forest. But even though all proof has been dissolved away by the liquid termite that the association stowed in my crash kit, I feel compelled to go back to that place from time to time.

Tonight, the first thing I do when we return is thoroughly wash my calloused hands of the excess grease and grime that comes with fixing vehicles. Working at the auto shop is my only steady income, but I don't need much, and I like the work. When I was at the academy, there were various programs and career opportunities I could have pursued further, and mechanics was something I seriously considered, but I was guided into other endeavors.

I climb the steps to my bedroom, kneeling to withdraw a large, metal box I store under my bed. Wildly out of place with the rest of the house, its cold, shiny exterior is truly alien compared to the green life surrounding it. I lay the box on the bed and open it with my thumbprint—the only way to unlock it. It scans the indents of my skin before the lid slowly rises. The box holds more than one function: it stores items, of course, but also acts as a console with a screen and touch pad that can be used for intergalactic communications. Housed inside are remnants of my crash kit and a few personal items. I have a tin full of a healing elixir that can cure wounds and broken bones within seconds simply by rubbing it onto the affected area. I've only had to use the ointment twice since landing here, sparing it in case there's a major emergency someday. I also have a BioXscanner, a device that can detect internal damage and ailments that may otherwise go undetected, and then a stellar atlas. I briefly opened it once, just to make an estimate of where I was in this vast galaxy, but when the map of stars appeared before me, I realized I didn't want to know. All that mattered was I was far, far away. Underneath the atlas is a small photon gun—which I've never touched—what is left of the liquid termite, and the translator, which no longer seems useful but I kept anyway.

However, the last item stored within the box is what I retrieve daily—the photon drive. The thin device is small enough to fit in my palm as I slide it into the slot on the side of the box, watching as the screen inside turns on automatically. I tap the screen a couple of times to get it set up.

I always check to see if the transmitter has detected any incoming signals, but just like every time before, there's nothing. The same four words appear on the screen:

Zero incoming transmissions received.

I usually transmit my signal for a good twenty minutes before shutting it off. Initially, I switched it on a few times a day, especially during the first year after I arrived here, but now, I get around to it once a week, give or take. Programmed into the transmitter is a homing device, and it's the last scrap of my previous life, giving me hope of making contact beyond this planet's realm . . . or with the person who gave it to me. The moment he placed the drive in my hands was also the last time I saw Nate, my best friend.

I can still hear his voice as clearly as if I were standing before him once more.

"The drive holds a signal that can only be traced by me. Turn it on as much as you can, and I will try to find you. Get far, far away from here, and don't look back."

So much more could have been said in that chaotic moment, but we were out of time. Every day, I wish I could have told Nate how grateful I was for his friendship, but at the end of it all, I think he knew, even if I never said it out loud.

I press the button to begin the transmission. The incessant beeping echoes from loud to soft, indicating the beacon is working. Then I head downstairs to get Shy her dinner. The chirp from the transmitter can be heard even as I enter the kitchen. Its eerie tone drifts through the house, but the sound is so familiar to us that Shy doesn't seem to mind as she spreads out on the couch, patiently waiting for her food.

"Do you truly like me? Or do you just use me to take you on walks and serve you food?" I say, and she lifts her head slightly. "Yeah, I thought so."

I pull out the dog food, and she trots over, tail wagging happily and huffing at me almost as if saying, "Took you long enough."

Replacing the bag in the cupboard, I take a moment to watch Shy devour her meal. I smile, grateful to have found her. Her previous owner left her in a small, cardboard box near the roadway one day, not long after I arrived here. Shy had clearly been abandoned, and it angered me that someone thought leaving a puppy at the mercy of the elements was a good idea—completely helpless to the weather and wild creatures of the forest.

Training her was easy; she's smart, but also needy, which is why I love her, to be honest.

Feeling my gaze, Shy glances at me, and I swear her eyes roll in annoyance. "Fine," I say, raising my hands in surrender. "I'll leave you to it." With that, I return to the bedroom to check the transmitter. I already know what I'll find, but I confirm the results anyway.

Signal transmitted.

No targets detected.

Every time those words appear, it only verifies time and again that my worst fears are most likely true. I set the photon drive back into the box and slide it under the bed before I plop down on top, putting my hands behind my head as I stare out the skylights above my bed. I play my day over in my mind, recalling the things I said and did—a mental checklist of sorts—making sure nothing slipped or could be seen as suspicious. For years, the only thing on my mind was the next task at hand, whether it was learning more about the people here, the planet, or finding means to live. But now, everything is settled. Finished. This *is* my life. No one is looking for me, or at least hopefully not my enemies. There's no one left to fool, nothing else to overcome. But what's surprising is that I still, even after all these years, can't shake the overwhelming sense that this is exactly what I was searching for all along in my travels in space.

Or maybe I was so close to death that it was the only thing left to hope for.

I feel the weight of the box sitting under my bed, and for a moment, I wonder what would happen if I never opened it again. What if I truly leave it all behind? Every day that passes, the chances of being discovered dwindle immensely.

Shy jumps onto the bed, startling me from my thoughts, and places her head on my stomach.

"I guess you do like me, and not just because of the food, huh?" She keeps her eyes closed, satisfied as I scratch her ears while I contemplate everything I think I know for what feels like the millionth time.

CHAPTER FIVE

Maven

I meet Tasha bright and early at the bookshop where she already has a lovely cup of hot coffee from the new Summit Coffee House waiting for me.

"You're the best," I say, taking a long sip and letting it sink all the way into my bones.

"Did you really think I wouldn't have a coffee ready for you? You're not much of a morning person, and besides, I know how you like it by heart," she remarks through a yawn.

"You know me too well and thank you."

We both have our hair pulled up and are wearing comfortable clothing—not bothering to put much effort into our appearance for the task we have ahead of us. There's really no need, especially since we won't be interacting with customers, just the hundreds of volumes waiting to be cataloged. We sit and drink our coffee for a few minutes, waiting for the caffeine to kick in before starting our task. The bookshop is so serene in these early morning hours that it only contributes to my sleepiness as the scent of the coffee and books mix together, creating a perfect aroma of coziness, just like it always has.

Since Tall Tales has been in Tasha's family for ages, I spent many playdates here as a child, and when I was older, Tasha and I would browse and read all the books we possibly could, drinking in words and leaving our young minds full of wonder. It never got old, and it still hasn't.

I waited until we got home last night to divulge my plans with Tasha, in case my mom was annoyed and didn't want to talk about it. She seemed a little irritated at first, but when I pitched her the idea that she may need some alone time to look over Dad's belongings, she changed her mood. For a moment, I thought she'd bring up what I'd heard her talking to Mina about, but her only reply was, "That sounds great, honey. I'm sure Tasha will love having company, and it will give you more time to catch up."

Eventually, Tasha rises from her chair, the creaking wood bringing me back to the task at hand, and I watch as she lazily makes her way to the counter where a pile of cleaning supplies are stacked.

"So, I was thinking we could start from the back and work our way across. You start on one end of the bookcase, and I'll start at the other until we meet in the middle, then we can move on to the next row," she recites with practiced orders.

Tasha had been doing this longer than me, so who am I to argue with her tactics.

I nod, absently surveying the shop. There are about thirty rows nestled in the tight space, and each bookcase is at least ten shelves high, their length as wide as the shop. I have no idea how long this will take us, but now that the caffeine has kicked in, I feel alive. I stand, stretching my arms above my head.

"Let's do it."

Tasha instructs me to thoroughly check each and every book, remove it from the shelf, flip through the pages, and check for any damage. For all the leather-bound books, I need to wipe them down with a cloth and apply a protectant so the leather remains in good condition. Most of the books are in excellent shape, no surprise there, the shop and books are in good hands. In the first half hour, we seem to be moving at a good pace, and thankfully, she doesn't bring up our mom's conversation we overheard the night before. I start to think that we'll be done in a couple of hours, but then I make the mistake of reading the books I pick up, and before I know where the time has gone, it's taken me a good five to ten minutes to "check" each book before placing it back on the shelf or into a donation box.

"Are you helping, or just reading?" Tasha teases.

"Both."

"We're going to be here all day!"

I chuckle in response. The rest of the morning is filled with laughter and reading, and I truly can't think of anywhere else I'd rather be, or anything else I'd rather be doing.

At some point, Mina calls us upstairs for lunch, and as we eat, I realize how grateful I am to be sitting here, talking with two of my favorite people in the world. For so long, I wondered if I would ever have the chance to live a normal life again, and I am lucky to say that, for the most part, I am.

We haven't been back to the book inventory for very long when the bell chimes, announcing someone has entered the shop. I don't really think much of it until I hear a man speaking in a deep voice and Mina's peppy tone responding to whatever they are saying. I go back to the books but pause again when I hear a boisterous laugh. I can't explain it, but I want to see the face behind that beautiful sound. It feels familiar somehow, even though I know I've never heard it before. Weaving my way through the rows, I find a spot where I can peek through the shelves to clearly see the checkout counter yet remain hidden.

The first thing I notice are muscled forearms leaning against the counter. I shift, standing on my tippy toes to see his face, and when I do, I can't help the wave of heat that travels through my body. The man talking with Mina has dark-blond hair, cut short on the sides and longer on top. There's stubble on his face, showcasing the strong angle of his jaw, and despite the distance, I can tell he has green eyes.

"What are you doing?" Tasha's sudden appearance makes me jump so hard that I knock a few books off the shelves.

"You scared me!" I whisper loudly, clutching my chest as my heart beats wildly. I don't even try to pretend that she hasn't caught me spying. "Who is that?" I ask in a whisper, motioning toward the front of the shop. Tasha walks to where I was standing to check, and when she turns to face me, her smile is positively wicked.

"That, my friend, is another thing that happened while you were away."

I shake my head. "What do you mean?"

Tasha covers her mouth to stifle her giggles, only making me more confused. "The look on your face is priceless." She snickers as I roll my eyes. "You're not the only one who responds that way the first time they see Renn."

I turn back to the shelf to peek through again.

Renn. I replay his name in my mind. It's different, but not too unusual. Simple. I decide I like the name, probably because of who it's attached to, but nonetheless, I do.

"Do you want to meet him?" Her question causes me to knock a few more books off the shelf.

"What! No!"

"Tash? Everything okay?" Mina calls. Tasha grins and grabs my hand, pulling me before I can protest.

"We're good. Maven was just . . . *checking out* a few books," she says devilishly as we round the corner.

I'm now severely regretting my clothing choice. They turn to face us, and as we get closer, Renn straightens fully. Oh, goodness, he is *tall*, at least six-three. If I had to guess, he seems to be around our age—late twenties, maybe even early thirties. He's wearing a white, short-sleeve v-neck, with dark pants and black boots. Tasha, still pulling me along, stops a few feet in front of him.

"Renn! I want you to meet someone. This is my best friend, Maven. Maven, this is Renn." His eyes meet mine, and I suddenly don't know what to do with my arms and hands. Luckily, he saves me when he extends a hand to me.

"Nice to meet you, Maven," he says, grinning. I take his hand, large and rough against mine.

"You too," I respond, and he lets go. His smile is so inviting, I easily return the sentiment.

"I was just talking to Maven about you, actually. She just got back into town," Tasha enthusiastically tells him, and I smile awkwardly, making a note to remind her later how weird she's making this moment. Renn's green eyes, that appear to be more of a grayish green up close, look at me again as he cocks his head.

"Back?" he asks, casually folding his arms. The gesture makes me feel like he really is interested. I clear my throat nervously because his eyes never leave mine.

What is happening right now? Am I blushing?

"Yeah. I, uh, we haven't been back to town . . . for a while. My mom and I got here last night." He nods.

"Maven and her family have been coming to Solitude Ridge for many years. We've known each other for a long time," Tasha explains.

I can't think of what else to add so I give her a validating, "Mm-hmm," in response.

"Well then, welcome back," Renn says, beaming. I'm relieved he doesn't ask more questions.

"Thank you. It's good to be back." There are a couple of moments of silence before I find myself asking, "When did you move to Solitude Ridge?"

Renn rubs a hand under his jaw and stares off for a moment, seeming to consider his answer. "It's been about four years."

We just missed each other, I think to myself. Not that it matters.

Mina pipes in. "Renn graciously stopped by to take the donation boxes for us."

I glance at Renn just as he blushes at Mina, rubbing the back of his neck. It's not hard to miss that he exudes confidence, but it's not in any way cocky. Even though I've just met the man, I can clearly see it in his body language and the way he speaks—he gives off a sense of ease. But I also can't help the nerves building inside me. The only way I can describe it is that he has a presence, and by the way we're all admiring him, I'm not the only one feeling an aura radiating off of him.

"Oh, I don't mind one bit. Happy to help."

Tasha looks at me with an expression that says, *Can you believe this guy?*

Before anything else can be said, my mom bursts through the shop's door. "Mave, did you get my messages?" She's frazzled, but I'm familiar with her in this state, especially when I don't respond to her messages in a timely manner. It happens more than I wish it would.

"Oh, no. Sorry, Mom. I don't have my phone on me. I must have left it upstairs."

She opens her mouth to say something, but then realizes there are other people in the room, her eyes pausing on Renn for a few extra seconds. "I needed a break from unpacking, but I haven't heard from you. I was wondering if you were close to being finished here." Pivoting to face Renn, she cocks her head. "But now I'm wondering who this handsome young man is," she coos flirtatiously, making me blush with embarrassment.

"Renn, this is Maven's mother, Tova," Tasha says, and they shake hands.

"Nice to meet you, Tova." They exchange friendly smiles.

"I see you've already met my daughter."

My cheeks burn.

"Yes. Just a few moments ago," he replies, eyeing me.

"Did you need help, Mom?" I say, cutting in before she can respond, because I get the feeling my mother is about to embarrass me further. "I can come back with you to the cabin if you need me."

My mom's head sways. "Oh, no, I'm good. I did, however, discover that the sink in the kitchen is leaking, so I need to stop by the hardware store."

"I can take a look if you need me to," Renn says cooly.

"Oh, no. We can figure it out. No need—" I start to say, but Mina interrupts.

"We can vouch for Renn. He's a good one to have around."

"No. I can fix it," I say, and Tasha looks at me skeptically.

"Have you fixed a leaky sink before?"

"Well, no, but . . ."

"Don't you remember how small towns work, Mave? We help each other. You know we're a close-knit community."

The way she says "community" makes me roll my eyes. Tasha is still laying it on thick for catching me spying on Renn. He hasn't moved during this exchange, but he seems to be enjoying the conversation unfolding in front of him, and gives me a look that suggests he's used to Mina and Tasha's theatrics.

"Don't let them guilt you into helping," I tell him, glaring at Tasha and Mina.

He chuckles lightly, a deep vibrato I can practically feel vibrating through my body. "Tasha's right. That's what we do."

I shake my head at him but can't help but smile. Not only is he good-looking, he's charming *and* helpful, too.

Tasha wraps an arm around my shoulder. "Welcome back to Solitude Ridge, Mave."

Everyone laughs, except for me because I'm too busy staring Tasha down. I guess if I'm going to be living the small town life permanently, I need to accept everything that comes along with it. I forgot how different this place really is sometimes. The genuine care of checking in on your neighbors and supporting each other is not common elsewhere these days.

"I was planning on taking the books to Greenhaven, but I could come by afterwards. It's about a two hour trip there and back," Renn says, looking at my mom.

"Oh, of course. No rush! Thank you for the offer." Her eyes crinkle from her grin. "Well then, I guess I'll be seeing you two later," my mom adds with a quick look between Renn and me—a look I do *not* like. Then, she's heading out the door.

"Bye, Mom!" I call quickly before the door closes.

Mina sighs and claps her hands. "So, Renn, the boxes are over here."

"Lead the way." He moves to follow her, and just when I think he will leave without saying anything else, he stops and turns to me. "It was nice to meet you and your mom, Maven, truly." His green eyes peer down at me, the color so cool, yet they hold so much warmth. "See you later?" I'm stunned by the genuineness in his voice.

"You too, and yeah, I guess I'll see you later," I say nervously. He gives a curt nod, then follows Mina. I wait until they're out of sight then turn to Tasha, hitting her arm.

She mouths, *Ow* at me.

"Care to explain why you left *that* out of your updates last night?" I bite, tossing my thumb in the direction of where Renn disappeared.

Tasha's grin is full of mischief. "That whole exchange was worth leaving it out, but since I'm feeling bad now . . ." I glare at her again, playfully this time. "Where would you like me to start?"

"How about from the beginning!"

She giggles. "Hmm, okay. Well, as you saw, he is *insanely* handsome."

I certainly did, but I'm not sure handsome is sufficient to describe Renn's appearance. From his observant and alluring eyes, to his sculpted features . . . I know there's more to him, but I can't put my finger on what it might be.

Tasha continues, "He just showed up one day and stayed. It was about a year after you . . . left." I know she was about to say something else, and I'm glad she didn't.

"Weird, but go on." It was unusual for someone to randomly stop by and decide to stay for so long.

"Well, he's probably one of the nicest people I've ever met. Always willing to lend a helping hand, as you saw. He's basically the town's hero. Last summer, a little six-year-old girl wandered off from her family on a hiking trail and was lost in the woods. Everyone in town was searching for her, but Renn was the one who found her. He acted like it was no big deal."

I nod. "Wow, that's admirable."

"Tell me about it!"

I can't remember the last time Tash and I talked this excitedly about a guy. Probably not since we were teenagers. Neither of us has ever had a serious boyfriend, well I've had *one*, technically, and as far as I know, Tash still hasn't. Dating hasn't really been on my mind since the accident. I've never really had time to.

"But there is one thing . . ." she continues, tapping her nails against the bookshelf and scrunching her lips.

"What *one* thing?"

She hesitates, giving me a knowing look.

"Wait, did something happen between you two?"

She snorts. "No, nothing like that. He's just a good friend, and besides, he doesn't have flings with anyone as far as I know."

"Okay . . ." I urge, motioning with my hands to keep going.

She purses her lips again. "He's a bit of a mystery. He's never spoken much about where he moved from, or about his family, and he doesn't date." It is a little peculiar, but nothing completely out of the ordinary.

"It is strange, I guess," I say with a shrug. I don't know why I care to ask, but I do. "How can you be sure he hasn't had a relationship with anyone since he's lived here?" I hate being so nosy, but my interest is definitely peaked.

Tasha snickers. "Because myself and every female in this town talk!" Both of us chuckle, and then I laugh harder because I love when Tasha cracks herself up like this. I've missed that.

"Fair enough."

Tasha stretches her arms above her head, turning back to the bookshelves.

"Anything else you've been holding out on?" I ask skeptically.

"Nope, that's it," she says with a smug expression. I stick my tongue out at her as she walks to the end of the row of books.

At this point of inventory, I'm more distracted than ever, and it has nothing to do with books. I wish I could say that I haven't given him another thought, but I'd be lying. I don't share it with Tasha, but I'm more curious about Renn than I made it sound, especially by the mysterious past she claimed he has.

I bet Valery knows, I think, and I bite my lip to keep from smiling, thinking about how pleased she will be when I ask her about him. Four years is a long time to avoid questions and give no real answers. I would know, because I've done it myself.

The "how" he did it isn't what causes me to think about Renn for the rest of the afternoon, it's the "why."

Why would he avoid his past?

I can't help but wonder that maybe he's running away from something too.

CHAPTER SIX

Renn

I've driven past Spruce Road countless times, but never ventured down it until today. When the cabin comes into view, my first thought is that it seems well-loved. It radiates warmth, with large, inviting windows and a deck that appears to wrap around the entire cabin.

I step out of my truck as Tova opens the front door and waves, meeting me at the steps leading up to the deck.

"Thank you so much for coming. To be honest, I probably would have made it worse if I attempted it myself."

I chuckle lightly. "I don't mind taking a look." I follow her through the front door, and the inside is just as welcoming as the exterior.

"So, this is it," she says, waving her arm over the expanse of the cabin. Despite being empty for years, it still feels snug and inviting, which I know is thanks to the presence of Tova and Maven, like the imprints they left behind have come alive again. "There's a loft upstairs, a bedroom and bathroom on the main floor," she says, pointing to each. "And this is the kitchen," she adds, leading me across the space.

It's very much like the layout of my cabin, but it has a larger kitchen and is more open overall. Plus the expansive windows let in a wealth of natural light.

"I like it," I say. She nods, her smile fading as she faces me. For a moment, she seems lost in thought, but before I can consider it further, she clears her throat and grins.

"So, the sink," Tova continues. "We have a toolbox that should, hopefully, have everything you need." She motions over to the round, oak table where a worn, metal box sits.

I peek through it for a few seconds. "Yeah, this should work, but I have some tools in my truck if I need them." She shows me where the problem is, and I take a quick glance underneath. The leak is significant, but I can manage. "It looks like it hasn't been leaking for too long, so, damage-wise, I think you're okay. You might want to leave the door open for a few days if you can to let it dry out."

Tova looks relieved. "Oh, thank goodness."

"It should be any easy fix," I say, lying on my back and scooting under the sink for a closer look.

"Great! I'm just going to keep putting things away. Will I be in your way?"

"Not at all." I scan for the valve to turn off the water source, and I discover the leak is from the sealant coming loose. "It looks like a few things just need to be tightened and resealed," I say, emerging from the cupboard.

"Oh, perfect!" She looks up at me, pleased. "I knew if Mina and Tasha liked you, you had to be a good one." That phrase rings in my ears again, causing me to pause.

I clear my throat. "Well, don't believe everything they tell you about me. I know how they can be."

She gives me a knowing smile. "Oh, I wouldn't dream of it," she says.

I wipe my hands on my black pants before heading back outside. "I just need to grab a couple of things from my truck. I'll be right back." I always keep a few things handy wherever I go, never knowing what Grant will need help with when I check in on him. *Always be prepared*—another credit to my extensive years of training that was drilled into me. At this point, it's all second nature. I grin to myself, thinking about what I would have thought if someone had told me six years ago that I'd be fixing leaky sinks and cars.

Finding the can of sealant easily, I head back inside.

Tova opens a few more boxes, laying items out on the floor as I get to work. "Sorry for the mess, just trying to get things organized," she says sheepishly.

"No worries. Unpacking is a process."

She exhales loudly, placing her hands on her hips. "You've got that right."

I give her a reassuring smile, turning back to the leak. The sounds of her unwrapping items and placing them inside the cabinet shelves is the only thing between us for a few minutes. A couple of times, I see her glancing out the window anxiously and wonder what's on her mind.

"Alright. I think you're good to go."

"That was quick! Thank you."

"No problem." I stand with a small groan, turning on the faucet to ensure it won't leak.

Tova places her hands on her hips again, scrunching her lips in thought and tapping her foot. "Would it be too much to ask for you to fix one more thing while you're here?" she asks apologetically before looking out the window again.

I smile, shrugging my shoulders. "I mean, as long as I'm here, you might as well use me, right?"

Tova is quickly catching on to my sense of humor.

"Exactly! Might as well make use of your time." She surveys the space, as if looking for something in particular. "We brought a new light with us. This old one isn't big enough for the room—we always meant to replace it." She gestures to the small light fixture hanging above the table. "Never got around to it before, but Maven insisted we get a new one. Now that I look at it, though, I fear it may be a bigger job than we can handle." Weaving through the boxes, she snaps her fingers. "Ah, here it is!" She drags a heavy-looking box across the floor, but I step in to help her carry it to the kitchen table. "What do you think? Can you swap them?" she asks.

I scan the details on the box. "Looks simple enough. I'll give it a shot."

Squinting at the directions, I wish my AI had been able to teach me the written language, but that wasn't part of the mission. I've tried my best to learn on my own, but I'm still not an expert. However, based on the design of the light and the images included in the instructions, I feel confident I can figure it out.

"I've got a step stool if you need it. You're tall, but probably not tall enough to reach the ceiling with ease."

I chuckle. "Yeah, not quite. A stool would be great."

She strolls off as I unpack the new light. Installing it will take longer than fixing the sink, but I don't mind. Soon, we go back to our tasks, Tova unpacking, me pulling wires and twisting screws into place. After some time, headlights flash through the windows.

"Finally! I was starting to wonder if she was ever coming home," Tova says, peering out the window. I now understand why she was anxiously observing it before; she was anticipating Maven's arrival. "Maven, I thought you'd be home hours ago," Tova says as the front door creaks open.

Maven steps inside, and her eyes immediately find mine as I practically hang from the ceiling. I feel a little vulnerable in this position, especially with those piercing blue eyes on me. Those eyes—they were the first thing that grabbed my attention this morning. I could hardly pull away from them then, and I'm having a hard time doing so now.

"Sorry, Mom, I went to Val's and we got to talking. You know how it can be with her."

"I do, but you could have texted me."

Maven inhales sharply, regarding her mom for a moment before she exhales, as if she's contemplating saying something harsh, but instead says, "I know. I'm sorry, but here I am, safe and sound." Her smile is tight, almost appearing forced. It's hard not to notice the sudden tension in the room. "So, you've got him working on other projects already. You've known him for, what? Three hours?" Maven adds, crossing her arms and giving her mom a disapproving smirk, but Tova completely ignores the last half of her statement.

"He was already here, so we thought he might as well."

Maven snaps her eyes back to me. "We?"

"It's true. I offered a hand," I say.

She glances at her mom and then back at me. "You don't have to do everything she tells you."

"Oh, Maven, honestly," Tova scoffs, turning her back to us as she places something into the cupboard.

Maven rolls her eyes and then mouths, *Sorry.*

I shrug and mouth back, "It's okay," then wink at her. She blinks, averting her gaze, but I notice the way she nervously plays with her hair, wrapping it around her fingers repeatedly.

"Well, I'm gonna take a shower," she announces loudly, placing her hands behind her back, almost like she's anxious.

Tova doesn't bother returning the stare as she responds, "Mkay. We'll just be out here."

Maven promptly walks away without another word, and I watch her until she reaches the set of stairs leading up to the loft. I return to the light as Tova continues placing more items into cupboards. The odd strain in the room lifts slightly.

As I twist the last screw into place, I hear Maven making her way down the stairs. I pretend to be preoccupied with the light, but I catch her out of the corner of my eye, slipping into the bathroom, followed by the sound of running water.

"Oh my," Tova says in a revenant voice. She stands, holding a worn notebook in her hands. "I was wondering where this ended up. I thought it might have been lost forever." She skims through the pages, and I notice the care in which she handles them. I can't help my curiosity getting the best of me.

"What did you find?" I jump down from the stool to move closer. She glances up, smiling, but I notice tears in her eyes.

"Sorry," she says, dabbing at her eyes. "This was my husband, Marc's, old sketchbook. We always meant to get these framed." She gestures for me to come closer. I hesitate because it feels like whatever she's holding is deeply personal, too important for a stranger. As I look at the notebook, I see what appears to be building plans for a structure of some kind. "Marc was an architect," she explains, noticing me inspecting the images. "The first thing he designed was this cabin. I wanted to hang these up somewhere, but kept putting it off." She surveys the room, as if picturing where to hang them. "Maven will be happy to see these."

I can still hear the shower running, and for a moment, I think about not saying anything, but the question is out before I can stop myself. "What happened to Marc? If you don't mind me asking."

Her focus dips to the sketches, a solemn smile on her lips. "It was a car accident. About five years ago. Maven and Marc were driving back to the cabin after going into town one evening. Marc passed, and Maven . . . well, she somehow survived."

A handful of stories the town locals mention from time to time come to my memory. Major incidents have occurred in the town's history—lost hikers and such are spoken about regularly. But I have heard more than one reference to "the accident," like it stood out from the rest for some reason, and now I understand why. I never inquired more about it, since it happened before I arrived in Solitude Ridge. Still, hearing this now, I realize the significance of these two returning to town—it's much more than an overdue visit, they haven't returned because of tragedy. I feel guilty for asking, now that she's telling me so much about their story, and without Maven present, it feels a bit invasive, but I'm not sure what else to do.

"I'm sorry for your loss," is all I think to say as she dabs at her eyes again.

"Thank you for saying that. I don't mean to blubber over every small thing. After all, it's been years now, but I still miss him, you know?" I only nod in response because I do, but in a different way. "Every day I'm so grateful Maven survived. I'm not sure what I would have done if I lost them both."

I try to think of something comforting to tell her, to let her know I understand loss on a major scale, but instead, I say, "I'm glad you have each other." She smiles warmly, both of us sitting in silence for a moment. I look back at the light. "I think that should do it," I say, breaking the silence as I switch the light off and on a couple of times to make sure it works. "I'll let you two get back to your unpacking."

I feel bad, trying to rush out, but then she rests a hand on my arm.

"Thank you so much, Renn. Hopefully, I didn't ask too much of you, especially after just meeting you . . . this morning." She smiles but then winces, sagging her shoulders like she's just realizing it was a bit odd.

"Not at all. Like Tasha said, that's how we do things here." And I mean it.

The shower is still running, and I decide it's probably best to leave before Maven returns. Tova clearly doesn't seem to mind one bit that I'm observing so much of their lives, but I doubt Maven would feel the same. I picked that up from our small exchanges already.

"Well, if anything else comes up, let me know," I say, heading toward the door.

"I will, and thank you again, Renn. It was very kind of you."

"Of course. I gotta keep up my reputation around here." I give her a quick wink as I pull open the door. "Have a good night, Tova."

"You too. Drive safe!"

I drive home with the windows down, letting the cool air stream in. The night is a blanket over the forest, even with the moon full and bright, and I let my thoughts roam as freely as the wind, traveling down the ominous, winding road. I will never be able to drive these roads again without thinking of Maven and Tova, about the heartbreak that took place somewhere along here, a permanent marker of how their lives changed instantly. It stays with me the whole way home, thinking about how the three of us had our lives turned upside down nearly five years ago, but for different reasons.

The timing of it all isn't lost on me. My actual arrival on this world must have been eerily close to when the accident occurred. So much impact and change in a small corner of this planet. Tova lost a partner, and even though our time together has been little, I could see the love in her eyes and the longing in her words when she spoke of Marc. Maven lost a father, and I bet it isn't the only thing she lost somewhere along the road, just like I had lost pieces of myself in the vast unknown of space—pieces of myself that died along the way, never to be resurrected again.

I find myself back in space often. If I don't have a nightmare of explosions and death, I dream I'm back on the ship, drifting and withering away, waiting for the end. It gives me chills as I drive through the shadowy woods, a blur of black whooshing past me.

It's unfair that these tragic events take a piece of our souls from us. And for some of us, instead of filling those missing parts with something to make us whole again, the grief only settles in and leaves us broken and incomplete.

CHAPTER SEVEN

Maven

The warm sunlight streaming in from the skylight above my bed wakes me the next morning. I'm so exhausted, physically and mentally, that I slept in longer than I meant to. My arms are stiff and my lower back is achy from bending and reaching repeatedly with arms full of books.

Thinking about the bookstore makes me think of Renn being in my house last night. By the time I got out of the shower, Renn had gone. I took my sweet time because I really didn't want to emerge fresh from a shower with him there. It felt too personal for someone I had just met to see me so exposed, and well . . . it was just weird. All of it is weird. Why I care so much about a stranger is a mystery to me.

It seemed my mom had been stalling, or attempting to at least. Whatever her agenda was in keeping Renn hostage wasn't a conversation I was ready to have, so I said a quick good night and headed upstairs, where I spent the rest of the night thinking about my conversation with Valery.

When I walked into The Peak, I'd known within seconds I was in for a long conversation. Val hadn't given me much time to protest as she dragged me into her small office in the back of the store. After an in-depth recap about my recovery, which I knew I couldn't avoid, I steered the conversation to what I really wanted to talk about. It was so out of character for me, but I did it anyway.

"So . . . I met Renn at the bookshop this morning," I say, doing my best to sound casual.

"Oh, really? And?" Val says with eyebrows raised. Her face lights up with a mischievous grin.

"He seems like a nice guy." I try to keep my tone as neutral as possible.

"Renn is a lot of things. Nice. Smart. Helpful. The list is long, sweetheart." Valery talks about him the way a proud mother would, and it surprises me.

I cock my head, realizing Renn is more than just the "new guy" in town, and Val clearly sees him the way Mina and Tasha do. "Goodness, he certainly has made quite the impression in such a short time." It's obvious he's beloved, and yes, the community of Solitude Ridge is welcoming and kind, but it feels like Renn is treated as if he has always been here, or at least that is the conclusion I've come to.

"Well, it has been four years, Mave. It didn't happen overnight." I purse my lips, not totally convinced. She clearly sees the uncertainty in my face. "When you get to know him better, you'll get it. Trust me." She beams at me, implying something. "So, what do you want to know about him, exactly?"

"Does he have any family?"

Val leans forward, resting her arms on the desk. "He must have made an impression on you too, not that I would blame you. If I were twenty years younger, I'd . . ."

"Val!"

She laughs, covering her mouth while I roll my eyes at her.

"You are ridiculous! Can you please be serious for a minute?" I tease her. She clears her throat and sits a little straighter.

Here we go, *I think. I could always count on Val being Val.*

"I won't lie, it took a long time just to get an idea of what his story was, and to be completely honest, I still don't know everything. No one does. All I know for certain is he had a job similar to something in the military. My guess is he's been through something that he doesn't like talking about." She pauses, and her stare intensifies on me for a moment, but I pretend I don't understand the not-so-subtle

hint. "Anyway . . ." She clears her throat again. "This is, of course, just what I gathered. He hasn't ever said this exactly to me, or anyone, from what I know." I nod for her to keep going. "He doesn't have any family. He was raised by his grandparents from what it sounds like. No siblings."

"And?"

"And that's really all I know, dear." I raise my eyebrows subconsciously, and once I realize she's serious, she giggles softly.

"Wow. Okay. Tash wasn't kidding," I say, leaning back in the chair.

The rest of our conversation naturally came back to my mom and me. Her eyes teared up once at the mention of my dad. But I wasn't going there, not even with Val, and I love her like a mother. I haven't even had the courage to have an in-depth conversation with my actual mom about my dad in a long time. Of course, we talk about him here and there, but nothing like a proper sit-down. Eventually, I told Val I needed to go home to unpack, so she let me go.

The sound of a bird singing in a nearby tree brings me back, so I reach for my phone on the nightstand and type out a message to Tasha.

Me: Guess who was still at my house when I got home last night?
Tasha: And that's a bad thing because???

She doesn't even need to guess.

Me: I don't know. We don't know him, so it's weird.
Tasha: Well, I do! He's a friend. Don't you trust my judgment?
Me: Of course I do, but still.

A few minutes pass before she sends a response.

Tasha: Don't take it so seriously. Relax. I do have a question though?
Me: What?
Tasha: Would you be opposed to something happening between you two?
Me: Please don't play matchmaker. I beg of you.

Tash: When was the last time you went on a date?

I scoff.

Me: Spare me, please? My mom's shenanigans are plenty. But okay, yeah, it's been a little while, I guess.
Tash: Interesting. Well, we'll see what happens...

I roll my eyes as I quickly type back.

Me: Don't DOT DOT DOT me. Nothing. Is. Going. To. Happen.
Tasha: If you say so...

I toss my phone onto the bed and head downstairs where I find my mom already sitting at the kitchen table, reading a book with a cup of coffee nearby.

"Good morning, sleepy head!"

I rub my eyes, sitting in the chair next to her. "Morning. I didn't mean to sleep in so late. How did you sleep?"

She lifts her mug, taking a long sip. "Pretty good. I got up early to go on a walk down the trail. It was nice."

The trail is our own little spot behind the house that no tourists know about. It's only about a mile long and leads to a quaint pond where I would skip rocks or make tiny boats out of bark and leaves to float across it when I was a kid.

"I'll have to go down there soon."

She nods. "You should."

I stand, looking through the fridge for something to eat.

"What do you have going on today?" she asks, attention back to her book.

"I'll probably stop by the bookshop again and then go on a walk through town, maybe check in on a few people. What about you?"

"I got a lot done yesterday, so I was planning on just staying here to relax today. Mina said she would stop by if things are slow at the bookshop."

"Sounds good."

She lazily sips her coffee while I continue to rummage for food.

"I noticed there was a patch on the roof that looked like it needed some repair," she says, but I hardly pay attention, my hunger at the forefront of my mind at the moment.

"So I asked Renn if he could come take a look," she adds, and I eye her over my shoulder, noticing she doesn't even bother to look up. The bowl I retrieved from the cupboard clanks against the counter as it slips from my grip.

"What? Why?" I fold my arms, annoyed she still isn't making eye contact. "When did you ask him? Do you have his number?"

She chuckles, ignoring the panic rising in my voice. "I asked Mina for it, and then I messaged him a little while ago. He said he'd come by this afternoon."

I walk to the table, flopping into my chair dramatically. "Mom. I'm sure he has better things to do with his time."

"I told him there was no pressure. He could have said no."

"People never say *no* when people say *no pressure*."

She finally puts down her book and looks at me directly. "Mave, honey. He offered to help yesterday, and he told me to let him know if I needed help with anything else. There are a few things that I'd like to get done around here before I go back home. And I'm certainly not getting up on the roof." I open my mouth to interject. "And neither are you!"

It's these moments with my mom when I have to bite my tongue from saying what's on my mind, because I owe it to her to be better. She was with me every step of the way in my recovery. And as her only child, I want to be the best daughter I can be. I want to make her happy, especially after what she has been through.

"Can't you ask someone else?" I groan.

She observes me with narrow eyes as she thinks over her response. "Probably, but wouldn't it be nice to make more friends?" And the puzzle suddenly comes together.

"Mom. You don't need to help me make friends. I have friends here already."

She shakes her head. "Maven, I'm your mom. Is it so bad I want you to have some more support here? If you need help with something like a leaky sink or roof, you know you can call him." I'm unsure if my mom is implying that I'm a loner, or that I am incapable of making new friends. "I'm just looking out for my daughter. That's what mothers do," she says very matter-of-factly as I roll my eyes.

She dives back into her book while I munch on my food, making a mental plan for my day. Maybe, while I'm in town, I'll run into Renn and explain that my mother's actions are based on her own crazy agenda, not mine.

She casually continues to sip from her mug, followed by the soft sound of her turning another page, and my heart goes from icy to warm. I can't remember the last time I saw my mom so relaxed, and it's been ages since she's read a physical book. I slide my hand over the table and grab hers.

"I'm sorry, Mom." She looks up, surprised, setting her book to the side. "I know you just want me to have a good life here, but you don't need to worry, okay?" She squeezes my hand, tears forming in her eyes. "I'll be fine. I'll have Mina and Tasha always checking on me. I'm sure Tasha already has plans to keep me busy. This place is my second home, so many people here are like family to us. I won't be alone."

She nods, wiping a tear off her cheeks. "I'm sorry, too. I went a little overboard with Renn, didn't I?" she asks, apologetically.

I pinch my fingers together for emphasis. "Just a little." But I clasp her hand again with a reassuring smile.

"I can tell him not to come."

I shake my head. "It's fine, Mom. He seems like he knows what he's doing." She raises her eyebrows at me to say what else I'm thinking; she knows me too well sometimes. "And he's not bad-looking."

She covers her mouth to keep from giggling. "Finally! I was waiting for you to say something."

"Mom!" I scoff. "You're almost as bad as Valery. You're old enough to be his mother."

"Oh, stop. I didn't mean it like that. Besides, I'm not so old that I can't appreciate a fine-looking young man."

"Okay, wow. I'm definitely telling him to not come over now!" I joke.

We smile at each other, our laughter drifting through the cabin, and it's that familiar sound that makes me recall how things used to be, especially in this place. A home filled with joy and fun, only to be followed by the reminder that things will never be the same again.

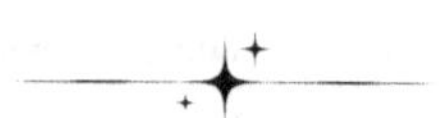

I message Tasha, letting her know I'm on my way to town, and we plan to meet for coffee at Summit Coffee House later. In the meantime, I want to go to another one of my favorite spots: the lounge at one of the resorts called Snowbird. The lounge has an amazing view because it sits high on the mountainside, and the added bonus is that they have great food. It's about a twenty-five-minute drive from Main Street, so I stop to get gas.

My father always taught me to never let your gas tank get below half full because you never know what could happen, especially on mountain roads. I start filling the tank, glancing across the street to watch the floods of people walking by, when I spot Renn coming out of the hardware shop. Perfect timing. *Let's get this over with.*

I finish filling my car, then give my reflection a quick one-over in the car window, tucking the loose strands of my long hair behind my ears. I kept my attire casual, with a dark blue t-shirt and light jean shorts. The shirt is basic, but one of my favorites because it makes my eyes an even more prominent hue of blue. Taking a deep breath, I jog across the street toward him.

"Hey! Renn!"

He turns, and when he sees me, he smiles wide, giving me a little jolt in my stomach. "Hey!"

His face is smooth and freshly shaven. He has on a dark jean jacket over a black shirt accompanied by a pair of dark pants and boots.

"I was hoping I'd see you," I say, biting my lower lip.

"Oh, yeah? Why's that?" he says, his eyebrows raised in surprise. As the sun hits his face, his green eyes shift to a richer hue—although still outlined with a smoky gray ring.

"I wanted to say thank you for all your help yesterday, and also to apologize." I could tell that he was about to say, "You're welcome" until I added that last part.

"Apologize for . . . ?" he asks, cocking his head.

"My mom. I was just hoping you didn't feel pressured in helping with the light and now the roof. You don't need to come over tonight if you really don't want to."

He nods, running his tongue over his teeth. "I see." He shifts the items in his arm. "I volunteered to help with the sink, and I don't mind helping with other things if you need it."

The last thing I want him to think is that I am helpless, so I quickly retort, "I probably could have done both the sink and light myself. She just worries about me doing too much."

I didn't mean to say that last part, and he gives me a questioning look before he says, "Oh, I'm sure you could have." His tone is in no way mocking, his face serious as he peers at me. A breath passes before he asks, "Does she do that with you a lot?" I subconsciously scan the area to make sure no one I know is nearby.

"Yes, and no. She thinks I am going to . . . overexert myself." I weigh the idea of how much to share with him, and if it weren't for the kindness in his eyes, I probably wouldn't say anything at all. "I was . . . injured a few years ago, so she tends to see me as too fragile. I have to remind her that I'm fine now."

He steps closer, until he's a couple of feet away. "Yeah, she kind of hinted at that last night," he says softly, and I'm sure the look on my face makes him regret saying it.

I furrow my brows. "She told you what happened?" I ask slowly, trying to keep my irritation under control.

I'm not mad at Renn. My mother, on the other hand, just happened to forget to tell me she shared this information. We've been here for less than forty-eight hours, and she has already embarrassed me in front of this guy more than once.

"Just that you were in a car accident. That was all."

I lift my chin slightly, scanning his face, and I get the feeling he's holding something back, or maybe he wants to know more but isn't asking.

"It's true, and I was injured, but I've recovered. Good as new," I say, holding out my arms like he needs to see all of me to prove it. This time, Renn scans all of me, his gaze sliding over my body with his stormy eyes, like something is brewing behind them. They root me to the ground, like I'm standing in a spotlight on a stage. I can see it all there in his face—his unspoken thoughts lingering as if he wants to ask, *"Have you recovered? Really?"*

I gulp, hoping he doesn't notice, and he finally breaks the silence. "It sounds like your mom is doing what most parents do. They worry because they care." He smiles. "Sometimes too much," he adds with a wink.

"Is that what your mom does with you?" The question spills out before I can think if I should ask it or not, my tone harsher than I mean it to be. His lips turn up slightly.

"She probably would if she were alive." I gulp again. *So you know what it's like to have lost a parent?* "She died a long time ago," he adds, and I wait for him to say more. "Take this with a degree of skepticism: time helps, but it's always there, the grief. It doesn't ever go away, but the way we grieve . . . evolves." His words are refreshing from the typical "time heals all wounds" remarks I always hear.

For reasons I don't fully understand, the next thing I say is surprising, even to me. "My dad hasn't been . . . gone for very long."

He sets down the items in his arms, then folds them across his broad chest. I try to act like the gesture doesn't affect me as much as it does. But I never talk about my dad like this, especially with someone I just met, and Renn is giving me his full attention.

"Everyone processes time differently. I don't mean that—" he says almost nervously.

"I know what you meant," I interrupt.

"Good." He puts his hands in his pockets, leaning back on his heels, studying my face once again. He clicks his tongue. "Well," he says, bending to retrieve his things, and I realize what he's been carrying.

"Are those things for the roof?" I ask, nodding toward them.

"Yes."

"My mom said she'd pay you, right?" I wonder, eyeing the items in his arms.

"She did." I don't notice the smirk on his face until I look back up at him.

"Okay. Well, good." My face grows warm. What is wrong with me? I've never been this nervous around a guy before.

"I guess I'll see you later?" he asks.

I could say I have plans, or make up an excuse not to be home later, but instead, I reply, "Yeah. I'll see you later, Renn." I say his name slowly, not really meaning to, but I think he notices too because I see his mouth turn up again before crossing the street.

I watch him for a few more seconds, but before I can look away, he looks back to find me still watching him. I hold his gaze as he winks. That damn wink. I roll my eyes, making sure he sees, and I can hear his laugh even from my side of the street as I walk in the opposite direction, trying to push away the thought that I am, in fact, very much looking forward to seeing him later.

CHAPTER EIGHT

Renn

Tova is waiting for me on the deck, sitting in one of the rocking chairs with a book in hand. As soon as she hears my car on the gravel driveway, she shoots from her chair, waving to me.

"Hey, Tova. Good to see you again," I say, opening the door of my truck.

"Thank you for coming. I really hope you don't mind."

"Not at all," I say, shaking my head.

She gestures up to the roof. "I noticed it yesterday. The hole looks small, but with the colder weather around the corner, I don't want it to get worse, especially since Maven is going to be staying here for awhile."

I had assumed they both were here for a visit, not for good, and I can't help but smile as I squint up at the roof, noticing the patch she was concerned about, right before the roof drops to the back of the cabin.

"Better to be safe than sorry," I reassure her.

"Let me know what I owe you for the supplies."

When she messaged me earlier, Tova mentioned she wasn't sure what materials I'd need to patch it, so I offered to grab some items on my way through town.

"You bet."

"There's a ladder in the shed, and if you need other tools, I left the toolbox in there as well."

"Sounds good." I turn to leave, but I spot a simple telescope on the other end of the deck that wasn't there yesterday. Tova follows my gaze.

"Oh, that's Maven's. I found it stored in the shed earlier. It's an amateur scope, but you'd be surprised what you can see on clear nights with just that little thing." The mention of anything galactic makes me more nostalgic than I want it to, but I can't help it. Space was my home for such a long time, something I can't easily forget, even if I wish I could.

Tova doesn't seem to notice I'm lost in thought as she returns to the rocking chair with her book, so I make my way to the shed to grab the ladder. It's old and wooden, but seems sturdy. I climb onto the roof, and it's steeper than it appears, but once I reach the top, I put a leg on either side while I cut out the damaged area, then seal it before adding the new shingles. All the while, Tova quietly reads below, letting me handle the task without conversation.

As I'm wrapping up, a noise coming up the driveway draws my attention. I can feel Maven watching me as she gets out of the car.

"I can't believe you actually made him get onto the roof." I hear her say before the car door slams.

"I didn't *make* him do anything." Tova turns to yell at me, "Right, Renn?"

I steady myself before looking down at them. "Right. I volunteered, remember?"

"Mom, don't distract him while he's up there!" Maven says, a tinge of fear in her voice.

I can't help but chuckle. "I'm fine, and I am almost done."

Maven narrows her eyes at her mom, then looks back up at me. "That's pretty high. Do you need help?" Maven calls, shielding her eyes as the setting sun is now positioned so the rays hit us in just the right spot to blind us. I move to respond, bringing my leg over from the other side to scale down, but my foot slips, and I grab onto whatever I can before falling all the way down the length of the roof.

"Renn!" They both shout in panic.

Thankfully, I am able to catch myself, the rough shingles causing burning friction and scraping my skin. I hope they didn't hear the vulgar word I muttered, even if it was in a language they wouldn't understand. My native language slips out from time to time, and this was one of those times. I honestly can't think of anything worse than falling off the roof with an audience. The pain I could get over, but the embarrassment, as much as I hate to admit it, would have taken much longer to heal from than any physical injuries.

"Renn?" Maven yells, louder than before.

"I'm okay. I'm okay. It's all good."

They both release identical heavy sighs of relief that make me smile.

"Renn, seriously, are you okay?" I hear Maven's voice, heavy with concern.

"Yeah. I'm coming down now." I feel their eyes boring into my back, a weight of worry with every move I make until I reach the bottom of the ladder. The second my feet hit the deck, Tova tugs me into a tight hug.

"You scared me to death!"

"Well, maybe you shouldn't have made him get up on the roof like that!" Maven says, waving her hand wildly.

"It's okay. It was my fault."

Maven stares at her mom with disapproval, her hands on her hips, and then looks me over. "Renn, you're bleeding!" She motions to my arm. I lift it, finding a deep gash on my forearm, which is also scratched up pretty good. Tova takes my arm softly, inspecting the wound.

"I have a med kit inside."

"Oh, I'm sure it's nothing. I can . . ."

"I wouldn't hear of it!" she says, completely ignoring me. "Let me at least clean it up for you."

Careful not to hit my arm, Maven urges me inside by touching my back gently.

"Are you actually agreeing with your mom?" I ask playfully, but she doesn't say anything right away, so I glance over my shoulder at her.

"Not at all. I'm just proving that I was right. You shouldn't have gotten up there." She eyes me passively, then raises a single brow as if to say, "Told you so" and follows Tova inside.

When I walk into the cabin this time, the boxes are cleared away, and there are pictures hung on the walls. Most of them depict Maven at various ages. The one closest to me is a photo of her holding up a fish, beaming from ear to ear. She probably isn't older than eight. The largest one is on the back wall, and it's a picture of Maven and Tova with a man that I know, immediately, is Marc.

They're sitting on the porch steps of the cabin, her dad and mom on one step and Maven behind them, resting a hand on their shoulders. Even from a distance, I can tell Maven got most of her genes from her father. He has the same striking blue eyes and dark hair. But the picture that catches my attention is the one next to it, a picture of Maven and Marc standing on the deck next to the same telescope currently sitting outside.

I'm so busy looking at all of the pictures, I don't notice Maven coming to stand beside me with a wet washcloth.

"Here you go," she says, handing it over and following my gaze to the picture, but she quickly looks away.

"Found it!" Tova says, walking into the kitchen area and gesturing for me to take a seat at the table. I don't bother protesting, knowing it would be of no use. I dab at the gash, and when I pull back the cloth, there's more blood on it than I was expecting. "You got yourself pretty good. Mave, can you grab another clean cloth for him?"

Without a reply, Maven walks into the kitchen, retrieving one in a drawer and soaking it with water. She motions for me to give her the bloody one, but I hesitate.

"It's okay. I'm not squeamish with blood," she remarks, holding out her delicate hand. I'm reluctant at first. It feels intimate to think of my blood on her hands, and as I offer it to her, I get the feeling she's thinking the same thing. She doesn't look at me as she takes it, careful not to touch me, and goes back to the sink to rinse it.

Tova takes her time cleaning the wound, and after a couple of beats, she casually asks, "So, Renn, do you have family around here?"

Maven goes still, and my guess is that she's giving her mom an incredulous look, but I keep my eye on Tova to answer.

"No. I don't have any family close by. I'm an only child, and everyone in my immediate family, unfortunately, has all passed on."

Tova pauses, studying my face, her eyes full of sympathy. "I'm so sorry to hear that."

Maven is staring at me as well, her bright eyes carrying the same sentiment. She had that same expression of tenderness on her face when I told her about losing my mother.

"Thank you, and it's okay. I've been on my own for a while, so I'm used to it."

They both remain quiet for a moment, Tova still cleaning my wound gently.

"Well, I'm glad you chose to make Solitude Ridge your home," Tova says warmly, rubbing anti-infection ointment on the wound before placing a bandage over the top.

Maven says nothing as she leans against the counter, arms folded across her chest.

"Me too." The stinging is slightly better now that it isn't exposed to the air, and I'm grateful for their care.

"It didn't look too deep once it stopped bleeding. I think it should be fine."

I glance down at the bandage. "I'm sure it will be. Thank you."

"Renn, would you like to stay for dinner?" Tova asks suddenly. I glance at Maven as she walks over to help return items to the medical kit, her expression unreadable.

"I really should get going," I say, but I catch a look of disappointment on Maven's face, or at least I think I do.

"Some other time, then. Especially after all your help. It's the least we can do. Right, Mave?"

"Yes. I think it's only fair that, since you almost died falling off our roof, *my mom* owes you dinner."

I lick my lips before smiling, but I can't deny I was hoping she would say something along the lines of *you should stay.*

"Some other time sounds great. Thank you."

They both follow me to the door and stand on the deck until I start driving away. I watch them go back inside through my rearview mirror, and I can almost hear Maven pestering her mother once the door closes. But Tova wasn't wrong about me helping. I could have said no, and despite almost falling off the roof, I grin at the thought of their concern for me. The feeling doesn't fade until I remember what Tova said about making Solitude Ridge my home. I want that to be true with all my heart. I don't want to be an outsider without a true place or people to call my own—nowhere to call home.

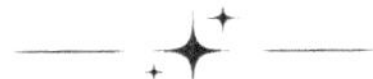

I start closing up the auto shop for the night, ready to head home for a couple of days off. I had only seen Maven and Tova briefly as they were leaving the bookshop one evening this week, and Tova immediately wanted to see how my arm was healing and inspected it thoroughly.

"I promise I won't be asking you to climb up on the roof again anytime soon," she said, followed by Maven's comment of, "How about you never ask him to do that *ever* again. That would be the better solution." Tova nudged Maven with her elbow, making me chuckle.

The memory makes me smile as I reach for the handle of my car door, but my attention is caught by a melody drifting down the street, tempting me to follow. I grab my jean jacket from the passenger seat, and after walking a couple of blocks, I discover the source: the coffee shop. The place is crowded, and there's a live band playing on the outdoor patio. The band members are a collection of some of the local teens, yet their sound is mature, with acoustic and soothing rhythms. Stepping closer, I notice the sign by the door that reads:

"One Year Celebration Tonight! Live music, free drinks and treats."

The cafe is buzzing with chatter and patrons enjoying the band as the aroma of nutty spices creates a cozy and welcoming atmosphere. Most of those inside are locals, grinning and waving as they see me. Before I can take in anything else, someone calls my name. I turn to find Tasha waving me over. Maven is standing beside her, wearing a stylish, wide-brimmed hat made of a velvet-like material. I weave my way through the crowd to join them.

We exchange pleasantries as the band transitions to a song with more tempo and volume, making it difficult to converse over the music.

"Did you just get off work?" Tasha asks loudly.

"I did. I thought I'd stop by and see what was pulling everyone over here tonight," I say, glancing around at the crowd.

"I can't believe it's already been a year since the shop opened." She looks over at Maven. "This place is just what Solitude Ridge needed if Maven is staying. She's a coffee addict."

Maven gives her friend a wary glance, but then says, in a playful tone, "It's true, so I won't complain." Raising her coffee, she takes a long sip for emphasis.

The three of us listen as the melody plays on, but when it ends, Tasha leans over and says, "Well, guys, I need to get going."

Maven looks at her with intense scrutiny, her blue eyes bright even in the dimly lit shop. "Yeah, I'm sure you do," she says through a tight smile. I try to stifle my chuckle but fail miserably, trying to cover it up with a cough. Maven shoots me a suspicious look.

"See you two later." Tasha's flirtatious tone makes Maven wince. We watch her walk away until she's out of the shop, then Maven turns to me and we lock eyes, both starting to laugh.

She moves a few inches closer to me and says, "I don't know what is wrong with all the women in my life. I'm so sorry about that."

I shrug my shoulders. "I think they mean well."

"It would be nice if they could mean a little *less* well." Maven rolls her eyes, laughing at herself, and I can't help but laugh along with her. As she gazes around the room, I shamelessly take her all in. Wearing a long, black, tank top dress, her raven hair drapes down her arms and back, and I can't take my eyes off her. She catches me watching when she brings her attention back to me. "Are you sure you're okay after what happened the other night?"

I snicker playfully. "It really is just a scratch. I'm fine." Her eyes flicker to my arm, even though my jacket is covering the wound.

"At this point, I'm not sure you'll ever have a chance to see us at our best. It's not always like this with my mom. I swear."

"Would it be weird if I thought it was actually pretty funny? Apart from when I almost fell off your roof, of course."

She squints in thought, biting her lip to keep from smiling. "I'm okay with that," she says, sipping her drink and watching me over the edge of the cup. "So, did you come to support the band?" I put my hands in my pockets as I reply.

"Sure. I just thought I would check it out, but I'm always happy to support."

She nods along while listening to the music. "Tash says you do that a lot. That you're supportive of all the local businesses and people here."

I shrug. "Yeah, I guess I am." She studies me, lips pursing to the side like she wants to say more, but decides not to. "So, what about you? Do you like to support local businesses? Or do you just really love coffee?" She brushes her hair back, and I inhale the warm scent of her shampoo or whatever perfume she is wearing. Maybe it's just the way she smells. I gulp a little at the thought.

"Both," she answers with a nod.

We stand side by side, taking in the music for several minutes. The band switches to a softer number, making it easier to concentrate and talk over the noise, and the silence between us isn't awkward in the slightest. Being with Maven is effortless. She looks very at-home with her cup, enjoying the band, and relaxed under her wide-brimmed hat. I can tell she's having a good time.

"Mave! Is that really you?" We both turn to see a man walking toward Maven with open arms.

"Jamie. Um, hi." He wraps her in a hug before she can say more. She has to move into an awkward position so he doesn't knock off her hat while she also struggles to keep her coffee from spilling. I take note that she doesn't hug him back.

"I heard you were back in town!" Jamie pulls away, scanning her face and body.

"Yeah, just a few days ago, actually." Her eyebrows furrow in confusion. "Tasha told me you moved."

His features puzzle, but he quickly recovers. "Oh, yeah, I did. I'm in town for a few days visiting my parents." Maven doesn't say anything for a few seconds, undoubtedly uncomfortable. "It seems like you've made some new friends," he adds, his tone carrying a hint of annoyance as glances at me.

Maven smiles awkwardly. "This is Renn. Renn, Jamie."

I hold out my hand, but he doesn't notice or care as he continues to stare at Maven intensely. I don't like the way he looks at her with hungry eyes, but who am I to do or say anything? They clearly have a past, and I'm someone she just met.

"We should go out while I'm in town. I'd love to catch up. You look amazing, by the way."

Maven stiffens next to me. "Um, yeah maybe," she says wearily, but Jamie doesn't pick up on the hint.

"Are you free tomorrow night? I'd love to hear how you've been, and the fact you're—" He stops abruptly as Maven moves closer to me, her shoulder brushing against mine, then she hooks her arm around mine, lightly placing her hand on my forearm where the bandage lies beneath my jacket sleeve like she knows exactly where it is. Without thinking, I lean into her like it is the most natural thing in the world. It's such a small gesture, but holds a significant meaning. Jamie gapes at us, understanding clouding his face. "Oh, I see. Well . . . it was good to see you again, Maven. Take care," he says quickly, then strides off, looking abashed, not waiting for either of us to respond. Once he's out of sight, Maven steps away, letting go of my arm.

"Friend?" I ask, watching to make sure Jamie is gone.

"Ex-boyfriend," she says, grimacing. "Maybe one of these days I'll stop saying this, but thank you. I probably owe you at least ten favors at this point." She blushes, looking up at me from under the brim of her hat. I sense her embarrassment, and I don't like seeing her this way. She has nothing to be embarrassed about when it comes to that asshole.

"He clearly can't take a hint very well," I remark casually.

"Nope. Never has," she says, taking a deep breath and looking a little flustered. "You want to know something?" she asks as if she's thinking out loud, but she doesn't wait for me to respond. "He didn't even bother coming to see me after the accident, just sent me a few messages. Never called. It just ended." Worry spreads across her face like she has shared too much.

"It's okay. I get it," I say, trying to reassure her. She looks down at the drink in her hand, the hat covering her face.

"I guess we all probably have regrets when it comes to relationships," she mutters. Regrets were something I'm in no short supply of, but relationships . . . perhaps my only regret is I've never been in a serious one. There have been a few women over the years, but never anything worth noting.

I try to let my curiosity fizzle, but the longer I stand beside her and talk, the more I want to know.

"Can I ask you something?" I ask.

She glances up, looking relieved that I am changing the subject. "Sure," she says, amused.

I lick my lips. "Why is everyone so worried about you?"

A flash of surprise skirts across her face, and she blushes as she sips from her coffee, like she is contemplating how to answer. "The truth?" She sighs, and I nod. "It's a lot of things, but the biggest reason is because . . ." With a pause, she stares off into the crowd before she continues. "They think I'm running away from my problems." She appears to be lost in thought for a second or two before she looks up at me, her bright, blue eyes full of complexities. I inhale a breath just looking at them. She snaps out of whatever memory she wandered to. "Anyway. I'm good. Everything is fine. I just wish *they* would believe me."

She hides under her hat again, and just like every encounter I've had with Maven since meeting her, I'm compelled to uncover what's beneath. I feel like I can see it, hints of an untold story in those deep pools of blue.

I shouldn't, but before I know what I'm doing, I hear myself ask, "So, what are you running from, Maven?"

She snaps her head up, her eyes wide, searching my face before her gaze narrows. It takes everything in me not to look away from those icy eyes staring straight through me.

"I could ask you the same thing."

An hour later, I'm lying on my couch while Shy sprawls out next to me on the floor. The smell of coffee lingers on my clothes, and when I close my eyes, I see Maven in that hat, sipping her coffee. I think about her jerk of an ex-boyfriend who I wouldn't mind seeing again, only to punch him. I saw the complete truth in her eyes, as if she could read my innermost thoughts. This woman, someone I barely know, can read me like a book . . . perhaps she could even decipher the secrets between the lines, too.

I could ask you the same thing.

It rattled me—*she* rattled me. Because if I could recognize the shadow of her past in her eyes, she could distinctly see something in mine—a shadow trying to cloak those dark places neither one of us wanted to go. Shadows concealing secrets. I doubt her secret was as shocking as my own.

But what frightens me is how easy it would be for her to unveil my secrets one by one. For the first time in five years, I worry that the discovery of what I am and where I come from is at risk, all because of a single look. I'm enveloped in the unnerving feeling that if she truly asked me about my past, it would all spill out of me, willingly.

I've always played this game well, always had the upper hand. But now that Maven has entered my life, I'm not so sure. One thought keeps me awake into the early hours of the morning. I know the solution is to ensure things remain as they are. They have to stay that way, no matter my feelings, so no one else will get hurt.

The smart thing to do would be to keep my distance from her, but the problem is, I don't want to.

CHAPTER NINE

Maven

Four weeks in Solitude Ridge have come and gone, but my mom and I have enjoyed every minute of them. We spent many days hanging out at the bookshop, having dinners with other friends in town, and even enjoying a spa day at one of the fanciest resorts in the area. Of course, there was the occasional awkward pause in the air when someone would ask us, "So how have things been?" or make the comment, "Maven, you're looking great." I always answered with a polite "thank you," and the conversation usually shifted quickly.

My mom never brought up what I'd heard her and Mina talking about the first night back, and she still doesn't say anything as she holds me tight in her arms.

Today, she's going back home. I can tell she's overly stressed about leaving, and I don't know what else I can possibly say to reassure her I'm going to be fine.

This is what I want, this is where I belong, and not only as the little girl who came here with her parents, but as a woman who is making a new life for herself, or is at least trying to. I want to fight for this new version of Maven. The version who is stronger, whose life isn't about everything that happened in the past, but about starting a new chapter—which was my ultimate goal for coming here in the first place.

Pretty much everything has gone exactly as I had hoped it would, and yet the thing nagging at me is Renn. Weeks have passed since that night at the coffee shop, and he hasn't said much to me since, only a few hellos or a wave here and there, but nothing more.

My counter to his question obviously hit harder than I meant it to, and it wasn't my intention to make him uncomfortable, but why did he react the way he did? He made up a not-so-convincing reason to leave and was out of the coffee shop before I could say anything else. To be honest, I'm annoyed. If he felt like he could ask me questions, why shouldn't I be able to ask him in return?

When I told Tasha about our conversation the next day, first pointing out how obvious she was in leaving the two of us alone, all she said was, "I told you. He doesn't talk about his past."

I'm supposed to just accept that and move on like everyone else in town, but it doesn't sit right with me. Maybe I could if it wasn't for his change in demeanor toward me. And while I was beyond grateful for his help when Jamie showed up, I'm only more motivated to find out why he felt the need to react this way. Could his past really be so sinister that he wouldn't share it with a single person? Not a single detail? My mind warns me to be cautious, but my heart is open and curious. It seems absurd to be wary of someone so courteous and friendly as Renn, but it still leaves me confused. At the same time, I keep reminding myself we just met. He's still a stranger, more or less. I shouldn't overthink it, so I pretend I don't care, hoping I can convince myself.

"I wish you could stay for one more night. You'll be missed by everyone at Firefly Night," I say through a sad smile.

"Me too, but I really need to get back to the business."

"I know, and they need you. It's okay, Mom. I promise."

She holds on to me a little tighter before she says, "Call me immediately if you need anything, okay?"

"I will, Mom. I promise."

"I'll be up in a few months for your birthday, but if you need me to come before then, just tell me." I can hear the quiver in her voice and know she's holding back tears.

"I'll call you all the time and message you at least once a day, I swear," I tell her, but I mean it with all my heart. I'll miss my mom, but I need to be on my own. She raised me, then nursed me back to health, but she has a new life to live, and I'm not going to let her love and worry for me hold her back anymore. I want her to move on, too.

She draws away, taking my face in her hands. "So much like your father. Independent, strong, and stubborn," she says, smiling. I look into her copper-brown eyes and wonder what else she sees when she looks at me. Does she feel resentment? Disappointment? Maybe it's none of those things. She's a more forgiving person than I am, and I wish I could be more like her in so many ways, but she isn't wrong. I am very much my father's daughter.

"Call me when you get home," I say, giving her one final, tight hug.

"I love you, and I'm proud of you," she says into my hair. I swallow down the emotion building in my chest; I can't cry now, or she will never leave.

"I love you too, Mom."

I watch her pull away and drive down the lane until she is out of sight. *So this is the true test.* I smile nervously to myself, making my way back inside and leaning against the door after I shut it behind me. I take a few deep breaths. "This will be good for you," I tell myself.

I clean up around the cabin, not that it needs it, but I want to keep myself busy. It's not too long after she departs that my phone buzzes with a new message.

"Already?" I smile to myself as I see it's from my mom.

Mom: I know it's none of my business . . . I'm not sure what happened with Renn, but he came to say goodbye when I stopped at the bookshop. Just wanted you to know. Love you sweetheart.

I don't know what to type back. I wonder for a moment if I were the one leaving Solitude Ridge, if he would have bothered to say goodbye to me. There's no denying that it stirs something in me. I land on something simple, not wanting to open that door more than it needs to be.

Me: I love you too, Mom.

It's still early in the day, so before I talk myself out of it, I grab a blanket and a book and walk down the trail to the pond.

It's a flat path, perfect for an easy stroll through the dense, evergreen woods, and I take my time to study the fallen leaves and pluck some wildflowers. When the clear, glass surface of the pond comes into view, I can't resist the urge to touch the water, carefully weaving through the brush to the water's edge. I graze a finger across the surface, then gradually wade my hand back and forth, watching the ripples expand in every direction.

Before long, I'm captivated by the intricate dance of cause and effect. The slightest touch upon the surface, or the tossing of a stone, every action, even the most subtle of movements will reverberate throughout the entirety of the tranquil pond. It causes me to think about my own life, about how every choice and every action I make affects those closest to me, my little circle of special people.

Five years ago, a heavy consequence from a terrible choice unexpectedly dropped into my pond. The water has finally stilled, and I hope my decision to stay in Solitude Ridge will be a positive ripple in my pond. For a long time, the ripples felt more like tidal waves, engulfing and drowning me. Isn't that why I am here after all? To iron out the past, hoping for smoother seas ahead? There would've been no harm in staying where I was before—working, and keeping busy—but I knew deep down that I would never truly be able to move on until I was here again. It was a personal experiment I created for myself. A test to see if I was really as strong as I felt—as strong as I knew I could be if I reached deep in myself.

I crave for my life to be like the calm stillness of the pond, but no matter how badly I want it, something whispers to me in the back of my mind that the peaceful life I desire is fleeting, and the next great wave will soon wash me away once again.

CHAPTER TEN

Renn

Firefly Night is one of the town's traditions that is known only by locals and Solitude Ridge regulars, and we try to keep it that way. The town is always welcoming to the crowds of tourists, but we like to hold on to the small town aspects when we can. For example, there are a handful of lakes in the area, but Mirror Lake has been kept away from the flow of tourists for many years, and I hope that never changes.

It was a happy coincidence that I saw Tova stop at the bookshop to say her goodbyes to Mina and Tash, and when she spotted me loading up my truck with folding tables and chairs to take down to the lake, she of course waved me over. I was honestly disappointed she had to leave, and when she gave me that warm, motherly hug asking me to look out for Maven, it made the guilt stab again because I couldn't tell her that I was trying to keep my distance since that night at the coffee shop.

Shy and I make a quick detour to pick up Grant, since he doesn't drive on his own much anymore, and now the three of us are driving down the bumpy, beaten road to the lake. Shy sits in the middle of Grant and me, ears perked and alert because she loves playing fetch on the lake shore, running through the water and retrieving sticks over and over again. There's already a line of cars parked on the beach, with grills and fires going when we arrive. It is a potluck of sorts, everyone contributes in some way.

I spy Mina and Valery directing people where to set up food and supplies. Shy stays in the truck, waiting for my command that she can get out. "Now don't get into trouble," I say to her, rubbing her ears.

"You've got that dog trained so well, she doesn't know what trouble means," Grants scoffs, slowly getting out of the truck.

"I know. I know. I just like to remind her." I pat Shy on the head one more time. "Alright then. Go ahead." She jumps out and makes a beeline for the lakeshore where a group of kids are laughing and already splashing around in the water. They welcome her with excited screams and giggles.

"Hey you two!" Tasha calls out, making her way over to us.

"Tash, help an old man out, would you?" Grants asks, beaming at her with his full gray beard and all.

"Of course. Anything for my favorite guy in town," she replies, taking his arm and helping him toward the camp.

"I thought I was your favorite guy in town," I say with a smirk.

She rolls her eyes playfully. "I'll be right back to help you unload those." She nods to the back of the truck.

I start pulling out the tables and chairs, and soon, Tash joins me. "You're so sweet, always taking care of Grant," she says, gathering a couple of chairs.

"He looked out for me when I first came here, so it's the least I can do," I respond, wrapping my arms around one of the tables, just wide enough for me to manage on my own. She snickers next to me. "What?" I ask through a smile.

"I've known you for years now, and I still can't get over how kind you are sometimes. You're a good friend," she says. She's looking toward the lake, so she doesn't see the flicker of guilt that I quickly push away. "*Good*." That word again. It still stings just as much as it did earlier.

"And what about you?" I ask. She looks at me a little surprised. "You're a good friend too." Her cheeks blush faintly as she grins up at me, finding I'm completely serious. "Don't think I've forgotten all the things you did for me when I showed up here too. I know you don't get new people who stay often, and you made it easier on me with your kindness. You and Grant were my first friends."

She grins wider now. "I take back what I said earlier. You are most definitely my favorite guy in town." She laughs, hitting me lightly in the arm with her free hand. "Speaking of friends..." I follow Tasha's gaze to see Maven pulling up next to my truck. All at once, nerves spark to life. *What is wrong with me?* I can't help but watch Maven get out of her car, her blue gaze flashing over me for a millisecond before looking at Tash.

"Mave!" Tasha exclaims, setting the chairs down before running over to her and wrapping her in a big hug. "It's Firefly Night!" she shouts, and they both chuckle.

"I know! My favorite Solitude Ridge tradition!" Maven says smiling. They both giggle excitedly like little kids for a moment.

"Come on!" Tash says, pulling her along.

I don't know how it happens so fast, but suddenly Shy starts running toward Maven and Tasha as they're locked arm in arm, barking happily.

"Shy! No, no, no!" I shout, but she completely ignores me and jumps on them, knocking them both to the ground. I'm not sure what I expected, but a jumble of laughs and Shy whining happily, licking Maven's face was not it. "Shy! Get off!" I yell, grabbing her by the collar and trying to pry her off.

Why do embarrassing things keep happening to me in front of this woman?

Tasha is on her knees clutching her stomach from laughing. Maven is flat on her back, stunned, but looks unharmed. I finally pull Shy off, but she still whines loudly.

"Sit," I say to her sternly, then look back down at Maven. "I am so sorry," I say as she sits up on her elbows, avoiding my eyes. "Are you okay?" I ask, kneeling beside her.

She wipes her face with her sleeve, her hair falling loose from parts of her long braid which is currently draped over her shoulder. She looks at me expressionless for a moment, but then she bites the inside of her cheek, trying to stop from smiling.

"I've never seen Shy do that to anyone!" Tasha exclaims.

"Uh-huh," Maven breathes out, narrowing her gaze at me while still holding back a smile the best she can.

"It's true. I swear," I add, but she doesn't look at me. Instead, she glances at Shy who is staying put, her tail thumping on the ground as it wags happily. Maven looks at Shy then back to me, and then the wonderful sounds of her laugh pours from her. Before I know it, all three of us are laughing, and I swear, if dogs could look smug, Shy's expression looks like she is quite proud of herself.

"Thanks for the warm welcome, Shy," Maven says cooly with a wide grin, rubbing a hand over Shy's ears.

"I really am sorry," I say as she continues to pat Shy's back.

"I forgive you, Shy. It's okay," she says while looking at me. Tasha flashes me a smirk. I stand and reach down for Maven's hand, and she squeezes it tightly as I help her to her feet.

"Don't worry, I've got it," Tasha says, standing. "Anyway. Let's go. Mom and I got our spot all set up." I give her an apologetic look.

I watch them walk away before I say to Shy, "Not really helping 'the keep my distance' plan, you know."

Shy's tongue sticks out of the side of her mouth, and she's staring at me like it was nothing at all. Then to top it all off, she leaves me to follow the two of them. That little shit, but I will love that dog forever for breaking the tension. I watch Shy trail Maven and Tash all the way to where they have a group of chairs arranged together. Shaking my head, I walk over to sit next to Grant.

"I guess Shy isn't as well trained as I thought," Grant says to me as I sit down next to him.

"I guess not," I mumble, rubbing my jaw as I watch Shy sit right beside Maven like she's done it a thousand times. Grant follows my gaze.

"Looks like you've been replaced," he adds, chuckling.

"I'll say."

"Renn! What happened over there?" Val asks as she walks over to us.

"I have no idea."

"Looked pretty funny from where I was standing," she says, giggling.

"It was not funny! More like, awkward." I bellow. I can't help but glance back at Maven as she runs her fingers through Shy's fluffy, brown fur. Shy looks like she's in heaven.

"Renn, are you blushing?" Valery asks, her tone rising an octave.

"What? No!" I say, standing.

"Where are you going?" she asks, giving me a look.

"To see if the food is ready. I'm hungry."

"I think you're right, Valery. He is blushing," Grants says, chuckling.

"Okay, thank you! You can stop now," I say, walking quickly toward the large tables with plates of food on top. This is going to be an interesting night to say the least.

No one really knows why, but every year without fail, a glow of fireflies make their home on the shores of Mirror Lake, and their lights shine the brightest against the still surface of the water at this time of the season. This phenomena is the closest thing I've found on this planet that can compare to the wonders I've seen in this galaxy. That is, until I saw Maven's eyes. That thought alone heats my blood. *Get a hold of yourself.*

Eventually, dinner gets cleaned up, and we all start to gather together on the lake's edge as the sun begins to set. It's moments like this that make us feel more like family than just neighbors. Shy hasn't left Maven's side the entire afternoon. We make eye contact a few times, but I stay by Grant's side for the majority of the time until the sun starts to set and an excitement starts building because we all know what is about to happen. I use this as my opportunity to walk over to Mina, Tash, and Maven.

"I hope Shy hasn't been bothering you all too much," I say, standing beside Mina.

"Not at all. She's always such a sweetheart," Mina says.

"She certainly has a thing for Maven," Tasha adds, giving me a knowing look.

I give her a tight smile. "It looks like it," I reply.

We all wait a second or two for Maven to add something to the conversation, but she keeps her attention on the lake, like she might not have heard us at all. Tasha and Mina both give her a look of sympathy.

The last rays of the sun dip under the mountain peaks, and at this exact second, the fireflies start to emerge from the foliage and begin dancing over the lake's surface. Even though most of us have witnessed this several times, many still *ooh* and *ahh* at the sight. Everyone watches for several minutes without a word, taking it all in.

"I'm so glad to be here with you all," Tash says reverently as she looks at each of us. I give her a wink when her eyes catch mine.

"Me too, sweetheart," Mina says, wrapping her arm around her daughter. "I wish your mom was here with us, Maven," Mina adds, and Maven takes a deep breath.

"I wish both my parents were here," she says softly, her eyes still entranced by the glow of the fireflies, like she hasn't realized what she said aloud. Mina and Tash look at each other, but before either of them can reply, Valery comes over to us, pulling their attention away. I don't hear a word they say to each other as I watch Maven out of the corner of my eye. I don't think she notices me, but I catch a small tear falling from her eye. She bats it away quickly. The urge I have to walk over to comfort her hits me so deeply that I take a few steps away from her, hoping some distance will help ease that pull. Unfortunately, it doesn't. It seems the weeks I was able to stay away did little, and now I'm right back where I was that night in the coffee shop, wondering, and wanting to know her more and more.

It seems like everyone gives Maven her space for the span of the fireflies' intricate display. The only one to never leave her side is Shy, but I get the feeling that is what Maven prefers, because she never looks away, not once.

When the display ends, I don't know if she ever looks my way as I walk back over to Grant's side to help him back into my truck. Everyone disperses, so I can't see Maven or Shy through the crowd, so I whistle for Shy to follow, and to my surprise, she actually obeys. I thought I was going to have to pry her away from Maven. Shy runs to my side and looks up at me, blinking a couple of times, and even though her golden irises aren't human, they seem to match mine. Because all I see in her eyes is a sadness and a want that neither of us can explain, but it's clear we both are thinking of the same woman.

CHAPTER ELEVEN

Maven

Tasha and I go to The Blue Bird after the lake for some scones. It's obvious the night was an emotional one for me, so I appreciated her asking if I wanted to go for a late night treat. She wasn't wrong, I need it. For one thing there was the Shy fiasco, which was actually hilarious and ended in my favor as I came away with a new furry companion, even if it was embarrassing for a moment or two. I've never been a dog person, but I guess I am now.

And then there was Renn.

How could he make me feel on fire one minute, then like I was being submerged in cold water the next? It makes no sense—not to my mind or my heart. Every moment with Renn is an up and down from one emotion to the other. Sometimes good. Sometimes bad, but no matter what, it is always intense. I didn't get a chance to talk to him as much as I was hoping tonight.

Then there were the images of my dad flashing through my mind as I watched the fireflies dance over the water. Attending an actual Solitude Ridge event without him had hit me deeper than I thought it would, and I don't want to face the idea that maybe I'm not ready for this—to be back here—after all.

"So . . ." Tash says, pulling my thoughts away from me, "how would you feel about going on a hiking trip with me?"

"A hiking trip? What do you mean?" In all the years I've known Tasha, she's never been on a hiking trip. Hiking, yes, but an entire trip? No. Once I notice her mischievous grin, I start to worry.

"Well, it's more of a retreat, so to speak. It's only for a few days. One of the tour companies in town started doing this huge end-of-the-year retreat for the last few seasons, it's kind of a big thing now. I signed up to go this year, and . . ." I glare at her. "I was hoping you might want to come with me." She intertwines her fingers. I wonder how long she's been contemplating asking me about this; she's certainly nervous.

"When is it?" I groan, trying to sound as uninterested as I can.

"Next week."

I choke on my coffee. "What? Why didn't you ask me about it sooner?"

She grimaces. "Honestly, I didn't want to tell you too far in advance in case you said yes and then started to overthink it."

I scoff.

"Come on! I know you. You would find some reason not to go the more you thought about it. This way, by the time you talk yourself out of it, we'll already be on the retreat so you won't be able to back out."

"Ha ha ha, very funny," I say, folding my arms, unimpressed, even though it is absolutely true. I ponder her request before responding, really taking into consideration what I would be getting myself into if I said yes. "I don't know, Tash. I'm not really in the best shape."

She shakes her head fiercely. "What are you talking about?" I shrug, and then it hits her as she realizes what I meant. "Are you worried about your legs?" she asks softly.

I nod. "Kind of. How difficult are we talking here?"

Her face turns serious. "I mean, I'm sure it's not going to be easy, but you can do it. I know you can." She smiles hopefully. I purse my lips to the side and scrunch my nose in thought. "And it will be so beautiful this time of year," she adds. "Have you ever actually been to the overlook before?"

The overlook is where Solitude Ridge got its name. At the highest peak, you can see the space in between the two mountain ranges, making the forest and valleys nestled between totally secluded. Solitude. Isolated from everything as the mountains provide a refuge, or a confinement, depending on how you look at it. Though I've only seen pictures, it's supposedly a summit of beauty and serenity.

I shrug bashfully. "I'll admit, I've always wanted to see it in person."

Tash bites her lip, waiting for me to agree; she knows she almost has me convinced. Ideally, it sounds perfect, but in reality, I'm not completely confident my body can handle the journey. I've learned the hard way how bodies can be easily broken, but at the same time, I battled through hell to heal and get to where I am, and I'm not going to waste it.

"If I say yes, what exactly would I need to do?"

Tasha claps her hands excitedly. "Yay! Okay! I'm so excited. I'll take care of everything. I'll get you a packing list of what you need, which I'm sure you already have most of, and if you don't, you'll be able to find it easily in town."

What do I have to lose?

My pride, for one, but why not push myself? That's why I came here, to move forward and up. I didn't really intend it to be literal by climbing a mountain, though.

"Alright, fine. Count me in."

Tasha grabs my hands, beaming, her hazel eyes bright. "It will be amazing. I just know it!" Her smile stretches from ear to ear. I'm not convinced it will be amazing, but what was the point of surviving the accident if I don't embrace life?

"I'm excited too." And I mean that with all my might, saying a little prayer in my mind to anyone who is listening that I can make it to the end of the journey.

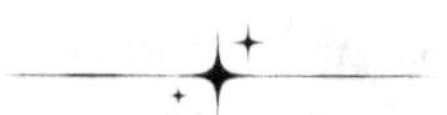

A week later, Tasha and I arrive at Solitude Ridge Adventure Tours at exactly 5:50 a.m. We grab our packs and gear from the back of Tash's car and head over to the group gathered near a folding table, where participants are completing paperwork. I signed all of the forms a few days ago, making note of how many times the word, "injury," and the phrase, "life threatening," appeared before signing. This was either going to be a great test of my abilities, or something I would regret severely. Either way, I was planning for the "experience of a lifetime," which was another phrase mentioned often in the forms. No doubt to distract people from the clear warnings of potential doom. Tasha also forgot to mention that we will be eating a variety of dehydrated meals where you simply "add water to consume." Sounds tasty.

When I brought this to her attention, she just said, "It will be fine."

"Have you had one before?" I asked.

"Well, no, but they can't be that bad, right?"

I have an inkling they will, in fact, be as horrible as I imagine.

"I'm going to grab a coffee. Want one?" Tasha asks, nodding toward the coffee house.

"Yes. Please." Coffee sounds divine.

She gives me a thumbs up and sleepily walks away to grab our much-needed jolt of caffeine. While I wait for her to return, I take in the group. It's a much larger gathering than I expected. The thought of this many people watching me fail ties my stomach in knots.

Awesome.

Some are gathered in smaller groups, a few I know, and they offer me friendly waves or nods when I catch their eye. The rest of the group is made up of excited tourists who have probably been preparing for this for months, while I had only a week's notice. Everyone is wearing the typical, outdoorsy dress code. Most of the women are wearing tight-fitting shorts and tank tops like myself, and like a few others, I have a jacket tied around my waist. Layers. Tasha told me to focus on light layers when packing my not-large-enough backpack. On top of my many clothing options, I managed to smash not only a sleeping bag and small tent into the bag, but a cot as well.

I check my phone for the time, 5:55 a.m. I look in the direction of the coffee shop to see if Tasha is making her way back, but instead of finding her, I see something I wasn't expecting. A man driving a motorbike, with an impressive-sized backpack strapped to it, pulling into the parking area. I immediately know who it is, even though he's wearing a helmet with the visor covering his face. The flip my stomach makes at the sight of him makes me a little queasy.

Surely Renn isn't coming on the retreat.

Sure enough, it's Renn who steps off the bike, removing his helmet in a swift movement.

He has on a long-sleeve, white shirt, dark pants, and hiking boots. His hair is extra messy until he runs a hand through it, smoothing it somewhat into place. I stare, unblinking, at him. I can't help it, and I'm not the only one enjoying the show. Several women and a few men are side-eyeing him too, trying to act like they aren't watching his every move when they most definitely are. What's annoying is that he's not even aware of it.

The butterflies in my stomach grow as he moves to undo the straps holding his pack in place. *He's coming on the retreat.* Panic settles over me, and suddenly, I'm sweating. He doesn't seem to notice me as he walks over to a group of guys who have waved him over.

"Renn's coming?" Tash asks, approaching with our coffees in hand.

"It looks like it," I reply, taking mine from her.

"Well, well, well, this is interesting." Tasha says, bumping me with her elbow. I give her a sidelong glance, then look back to find Renn in the crowd, and when I do, he's watching me. We make eye contact, and he starts walking toward us.

"Great," I mutter under my breath so only Tasha hears.

"Relax," Tasha whispers back. "Renn! Hey! Happy to see you're joining us," she says a little too loud. I give her a look of warning, telling her to cool it, but she ignores me.

"Yeah, I decided to join at the last minute," he says, looking at Tasha and then me.

"What changed your mind?" My tone sounds a little frantic, but he only smiles back.

"I guess I've been so busy that I didn't realize how close it was for good hiking weather to almost be over, so I thought I'd better join before it's too late." Those stormy eyes remain on me as he speaks.

I take another sip of my coffee, acting like it doesn't affect me if he is joining.

"Yeah, that's totally why you came last minute," Tasha says with a wink, causing me to choke on my coffee. She slaps me on the back. "You okay there, Mave?"

I clear my throat and cough. "Yep. All good." And this time, I glare at her and I don't care if Renn notices.

"Have you ever been to the outlook, Maven?" he asks me.

Finally able to catch my breath, I peer into his eyes. They're more gray toned than green today.

"No. *We* haven't been to the outlook."

Renn bites the inside of his cheek. "Well . . ." he says, rubbing the back of his neck, and I spy a small chain there, the same one he's worn every time I've seen him. I've only ever noticed the outline through his shirt. He glances between us. "I'll see you guys on the trail then." He smiles back at Tash and bites his lip like he's trying to hold back a laugh when he looks at me like he knows what I'm thinking. I watch him return to the group of guys he joined earlier.

"Thanks for that," I say, hitting Tasha on the arm. She snorts.

"Oh, come on. We clearly know why he's here."

"Do we?"

"Yes! He's here because you are!" she says, poking my shoulder.

"No way!" I mock.

"Maven, he's never come on this retreat before. The only thing different this year is *you*."

I shake my head fervently. "I can't tell what he is thinking. One minute it seems like he wants to keep his distance, the next ...I don't know. He is such a mystery." I sneak another glance over to where he's listening to one of the guys in the group.

"Well, he obviously doesn't want to keep his distance now," Tash remarks, giving me another nudge.

"Whatever." I roll my eyes. That can't be why he's here . . . Can it?

"Whatever, nothing! I can sense the tension between you two!" A few people nearby glance in our direction.

"Shhh!" I laugh, hitting her in the arm again.

"This is going to be an *interesting* few days, that's all I'm going to say," she says, putting her free hand up in defense.

At that moment, a group of people wearing matching shirts, who I assume are the guides, steps in front of the group. The one who appears to be the leader shouts over the crowd for everyone to come closer. Tash lifts her pack from the ground, and I reluctantly sling mine over my shoulders, rolling my eyes as I follow. I don't know if "interesting" is the word I would use, but I guess we'll find out.

After we receive the general information and instructions for our first day, we pile into the shuttles waiting to drive us to the trailhead. Tash conveniently chooses the shuttle Renn boarded. I try not to make eye contact with him, keeping my gaze toward the window, but there's no force that can stop me from watching him lift his pack into an overhead bin, his forearms flexing and shirt rising to reveal a sliver of skin. *Get a grip on yourself, Maven. Is it going to be like this the entire retreat?* Throughout the forty-five minute drive to the trailhead, people talk excitedly, becoming more alive as the morning sleepiness wears off. Despite my best efforts, I find myself stealing a glance over my shoulder at the group Renn is sitting with. He's bent over, arms resting on his knees as he talks with the people near him, all of them leaning in to listen. Whatever he's saying must be compelling.

"Okay, but for real, are you okay?" Tasha says. "I didn't mean to give you a hard time because *you know who* is coming along."

I don't want to make a big deal about it either. Because it isn't. Renn can do whatever he wants, and I'm not upset he's here, just startled. He keeps taking me by surprise. I want to focus on what this hiking retreat is for me and me alone, and I'm not going to be distracted, even by *him*.

"Yes. I'm fine." I say.

She gives me another *I'm sorry* look. "Okay. If you're sure."

"I am." We sit in silence for a beat or two. "So, he's really never been on the retreat before?"

Tasha grins. "Nope. Never."

I let out a small giggle. "Interesting."

And that's the last thing we say to each other for the rest of the drive as the butterflies in my stomach dance wildly.

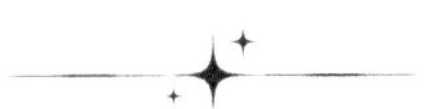

Once we reach the trailhead, the group is anxious to get started. A light breeze ruffles the leaves and branches of the dense forest around us. Yellows and reds contrast against the dark evergreen, creating a breathtaking view. The guides gather everyone together to hand out maps for reference on our journey, indicating how far we will go each day and where we will camp each night. They also pass out a schedule of who will help collect firewood or assist with cleaning each day. After another quick safety reminder to stay with the group and not wander from the trail, we head out.

According to our itinerary, we will hike eight to twelve miles a day with a couple of breaks before we make camp each night. Six days in all—two days to get to the outlook, two days camping near it, then two days to hike down to home.

I don't see where Renn ended up as we follow the people in front of us and start to move forward. Soon, the trail narrows, so we have to walk two by two for the next stretch. The first few miles are fairly flat, making it easy to keep a conversation going without getting too winded. Tasha and I talk about a variety of topics, but by the time we're at mile five, the steepness of the trail drastically increases. The guides are spread throughout the group, and a few mention this bit as the first of the steeper stretches of the trail and to watch our steps, saying things like "it's a bit rocky here," or "watch this log, it's unstable." It forms an instant comradery within the group as we point out the bits in the path that could be hazards. I've heard that being in the wilderness has this effect on people. It's a comforting thought that, for the next few days, everyone will be looking out for each other, even though many of us are complete strangers.

The guides aren't exaggerating about the steepness. By the time the trail evens out again, I'm panting and sweaty. I shouldn't be surprised since, according to the map, we will experience an elevation gain of about six thousand feet by the time we are through. Luckily, we're toward the front of the group, so once we reach the stopping point, it gives us extra time to rest for lunch. I welcomed the burning in my legs as my muscles worked to carry me forward, but I'm equally grateful for a moment to sit. Tasha and I settle near a group of women around our age as we snack on granola bars and nuts.

I'm not paying much attention to what they're saying until I hear one of them say, "I already know who my retreat crush is." The others in the group giggle.

"Oh, yeah? Who?" another one asks.

"I think someone said his name is Renn."

Tasha glances over to them and then gives me a mischievous look.

"I think he's a local," another adds.

Tasha and I both stare at each other, grinning. Of course he caught their attention already. I don't blame them; he had the same effect on me when I first saw him. Still does.

"He's so attractive. I'm tempted to just pull him off into the forest for a quick . . ." She stops abruptly, and the others make shushing sounds because, right on cue, Renn walks over to Tasha and me.

"Hello . . . Renn," Tasha says slowly and loudly, to be sure they heard.

"How's it going?" he asks, his voice cheery.

"Good. Not too bad so far," she replies. "How about you?"

I look up, craning my neck to watch him as he answers. Sitting makes it more difficult than usual to actually make eye contact with him. He notices my strain and sits on a rock in front of us. I notice that he doesn't seem winded at all. Of course he isn't.

"It's been great," he says, reaching for his water canteen. I notice the group next to us has suddenly gone deathly quiet.

"Hmm," is all I say in response, followed by a few seconds of silence.

"Who's watching Shy while you're away?" Tasha asks, sensing the "tension" she mentioned earlier.

"I left her with Grant. I think he'll enjoy the company."

"Nice," Tasha says and then looks at me like it's my turn to add to the conversation, but I pretend to be searching for something in my backpack. "So—" Tasha starts, but I interrupt.

"So, Renn, Tash says you've never been on the retreat before." He stares at me with a shocked expression, and I can feel Tasha's wide eyes drilling into me.

"I have not," he says as he cocks his head to the side, trying to get a read on me. I keep my eyes locked on him, waiting for him to look away first, but he keeps watching me too.

"So, why now?" I ask.

Tasha acts like she's more interested in the trees, studying anything besides me and Renn. The group behind us whispers. I'm not sure what it says about me that I'm enjoying them listening in on this flirtatious exchange. I've never considered myself very good at flirting, but with Renn it comes to me easily.

"I don't know. There was just something different about this year," he says in a calm manner. If flirting was a competition Renn would win every single time. He gives me a wink and smiles. My face feels hot because I can't stop myself from blushing at that smile. I try to think of something to say to calm the nervous excitement continuing to rise in me.

"My mom said you stopped by the bookshop to say goodbye," I say flatly.

"I did."

"And?"

He leans forward, resting his elbows on his knees. I catch his scent—rain and something else I can't place at the moment. "It was nothing really. I mostly just wanted to show her the nice-looking scar I now have on my forearm from the roof."

Tash guffaws, but I squint at him, challenging him to see if he's all jokes or if he'll say what I think he wants to.

"Okay, fine. I like your mom, so I also wanted to let her know I was sad to see her go, but that I look forward to when she returns."

I cock my head this time. "Really?" I wonder.

"And," he goes on, a bit softer this time, as if bashful about his next statement, "that I would look out for her daughter even if I think she can take care of herself. Regardless, I will still come if she calls."

Tash sighs, and I'm interrupted before I can say anything.

"Alright, everyone! We've got four miles until we make camp for the night. Be ready to move in five minutes," one of the guides calls out.

Renn stands. "I guess I'll see you two around." He smiles at me for a second longer, and I hold back the urge to grin back and settle for a smirk. I feel like he understood the frustration I was feeling toward him, and that in some underlying way, he was saying sorry.

Once he's a safe distance away, Tasha eyes me suspiciously. "Is it just me or is the tension between you two reaching out of this world heights?"

I shrug, and we gather our packs, strapping them onto our backs once again. Then I turn to Tasha, grinning.

CHAPTER TWELVE

Renn

I wasn't exaggerating when I told Tasha and Maven that it was a last-minute decision to join the retreat. Luckily, I already had all the gear I needed for the journey. The hard part was deciding what else to take with me. I tossed and turned about it the night before, wondering if I should bring the beacon, but thought better of it for the fact that someone might discover it and start asking unwanted questions. It is much safer to keep it at home, even if that means it'll be awhile until I can check it. I didn't expect how strange it would feel leaving it behind, like a weight has been lifted off of me. It's freed me from having to make the choice to pull out the transmitter or not, waiting for the unchanging results again and again. It was a risky move, so I left the transmitter on, but the likelihood of anyone picking up or sending a message while I'm away is near zero since it hasn't happened a single time in five years. And besides, watching Maven's face as I rode up this morning was both satisfying and amusing.

Worth every worry I had. And yes, I *was* watching her.

It took some serious control not to laugh at our exchange this morning, but I know I saw something else in the radiant blue of her eyes—I may even dare to say it was enthusiasm, knowing that I would be coming along.

I'd ended up toward the back of the group as we set off this morning, and every once in a while, when I would glance up the trail, I would spot Maven, her long, dark hair pulled back, swinging as it draped down her back. I also couldn't help but notice the scars on her knees and legs. The largest is on her upper right thigh, while others aren't as noticeable, but because of the shorts she's wearing, it's hard not to stare. Some marks seem to have been made with precision, while others are more jagged. I assume they must be from the accident and possibly surgery, or surgeries. Seeing them on her skin made me realize just how severe the accident must have been, but what struck me most of all was that she isn't shy about revealing them to the world. She carries them with grace, and I decide it's the most attractive thing about her—that she bears it all with pride and won't let anything limit her, not even people's stares and whispers, which are hard to miss.

When Valery just so happened to mention, the night before the retreat, that Maven was going this year with Tasha, I immediately felt an internal pull, a gravitational force, drawing me to her. It wasn't going away, it only seemed to be getting harder to ignore.

And so, a few hours later, I find myself hiking through the thick wilderness with people I know and some I do not, but it doesn't matter who's here, because I'm only here for one reason—one person.

We continue our journey after the break, and I stay close to Tasha and Maven for the next few miles. One minute, the group is moving at a good pace through the evergreen landscape, the next, we abruptly halt when a scream of pain rings out through the trees. I don't see it happen, but the sound alone tells me that it's not good. Without thinking, I push through the gathered crowd and discover that one of the guides has twisted their ankle. It already looks swollen where she lies on the dirt path. I hadn't intended to intervene, but Asher, our head guide who is supporting her, spots me.

"Renn. Would you mind taking a look?" Asher has been leading these hiking retreats for the last few years, and when a little girl went missing a couple of years ago, he and I covered a lot of ground together, so he's familiar with my skills and background.

"Sure," I say, sliding off my pack before kneeling next to Talla, a local, but I don't know her well. She looks up at me with tears in her eyes. "I just need to examine it closer. I'll be gentle, but it may hurt a little," I say, keeping my voice calm.

She only nods in response. She winces as I place my hands on the swollen ankle, turning it ever so slightly, causing her to grip the arm of another guide, holding her tighter.

"It could be a bad sprain, but I think it's broken." I pause. "I'm sorry," I say, looking at her, and she gives me a tight-lipped smile.

"I'm so sorry, everyone," she says, glancing around the group, tears in her eyes.

"It's okay, T. It could have happened to any of us," Asher says, kneeling to lay a reassuring hand on her shoulder. "Let me get in touch with the office crew to see what we can do." Asher steps away to search for a clearing to make the call using the satellite phone. The rest of the hiking group waits, some taking the opportunity to rest while others appear a little on edge with concern. One of the other guides briefly goes through the group to explain the situation.

After a few minutes, Asher returns, looking slightly relieved. "I radioed in, and a team can be at the trailhead within a couple of hours. If we can get back down to the first marker, they should be able to meet us with a stretcher to get her down from that point." We nod along. "The problem is, that means two of us will have to abandon the group. Leaving only two guides to lead the rest of you to camp for the night." The group exchanges worried glances, and I already know what that means.

"I can do it," I say. They all look at me and then at Asher.

"You sure?" he asks.

"If you're concerned about leaving only two guides here with the group, I'd be happy to go with one of you to get Talla to the meeting point. If we leave now and then hike back at a fast pace, we should be able to get to camp before we completely lose the light."

Asher glances to the other guides for their reactions. "Renn, can you give us a moment?"

"Of course." I step a few feet away as they talk.

I search through the group until I find Maven and Tasha looking on from afar, both of them wearing worried expressions. For a moment, Maven's eyes meet mine, and maybe I imagine it, but the worry in her eyes seems to deepen before she quickly looks away, saying something to Tasha. Tash shrugs in response. Soon, the guide group breaks from each other and Asher steps forward.

"Talla is comfortable with it, so we all agreed it would be okay for you to go." He leans in closer so only I can hear him as he says, "Of course, I know you're more than capable with your experience."

I nod. "I understand."

Asher slaps me lightly on the back before instructing the other guides to prepare for next steps. Maven and Tasha keep watching me intently, and I make my way toward them to give them the news. Tasha parts her lips to speak as I approach but is interrupted.

"Is everything okay?" Maven quickly asks.

"She needs to be carried down to where a medical team can meet up to take her the rest of the way." They seem to already know what I'm going to say next. "I'm going with another guide to take her, and we will hike back as quickly as we can to get to camp before sundown."

Maven doesn't say anything at first, staring at her boots.

"Do you need us to carry anything for you? A lighter load may help the journey back," Tasha says.

"That would actually be great if you don't mind."

"Of course we don't," she replies. I rummage through my pack and give them my tent and sleeping bag, both bulky items, but not too heavy.

"You sure you don't mind?" I ask, zipping my pack back up.

"Not at all," Tasha says. I turn to Maven, but she's looking away, adjusting the straps of her pack with the added items.

"I'll be seeing you two at camp before nightfall. Hopefully," I say, winking just as Maven's eyes meet mine again.

"See you later," Tasha says.

I turn, taking a few steps, but before I'm too far, Maven calls out to me, "Be careful, Renn." Her voice is smooth, but it carries concern. I turn around to meet a gaze of azure.

"I will," I say with a smirk.

Maven fully smiles back this time, and it gives me a boost of confidence I didn't know I needed. I don't look back to see if she watches as me and another guide, Trey, situate Talla, placing her arms around our necks while we support her legs and lift her between us. We say our farewells and start the trip back down while the rest of the group continues up the winding path through the forest. I don't get a chance to find Maven again in the crowd, but I can feel her eyes watching me until we're too far away to be seen, vanishing from view.

Sure enough, the medical crew met us about a mile out from the trailhead. Trey and I said little to each other as we carried Talla down the trail, mostly just to conserve our strength, but I encouraged her to talk to us, if only to distract her from the pain, and it seemed to help. She was extremely grateful for the help, and I was happy to offer it, because by the time she was strapped into the stretcher, her ankle had almost doubled in size. I feel a little bit guilty, because I did bring the tin of healing ointment, and I was tempted to use it, but I couldn't risk it. At least not yet. The only reason I would ever consider using it would be in a life or death situation, or on myself if no one could witness the medical miracle. It had been an adjustment, having been used to my planet's more advanced medicine for so long. But there were no body scanners or instant healing remedies here. As soon as the medical team gets her settled, Trey and I make the trek once again up the mountain. We move at a decent pace, both of us experienced and in shape enough to take on the challenge.

"Have you worked in the medical field?" Trey asks when we stop for a quick water break.

"I know some of the basics, but that's all."

He takes another swig of water. "So you served in the military, right?"

I know he's just trying to make small talk, and similar questions about my background have often been brought up before. Truthfully, a military career might be the closest thing to what my line of work used to entail. I always answer that inquiry with the same response.

"My previous profession was very similar to military work, but I left some time ago due to personal reasons."

That phrase usually makes people stop asking questions, or they will change the subject, just as Trey does now as he straps his water canteen back onto his pack and says, "Nice."

We don't speak the rest of the way, focused on our steps, moving quickly. The sun's rays cast long shadows through the trees. The air nips with a chill, but the cold is welcome as it cools our overexerted limbs. We're hot and sweaty from the intense speed, but I can tell he likes the challenge as much as I do.

The forest was already quiet, but as the night creeps in, the stillness becomes more menacing. Pitch blackness is familiar to me. I witnessed a very different kind of darkness in space—the abyss and void that never ended. Those images remain with me and always will. There's nothing like it.

I'm about to pull out a flashlight to help guide us in the failing light, but spot the warm glow of a campfire, and soon we come upon camp, the light from the small city of tents helping to guide us the rest of the way. Someone must have spotted us, because I hear a whistle, and the hikers still lingering by the fire jump up and start clapping.

Asher is the first to get to us, shaking our hands in gratitude. "Well, you waited till the last minute, but you made it just like you said you would. Thank you both." I nod, and Trey starts to give Asher the details of the journey and the update on Talla. I scan the camp, many people chatting happily, and then I see her. Maven sees me too and speed walks over to me.

"You made it!" she says, relieved.

"Cutting it close, but we did indeed," I say.

We hold each other's gaze for a few more seconds before she says, "You must be exhausted. Come sit down." I follow her to the fire, and she leads me to where Tasha is sitting.

"Renn! The hero once again!" Tasha exclaims as I sit next to her, shrugging off my pack and rolling my shoulders.

"I'll go grab you something to eat," Maven says and walks off.

"So, how tired are you?" Tasha asks. I stretch out my legs in front of me and then loosen the laces on my boots.

"Honestly, not too tired," I say.

"Show off," she says, hitting me in the arm. "I knew you'd be fine, but Maven has been on high alert since you left. She's been overly anxious," she says, pursing her lips with raised eyebrows. Her very subtle way of saying *Maven was worried about you*. I give her a sidelong glance as I take a swig of my water.

Maven appears again with food in hand, which appears to be some kind of rice and vegetable plate. She hands it to me as she says, "It's actually not bad, but I won't lie, I'm already looking forward to fresh food again."

I smile up at her. "Thank you."

"Will Talla be okay?" Tasha asks.

"I think so," I say before taking a bite of the food. A few people come over to offer their praise. "I was happy to do it," I say what feels like a hundred times.

The crowd disperses as people begin to retire to their tents for the night. I quickly finish the food so I can get my own tent up. "I better get set up before it's too dark," I say to Tasha. Maven has her back to me and is in the middle of a conversation with Larissa, another local.

"We got it set up for you," Tasha says, looking pleased. "Well, actually, I set up our tent and Maven set up yours." I turn back to Maven, but Larissa is stealing her attention.

"Will you tell her I said thank you?"

"Of course. Let me show you where your tent is," Tasha says, and I follow her. I glance over my shoulder again, finding Larissa still talking to Maven, seeming to be in a deep conversation. "She gets that a lot," Tasha says, following my gaze.

"What do you mean?" I ask as I walk beside her.

"I'm sure Larissa has been dying to ask her about everything," she states, very matter-of-factly. "She puts on a brave face, but she hates it," Tasha adds. I don't say anything, thinking back to that night at the coffee shop—Jamie's utter disbelief at seeing her standing there in front of him, like it wasn't true. "She's used to it, all the questions and what not. I worry about her, too," she says.

"I'm not worried about her," I reply a little too quickly, completely giving me away. Tasha's lips turn into a smile.

"Your face says otherwise," she retorts, and I bite my lip to keep from saying more. "Anyway, here we are." She motions to the two tents nestled near each other.

"Thanks again for your help. I appreciate it."

"No problem. Glad you made it back safe." She pats me on the arm before disappearing into her tent.

The low chatter of people settling in their tents drifts through the camp, and beams from flashlights appear here and there. I look back one last time to Maven, still sitting by the fire with Larissa. Tash is right; I do worry about her, but not in the same way I suspect Tova, Mina, and Tasha do. I worry because I know how utterly terrifying it feels to face the things we've kept hidden away for so long.

CHAPTER THIRTEEN

Maven

When I was finally able to join Tasha for the evening, she was already fast asleep on her cot. I'd seen Larissa in the crowd earlier that morning and had tried to avoid her, but she'd found her opportunity and practically held me captive, asking for all the details on my recovery and "how I was doing after such a tragic event."

There was a small glow coming from inside Renn's tent as I passed by. For a moment, I thought of saying something, but decided to leave it till morning, quickly zipping my tent flap.

Breakfast today is a pouch of dehydrated sausage, eggs, and peppers. It honestly isn't as bad as the beef and vegetables from the night before, but as I watch Tasha take her first bite, she very painfully smiles through it. She'll never admit she's miserable.

Renn must have woken up much earlier than us, because by the time we emerged, his tent was already packed up. It doesn't surprise me that he's a morning person—laziness doesn't seem to be in his character.

As we help clean up the rest of camp, I find him assisting a couple of women who had overheard our conversation yesterday. He's patiently instructing them how to store everything from their tent back into their bag, but I doubt they're as helpless as they're pretending to be.

However, not even that could distract me from this first, beautiful morning out in the wilderness. It's been years since I last went camping, and I forgot how special it is, waking up in peaceful nature. I love the cold, early morning air hitting my cheeks, the crisp air filling my lungs. Last night, we made camp near a grove of trees with bright-yellow leaves, and the first sun rays illuminate them so much that it looks like they will catch fire.

"Beautiful," Tasha says, coming to stand next to me.

"Yeah, you definitely weren't exaggerating about this part of the retreat."

Someone whistles loudly, and we turn to find one of the guides calling us over now that the rest of the group is ready to go.

"Ready for another day of fun?" Tasha asks with a hopeful smile.

"Not sure if I'd call it fun," I say, giving her a look.

"So far, it's nothing like I thought, but I'm still enjoying it. You know what I mean?" she asks, and we make our way over to the group where I see Renn shrugging on his backpack now that the not-so-helpless women are packed up.

"Yeah, I do," I say just as Renn catches me looking at him and gives me a wink.

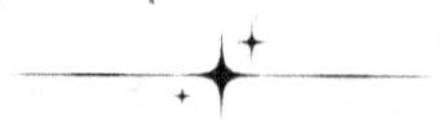

My right knee and thigh start to ache with the constant incline about two miles after we stop for lunch. The left is managing it well enough, but the right—it hurts more and more with each step. The pain is unwelcome, but not unexpected. My right leg was injured worse than the left and didn't recover quite as well. At first, I hold back the groans and winces of pain, but soon, the release is the only thing that keeps me pushing forward.

"Mave, we can stop. It's not a big deal," Tasha says.

"No. If I stop, then I might not be able to get going again. The momentum helps."

She's unconvinced, cringing at the sound that escapes my mouth with the next step I take.

I sigh heavily in defeat. "Okay, fine. But just for a minute."

We step aside, letting people pass, and I pull out the bottle of pain relievers from my pack. I had hoped I wouldn't have to resort to them, but right now, I'm beyond glad with my decision to bring them. I ignore Tasha's worried look, pouring a couple into my palm and plopping them into my mouth.

People continue to pass us, some offering encouraging looks, others with sympathy, and both annoy me. I know people are trying to be nice, but it just makes me frustrated. We still have the rest of today and most of tomorrow before we reach the summit. The frustration spirals through me, and I hate myself for it, that I can't hold on just a little bit longer—that I'll let the broken part in me win again and again. I begin to wonder if coming back to Solitude Ridge was perhaps the worst decision I've made since the day my dad died, and the only thought in my mind is that I should have never come back.

What if I can't make it? I'll probably have to be carried down the mountain. Will Renn carry me like he did Talla? That thought makes my cheeks warm just in time to see that Renn is about to pass. I keep my head down, not wanting to see the pity in his eyes. I can handle anyone but him.

"Hey, guys. You good?"

I look up, meeting his cool, gray eyes, and I'm surprised by what I find. It's not pity—it's something else that I can't place. And then I notice he's holding what looks like a small, metal container.

He follows my gaze as he says, "I . . ." He clears his throat, almost as if he's nervous. "I noticed that your leg was bothering you." My cheeks flush again with embarrassment, but he offers an encouraging smile. "I have something that may help." He holds out the container. It doesn't have a label or any indication of what it is, so I look up at him, confused. "It's an ointment for injuries."

I glance over at Tasha, and she bites her lip, trying not to say something. I know whatever it is she wants to say would have my cheeks flushing redder.

"So, it's a numbing cream of some kind?" I ask.

He licks his bottom lip. "Yeah, something like that." I give him a skeptical look because I've tried other pain relief methods over the years and they've never done much. He picks up on my doubt and adds, "Trust me, you've never tried this before."

I curiously eye the container. "How do you know?" I ask.

He chuckles lightly. "Because it's very special."

"And you have it because . . . ?" I ask, squinting my eyes, head cocked.

"Isn't that already obvious? I'm special, hence the special ointment," he says, followed by a wide grin, like that alone can convince anyone of anything. To his credit, it does help a little bit. I'm suddenly at a loss for words, and I don't know if it's because of what he's offering, or because I'm worried about my knee. My eyes sting for a moment, unwanted tears brimming. I'm on the brink, my tears waiting for me to crack—the crack that is becoming deeper as I realize there's a chance that I'm physically too weak to make it through this retreat. But Renn's act of kindness is so pure that it lights a little spark of hope in me. I take a deep breath and look back at Renn, golden sunlight catching the edges of his frame, and I feel like I can read everything there in his eyes.

I don't want to see you hurting. I know this isn't much, but I want to help.

He makes everything better—he makes everything okay. Bearable.

"Or I can carry you, if that's what you prefer," he says, his grin somehow brighter than his eyes, and I can't resist the smile that appears on my face. Tasha covers her mouth, trying to suppress the giggle that wants to slip out.

"As nice as it would be to have my own pack mule"—he chuckles—"I'll try the ointment," I say.

Renn bends down to meet me at eye level, then unscrews the lid from the container.

"May I?" he says, motioning to my knee.

My cheeks aren't the only thing that suddenly goes hot. "Um, yeah. Go ahead."

Renn uses two fingers to scoop up a small dab of the clear ointment, then sets the container on the ground. He looks at me, his eyes seeming to say, "Are you sure?" and I nod for him to proceed. He tenderly places a hand on my calf to raise my leg slightly so my foot hovers above the ground, using the other to smooth the ointment onto my knee. I watch his fingers trace over the scars, his touch so soft, featherlike. My leg burns, and I can't tell if it's from the ointment or his touch—probably both.

He looks up at me. "You okay?" he asks.

I gulp. "Yep."

"It should start working fairly quickly," he says, then lets go of my leg, setting it back down.

"Renn, everything okay here?" The guide, whose name I don't remember, walks up, bringing the last of the group. I notice that Renn quickly places the tin back into his pack, almost as if he wants to hide it.

"Yeah, all good here. We just need a minute or two. My legs are pretty sore from the double hike to catch up with you guys yesterday," Renn says casually, sneaking a wink at me.

"If you don't mind bringing up the back in case anyone else needs a break, take all the time you need," the guide says.

"No problem at all. We've got it."

He gives Renn an appreciative nod and leaves the three of us behind.

We sit for a good twenty minutes before we get going again, and Renn wasn't kidding when he said I should start to feel the effects of the ointment quickly. Within minutes, the pain is completely gone, and once we start moving, I expect it to wear off, but it doesn't. For the next few miles, it's just the three of us, and time seems to go by quickly.

At some point, Renn starts rattling off facts about the area and points out different kinds of wildflowers and plants that we pass.

Eventually, I ask, "How do you know so much about all of this?"

Tasha pipes in with, "Yeah! I've lived here my whole life and don't know half of what you know. Show off!"

Renn grins with an innocent shrug. "I just like knowing my surroundings, I guess. I've read a lot about the area since arriving here."

Must be some of that military jargon that has lingered. But "arriving?" There's something about that choice of wording that sounds odd.

"Sounds like you didn't come here by choice." I don't realize I say this aloud until I almost run into the back of Tasha because Renn has stopped abruptly ahead of her.

"What the—" Tash stumbles to keep her balance, and I grab her arm to steady her.

"Renn, you okay?" I ask.

Renn turns around, realizing that the three of us nearly collided. "Sorry. I just . . . No. I didn't come here by choice."

I scrunch my eyebrows together, confused. He licks his bottom lip, and I wonder if it's a nervous habit of his, but why would he be nervous about this?

"I guess you could say it found me."

I open my mouth to say more, but Tasha doesn't see because she still has her back to me. "Right. You were looking for something small and quiet," she says very matter-of-factly. Like everyone knows that, even if he's never said it. My thoughts go back to what Valery said, that a lot of what people know about Renn are assumptions.

Renn starts moving up the trail again and says over his shoulder, "Yeah, something like that."

Tash follows without hesitation; like nothing out of the ordinary just happened. But I stay where I am, my mind going everywhere all at once. So he *is* running away from something. What it is remains a mystery, but I was right after all.

"Mave! Are you coming?" Tash is up ahead of me, further than I realized, and waits for me to catch up to her. "Everything okay?" she asks.

I think about saying something, but decide to let it go. "Yeah, I'm good."

We walk beside each other, Renn ahead of us. I keep my eyes on him, wondering what could ever cause him to run.

CHAPTER FOURTEEN

Renn

When the three of us finally arrive at camp for the evening, most of the group already has their tents up and fires going for the night. I glance over at Maven as I hear her walk up beside me, her troubled expression taking in the campsite.

"We made it!" Tasha exclaims with a huff, coming up on the other side. She quickly scans the scene. "It looks pretty flat over there. Should we set up the tent, Mave?" she asks.

Maven places her hands on her hips and takes a deep breath, and with a sharp tone replies, "Sure."

"If you need to rest, I can set it . . ."

"No. I'm fine," Maven snaps, cutting her off. Tasha is taken aback, so she adds, "Sorry. Yes, I'm good. Let's go." She walks past me without giving me a glance or goodbye.

Tash shrugs with wide eyes, and she mouths *I don't know.* "See you later, Renn," she says out loud, then follows her.

"Later," I say, raising a hand in goodbye. I watch them for a moment as they begin to pull out the supplies from their packs. Tasha watches Maven carefully, as a concerned friend would, but they don't speak.

There's a clearing a little further off from the group, beside two large spruce trees, and I decide to unpack there. It takes me longer than normal to get my space set up and secured—I'm distracted, playing through the day in my head. I change into a dark green sweatshirt and grab a beanie from my pack before I make my way over to the larger fire set up in the middle of camp. The sun is almost completely gone as the heaviness of darkness in the forest sinks in for the night.

The voices surrounding the fire become more clear as I inch closer. Maven and Tasha are already eating dinner, which is some sort of a beef stew. Tasha is engaged in conversation with a few other people sitting around them, but Maven stares blankly into the fire as she holds her bowl of food in her hands, untouched. She changed into a gray hoodie and black beanie, looking cozy but not content. She looks up, her eyes immediately finding mine over the flames. Her eyebrows knit together, her mouth parting slightly. I give her a small smile, and she smiles back, but it doesn't reach her eyes. We study each other for a few seconds, and then she rises from her seat, sets down the bowl, and wanders toward the trees.

My gaze follows her until she disappears into the dense forest, and without a second thought, I grab a lantern nearby and follow her. I have a feeling she wants me to follow her, but I still feel my heart make a nervous jump in my chest as I navigate through the maze of trees. The air is chilly as it touches my skin; every step gets darker and colder, but I chase her, knowing where it will lead me. After a few more yards, I see her in a clearing, sitting on a fallen log and looking up into the night sky. The moonlight illuminates a perfect spotlight around her, and she doesn't turn to face me as I set the lantern down and sit beside her. I gaze up to the sky too.

"Do you want to be alone?"

She sighs heavily. "No."

There's a sad smile on her lips as she gazes up into the firmament above. I want her to go on, but I don't want to push her while she's clearly working through something. The stillness of the forest around us invokes a calming essence.

"Sorry about earlier," she says, finally looking at me. "It's been a hard day. I didn't mean to take it out on you and Tash. It was very kind of you to stay back with us."

"I was happy to."

She scoffs lightly at this.

"What?"

"Nothing, it's just my wounded pride, I guess."

I mull over her words for a beat or two. "What do you mean?" I ask, cocking my head.

She looks at me with an intense gaze. "I didn't want you to see me struggle today. It's . . . embarrassing, and even with that magic ointment stuff . . . What is that exactly?" I shrug to play it off like it's no big deal. "Well, whatever it is, it helped a lot, but I still fell so far behind. I didn't realize how far we really were until I saw camp was already completely set up."

I'm surprised by her response, not only for the fact that she thought it was an inconvenience to me to stay behind with her, but also because that wasn't what I saw at all. I feel a sharpness in my chest.

"Maven. You have it all wrong."

Her eyebrows raise in surprise, and I search her eyes like I'm still looking into the never-ending night sky.

"I watched you overcome something difficult. Which you handled with grace, by the way." She swallows nervously. "You were fighting, not struggling."

She takes a sharp inhale of breath, looking down at her feet, then shakes her head, chuckling. "Renn. You don't have to say that."

I scoot closer to her, the movement causing her to bring her eyes back to mine. "I'm serious. I'm glad I got to experience it with you."

"Why?" Her voice is soft, almost a whisper.

The lantern light casts a soft glow across her face. She's beautiful. Her blue eyes sparkling in the darkness as she searches mine. My heart beats fast in my chest, and I don't remember ever having this nervous, exhilarating feeling with anyone. I get the overwhelming urge to lean over and kiss her, but I won't.

"Surely I haven't been hiding it that well," I say, looking at my hands, locking my fingers together. I feel her eyes on me, but she still doesn't say anything. I take a deep breath before looking back at her. "I came on this retreat to be close to you, Maven."

I lick my bottom lip as she shyly grins at me. "Then you should know how happy I was when you showed up. Even though it made me nervous, I felt safe knowing you would be here."

My body instantly relaxes a bit.

"Why were you nervous?"

She hesitates for a moment. "I'm always nervous around you, Renn." She blushes and looks up to the sky, biting her bottom lip. Heat rushes through me at the sight, and I can't help but smile wider. She turns to see my smirk and hits me lightly on the arm. "Don't look smug!" she says, laughing, and I only laugh back.

"You don't need to be nervous around me. I'm sorry if I made you feel that way."

She rolls her eyes.

"What?"

"You would have to be blind if you don't see the effect you have on people." I can't help but chuckle, and she hits my arm playfully again. "Renn!"

"Okay, fine. Yes, to an extent. But you have an effect on people too, and I *know* I haven't been hiding the effect you have on me." I can see her cheeks blush even in the lantern light.

"Okay, fine. Yes, to an extent," she says, using my words. "I can tell you like me. There, I said it."

"Thank you!" I say loudly, and we both chuckle.

Maven's laugh is infectious, and just like the first time I heard it, I can't help the reaction of my body to the sound of it, the warmth singing through my body.

After a few moments, we both go quiet again. She leans her head back to look up to the night sky once again, but I keep my eyes on her. Her dark hair cascades down her back and shoulders, her neck more exposed the more she leans, taking in the stars above. I see sadness creep into her eyes just as it did on Firefly Night.

"My dad and I loved to stargaze." Her voice is steady but mournful. "We were always fascinated with space. I guess you could say it was a hobby, in a way. He always had a random fact or two to share. We read books, watched movies. He even bought a little telescope for us one year." I get the feeling she hasn't spoken about him with anyone for some time, based on her reverent tone. "It made me feel so small in comparison to everything we could see up there, and it always left me in awe. From our little spot on the ground, with so many stars shining right in front of us, it was almost like we could reach out and touch them."

I follow her gaze. "And what about now?"

She is quiet for a few beats, then turns to face me again. "Do you think there's life beyond this world?"

I stop breathing. The question shakes me to my core. I try to keep my face as neutral as possible, my mind racing, thinking about what to say, what to do. This is the second time today she's caught me completely off guard. Or maybe I've been letting my guard down around her without even noticing.

"What do you mean?" My voice sounds off, but I hope she won't notice. Maven leans back further, placing her hands on the log as she arches her back and rolls out her shoulders. The casualness tells me she meant it as an innocent question. Of course she did.

"There has to be something else out there, right?"

I wish I could tell her how right she is. That I've seen things beyond her wildest imagination. I'm compelled to tell her everything, but if I do, she will look at me like I'm crazy and most likely run in the opposite direction. And even if I tell her the truth, how would I go about that exactly?

Yes, Maven. There is life beyond this world. How do I know? Because I'm from another planet.

So, instead, I try to validate her wandering thoughts with a half-truth.

"I think you're right. I think there is more out there." I inhale. "Worlds and stars without end." She doesn't respond, her gaze only intensifying on the sky as she contemplates my words. "I actually know a thing or two about space myself," I add, ashamed to play it off, but I don't know what else to do.

"Really? Tell me something about space, Renn." She swings a leg to the other side of the log, straddling it to face me full on. I try to keep my breath even.

I squint my eyes in thought. "Hmm, let me think." Maven smiles, waiting patiently. "What do you know about nebulas?"

She shakes her head. Here goes nothing.

"Nebulas are common throughout the galaxy, but they can only illuminate by reflecting off nearby stars. The more starlight they capture, the more colorful they appear. Most reflect shades of blue."

She ponders this for a moment. "What are they exactly?"

I'm pleased by her curiosity. "They're remnants of stars that have died, or new stars forming—star dust that is gathered together."

She hums in response, glancing up to the starlit sky again.

"They don't always appear that way though. They can also be incredibly menacing. Without light, a nebula can become so dark, that it appears as an endless void of blackness. Both are beautiful in their own way."

"Goodness." Her body shivers at the words, and we both chuckle. If I were braver, I would tell her that her eyes remind me of a nebula. I've witnessed so many, ranging in intensity and brightness, but the color of her eyes is one of a kind, even in comparison to the universe. Her eyes look like they encapsulate millions of stars, making them truly stellar, but it isn't just the vividness that hits me, it's also the fact that they contain a darkness—something inside that she wants to keep hidden. That kind of darkness recognizes itself, and when it comes to Maven, I see it as clear as day—light and dark coming together to create a devastatingly beautiful thing.

We remain quiet for a while, the constellations glittering above us.

Maven's smooth voice breaks the silence as she asks, "How do you know so much about space?"

I stare at her face again, one side illuminated by the moonlight, the other by the lantern glow. The light and the dark. "I guess you could say it's a hobby of mine, too."

She glances back at me, a small smile on her lips. Then she does something I wasn't expecting. She reaches out and places a hand on my knee. "Thank you, Renn."

I'm not sure if she's thanking me for reassuring her, or distracting her. Maybe both. I hope I was able to comfort her in some way, and I let my thoughts wander, wishing I could do more for her—*to* her, if I'm being honest. Because as I look at her lips, I want to know what they would feel like against mine. How her dark hair would feel on my fingertips. The sensation of having her bare skin against mine. The heat in me blazes brighter just from her touch. Before I can dare to touch her back, she removes her hand.

"We should probably get back to camp." She stands, wiping off the bark sticking to her palms before wrapping her arms around herself. I didn't realize how much the temperature had dropped as we sat here, side by side in the twilight.

"Yeah. Probably a good idea." We stroll back to camp in silence, the glow of the fire and lantern light guiding us.

"There you guys are!" Tasha shouts, running up to us—a look of relief on her face. "I was about to come look for you two."

Maven clears her throat. "Sorry. We didn't mean to scare you."

Tasha's eyes move to Maven, then to me, looking us up and down. "What were you guys doing out there anyway?" She crosses her arms, giving us a suspicious look.

"Nothing. Just talking," Maven says, moving forward and grabbing Tasha's arm to lead her away. "Let's get to bed." Tasha winks at me and follows Maven toward their tent. "It was nice talking with you, Renn. See you tomorrow," she says, looking over her shoulder while continuing to pull Tasha along.

"See you tomorrow."

Maven and Tasha start to speak in low whispers as they move further away. I watch them walk into their tent, still watching as it illuminates from the inside. The camp is quiet now; the low light of the glowing tents and lucent embers in the fire pits are the only signs of life. I try to be as quiet as I can, climbing into my tent and unwrapping a granola bar from my pack after I realize how hungry I am. I scramble into my sleeping bag, chewing on the bar. I had been worried that coming on this trip may have been a mistake, that maybe I was intruding on what was clearly much more than a hiking retreat to Maven. The look of determination and sheer will she possessed today made that evident. But after tonight, my mind is free of doubt. That conversation under the stars with her was worth the risk of leaving the transmitter behind, worth giving her the ointment. It was worth everything. Perhaps this was the first indication that a true friendship has grown between Maven and me, and maybe that was my intention all along. If Maven sees me as a friend, that will be enough . . . for now. But the final thought that enters my mind before I sleep is that the real truth is, Maven is quickly becoming so much more than just my friend, and I want that more than I care to admit.

CHAPTER FIFTEEN

Maven

"Okay, seriously. Tell me what happened!" Tasha semi shouts, sprawled out on her cot.

"Shhh! Keep it down, would you?" I pull off my beanie and run my fingers through my hair.

"Tell me!" she whispers loudly.

"Okay, first of all, that wasn't even remotely quiet. Second, nothing happened, we just . . . talked," I say flatly. Tasha rolls onto her side so she's facing me fully, her expression unconvinced. "We just talked, I promise. I would tell you if there was anything else." I mean it genuinely, and she knows it.

"Alright. Alright." She pauses for a moment, eyeing me. "Did you *want* something else to happen though?"

I roll my eyes at her. "You are ridiculous!" I say, throwing my hat at her.

"Hey!" She laughs, throwing it back. "Look, all I'm saying is that this is so unlike normal Renn behavior. And you have never been this nervous around a guy. I can tell he likes you and you like him."

I can tell you like me. There, I said it.

His laugh was deep and *so* very good. I can almost feel it reverberating through my body, a warmness pooling within me just thinking about that sound. It makes me feel things in places I don't dare admit, even to myself.

"Fine. You're not wrong. I like him probably a lot more than I should." I look down at my hands because it is the truth, and I didn't intend to share it, not even with Tasha. But I'm too timid to say more.

She scans my face, her expression suddenly serious. I wait for her to say something else, but instead, she only smiles and turns to lie on her back.

"By the way, I'm so proud of you," she says quietly, staring at the roof of the tent. My eyes prick at her words, especially because today wasn't my finest moment.

"Thank you for nudging me to come on this retreat. And I'm sorry about my grumpiness today."

She laughs lightly. "It's okay, and maybe thank me after. It's not over yet."

"Okay, deal."

I lie flat on my back, but I don't feel tired with the butterflies still fluttering in my stomach.

I meant what I said, Renn makes me feel safe. He calms me, enough to share more with him, allowing me to be myself. I haven't even been able to do that with Tash since everything happened. She's always been supportive of me, but with Renn . . . he compelled me to share more, and what's crazy is that I wanted to.

I close my eyes, trying to find sleep, but I hear Renn's voice in my head, his words a song in my mind. One thing in particular I can't seem to shake from my consciousness is the look in his eyes when he spoke of space.

I think you're right. I think there is more out there. Worlds and stars without end.

The tone of his voice when he said it sent a chill through me. It touched me somewhere deep within, and when I gazed into his eyes, I could have sworn I truly saw worlds without end flashing across his face, like he was reliving something that he knew to be true—like he wasn't just satisfying my curiosity.

Eventually, the forest's soothing sounds help my mind rest. I need to sleep to help my legs recuperate. I made it to the camp, but I haven't been that sore in a long time, and like Tasha pointed out, the journey isn't over yet. I worry that, while I have come a long way, there is a chance I won't make it to the end. As soon as the thought comes to mind, another one quickly follows. Even if I slip, fall, even if I need to rest a hundred times before we make it to the end, I know Renn will be there. That comforting thought swiftly takes away all my fears and doubts, and I fall into a deep sleep at last.

I hear the camp coming alive, long shadows of the trees from the morning light crossing over our tent. Excited chatter drifts throughout the camp, and I can't help the rousing feeling growing in me as well. Tasha stirs in her cot.

"Good morning," she says through a yawn.

"Morning!" I unzip my pack quickly, grab my toothbrush, and push through the tent flap, pulling on my dust- and dirt-coated hiking boots.

"Geez! How are you so awake already?" she groans into her pillow. I don't stop to respond. I use my canteen to brush my teeth, quickly stuff it back inside my pack, and make my way over to the center of the camp, scanning for him. Many have already packed up their tents and are eating a breakfast of dried fruit and oatmeal; I don't care nearly as much today that I have to eat the rubbery meal. Then, I spot Renn talking to a group of guys, his arms across his chest as he speaks. He's wearing the same black beanie from last night, but has changed into a white shirt under a black jacket with dark jeans. As if he can feel my gaze, he turns, and when he sees me, he puts a hand up to excuse himself from the group and makes his way over to where I stand.

"Good morning." His voice has a raspy, morning tenor to it, and I try to ignore the heated feeling it gives me.

"Hey. Did you sleep well?" I ask.

"I did. Very well, actually." He nods, putting his hands in his pocket.

"I did too," I say.

"Good."

We smile foolishly at each other. His bright smile is even more radiant in the morning sun. The stubble on his face is the longest I've ever seen it—more rugged. I decide that Renn in a beanie is my favorite look on him, and if he added that jean jacket, I would be a goner.

"So, last night. It was . . . nice," I say nervously. He steps a bit closer to me, and I feel my blood warming up.

"It was nice for me too."

It's undeniable that something is different between us now. If I had to attach a name to it, I'd call Renn a friend now, but is there more? While he's still intimidating in many ways, I feel like the relationship growing between us has come about fast and easy, maybe with a couple bumps, but now we're at a turning point. The more time we spend together, the stronger it grows, and last night, he made it clear he wanted to spend more time with me.

"So, are you ready for today?" he asks through a grin.

"I think so."

For a split second, he looks down to my leg then back to my eyes as he asks, "Feel okay?"

I reach down to rub it, stretching it a little to test the soreness. I was so focused on finding him, I didn't even register the tightness in my muscles until now.

My knee is a little tender.

"I feel good. I know the ointment helped a lot yesterday."

He inhales deeply. "I'm glad. Really, Maven. I'm happy it helped you. And if you need to take breaks today, don't feel bad about it. I'll be with you the whole way."

I assumed he would be hiking with Tasha and me today, but hearing him say it fills my heart with warmth, and the fluttering feeling in my stomach grows.

"Well, I better help Tasha pack up." My nerves get the better of me. "See you on the trail?" I ask.

He smiles wide, eyes crinkling. "See you on the trail, Maven."

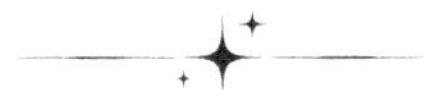

My nerves only grow the closer we get to the ascent, and for some strange, but welcome reason, my knee is still holding up well. I really need to ask Renn more about that ointment.

The ascent is only half a mile, but it's the steepest section of the entire hike. The group as a whole seems to move at a faster pace in anticipation of finally getting to our sought-after destination, and even though Tasha, Renn, and I are at the back once again, we keep up well enough. Maybe it's the adrenaline that pushes me forward, helping me to ignore the burn in my muscles, or maybe Tasha and Renn's presence gives me motivation.

If I'm being honest, it's probably both, and I'm grateful for it.

The last ascent before the overlook is narrow and rocky, with sections of nothing but sheer drop-offs on either side. The guides instruct the group to go single file and to leave plenty of room between each other. Because of this, we have to wait for our turn to go one by one. I'm thankful for the extra time to rest and review everything I know about the ascent. The narrowest, most dangerous sections of the trail are guided with rope tied to metal stakes which are anchored into the rock. I've heard many stories about this part in particular over the years, and it's where people actually fall off the cliffside every few years.

"*If people would just do what they're supposed to, they wouldn't fall.*" I hear my dad's voice in my mind.

"The key is to not look down, keep your bearings, and go slow," Trey says, giving the group tips. My knee starts to bounce nervously with anticipation.

"Do you want me to go before you, or after?" Tasha asks. I watch those already scaling the mountain, taking note of what's helping make it easier, and what to avoid.

"I'll go last."

The sun beats down on us. Trees are more scarce now that we're near the top of the mountain, which means less shade as we wait. Maybe going last isn't such a good idea. I can feel the heat stealing my strength little by little.

As we wait, Renn spends most of his time talking with the same group of guys from town, but at one point, the woman who said she wanted to take Renn into the woods for a hookup approaches him. She's pretty with short, blonde hair. She's bold, I'll give her that, but a pulse of jealousy pumps through my blood when I watch her put a hand on Renn's forearm. She had to touch him there, of course. He catches my eye as his expression says something like "help me." I shrug and flash him a wicked grin, the jealousy gone.

When our turn finally arrives, without a word, Tash pulls me into a tight hug and holds me for a long moment. I hold her back just as tight.

"You've got this," she says, pulling away. Her wide, hazel eyes are full of hope and worry as she looks at me, unblinking.

"I've got this, and so do you," I say, giving her an encouraging smile.

She gives one last squeeze, then tightens the straps on her pack and starts scaling up the rocky path. Her curly hair is pulled up high on her head, and she looks graceful as she moves onward and up. A beam of pride for my best friend burns in my chest.

Renn comes up next to me, watching her for a moment, then bends down to tighten his shoelaces and the straps on his pack. "Well, this is it," he says. His eyes are more green than I've ever seen them. I wait for him to give me the same encouraging sentiment as Tasha, but instead, he moves closer to me so I have to tilt my head back to look him in the eyes. "Keep looking forward, one step at a time," he says, low and calm. The sound of it grounds my nerves and thoughts of excitement. For a moment, I think about hugging him, but instead, I just nod. "I'll see you at the top," he adds, his eyes clear and captivating. I read it all there, the things left unsaid. The belief, not hope, that I will make it—and that is the final push I need.

"Don't worry about me. Just keep going. I'll catch up," I say.

He smiles wide and then turns to face the mountain. He takes a deep breath and starts to climb, his broad chest moving in and out, slowly. I try not to let my mind go wild as I take in every move he makes, his arms flexing as the muscles tighten across his back, his long fingers gripping on to the rock when he needs extra leverage. Even through his shirt, I can see the material moving against him, stretching against his muscles, leaving little to the imagination.

Stop thinking about Renn's muscles. Focus on the mountain, I tell myself, laughing lightly. Once he's several yards ahead of me, I close my eyes and take a collection of deep breaths.

Steady yourself. You've got this. They will be waiting for you.

I say the mantra to myself a few times, then open my eyes and begin. I don't think of the path as a whole; instead, I do as Renn said and take it one step at a time.

Make it to the bend. Now the rock ahead. I take the path in small stretches to get me to the end, little by little.

I can spot Renn from time to time up ahead of me, catching quick glimpses of his red backpack for a moment or two when the path isn't obstructed by trees or rocks, and every time I do, it gives me that extra motivation to keep moving. When I arrive at the first rope section, it becomes clear that people didn't exaggerate when they said it's narrow. It's so slim that I have to walk almost as if I'm on a tightrope, one foot in front of the other while clinging on to the rope, the roughness rubbing against my palm, almost burning from my tight grip. My heartbeat thumps in my ears, and my hands are sweaty, probably from a mixture of nervousness and exhaustion. I try to keep my eyes ahead, but steal a glance to the side at the sheer drop off, and all at once, my body goes stiff, my legs feeling like they weigh a ton. I try to step forward, but can't. I close my eyes, taking deep breaths, trying to control the fear building inside me.

Deep breaths. Just take a step. One step, that's all.

But no matter how many times I say it, I stand, frozen.

Not sure what to do, I do something I haven't done in a long time.

"Dad," I say aloud, the vibrations of my voice echoing off the rocks around me. "Dad, if you're there, if you're somewhere . . . anywhere, I need your help." I pray that maybe there's a part of him here—an imprint because of how much he loved this place. Maybe that's why I do it, but no matter the reason, it's comforting the more I speak.

"Dad, help me." I keep my eyes shut tight, waiting for a feeling, anything to give me a sign. I take long, deep breaths, trying to hone in on the mountains and nature surrounding me, focusing in on the soundscape until it becomes a soothing source of solace. It begins to call to me, igniting my soul.

Maven, you are not alone. You can do this. Don't give up now.

Then, almost as if I can feel a reassuring hand on my shoulder, I keep going. My legs are light but strong. I don't know what to make of what's happening on this mountain, but the closest thing I can call it is a spiritual awakening. Whatever it is, it gets me to the end. When I turn the final corner, I'm welcomed by the setting sun's rays. Most of the group has their backs turned, looking out toward the overlook.

The first person who spots me is Tasha, and I hear her before I see her. "Maven!" she yells. A few people look our way, but I don't care if we have an audience as she runs to me with tears in her eyes. My eyes fill with tears of their own. She pulls me into a tight embrace.

"Were you worried about me?" I ask through a chuckle.

She squeezes me tighter. "Maybe a little, but I knew you could do it," she says as she pulls away. My eyes dart ahead. "It's even better than I imagined," she says, following my gaze to the edge of the mountain. "Come on." She takes my hand and we walk side by side, arms linked together.

The vista slowly comes into view, step by step, and soon, all I see ahead of me is majesty and wonder.

I had an image in my head of what the overlook of Solitude Ridge would look like, but in person, it leaves me speechless. The sweeping, vibrant colors, ranging from deep red to bright yellow, cascade over the hills—the beautiful colors brilliant against the dark green of the evergreen trees.

I lean on a nearby rock, slowly lowering myself to sit. My eyes sting with tears. It's so beautiful, and I can't believe I made it.

It is overwhelming.

I don't know how long I sit, but suddenly, I remember who else I want to see. I stand, and the first person I notice when I turn around is Renn. Before I know what I'm doing . . . I run to him—my achy legs not nearly as sore as they were seconds before. He wears an expression somewhere between relief and joy, and the closer I come to him, the wider he smiles. I wrap my arms around his neck, and he lifts me off my feet and spins me before placing me back onto the ground.

"You did it, Maven. You did it," he says into my hair. I feel his broad chest move in and out, inhaling me, and I don't care if I smell of dirt and sweat. I can sense it on him too, but for some reason, the salt and earthiness adds to his already intoxicating scent. I let go of his neck and lean back to look into his shining, green eyes. I try to think of something to say—something equally profound that can match the feelings flowing through me, but I'm at a loss for words. Renn seems to be as well, because he just beams down at me, the brightness in his eyes lighting me up inside.

"Let's get a picture!" Tasha calls out to us, interrupting the moment as she pulls out her phone and hands it to someone nearby.

Renn moves to step away, but I pull on his arm, encouraging him to stand next to Tasha and me. He parts his lips to protest, but doesn't as Tasha pulls me to stand beside her so that I'm nestled between the two of them. The woman holding Tash's phone takes a few photos, rotating the phone to give us a variety, then hands it back to her.

"Thank you so much!" Tash says while I still have my arm looped around Renn's. I slowly let it drop to my side. "Ooo, these are so good!" Tasha exclaims, swiping through the pictures and handing the phone to me to look.

We all have huge smiles on our faces, the backdrop of the overview behind us breathtaking, but the only thing I focus on is the three of us—my best friend on one side of me and Renn on the other. At this moment, the word *friend* seems so small compared to what they both are to me. Tash is more like a sister, and Renn . . . I don't know exactly. I pray I can hold on to this feeling long after the day comes to end, but no matter what, I will always hold this memory close to my heart.

CHAPTER SIXTEEN

Renn

Maven arriving at the overlook is a memory I want etched into my mind forever. The pure joy lighting her face was more striking than the view that took almost three days to get to. While everyone looked out to the vista, I couldn't take my eyes off her. She was unmatched by the beauty that surrounded us. She was transcendent. I had never seen or felt anything like it before as I watched her from afar. I wanted to give her a moment, but when she finally turned around to search for me—when she ran to me . . . neither one of us hesitated to hold on to each other . . . It was perfect. The way her body lined up with mine; how I didn't pause to pick her up off her feet and hold her tight against me. Just thinking about it makes my chest ache. For a moment, it felt like there was only her and me on top of that mountain, a feeling I didn't realize I had been chasing this whole time until she was in my arms.

We spend the rest of the day lounging and drinking in the scene, and I'm just as surprised as everyone else when the sun begins to set and we realize we still have to set up camp. At least we still have a couple of days here to relax and enjoy.

We set up camp a good distance away from the outlook—firstly for more even ground, and secondly for safety, because in the pitch black, it would be easy to accidentally get too close to the ledge. By the time dinner is consumed, the tiredness has set in with everyone, including myself. Maven and I exchange glances across the fire. She's so different from how she appeared last night. Now she's smiling and laughing—happiness radiating off her even under the cloak of night. I'm proud of her, and if I wasn't already entranced, this day would have made it undeniable.

The alarms on the ship echo throughout the labyrinth of hallways as crewmembers run for the nearest escape pods. We've all been trained for a variety of emergency situations, but to actually live it—it's something else entirely, and it doesn't matter how many times I relive it in my dreams, it never makes it easier.

I'm sprinting down the white hallways, the shiny surface of the floor showing my reflection as my boots pound onto the floor. I turn the corner, and instead of seeing the next corridor I see . . . Maven. She has her back to me, and she is looking over Solitude Ridge's outlook, the perfect picture of how she looked when she made it to the top. The ship slowly fades away around the edges of my dream as I approach her, and when she turns around to face me, her expression goes from full of happiness to confusion as she takes me in.

"Renn?" she asks, looking me over slowly.

I glance down and see my uniform, the dark-blue, form-fitting outfit made of sleek material, with my badge engraved with the insignia of my rank on my right shoulder. I look back up, meeting her confused, bright eyes.

"Maven, I can explain."

She steps backward, putting a hand up. "Who are you?" she asks, her voice trembling.

"Maven. Please," I beg, reaching for her, but she keeps moving backward toward the edge.

"Who are you?" she screams, her eyes full of fear.

"Maven! Stop!" I reach for her, but she disappears over the side of the cliff. I leap to catch her, but instead of falling over the edge with her . . . there are hands on my shoulders shaking me.

"Renn! Renn, wake up!"

I open my eyes, sitting up in a panic. Maven is kneeling beside me, her eyes wide in shock and worry. My heart races, a trickle of sweat on my brow.

"Renn?" I calm myself enough to focus; her hand rests on my arm. When I look down at it, she pulls it away, quickly standing. "Let me get you some water. I'll be right back."

I don't say anything, still trying to catch my breath as she swiftly leaves the tent. Based on the light I can see through the tent walls, it appears to be the very early hours of the morning, meaning most of the camp is still asleep, or at least I hope they still are. Maven quietly enters the tent again, handing me a canteen. Avoiding her eyes as I remove it from her hands, taking a long drink of the cold, crisp water inside.

She kneels next to me again, her movements slow. When I pry my lips away from the canteen, I finally allow myself to look at her. I didn't know what I would find in her blue haze stare, but I discover genuine concern without a hint of judgment.

"I'm sorry," I say, my voice barely above a whisper.

Her brows furrow. "Sorry? You don't need to be sorry about anything, Renn." She stares at me for a beat or two before she goes on. "All I want to know is if you're okay."

I take a deep breath, thinking of what to say, wondering what she heard or saw. My vulnerability is now on full display, but instead of feeling uneasy about it, with Maven beside me, I feel relief. I decide to tell her the truth, or at least a part of it.

"I have nightmares. Sometimes they're minor . . . sometimes worse."

Maven moves to sit down fully next to me, bringing her knees to her chest. The action stirs something in me.

I pause a moment before I continue. "It's usually the same dream every time. A day from my past, but this time, it was different." Maven keeps her cool, comforting gaze on me. "I saw you . . ." I start to say, but look down at my hands. I hear her breathing change slightly. "I saw you standing at the edge of the overlook, and you . . ." I bite my lip, wondering if I should go on. "You fell." I close my eyes at the last word, rubbing the heels of my hands into my temples to push out the image.

"I heard you," she whispers. "I heard you say my name." She takes my hand, gripping it tight as she looks at me so intensely, I don't dare look away. "Do you want to talk more about it?"

I exhale a breath, studying her face.

"It's okay, Renn," she adds.

My voice is caught in my throat for a moment, but I manage to speak. "I don't know if I can."

Maven smiles sadly at me. "I'm sorry. I wish I could think of something better to say, but I mean it. I'm so sorry."

I believe her, because in the short time I've come to know her, she has somehow irrevocably changed me. Because for the first time in a long time, I feel seen.

"I'm not going to lie, I wish the first time you dreamt of me wasn't a nightmare. Maybe next time you could make it a happier one?" she says through a smirk. I smile wide at her as I sit up more, bringing my face closer to hers. Her smile fades slightly, but her eyes stay bright.

"I never said that was the first time I dreamt of you. Sometimes I have very good dreams," I say with a wink, and she gasps, hitting me in the shoulder.

"There he is," she says, laughing. We smile at one another for a moment. "Well, we still have a few more hours until sunlight breaks. Try to get some sleep," she says, standing.

But before she leaves, I quickly say, "Maven." She pauses, turning to me. "Thank you."

"You're welcome." She smiles at me warmly then leaves the tent.

I lie there, staring at the top of the tent before coming to the conclusion that I'm not going to go back to sleep. My body is electrified with tension—the good kind. After some time, I quietly slip on a jacket and boots before heading outside. The woods are dreamy and dark, waiting for the morning sun to break over the mountain tops. I walk through the camp, light on my feet, and head toward the lookout point to watch the sunrise. I find a smooth, wide rock to lie down on so I can look directly up into the sky, watching the stars slowly fade.

I can't shake the nightmare from my mind, but I realize why. Maven's presence not only calms me, but she's ignited something: a spark of hope that there could be more to this strange life I'm living. It never gets easier being deceptive. I'm a friend, but always a stranger. A neighbor, but an outsider.

But a dangerous question comes to my mind. What if? What if I could really shake off those chains of my past? It feels like no matter how much time passes, they won't ever let me go. It's been five long years, and nothing has happened, no one has found me. And I realize, staring up into the stars, that maybe there's no one looking for me in that great night sky—not anymore.

Maybe all this time, what I was truly looking for is right in front of me. And that is perhaps the most frightening realization of all.

CHAPTER SEVENTEEN

Maven

I t was refreshing not having to pack up immediately when we woke the next morning. Instead of bustling about after breakfast, everyone was still and quiet, settling into our home for the next couple of days. Eventually, most of the group ventured back to the overlook; some had binoculars and were scouting for wildlife, others were writing in journals, and some even seemed to be meditating in one form or another.

All I wanted to do was look. And for the most part, so did Tasha. We just sat and talked and looked over the scenery at the most colorful time of the year. Those days we had at the outlook were full and inspiring. I think my favorite part was sitting around the fire with everyone in the evenings. I'm not sure what it is about people sitting around a fire, but it brings you close together. It makes you forget the bad things in your life by burning away your troubles, and all you have to do is sit and take it in. Every night, I sat next to Renn, the two of us stealing glances at each other the entire time.

I haven't told Tasha about what happened with Renn that night, and I never will. He seemed fine the next day, but I couldn't help feeling sad for him, knowing he has to face every detail of his trauma in his dreams, while I have no memories of my life-altering night. I don't remember the crash itself, but when I woke up, that was when my nightmare began. I wish I could switch places with him, because it doesn't seem fair, especially for someone as good and kind as Renn to have to face something so dark that it plagues his dreams. To see that pain etched across his face, even for just a moment . . . it didn't fit the man I had come to know. For something so painful to torment him, and yet he is still so full of light.

I don't want to leave now that the day has come to head home. Everyone loads onto the shuttles, and unlike the drive to the trailhead, we're all a little somber on the way back to Solitude Ridge. I think there's overwhelming exhaustion settling on everyone as well. Some people even fall asleep on the drive, including Tasha. My body is sore, but my knee—my knee hasn't hurt at all, even after all of the hiking. It's sore like the rest of my limbs, but nothing like the throbbing pain that was once there.

I look for Renn, but I think he may have ended up on another shuttle after helping that blonde woman from earlier get her backpack loaded on the shuttle . . . again. Soon, we pull into Solitude Ridge Adventure Tours, and I try to quickly get off to find Renn, but before I can, I watch him get on his motorbike and speed off in a hurry.

Tasha follows my gaze as the sound of his bike fades down the street.

"Renn leave already?" she asks.

I shrug. "It appears so," I say, clearly disappointed.

"He probably just wants to see Shy. They haven't ever been apart for this long as far as I know," she says.

"Yeah, probably."

But I still can't help feeling a little underwhelmed that he left without saying goodbye.

The town of Solitude Ridge was swiftly hit by harsh and unforgiving winds just a couple of weeks after the retreat, officially bringing in the new season. Bright, sunny days were swept away, and the leaves seemed to have fallen from their place holders overnight. Overcast clouds transformed the once colorful and vivid landscape to dark green and gray.

While I enjoyed the warmth and color, the colder times of year are actually my favorite. I feel more at home than ever when the rain falls and snow eventually coats the town. Tourist season has slowed down with most of the resorts now closed, though a couple usually remain open with smaller staff and less amenities. Solitude Ridge is so secluded that we don't get many people venturing up the snowy mountains for the winter. Being snowed in is a yearly occurrence, with no roads open in or out for a couple of months at a time. Yet another reason why I love this time of year: the town is finally *ours* again, rather than just a flow of strangers passing in and out.

Most everyone in town has been busy closing up their shops for the season, including Tasha and Mina. During the slow times of the year, the bookshop is open for less hours and is completely closed for a few weeks when Tasha and her mom go on their annual trip to visit Mina's parents, who live further south where it's warmer for their "aged bodies," as Mina likes to say.

Tasha and I decided to meet up for one last coffee date before she leaves for the road trip. Her worry about my well-being is evident in our conversation, and she isn't wrong in feeling so. It's the calm before the storm, likely quite literally in this case.

"You know, you can totally come with us if you want to," she says, but I give her a scrutinizing look.

"Did my mom put you up to this?"

With a sheepish look, she says, "Maybe, but does it matter? You know you're welcome to join us either way."

"I appreciate the offer, but no, thank you. Besides, I like being here this time of year," I say, taking a generous sip of the earthy mix of coffee that is the daily special today.

"You've always loved it, haven't you?"

I nod cheerfully. "It could inspire me to maybe do some sketching."

Which wouldn't be a bad idea since I'm going to be without company for a few weeks. A couple of weeks ago, I might have said otherwise, but the weather wasn't the only thing that had changed dramatically. Renn had, once again, distanced himself, especially from me, it seemed. I had seen him in town, of course, but we never said more than a few words to each other. I'm not sure what I'd expected once we got back home, but it wasn't this vague interaction, like nothing had happened.

Surely I'm not that out of practice when it comes to relationships, but maybe the last five years have made me rusty. Even still, there were things I felt with Renn on that mountain that I've never felt before. The last person I had been with romantically was Jamie, or at least I thought it was romantic at the time.

Tasha continues to give me some space on the subject, but she can't help herself from speaking up about it when I spy him across the street. Shy trots next to him, keeping up as he seems to be in a rush to wherever he's going.

Tash follows my gaze out the window as she says, "He gets really busy this time of year." Her voice pulls my attention away from him.

My only response is, "Hmmm," before sipping from my coffee again. I attempt to convince myself that I don't care, but in reality, I'm maddened that I am, once again, experiencing the unpredictable ups and downs of what Renn wants or doesn't want when it comes to our relationship.

"So, nothing's happened since the retreat?" Tasha hesitantly asks. I peer back out to the street to find Renn gone just as quickly as he appeared. I sigh heavily.

"It's fine. It doesn't bother me." She raises her eyebrows skeptically. "I swear. The only thing bothering me is the fact that my mind is playing tricks on me, making me think my hair still smells like campfire," I say flatly.

Tasha covers her mouth with the back of her hand to keep her giggle to herself. "Oh, yeah, you're not at all bothered about Renn," she says with a wink.

I roll my eyes then stick my tongue out. I begin to tap my fingers loudly against my cup, anxious and annoyed until I can't keep it in any longer. "Okay, but seriously, what the hell?"

Tasha's mouth is in a tight line, shrugging her shoulders. "It's just Renn being Renn."

I don't want to accept that as an answer.

"But you said that he had never, you know . . . acted that way before."

Tasha's look of pity pains my stomach with embarrassment. "I know, and it *was* different, but I guess he's back to his usual nice-but-distant self." I stare into my coffee, taking in her words for a minute. "I'm sorry," she adds gently when I say nothing.

"It's fine."

Tash clears her throat. "Look, Mave, Renn is a loner, but I've known him for a while, and I feel like I can confidently say that I highly doubt he meant to hurt you. I may not know everything about him, but I know he would never do something like that on purpose." I bite the inside of my cheek. "Why do I get the feeling something more happened between you two than you're telling me?" she asks, but I don't answer for several moments.

"I thought maybe there was something, but I guess I was wrong."

She grabs my hand from across the table. "For what it is worth, I'm sorry that he made you feel that way. He loses a lot of points in my book, because you're my best friend."

I know in my heart what she says is true, but it doesn't make me feel any less foolish.

"There's nothing to be sorry about. He's just a guy right?" My own words don't convince me as I say them, so I change the subject instead. "But now that it is over, I am grateful that you persuaded me to go on the retreat. It was what I needed, truly. Regardless of whatever happened with Renn, I had an amazing time with you." And I mean it.

She peers at me, her warm, honey, hazel eyes twinkling. "Let's not talk about Renn anymore, okay?" she says.

"Deal," I say with a nod. "So, tell me more about your plans for the road trip," I quickly add.

We spend the rest of the afternoon in easy conversion and do not once mention Renn, just as we promised.

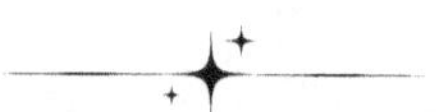

About a week after Tasha and Mina departed on their trip, I ran out of reasons to go into town besides food, and now I'm hunkered down in the cabin with no intention of leaving. It's the first time that I've been truly alone since moving back to Solitude Ridge, and it's in the loneliness that the shadows from the dark corners of my mind—where they've been lingering and waiting for the opportunity to overtake me—come alive. What was once cozy and quiet has become isolating and cold. I look out the window, the change of scenery reminding me that the beautiful parts of my life are like the now fallen leaves, short moments of brilliance, only to fall to the ground, crumpled and dead. I never meant for this downward spiral to get the way it has. It would be too easy to pick up the phone and call someone, or simply go into town just to be around some other living beings. But before I realize the path I'm treading down, it's too late to turn around, and I can't find my way back.

I used to be afraid of things that made sense to be afraid of, like the dark or heights, but the truest form of fear is when you become afraid of yourself. Some people fear that they may never accomplish their lifelong goals, never find out who they truly are, or fear that their life has no purpose. But not me. It's not about whether or not I know who I am or what my life means—it's the opposite. I know exactly who I am, what I've done, and what I deserve. The retreat only distracted me from the truth.

So now, instead of pushing it out of my mind, I welcome it in, all the grief, all the guilt and pain.

You don't deserve to be happy, something whispers to me. I've done a decent job of ignoring it for this long, but what that voice whispers rings true. So, I let it in and allow it to stay a while—that demon living inside, making itself at home.

CHAPTER EIGHTEEN

Renn

Four days. That's how long it's been since I last saw her. It's ridiculous that I've started keeping track, but it's odd not to have even caught a glimpse of her, even for a second or two as she walks by or drives through town. I even found myself going to the coffee shop one day to see if I'd spot her, but no. I knew Mina and Tasha were due to make their annual trip, and I naturally assumed that, with them gone, Maven was bound to be in town less frequently, so I didn't read into it too much.

It's the afternoon, and the sky is already darker than normal, yet there's no sign of the big storm that's predicted to hit town soon. I always have steady work at the auto shop, which I split with the other two guys who work here. But at this time of year, I always lend a helping hand wherever I can. Winter is not to be taken lightly around here; preparation is key, a habit I've been acquainted with for as long as I can remember. It's what I've always done. This time around, I welcome the work more than usual, if only to offer me more diversion from my thoughts drifting to Maven.

Those days on the retreat were some of the best days of my life, but once the distraction of it all faded away, I had a feeling something was off. I had an aching feeling in my gut that I had to get home as soon as possible and reality hit me like a wall of bricks when I came back to find that the transmitter's signal had picked up on something—or someone—while I was away. The hope I had felt just days before had been ripped away from me again. It had been for less than a second, but I saw the record of it on the screen. My transmission had been tapped into, and I had no idea if that means everything or nothing. Anomalies are possible, especially with a simple transmitter such as mine, but unlikely. My basic console is nothing like what the average space ship is equipped with, but it should still work for what I need it to do. I looked over the device multiple times, checking to see if I could determine if there was clear proof that it was something to worry about or maybe something hopeful. I searched the telemetry data and scanned the material thoroughly for hours, looking for any technical malfunctions, but I couldn't find anything that ultimately gave me an answer.

This is why you can't get too close. You need to stay away.

It's an emotional torture that has left me with gnawing regret. It isn't fair to her, but I don't know what else to do. The most important thing is to keep her safe and not drag her into whatever *might* happen. I wish it could be different, more than anything, but I can't let personal desires get in the way, no matter how much I want the outcome to be different.

My phone rings, and I look down to see Tasha's name flash across the screen. I know instantly that she's calling about Maven.

"Tasha. What's up?"

"Renn! Oh my goodness. I'm so glad you answered."

"What's going on, Tash?"

"I have a question."

"Okay."

Tasha clears her throat on the other end. "Have you, by chance, spoken to Maven recently?"

My chest goes heavy. "I haven't. I . . . actually haven't seen her around town for a few days." There's a long pause. "What's wrong? Is she okay?" The questions spill out of me, hurried and panicked.

"It's probably nothing, but I haven't been able to reach her for a couple of days."

"What about Tova?"

"She called my mom this morning asking if we had spoken to her. She said she got a text from her last night but still hasn't heard anything from her today. Her call went straight to voicemail. I've been trying to get a hold of Valery, but she must be busy."

I take a deep breath. "I'll go."

"Renn." Her tone is edged with worry, and for a moment, it's all she can say. "Listen. What I'm about to tell you has to stay between us, okay? As my friend, and as Mave's friend," she says softly through the phone.

"I understand," I reply, keeping my voice steady.

"She's been more distant than usual these past couple of weeks, and I thought she'd be okay, but . . ." Another pause. "I'm scared for her, Renn."

We're both quiet for a few beats.

"This is about the accident. Isn't it?"

Tasha doesn't answer immediately, undoubtedly wondering what she should share with me, questioning what I already know.

"Today is the day when it happened."

Tasha doesn't need to say anything else. I know what was left unsaid. She trusts me, even if I don't deserve it. "I'll go," I say abruptly. "I'll go make sure she's okay."

There's silence again on her end of the phone.

"She might not let you in."

I know she doesn't just mean inside the cabin. "I'm going to try."

"Okay . . . but can I ask you something, Renn?"

"Of course."

"Why did you lead her on? I thought something was going to happen between you two, but . . ."

I pinch the bridge of my nose then run a hand through my hair. "I know. I know. I, uh, I've been busy."

She doesn't say anything for a few seconds. "Are you sure that's all?" I don't know what to say. and when I don't reply, she adds. "Look I don't know what happened, but I do know the way Maven is around you, and even when she says she doesn't care, her face says something else."

I still say nothing.

"I see that same look on your face, Renn."

The tightness in my chest strains again, and I clear my throat before I reply. "I'm sorry. I should have done something sooner."

Even though I can't see her, I can hear the sad smile on her lips.

"It's okay, Renn." She sighs heavily, the rush of breath muffling the speaker. "Honestly, there's probably a lot of things we all could have said and done better, but I think she would have found herself at this point eventually."

I lick my lips. "I'll let you know when I get a hold of her."

"Thank you, Renn. I appreciate you looking out for her."

I haven't been looking out for her, not when she needed someone. It was cruel of me to give her all my attention and then none at all, but I intend to fix that now.

"You're welcome. Bye, Tash."

"Bye, Renn."

I immediately store my tools and let the guys know I'm leaving for the day. Then I make a quick stop at home, mostly to take care of Shy, but I opt for a speedy shower as well. And now my knuckles are white, gripping the handles of the motorbike as I try to steady my hands from shaking. I didn't even consider taking my truck. I just want to get to her as fast as possible. I typically follow actions based on logic, but there were many moments in my space endeavors when intuition played a major role. So, I follow that feeling inside me, the same feeling that brought me to this planet in the first place. Maven is in trouble, and it isn't just my inner pull that is leading me to do this, it's my own experience.

Flashes of images from when I was starving and floating in endless darkness come to mind. Even after all these years, whenever I recall those moments it still locks me up inside. I feel the chain lying against my chest underneath my clothing as I search for anything to comfort me.

She's okay. She's okay. I keep reciting it in my mind, revving the bike to go faster until the silhouette of the cabin comes into view. It's completely dark—no light pooling through the windows—but Maven's car is parked up front. I ease up the gravel driveway, now covered in dead leaves, and don't stall for a single moment as I jog up to the front door and knock, praying she will let me in and that I'm not too late.

CHAPTER NINETEEN

Maven

I'm startled awake by rapid knocking at the front door. Lifting my head off my pillow, I barely open my eyes as I feel for my phone on the nightstand. I tap it a few times, then realize the battery is dead. The clock on the wall reads 5:15 pm.

Is it already that late in the day?

The knocking sounds again, this time louder. There are no lights on in the cabin, so I hope whoever is here will just leave, and I pray it isn't someone in particular.

"Maven? Are you in there?"

Shit. Out of all the people in this town—no, the entire world—Renn is the last person I want to see. I'm not a pretty sight, having worn the same oversized hoodie and sweatpants for a few days now. A comfy, "leave me alone" outfit donned with zero intention of seeing anyone, especially him. He knocks again, softer this time, like he knows I heard him but don't want to come to the door.

"I just want to make sure you're okay." I can hear in his voice that his sentiment is genuine, but I still want him to go.

Now you care if I'm okay? I think.

"Tash called. She's been trying to reach you."

He talked to Tasha about me? Great. What did she tell him? I wait a few more seconds, praying he will just leave, but an ache in my heart hopes he won't.

"Maven?" he semi shouts now.

Is he really not going to leave? I sit up, ripping back the covers, surprised at myself for considering talking to him as my body keeps putting one foot in front of the other. I reach for the handle, letting my hand hover above it for a few seconds before I drop it back down to my side and lean against the door frame.

"You there?" His tone is heavy with concern—concern for me.

I take a deep breath. "Yes. I, uh . . . I'm fine. My phone died. I'll call Tasha and let her know that I'm okay." My voice is scratchy, having not actually uttered a word in days.

"You sure?" His voice sounds nearer, like he's leaning close on his side of the door, causing my heart to thud loudly against my ribs. Even with a door between us, he does something to me. I wish it wasn't true, but the reassurance I feel from him being here, that presence of calm radiating from the other side of the door, already makes me feel more alive than I have in days. But I didn't ask him to come, and I don't want him to see me like this. "Maven?" I would almost say he's pleading now.

I whip the door open to the sight of him standing on the doorstep, wearing that damn jean jacket and black beanie, his motorbike helmet tucked under his arm. Even in the state I'm in, I still get a warm feeling in my belly. He looks at me with a shocked expression, which tells me he wasn't expecting me to open the door, and in all honesty, I wasn't either.

"See? I'm fine, okay?" I'm on the verge of shouting, and I want to slap myself for being so brash toward his act of kindness.

Renn surveys me for a long moment, taking me in, his gaze going up and down the length of my body. Not in a judgmental way, but making sure that I am indeed fine—at least physically.

"Thank you for opening the door," he says with a small smile, and I swear I see a look of relief flash over his face.

"Yeah, well, I'm fine, so . . ." I say, trying to sound overly annoyed, when in reality, now that I see him face to face, my legs feel weak at the knees. Or maybe that's the lack of food.

"So . . . do you need *anything*?" he asks slowly, like he's hinting that he actually does mean *anything*. I give him a narrowed look.

"Nope."

"You sure?"

"Yes."

He stares at me with a crooked smile, putting his hands in his jacket pockets before leaning against the doorframe. I try to wait him out, but he looks pretty comfortable standing there.

"What?" I snap.

"Can I come in?" His demeanor is smooth, trying to make this painfully awkward situation less terrible by attempting that classic Renn charm on me, and the persuasion is working.

I purse my lips and look him straight in the eyes. "I. Am. Fine," I say in the most condescending tone I can muster and move to shut the door, but Renn puts a hand on it, stopping me. "What are you doing?" I groan, straining to push it closed, but it doesn't budge an inch.

"Can I come in for just a minute? Please?"

"No!"

It doesn't phase him as he continues to stand there, cool and collected, but now his smile is gone. The longer he's here, the harder it will be to convince him to go. I gulp, trying to swallow the tears that are forming. I'm yearning for him to come in, but I still can't seem to say what I want to—say what I really want from him. On top of all that, I know he sees right through the illusion that I'm trying to create. He can read the conflict in my eyes, the internal struggle. It makes me all the more fearful that if he really got to know me, he would regret coming here in the first place. The thought stings my heart as Renn continues to stand there patiently, like he has nowhere else to be tonight. I bite my lip, trying to think of something to say, but I realize there are no words that would leave him convinced. I back away slowly as he moves forward, closing the door softly behind himself and placing the helmet on the floor before turning to face me.

"May I?" he asks, reaching for the collar of his jacket. I nod, and he removes it and his beanie, placing them on the back of a chair at the kitchen table. His hair is messy, and the white, long-sleeve shirt he wears fits close on his body, highlighting his toned arms and chest so that the necklace he always wears is outlined underneath. I fold my arms, holding them close against my chest like they are a dam, keeping the feelings inside and locked away. "Maven, are you okay?"

No. I'm not okay, and I worry I never will be.

"I can't do this," I say, shaking my head.

"Yes you can," he says, taking a few more steps forward.

I look away from him and bite down on my lip. The voice in my head screams at me, a jumble of thoughts bouncing back and forth.

Tell him to go away. Tell him to get out. I swallow my empty words.

"I'm just going through something, and . . ." I pause. No, I won't do this, not with him. "Look, I'm not in the mood for this right now, and to be honest, I'm over this whiplash of you being here, then not here." His face looks defeated as I take a sharp inhale of breath before adding," I want to be alone, and I don't think you could ever understand the—"

"I think you're underestimating what I understand when it comes to you, Maven," he says, cutting me off. I stand, stunned. "I think I know exactly what's happening here," he says, his tone serious and commanding. I stare back at him, trying to read him—looking into his eyes that are more gray than green today. He steps closer. "I know I haven't been a good friend, and I'm so sorry about that, especially after the retreat, but I care about you. I was genuinely getting very worried, and after Tash called me . . . I had to see you. I know I'm intruding here, but I had to know if you were okay." He stops, taking a deep breath, then runs a hand through his hair before going on. "I don't know if I can be of help, but please let me at least try."

His voice is thick and deep with meaning, giving me goosebumps along my skin—as if the words now cover every inch of my body.

When I don't answer, he goes on. "Tell me to go and I will, but if there's any part of you that wants me to stay, I'll stay. I'll be here for as long or as little as you want me to be."

I inhale a shaky breath, trying to think of something to say, but my emotions betray me. "Why do you care? You don't even know me."

I immediately regret the words the second they leave my mouth because I don't mean them—not a single one. He takes a step back like the words hit him like a bullet. I'm pushing him away in anger because I don't know what else to do. I don't want him to know this person. This version of myself is ugly and unkind. I'm falling deeper into the darkness, and all I can think to do—the only thing I know how to do—is run. I turn away from him, and I start to walk back to my room.

"Maven," he whispers, and the reverence of his voice forces me to stop in my tracks.

Hearing him say my name like this pulls me back, but I don't turn around to face him. He said it with such care, and it's all I need to break, so I do the only thing I have strength or reason left in me to do: I close my eyes, drop my head into my hands, and cry.

I hear him move closer until I can feel him standing behind me.

"I can't . . ." My tears turn into full-on sobs, and I'm unable to speak through the heaviness in my chest and strain in my throat.

"I know I can't fully understand it all, Mave, but I don't want you to be alone. Please? Let me stay."

I breathe out a few sobs, shuddering as I try to speak until I'm finally able to form a word. "Okay."

I say it so quietly, I wonder if maybe I didn't say it at all, but then he moves around to stand in front of me. He isn't touching me yet; I know he's waiting for me to come to him. I may not have known him for long, but I know he would never force himself on me.

When did Renn the Stranger become the person I want to be around more than anyone?

I still can't bring myself to look at him like the coward that I am, so I step forward, covering those last few inches separating us, and bury my face in his chest. Renn instantly wraps his arms around me and rests his chin on top of my head. I embrace his warmth and the strength of his arms, anchoring against him as I cry harder with each passing second. He strokes my hair, holding me tighter as the tears keep falling. I'm lost on what to say or do, and instead, I focus on taking deep breaths, trying to control them, and each time I do, I inhale the scent of him. He smells like the forest and the rain with a hint of car grease from the auto shop, and it's so intoxicating that I can taste it on my tongue, the earthy pure goodness of him.

"I'm sorry," I choke out.

"There's nothing to be sorry about. Let it out. It's okay," he says softly against my hair. "I've got you."

And I know what he says is true. I know he won't let me go, and so I do as he says. I let it leave my body and breathe through it until it feels like I can't possibly cry anymore, like all the bitterness is being washed away until I feel empty and numb. I let myself sink deeper into his embrace until he's practically supporting me to keep me upright. The more I lean into him, the safer it feels. I don't know how long we stay like this, but at some point, Renn gently gathers me up in his arms and carries me to the bedroom. He does so with such ease, pulling back the sheets while still cradling me and then laying me down onto the bed. I literally cling to him, and the front of his shirt is soaked with my tears. I'm pathetic, but at this moment, I don't care.

He pulls the covers over me then turns to leave, but I grab his hand, strong and warm as he slowly wraps his fingers around mine and gazes down at me. Neither of us says a word, but we don't have to, he just knows. He kicks off his boots and lies down on the bed next to me. Being a chivalrous man, he refrains from getting under the covers, as much as I wish he would, but he's still close enough that I can feel his warmth. I need him closer, so I slide over, laying my head against his chest, and he naturally wraps his arms around me.

My mind and body unwind, and it isn't long until the heaviness of sleep overcomes me, his steady heartbeat in my ear lulls me to find peace, the sound reminding me he's here—he's real. I don't remember falling asleep, but when I dream, I dream of Renn. Because even with him right beside me, I want to keep him close, even as I sleep.

CHAPTER TWENTY

Renn

Maven sleeps for hours, and I'm relieved that she allowed herself to calm her mind and get the rest she needs. I got the inclination that she probably hasn't slept well for a few days at least. The moment she opened the door, I knew it was bad. It wasn't only the fact that she appeared emotionally spent, it was her eyes that hit me hardest. They were dull and empty. Those stunning pools of blue, absent of the light usually shining in them; it was like she wasn't really there. It scared the hell out of me, and I wondered if she heard that fear loudly drumming through me when I held her in my arms. When I saw her standing there . . . it was enough for me to almost fall on my knees and beg her to let me in.

God, I'd missed her. I didn't realize how much until she stood before me. There was a moment I thought she was going to send me away, so the total relief I felt when she allowed me inside eased that pain in my chest profoundly. I knew it was bold to practically demand that she let me in, a bit intrusive, but I needed to be here for her, if only to ease my own wanting, and I don't care that it makes me selfish—not this time. I meant every word I said. If she told me to leave, I would have. It would have killed me to do it, but I would have done whatever she asked, even if my need for her—to keep her from harm—is perhaps the deepest desire of my battered heart. It terrifies me that she has this hold on me, and I feel ashamed that I gave her a piece of myself, only to push her away like I had these past weeks. It seems that no matter what I do, Maven is bound to get hurt, and I hate myself for it.

I hope when she wakes up, she will still be glad about her decision. Through the skylight above her bed, the sunlight is turning the sky orange as it rises. My guess is that it's around 5:00 a.m. I need to get home to check on Shy. She has a dog door to go outside when she needs to, but she'll need to eat soon. My arm has gone numb, not that I mind in the slightest, and I slide it gingerly from underneath her, hoping to not disturb her slumber. She unconsciously buries her head into her plush pillow, and I pull the soft sheets around her before I grab my boots, leaving the room. As stealthily as possible, I slip on my jacket and beanie, then ease my way down the driveway, trying to keep the sound of the tires on the gravel to a minimum.

I can see Shy peering out the loft window when I pull up to the house, her ears sticking straight up before she quickly disappears to meet me at the front door. Before the door is fully open, she's whining happily, jumping up to lick my face.

"I'm sorry, girl. I didn't forget about you."

She huffs at me.

"I swear!" I say, patting her on the head. She prances over to her food bowl, and I don't take a second longer than necessary to get her fed. She dramatically chomps down on her food, acting like she hasn't eaten for days. *Very subtle.* Point taken.

I pull out my phone to check my messages and remember that I haven't updated Tasha as I see her name pop up at the top of my screen.

Tasha: Did you talk to Maven? Is she okay? Let me know when you can.

The last message was from an hour ago.

Tasha: Hopefully no answer means you got a chance to talk to her. Please let me know.

Renn: Hey, Tash. Maven is okay. I'm sure she will want to talk to you soon. I'm heading back over there in a little bit, just came home to clean up and check on Shy since I stayed the night.

A reply from her immediately arrives.

Tasha: You stayed the night?

I chuckle, typing back a reply.

Renn: I'll let her explain. She was still asleep when I left.
Tasha: Okay, okay. And Renn, thank you. Seriously.
Renn: No thanks necessary.

Shy is still happily gobbling away at her food, so I go into the bathroom and splash some cold water on my face, hoping the brisk temperature will make me feel more awake. I brush my teeth and run a comb through my hair, deeming it good enough. I want to be there when she wakes up, so I encourage Shy to finish her food and then beckon her to follow me back outside. The brisk air is biting with the first sun rays of the day just about to appear. Still no sign of the promised storm. Maybe it passed over us. When I return to Maven's, I softly open the door to the cabin and pause, waiting to hear if she's up yet, but I hear nothing.

Shy casually makes herself at home by climbing onto the nearby couch and closing her eyes before I can object. I go to the bedroom, peeking inside to see Maven still soundly asleep. Shy's ears perk up as I walk over to the couch to sit beside her, and she lays her head in my lap while I scratch her ears. I check the time on my phone to find it's nearing 6:00 a.m. I hope Maven will sleep in late, so I try to close my eyes for a moment, but sleep never comes.

Eventually, curiosity gets the best of me, and I start to wander around the cabin to get a better look at the new pictures adorning the walls. It's not until I'm standing directly in front of it that I notice one picture in particular. I gaze fondly at the photo of Maven, Tasha, and myself at the Solitude Ridge lookout taken just a few weeks ago. The sweeping landscape behind us is almost as striking as it was in person, but just like before, my attention remains on Maven's face, full of warmth and sunshine as her arm is wrapped around my middle. Her blue eyes are still captivating from inside the frame, and it pains me that what was such a happy moment mere weeks ago had faded. Here I am, still unsure of what to do. I'm at the crossroads once again, needing to make a definitive choice: whether to let her in or let her go.

Before I can lose myself further in my worries, my stomach growls loudly. Shy hears it from her spot on the couch, ears perking up again. "I guess you weren't the only one who needed breakfast," I say. She blinks a few times before setting her head back down on her paws. I meander over to the kitchen to look for something to eat, feeling a bit weird for meddling around. Luckily, it appears the cabin is well stocked with food, something I'm sure Tova did before she left. I notice the empty sink, no dirty dishes in sight. She probably hasn't eaten much in the last few days on top of not sleeping.

I click my tongue. "What do you think, girl? Should I attempt cooking?" Shy cocks her head to the side, blinking a couple more times. "Yeah, probably not the best idea." She jumps off the couch to sit beside me. "Of course, with your supervision, maybe I can make something edible." I kneel to rub her ears. "Let's start with coffee, and then we will see where that leads us." She places a paw on my leg as a token of support.

It's been some time since I've cooked a full meal for myself, let alone someone else. A couple of times a week, I heat up a frozen meal or two from Valery. Originally, I took them up to Grant if she wasn't able to, and then she started giving me my own, no doubt because she took notice of the things I purchased from the store and very lovingly thought I needed more variety. It's hard to get anything past that woman, but I'm grateful for it. Over the years, I've become comfortable enough with the food here. Once my food rations had run out, I had no choice but to acclimate my malnourished body to all the foreign aspects of this new, yet familiar world. It took months to gain the weight back, but eventually, I returned to feeling and looking like myself again.

It's strange that sometimes, when I stare in the mirror, I can still see myself in my uniform, adjusting the lapels of the jacket I would wear on special occasions. I used to take pride in that, but now, whenever I see my reflection, the man staring back at me is not the man of honor I had worked so hard to become. Now, this version of myself is a man of contradictions.

The greatest contradiction of all is the fact that I'm here, in Maven's kitchen, attempting to make her breakfast after spending the night holding her in my arms, asking her to trust me when I still don't know if I can ever tell her the full truth of who I was—who I still am.

You've already done things you say you never would, my own voice mocks me. It appears that all the things I promised I wouldn't do are slowly fading away the more I come to know every broken and beautiful piece of the woman sleeping in the next room.

CHAPTER TWENTY-ONE

Maven

I slowly open my eyes, and it takes me about ten seconds to remember how I got here, and who is in my house. I scoot out of bed and pad gingerly across the wood floor to the door, placing my ear against it for any sounds on the other side. I hear him in the kitchen, and then I notice a sweet aroma drifting into my room.

He's cooking. *Of course he knows how to cook too. What doesn't he know how to do?*

I quickly change into some clean clothes, run a hand through my tangled hair, and pull it up into a bun before I carefully open the door. Renn immediately turns at the sound.

"Hey, good morning," he says casually, like it's completely normal for him to be here, making breakfast in my kitchen, like he's done this a hundred times before. But then I notice he's still wearing the clothes he wore yesterday, and that does something to me.

He never left. He was here all night.

"You stayed," I say, softly. That's all I can think about at the moment, and I'm trying to hold back the emotion building in my chest.

"Well, I did go home to grab Shy," he says, nodding over to the couch where she nonchalantly lounges. "But yeah. I stayed." We stand there for a beat or two.

"I'll be right back," I say.

Without waiting for a response, I speedwalk to the bathroom to freshen up a bit and try to gather myself. I properly brush my hair, brush my teeth, and wash my face to try to liven up my complexion before I head back out to the kitchen. I find Renn sitting at the table with an assortment of breakfast food in front of him: some chopped fruit, perfectly fluffy pancakes, and a steamy, fresh cup of coffee next to the plate he laid out for me.

"Hungry?"

"Very." I smile taking a seat across from him. We eat in silence for a minute, the only sound is our forks scratching against the plates, but I fidget in my seat because I feel like I need to say something. But what? *Thanks for talking me through my emotional breakdown?* I mean that was exactly what he did, but would it feel weird to say it aloud?

"This is delicious. Thank you."

"You're welcome. I haven't had a breakfast like this for a while. I usually get something to grab and go."

"And you don't have anywhere to go this morning?" I ask, lighthearted but curious.

Renn grins. "Not at the moment, no."

I give him a smirk and take a long sip of coffee, hoping it can somehow give me courage. Be brave. *Let's get this over with,* I think to myself.

"So, about last night . . ." I pause when he looks at me with a serious expression. "That was probably the kindest thing anyone has ever done for me." And I mean it, but he knows there's something more.

"But?" He leans forward.

"I'm just a little embarrassed. Really embarrassed, actually."

He looks at me, confused.

"Why are you embarrassed?"

Is he really going to make me spell it out for him? I feel my face get hot.

"I mean . . . it was pretty pathetic. So, yeah, I'm embarrassed."

Renn rests his elbows on the table, crossing his arms in front of himself. His gray eyes hold mine, and I don't dare take my gaze away from him.

"That's not what I saw." His tone is so serious in that deep, luring voice. I can feel my face blush again, and the goosebumps rise on my skin. "I saw someone who is strong. Who is living day after day with a burden that they carry alone, and yet, you still go on. You're still here. You're trying." I want to look away from his stormy eyes, but it's impossible, so I just shake my head. "You are kind and genuine, even when you have every excuse not to be. That's not someone who is weak or pathetic. I saw someone being the strongest a person could be, and that's you, Maven."

Tears blur my vision, but this time, they aren't tears of sadness, rather, they're a revelation. That he truly sees this side of me but doesn't run away from it. That I'm not the horrible human being I see myself as. That he only sees *me*. But I need to tell him the whole story, and it's not surprising that being with Renn helps the words easily come to my mind.

"Has anyone ever told you about the accident? The whole story?"

He shakes his head. "Only that you and your father were in the car together."

I gulp and realize that the words I'm about to say are words I've never said out loud to anyone. Not even my mom.

"It was my fault that we crashed that night. I was driving. My dad was the passenger."

Renn's eyes stay on me as I say this, his face calm.

"My dad and I went into town that night—just the two of us—to get a treat after dinner. But what I didn't know was that my dad wanted to use this particular trip to talk to me about Jamie." Renn crosses his arms at the mention of Jamie's name. "He told me that I could do better, and he was worried about what could happen if I wasn't careful. I had just started my career, and things were going well, but I guess he was worried about Jamie messing it all up for me. I was young and stupid. I thought what Jamie and I had was a good thing."

I lick my lips. "Instead of hearing him out, I just became angry. I didn't want him to tell me what he thought was best for me. We got into a big argument, and I eventually stomped out of the restaurant to the car. As we were driving home, a bad storm came out of nowhere. My dad told me to pull over so he could drive, but I told him no." I take in a shaky breath. "And that was the last thing I remember before I woke up in the hospital three weeks later." Renn deeply inhales at the words but remains silent. "I had driven off the road and crashed into a tree. My dad had been killed on impact." I need to get through the whole thing. If I lose it now, I won't ever be able to get it out. "I broke both my legs and fractured my back. I was put into a medically induced coma because of my head injuries." As I say this, it doesn't go unnoticed that Renn's fingers flex slightly as they rest on his forearms. "When I woke up, I couldn't talk or move, but I could see and hear, and when I opened my eyes, my mom took my hand, and I knew from the look on her face that he was gone.

I choke on the words for a moment—the memory is so clear in my mind.

"The doctors told us that it would be a long and difficult road of recovery, and there was a chance I'd never walk again. Miraculously, my brain remained unharmed, but I wasn't able to stand on my own until a year later and couldn't walk without support for several months. It took countless hours of therapy and a handful of surgeries to get me where I am today. I pushed myself to my limits to heal. I threw everything I had into beating the odds. People tell me, 'You're amazing, Maven. You should be proud of yourself.' But I'm not proud, not even a little bit. The truth is, I did it because it was a distraction from facing what I had done. From the fact that my dad was dead because of me and everyone knew it, but they never said it, at least not to my face." I exhale and catch my breath. "My mom. I don't know how she can even look at me. I . . . I killed her husband."

Renn stands abruptly and walks over to my side of the table, pulling his chair with him so he can sit next to me, facing me. He subconsciously pulls the sleeves of his shirt up his forearms, and a flutter in my stomach goes wild as he rests them on his knees, leaning forward a little.

"It was an accident. Your mom knows that. Everyone knows that." I shrug in response. "You can't see it as all or nothing. No one knows what could have happened if things were different that night."

I take in his words for a beat or two.

"But it happened. I lived. He's gone. And now because of what I did . . . it's left a darkness in me that I don't think will ever heal. I can't fix it like my broken bones. It's like an open wound on my heart—this dark mark that is part of me forever."

Renn ponders this, and his face holds a saddened expression for a moment. "Maven." My name on his lips. "Everyone has some version of darkness in them. Some more, some less. It's not about removing the darkness, but how we learn to live with it. How to accept it as a part of us, and what you do next."

I like the idea, especially since it comes from Renn, but that can't be true for everyone. Right?

"How can you be so sure?" I ask.

He doesn't say anything for a long moment, but then he reaches under his shirt collar to grab the necklace he always wears, pulling it out so I can see it fully. On the end of the chain, there's a thin, metal rectangle with something engraved on it. I lean forward to look at it a bit closer.

He lays it flat against his palm so I can observe the fine-lined imprints of a small sun, moon, and a star.

"My father was gone a lot for his job before I was born, so he gave this to my mom."

I'm surprised he's speaking of his parents, because I know he never has with anyone.

He continues, "My dad kept this when my mom passed, then he gave it to me when I was older. He told me that he loved my mother as gentle as the moonlight but as fierce as the sun and endless like the stars." I can't help but grin wide at the sentiment. Renn chuckles softly. "I know, it's a bit much, isn't it?"

I shake my head. "Not at all. It's lovely." He smiles warmly at me, but his face becomes serious again as he looks back down at the necklace.

"My mother died when I was born. She had a rare blood disorder that made her pregnancy with me dangerous, and it was even more so when in labor." I watch as he rubs the indents with his thumb. It looks so delicate in his slender fingers and strong hand, and for a moment, he seems lost in a daydream. I try to picture Renn as a young boy and wonder if he looks more like his father or mother. "My dad was never around growing up. I was raised mostly by my grandparents—my mother's parents. They tried their best to cover the fact that it was difficult for my dad to be around me because I was alive and my mother was not." This saddens me to my core, and my heart breaks for him. "But I only lived with them for a short time before I went to a—" He stops, like he doesn't know the word to say, but then says. "A boarding school when I was fourteen."

So young. And to have grown up without a mother . . . then his father abandoning him. I think back to what Renn said that day on the sidewalk, that our parents would do anything to shield us from those difficult parts of life. I see that realization on his face, like he remembers the moment too. In this case, it was his grandparents.

"Renn, I don't think that's true. I'm sure he loves you."

"Maybe he did, but it doesn't matter now." He smiles sadly. *Did.*

"He died two years after I'd left for school. He had a dangerous job, so to speak."

I don't realize I am crying until I feel a couple of tears slide down my cheek.

He clears his throat, and I can see the emotion thrumming in him. "After some time, I realized that it wasn't about me. I think he loved my mother so much that, maybe with her gone, he simply had no love left to give."

I continue to let the tears fall, one by one, and I can't seem to stop them. My heart aches for him. I wonder what his parents would say if they saw the strong, wonderful man he has become. He lost both of them, tragically. And he said I'm strong?

The fact that he is the man he is—kind, gentle, smart—even after all he's been through, his own strength is far beyond what he thinks he sees in me.

"Are you grandparents still alive?"

He shakes his head. "They lived long, happy lives, but they have passed on." I dab at my eyes lightly, and Renn licks his bottom lip before he speaks again. "I've been through some dark times. There have been times in my life when those dark places were almost unbearable. Hopelessness was all there was, and it felt like there was no way out besides not being alive anymore to feel it."

He closes his eyes, his breathing changing, and then all at once, the realization hits me hard in the chest—the deeper reason he came here, and why he refused to leave.

"Oh, Renn . . ." I place a hand over my heart. "I don't know what to say."

He rubs a hand along his jaw, and I see tears brim in his eyes.

"I don't ever want to assume anything, but I have thought about it . . . that if I were no longer here, it would be better, and I didn't want you to think . . . I'm not saying that you would ever . . ." He stops, pinching the bridge of his nose before looking back at me. "I was out of line. I should never assume anything. I'm sorry."

I reach for him, pulling his hands into mine. He stares at our hands for a moment, fingers tangled together before he goes on. "I shouldn't have pushed into your life like that. I'm sorry if I crossed a line. That was never my intention."

"I know, Renn. I know," I say softly.

"I was just so scared, Maven." His voice is strained, and he has to look away. I squeeze his hand, hoping to reassure him that I understand. "I didn't want you to face it alone like I had to."

I wrack my brain, searching for something profound to say. My heart is just heavy with gratefulness for all he has done for me. Because he's not wrong; I honestly can't say what would have happened if he hadn't come over. I hope that I would have snapped out of it eventually, but it terrifies me that there's a part of me that knows it could have gone another way just as easily.

"Renn. It's okay."

Relief spreads across his face. "I still carry my own demons day after day. I hope someday I will be strong enough to tell you about them. But for now, I hope you understand why I did what I did."

"I do understand, and I'm not mad one bit. What you did . . . it means the world to me."

He parts his lips to say something, but his phone starts buzzing, breaking the moment. He pulls back his hands to check it while I sit there, awkwardly watching as he reads the message, the tension in the room shifting.

"Sounds like things are busy at the shop today and they need extra help." He slides the phone back into his pocket and quickly glances at my hands. I place them back in my lap and then fold them across my chest, not sure what else to do with them. "I was going to ask you if you wanted to go into town together, but . . ."

I start to shake my head. "Oh, it's okay. No worries." He smiles crookedly at me. "We can talk more later," I add. "I'll call Tasha and go to the coffee shop, but maybe . . . we can touch base later?"

The crooked smile turns into a wide grin, and my stomach does that fluttering thing again.

"Yeah, that would be nice." He clears his throat. "Well, I better head out then," he says, standing to grab his jacket and beanie off the back of the chair. I don't attempt to not stare as I watch his every move intently. He shrugs on his jacket and slides the hat over his head. His eyes lock on mine as he adjusts the collar, placing the necklace back under his shirt.

"Renn. Thank you." He scans my face. "Thank you for everything."

And then I stand up and do something that makes my senses go wild. I step forward and place my hands on his forearms for leverage as I stretch on my tippy toes to reach up and kiss his cheek. I let my lips linger there for a second or two longer, and when I pull away, I'm almost positive he's blushing.

He smiles down at me, our height difference more substantial standing this close to each other. "In case you didn't know already, I'm here for you, for anything, okay?" he says. I nod in response. Then he looks at me like he wants to say something more, *do* something more. I can't help watching his lips as they part slightly, but a second later, he says, "The weather seems to be letting up. Maybe if it's still nice later, you could come with me and Shy for a walk. If you want."

I grin. "That would be nice," I say.

"I'll let you know when I get home, okay?"

"Okay," I say with a bittersweet smile, because I don't want him to go yet.

"Come on, Shy," he says.

I had almost forgotten Shy was there as she bounds off the couch without hesitation at his command and they both walk toward the door. But before he closes it behind himself, he, of course, winks, then shuts the door softly.

I exhale, wrapping my arms around myself, as I hear his truck start up and drive down the road. I look over at the kitchen table and decide to take a shower before getting to the dishes. Before jumping in, I look at myself in the mirror to find I have a stupid grin on my face that doesn't want to go away, no matter how hard I try.

"What is happening right now?" I say to myself.

The basic answer is a friend came to my aid in a time of need. The complicated answer is that Renn, the man whom I have quickly developed feelings for, came for me. He had seen me at my absolute lowest and yet, he stayed.

He didn't treat me like some breakable thing, he just didn't want me to be alone. In this moment, I realize that sometimes being strong isn't about facing things alone, because no one, not even Renn, can take the pain away for me. But just knowing he was there gave me the hope to not give up. I have my demons, just as he does, but I don't have to endure them alone. I hope in some way I could do the same for him in one way or another.

For the first time in five years, I'm not dreading the future, instead, I face it, feeling lighter than I have in a long time.

CHAPTER TWENTY-TWO

Maven

I take a very long, very hot shower, taking my time to soak and breathe in the steam. Lying in bed for several days made me feel suffocated and gross; I needed the extra time just to feel alive again. I walk back to my room, a towel wrapped around myself with another one holding up my hair. I find my charger and plug my phone in. The cord is long enough for me to flop onto the bed while I wait for it to come to life. Once it does, I see I have three messages from Tasha and two missed calls from my mom. I message Tasha back first.

Tasha: Just checking in. Call me later.

Then there's a message from a few hours later.

Tasha: So, did you get a visit from a certain someone last night???

Then another one this morning.

Tasha: Call me!!!
Maven: Hey!

Tash messages me back immediately.

Tasha: Mave! Finally! So...did Renn come by last night?

I roll my eyes, smiling as I type back.

Maven: He did.
Tasha: AND?
Maven: I'll explain everything when I see you.
Tasha: You're going to make me wait? Seriously?
Maven: This is definitely an in-person conversation.
Tasha: Fine. Mom and I are heading back tomorrow, so we should be home in a few days at most, maybe sooner.

She sends another message before I can reply.

Tasha: So, are you okay? You kind of scared all of us for a minute there.
Maven: I'm completely fine. More than fine. And I'm sorry. I didn't mean to do that to you guys.
Tasha: GOOD! You know we love you, right? We want you to be happy.
Maven: Of course I do.
Tasha: Good! I'll see you in a couple of days.
Maven: Be safe coming home. Love you!
Tasha: Love you too! And you better not leave out ANYTHING that happened with Renn.

Next, I call my mom.

"Thank goodness. I was getting so worried." Her exasperated tone doesn't go unnoticed.

"Hello to you too, Mom, and let me start by saying I am totally fine."

"I got in touch with Tasha when you didn't call me back," she says, ignoring my response completely.

"And what did she say?"

"That she hadn't talked to you and that she was sending Renn over to check up on you."

I sigh heavily.

"So did he? Is everything okay?" she inquires.

I take a moment to think of how to approach this conversation. "Yes, everything is fine, Mom. It was just a hard couple of days."

"I should have come up there to be with you. That was a mistake . . ."

"Mom, no. You can't run up here every time things get hard. That defeats the purpose of why I'm here."

She doesn't say anything for several seconds, and I don't know how to tell her what Renn did for me, or if she needs to know at all. I find it difficult to think of the right way to say it without making her worry or having her ask too many questions. But something I know without a doubt is that my time with Renn showed me that strength isn't earned by doing things in solidarity, it's about having the courage to face your challenges. It means never facing them alone. I think about saying this to her, but I don't.

"It's still a bit complicated, isn't it? Not knowing how to feel or what to do," she sighs.

I smile sadly, her words resonating with me for the first time in a long time. "It is. I feel guilty when I don't feel sad all the time, but ashamed to think of what Dad would say if I was just wallowing. You know?"

It's strange that we've never really spoken about this before, but for some reason, thoughts keep pouring from us both.

"I may not know a lot of things, but I do know this: Your father would have wanted you to be happy and live your life to the absolute fullest. He would have wanted you to *live*."

I choke back the tears, and I know she hears the strain in my voice as I reply, "Thank you, Mom." I pause for a moment. "And I should have called. I'm sorry. I just needed to process some things."

"I understand. I stayed home all day yesterday, but I'm going out with a few friends tonight to get out of this funk." My heart feels a bit lighter at this.

"That's great, Mom. I'm glad," I say with a small smile.

"So . . . you didn't answer my second question. What happened with Renn?"

Here we go.

"Nothing. He just came over to see if I was okay and then we hung out."

"Mm-hmm."

"What?"

"Why do I get the feeling you're leaving something out?"

"It was nothing. Like I said, I had a couple of bad days. Tasha told him I might need some company, so he came over, and that's it."

It's quiet on her end of the phone, yet so much could be said in these few seconds of silence. I know she's contemplating if she should push for more details or drop it for another time. Thankfully, she chooses the latter.

"Well, I'm glad he stopped by then. What are you up to today?"

"I'm going into town for a little bit. I'm planning to stop by the coffee shop."

"That sounds great. Message me later when you get home."

"I will. Have fun with your friends. I love you."

"I love you, too."

I tap the screen to end the call. I wasn't planning on that conversation going the way it did, but I'm glad nonetheless. It was just a few words, but they were words that my mom and I have danced around for years.

I look toward the bed, picturing Renn and me lying there, side by side, his arm around me. I don't push aside the satisfaction I feel that what happened on the retreat wasn't all in my head. I had started to wonder if he had even spared a thought for me at all, but after last night and this morning—whatever he felt for me, whatever friendship we had between us, I can tell it had consumed him as much as it had me.

I walk over to his side of the bed, picking up the pillow he laid on, bringing it to my nose to inhale his scent deeply. The muskiness that I've learned to recognize so well washes over me. Catching myself in the moment, I quickly throw it back onto the bed.

"Don't be creepy," I say aloud, turning to my closet to find something to wear to take on the day, truly grateful that I have another day to live, and for the people in my life who make it worth living.

I walk into the coffee shop, book and sketchpad in hand. After a little while of reading, I soon find myself scanning the same sentence over and over again, so I pull out my sketchbook and pencils. I'm glad I grabbed them on my way out as an afterthought. I haven't sketched or designed anything in months, so I'm surprised how quickly I lose myself in the blank sheets of paper. It helps distract me from replaying last night, and this morning, over and over in my head.

What does this mean for Renn and my relationship? We are friends, but more . . . so now what? Just as I'm about to finish with my second cup, my hands now smudged with residue from the pencils, Valery walks into the shop and spots me by the window.

"Maven, my dear. So good to see you!"

"Hey, Val. Good to see you too!" I gesture for her to sit across from me. "Do you want to join me?"

Her bright smile fades. "I wish I could, but I need to get back to the store. We are a bit busy at the moment. I think everyone is stocking up for the storm." She must read the confusion on my face as she adds, "Did you not get the weather alert?"

I scan my phone and find no missed notifications. "I thought the storm had passed?"

"Oh, well, there's another one on the way. It may even snow. It's supposed to last a couple of days at least, if it doesn't blow over again."

The first snowfall of the year was never to be taken lightly around here, that much I knew. "Thanks for letting me know. I probably should be heading home soon if that's the case," I say, looking out the window.

"That would probably be for the best, dear. Are you going to be there all alone?" she says, raising her eyebrow.

"Yeah . . . probably." I give her a narrowed look. "Why do you ask?"

Valery makes a face that I know all too well.

"I just happened to overhear someone earlier at the store mention that they saw Renn turning onto Spruce Road last night. Or at least they thought it was him. It's hard to miss him, especially when he is riding that motorbike."

I have to force myself to not roll my eyes. I highly doubt that she "overheard" the conversation; whoever had seen Renn turn down my road probably couldn't wait to pass it along to Valery. Small towns are no good at keeping secrets, and gossip sometimes feels like a competition.

"I see. Well, yeah, Renn did come by last night. Just to check in." Valery raises her eyebrow again, hinting she needs more details. "And . . . we might see each other later, I don't know." Val's smile widens to a full, toothy grin, and I can't help but roll my eyes this time. "We are just friends, Val."

"Oh, of course. Of course," she says with a wink. It's pointless to try to convince Val of something if she already has her mind made up, so my only option is to get out of here before anything else can be said.

"Well, I guess I better head home," I say, starting to gather up my belongings. She watches me as I stand, pulling me into a quick hug.

"Be safe, and call if you need anything."

I squeeze her back, remembering that, while it's a bit intrusive, she did it out of love, pretty much how everyone does anything in Solitude Ridge.

"I will, Val. Thank you."

I pull up to the cabin and the storm hits. Perfect timing. It doesn't gradually begin either, the hard pounding of rain is almost instant as it bounces off the roof and ground. I quickly run inside, trying to cover my hair as best I can without a hood or umbrella to shield me. The cabin has a standard heating system, but if the power goes out, the fire will keep me plenty warm and cozy. I prefer it, especially on cold, rainy evenings like this one. I can still read and sketch, but the ambiance would be perfect in the firelight and crackling of wood.

"Looks like we aren't going for that walk then," I say to myself, looking out the window.

After begrudgingly changing into some comfortable clothes, I make a simple dinner, and just as I'm about to sit down at the kitchen table, all the lights suddenly switch off. Everything goes deathly quiet, the kind of quiet when you know the power is going to be off for a while. I can just feel it in the air, which isn't surprising with this storm. I pull my raincoat and boots on quickly to go out around the back of the house for some firewood, only to find none.

How did I miss that?

Without the fire to keep warm in a power outage, it could end up being a couple of extremely cold days, especially if it does end up snowing. I sigh, defeated, and run back inside. I pull out a lantern from a nearby closet, setting it on the table to eat the rest of my dinner.

I tap my finger against the table in thought. I do have the option of staying somewhere else until the storm passes, and I can't help the tinge of excitement thinking about the possibility of going somewhere in particular. My cheeks heat at the thought, a little embarrassed with myself. I dig around in my bag, looking for my phone, and find I have no missed calls or messages. Renn is most likely still at the auto shop, and he could be there a few more hours. He said he'd call, so I guess I'll have to be patient and finish my soup in a mood of boredom.

Soon, the lantern is the only source of light. I searched the supply closet to find more to spread throughout the cabin now that the normal mountain nighttime darkness is amplified, with the stars and moon nowhere to be seen. I try distracting myself with my books, snacks, and sketching, but it doesn't help at all as I keep checking my phone every few minutes.

It's a good thing I have a portable charger because I am draining the battery.

I figure I have three options. Tasha and Mina's place is empty and probably still has power since Main Street has back up generators. Any other time, I would have liked having the bookshop all to myself, but not tonight. I could call Valery, or pretty much anyone else in town, but option three is where I land. I won't deny this desire wishing I was somewhere else . . . with someone else. Plus, the storm hasn't faltered in the slightest; the rain is still coming down just as much as it was when it first started. I guess my fourth option is to stay here in the freezing, pitch-black but . . . I could just call Renn, my third option. His place *is* much closer—another thing to add to my list of reasons to call him and not anyone else. Before I can talk myself out of it, I pick up the phone and tap his name.

In one ring, he answers.

"Mave, you okay?"

"Hi to you too, and yes, I'm fine," I say, smiling.

"Sorry, it's just you've never called me before."

He's not wrong, and now that he's brought it up, I realize I should've just messaged him.

"Oh, well, yeah. Um, are you still at work?" I quickly ask to cover my faltering.

"No, I just got home actually. I was going to clean up . . . then see what you were up to." I blush with embarrassment. If I would have waited one more minute, I wouldn't seem so desperate. And maybe I am, but at this point, I don't think he thinks that based on his response. "Are you home?" he asks, and I can hear Shy's paws clacking on the floor on his end of the line.

"Yeah. I got home a few hours ago after going to the coffee shop for a while." I swallow nervously. "But my power went out, and I'm out of firewood."

The pause on his end is entirely too long. I hold my breath for what feels like hours.

"I'm sure it's just a breaker or something. I could fix it, but . . ." He inhales deeply like he's thinking. "It will probably have to wait until tomorrow, when it's not raining as hard." I hear the smirk on his mouth. I get the feeling that he could fix it now if he really wanted to. But no, he's going to make me work for it. "So . . ."

"So . . ." I play along, smiling to myself as it remains quiet on his side for another second or two, and for a moment, I wonder if he isn't picking up on what I'm hoping he will say, but thankfully, he puts me out of my misery.

"You could come stay at my place if you want."

The wide grin that comes across my face is nothing short of pure victory. "Okay, well, I mean, if you don't mind." I like playing this game with him.

"Not at all. Plus, it's not like we haven't slept together before."

I stand shocked and can't think fast enough. Then Renn starts laughing. Just when I thought I'd won . . . Damn him.

"I'm kidding. You can take the bed, and I'll sleep on the couch."

"No, Renn. I'll take the couch."

"Maven. No, I'm sleeping on the couch. You'll sleep in my bed." *My bed.* The thought of being cozied up in his bed, in his sheets that smell like him, gives me a tingly feeling in my core as I consider what that experience will be like—probably heavenly.

"I'll take the couch," I say sternly, blushing over the other thoughts I have of Renn's bed.

He sighs deeply.

"You're so stubborn, but fine, I won't force you."

"Thank you. I'll head over in a little bit. I just need to pack a few things."

"A few things? How long are you planning on staying, exactly?" he says, teasing, and it makes my stomach flip again. I like bantering with Renn, but I also secretly hope we aren't going to dance around each other all night in this flirty game of not talking about what's really on our minds. There are things that I still need to say, and so much more I want to know about him.

"Well, how long until I wear out my welcome?"

He goes quiet again for a few beats.

"You would never. Not with me."

And there it is, that flirtation turned serious, the tone of his voice making me weak in the knees. He always does this, charms me then hits me with something deeper, and it always feels unexpected but comforting at the same time.

"Well, I guess we will find out if you mean it." I say, cheeks burning.

"Do you want me to come pick you up?" He asks. I don't want to seem completely helpless, so I quickly respond, "Oh that's okay. I don't mind."

"Alright then."

"I'll see you soon."

"See you soon, and Mave . . . be careful. I'll be waiting for you." He ends the call and I realize that it's the first time he's called me "Mave".

CHAPTER TWENTY-THREE

Maven

I must look a bit deranged as I quickly throw items into a large bag. I have a moment of hesitation when I start up my car, glancing at the stuffed bag of my belongings next to me on the passenger seat. I can almost hear Tasha's voice in my head: *"How long are you staying? A week?"*

"Oh, shut up," I say out loud and then back out of the driveway. I'm cautious driving, probably overly so, because it takes me fifteen extra minutes to get to Renn's. Since I don't actually remember the crash from that rainy night many years ago, it doesn't give me anxiety as much as it makes me mindful when driving in these conditions.

I'm fairly familiar with Renn's place, but it's been many years since I've seen it in person. It's barely visible as the rain bounces off the windshield when I pull up the drive. As I move closer, I spot Renn on the side of the house, gathering firewood from a large pile sheltered from the rain. I pull the hood of my raincoat over my head, grab the bag, and brave the downpour.

When he turns to find me there, I call out to him. "Do you need any help?"

He jogs over quickly, meeting me at the porch steps. His dark green rain coat and hood cover most of him, but it still doesn't hide his broad shoulders and chest underneath.

"I got it," he says with a grin, glancing down at my bag. "So, a month then? I don't think your power will be out that long."

It takes me a second to realize what he means because I'm too busy drinking him in, but once I do, I hit him lightly on the arm. "Oh, stop! I'm just prepared, that's all. What if we get snowed in or something?"

Renn bites his lip almost nervously, and I think I spy a hint of blush on his cheeks again, which only makes me blush in return. "Always good to be prepared," he says, winking, then motions to the door. I carefully walk up the porch steps, him following closely behind as I push open the door. Stepping into Renn's house gives me a rush of excitement, and Shy is there to greet me, her tail wagging happily. It has a similar layout to my own, just smaller with fewer bedrooms. The space is open, a seating area and fireplace with a small kitchen at the end of the room and a back door that leads to the deck. To the left is a set of stairs with a door beside them for the bathroom. No pictures hang on the dark wooden walls, but it's tidy and inviting. A simple but cozy-looking couch sits in front of a large, greystone fireplace.

"This must be where I'm sleeping?" I ask, nodding to the couch. Renn gives me a bemused look as I set down my bag. We both remove our shoes and hang our coats on the hooks near the door.

"If I had it my way, I'd be sleeping there and you would be in the loft, but yes, that's one place that you can sleep," he says.

"So upstairs is your room," I say, walking further into the house and nodding toward the stairs.

"It is."

That was a dumb thing to say. Obviously that's where he sleeps. I pretend to be interested in the kitchen, hiding my embarrassment as I continue to look around.

"Are you hungry? Thirsty?" he asks, walking into the kitchen with me.

"Something to drink would be nice, thank you."

"I didn't stop at the store on my way home, so I don't have a lot of food options, but I do have coffee," he says, placing his hands on the countertop of the small island in the middle of the kitchen.

"Coffee would be great. I'm still feeling a bit cold."

"You got it." I watch him gather up supplies and a mug from a cupboard. "Please, make yourself at home."

I walk over to the couch and flop down. It really is as comfy as it looks, and Shy jumps up to join me, placing her head on my lap. I scratch her ears, busying myself as Renn makes the coffee. Soon, the warm aroma mixes with the fire . . . and the smell of Renn, that is, of course, everywhere in this house. I wish I could drink it all in, not just the coffee.

"Here you go." He hands me the mug, our fingers brushing slightly before he sits down on the other end of the couch with Shy between us.

"Thank you so much for this, and I don't just mean the coffee." I don't look at him as I say it, feeling silly that I'm so nervous sitting here in his house.

"Of course. Like I said, I'm here, for anything." I look up at him, and his green eyes are just as bright and deep in the firelight. I part my lips but can't find the words to respond. He looks toward the fire. "I better throw a few more on just in case the power goes off during the night," he says, walking toward the pile of logs neatly stacked near the hearth.

As he crouches to add the wood to the fire, I notice for the first time what he's wearing. He has on a pair of black, cotton jogger pants and a long-sleeve, light gray shirt that is, of course, rolled up on his muscled forearms. The pants stretch across his thighs as he leans in, adding a few more logs. I spot the chain of his necklace peeking over the collar, lying across the back of his neck. If he feels my gaze on him, I don't care. I don't try to hide the fact that I am completely and fully checking him out. Especially now that I know what it feels like to be pressed up against his body, what those arms feel like around me. I take a small sip of my coffee as he stands to retrieve the poker next to the wood pile.

"I'm not usually this helpless, you know." I blurt, and I don't know why, maybe to calm my nerves by talking—not that it's helped much in the past. But it's too late to take it back now.

He stands, turning with a confused expression.

"I never said you were helpless," he says, calm and serious. Renn mimics me by crossing his arms to give me one of his soul-piercing stares.

"I know you didn't. I just . . . Well, you seem to be saving me a lot lately. So, it probably looks that way."

Renn's reaction surprises me. It's not a look of pity, but I can't decide what it is. Maybe frustration?

"You think that's why I came over? That I thought you needed me to rescue you?" His voice becomes harsher

"Maybe? I don't know. We didn't really get to finish our conversation."

Renn's serious face suddenly becomes softer again, stepping away from the fireplace, walking toward me.

"That's not why I came over, but I think you already know that," he says, giving me a knowing look. "I told you I care about you, so why are you questioning it?"

I swallow before I say, "I guess I'm just worried about what you might think of me now. Now that you know everything."

He takes a couple more steps toward me. "So, you think I don't like what I saw, and now you're worried you scared me away?"

I shrug. "Yeah, in a way, I guess." He smiles at me, biting his tongue, and I can't help but smile back. "What?"

"You really think that's what the problem is here?" He motions to the space between us. I inhale nervously. "The problem isn't me liking you less the more I get to know you, Maven. It's the fact that the more you share with me, the more things there are to like about you." He sighs, defeated, almost like it pains him to say it.

"Why would it be a problem if you liked me?" I ask, my voice soft.

He's still as he searches my face, close enough now that I can see the rim of light gray circling his green irises.

"Maven, I've told you more things about me than I've ever told anyone here in Solitude Ridge, but there's so much more that I should tell you, more that I *want* to tell you." He pauses for a moment before going on, his voice dropping another octave as he says, "I guess I have the same fear as you, that if you really got to know me . . . I don't think you'd be standing here right now."

I shake my head. "No, Renn. That's not possible."

"It is. There are parts of me that I don't want you to ever know because it's better that way. Trust me."

I stare at him, trying to figure out what he means as the firelight dances across his face, but I can't find anything sinister there. I can't see or feel anything about him that would ever cause me to run from him.

"That's not fair. How can it be true for me and not for you? After yesterday, don't you think I would understand?"

I can see that he's at war with himself. Clearly, it's difficult for him to even say it, whatever *it* is, so I don't want to push him. I want him to come to me when he's ready, just like he did for me. At least now he knows that I'm here for whenever he *is* ready.

He never pressured me to tell him my deep, dark secrets, so I will do the same for him.

"You don't have to tell me now, but someday?" I ask.

He smiles faintly, and a few seconds pass. "Yeah. Someday."

We look at each other for a few more beats, and it's Renn who breaks his gaze first, turning to look into the flames, the firelight making his already sharp jaw more defined.

And before I even know what I'm doing I ask, "Can I ask you to do one more thing for me?"

He brings his eyes back to mine, a small smile edged with kindness and curiosity.

"Kiss me." I shock myself for being so bold. He goes very still, and after what feels like an eternity, he slowly takes a step toward me. It only makes the nerves in me build, and I start talking to try and calm myself down, but it doesn't help. If anything, it only makes me sound like a blubbering idiot.

"I just want to know," I say.

"Know what?" His gray-green eyes look a bit wild, making my heart jump.

"What it would feel like. Just once."

He tilts his head a little to the side, smirking before taking another step closer. My skin erupts with goosebumps, my heartbeat thrums loudly in my ears. And his eyes . . . they are almost too much the closer he moves toward me.

"I hope you know what you're getting yourself into," he says, a smirk playing on his lips.

Is he really teasing me right now about how good of a kisser he is? Not that I think he would be bad at it. I mean, how could he not be good at kissing, or anything else for that matter?

"Are you really that confident in your skills?" I ask, trying to tease him back, but it just sounds stupid.

He darkly chuckles and shakes his head. "No, it's not that. I just meant . . ." He steps even closer until we are inches apart, my body radiating just as much heat as the fire beside us. "I meant, do you really think I'd ever be able to kiss you just once?"

I inhale sharply. I think my heart stops beating for a second or two.

"Because if you ask me to kiss you, then you should know I've thought about it many times. About what it would feel like. What you taste like." I lick my lips nervously, and his gaze goes there for a moment before looking back to meet my eyes. His voice is low and dark as he says, "My imagination is pretty good at coming up with ideas, but it hasn't even remotely satisfied the thoughts I've had of you. So, if you're sure about this . . . I will kiss you. But I'm warning you, before you fully decide, it won't be once, not even twice. I don't think I could come up with a number that would satisfy me."

He brings a hand to my face, tilting my head back a little, placing his thumb on my chin to hold me where he wants me while he scans my face. I tremble at the sensation and can't help the sharp intake of breath I take at his touch. His movements are purposeful, like he truly has pictured this—like he's planned it all along and was just waiting for me to ask.

I believe him now.

His grip on my chin tightens a little. "Tell me, are you sure, Maven?" His breath dances across my lips, and I inhale again, gulping it down.

"Your expectations of me are much too high. You may be disappointed," I whisper, trying to tame the nerves and heat thrumming through every inch of my body. There's fire in my veins and he hasn't even kissed me yet.

"Doubtful," he whispers back.

I can't tell if I'm breathing anymore, and I want to say something back, but those eyes of an emerald storm steal my words.

"What's it gonna be? I need to hear you say it." His breath tickles my lips again. I breathe, finally, taking a deep inhale.

"Renn, I want you to kiss me. Right here. Right now. And if you don't, I'm never going to ask you again." My voice is breathy and wanting, and he chuckles, satisfied in seeing what he does to me. The vibration of his laugh is so good that I feel it all the way to my toes.

"Trust me, you'll never have to ask me ever again."

He leans down, and I melt. The touch of his lips are gentle on mine, the stubble on his face strangely satisfying against my skin. His kiss is soft, colliding with mine, but then he brings both his hands to either side of my face, his fingers trailing over my neck until they dig into my hair. It's painfully slow, but it feels so incredibly good.

I thought I knew what it felt like to be kissed, but kissing Renn is an entirely different experience. It's nothing like the boys I've fooled around with before, not like Jamie, who just wanted to take something—to use me. They all were lustful and sloppy, but Renn kisses to give me something, giving me a part of himself. He kisses to make me feel, and he's making me feel oh so many things.

I keep my hands at my sides, not touching him yet. I don't know why, but some part of me just wants to see what he will do with nothing holding him back, what he's thought about doing before I take it further. He slips his tongue over my lips and into my mouth, and I can't stop myself as I let out a sigh of satisfaction at the feeling of his tongue brushing against mine again and again as I kiss him back. I try to stay that way, but then he moves a hand to my hip and pulls me against him, and I can't keep my hands off him any longer.

I reach up, touching the sharp edges of his jaw as his strong body pushes up against mine. He hums in gratification. My nerves are out of control, but I feel safe. I always feel safe with Renn—even now, as my heart races and my mind is dizzy from the feeling of him touching me, kissing me, *holding* me like this.

This is really happening. Renn is kissing me, and God, I only want more. I stand up on my toes to kiss him harder, wrapping my arms around his neck, and he lets out a groan, sending chills through my body.

"This is probably a bad idea," he says, panting against my lips. His heartbeat thrums on my palms as I move my hands to lie against his chest. It's beating as fast as my own.

"Too late," I say, my breath shaky. He pulls back a little, our lips still danger-ously close together.

"You don't want to get tangled up with someone like me." His eyes glaze a bit as he says it, but I scoff.

"Someone who offers his place to a friend in need? Who cares enough to help her in a most dire situation?" He searches my face, and I notice a bit of disbelief in his eyes. "Renn, you are the kindest, most selfless person I know." His hand slides to my neck, tilting my head back a little as I look up at him. "I'm sorry to disappoint you, but I'm already tangled up with you," I say softly. Renn looks at me with concern in his eyes, but then he leans down and kisses me along my jaw. I close my eyes at the feeling of his lips trailing up until he reaches my ear.

"That's what I'm afraid of," he whispers, his lips grazing my ear slightly.

Just as I'm about to say something back, my phone rings. "That's probably my mom."

He leans in to kiss me again, but then pulls away. "Yeah, you better get that. She's probably worried about you with this storm."

Renn drops his hands, taking a step back. I notice a look of disappointment on his face, and it makes me smile as he walks back to the hearth, giving me some space. I reluctantly take my phone out of my back pocket before taking a deep breath and answering the call, not realizing how out of breath I really am until I try to speak.

"Hey, Mom."

"Hey, sweetheart. How are you?"

"I'm good. There's a bad storm that came through today and the power went out, but I'm fine."

"Oh, no! Are you staying at Mina's?"

Renn stokes the fire again, even though it doesn't need it.

"No. I'm actually . . ." I pause, and Renn glances over to me with a mischievous look on his face, trying to hide a smile. *Stop that*, I mouth to him. "I'm at Renn's place, actually."

There's dead silence on the other end for a few beats.

"You're staying at Renn's? All night?" I roll my eyes as Renn leans against the mantle, watching me.

"Yes, Mom. I'm staying here all night," I say the last part slowly, giving Renn a look like, *don't even*, but he ignores me.

"Probably tomorrow night too!" he yells.

I gawk at him and cover the phone speaker. "Would you shut up!?" I say, trying to whisper, but I laugh instead. He puts a hand on his chest as he laughs. "Ignore him, Mom."

"Oh! Well then . . . That's great." Her voice is edged with worry, but maybe also a hint of relief.

"Yeah, it is *great*," I say, giving him another look.

"Well . . . I'm glad you're okay."

"Yep, we're all great here," I say, quickly trying to end the call before Renn jumps in with something else to tease me with.

"Okay, good. Well . . ." She pauses. "Have a good night."

"Okay. Goodnight, Mom. I love you, bye," I say as fast I can and tap the end button aggressively. "You're ridiculous," I say, laughing as Renn walks back over to me.

"I don't know what you're talking about. I thought that was pretty *great*." He smirks, taking my hand and pulling me toward the couch. My heart rate intensely accelerates again, but just before we sit down, Renn's phone buzzes. He lets out an angry groan, dropping my hand.

"That's it. I'm throwing these damn phones outside, and I don't care that it's raining." I cover my mouth to keep from laughing too loud. He looks down at the screen. "It's Valery. It could be an emergency."

"It's fine. No worries." He smiles at me for a second or two before answering.

"Hey, Val." He looks at me and winks. I can hear Val's muffled voice but can't make out exactly what she says. "Not much, What's up?" There's another muffled response from her end, and Renn nods along to whatever she's telling him.

"I can be there in twenty minutes . . . Uh-uh. Of course. Yep. Okay, see you soon." He slides the phone back into his pocket. "There's some flooding on Main Street, and they need help getting some barriers set up to direct the water from the structures." He genuinely looks disappointed, and so am I.

"Sounds like they need you."

He takes my hands in his, and I'm pleased with how easy and quick it is, that he doesn't hesitate to touch me. "Hopefully I won't be too long. Are you okay being here by yourself?"

"Yeah. I've got Shy. I'll be good."

He squeezes my hand. "Okay, good. I'll try to hurry." He lets go of my hand, moving toward the front door to grab his raincoat. I watch as he shrugs it on. "We can talk about this when I get back, okay? I'm sure you have some thoughts," he says, winking. I walk over to hit him on the arm.

"Whatever. But yeah, I do." He bites his lip, trying not to look too pleased with himself. "Like what happens next, for starters," I add.

He takes my face in his hands again. "I don't know about you, but I hope more of this." He doesn't wait for my response as he kisses me again, practically taking my breath away. But this time, I push against his chest, and I can tell he wasn't expecting it as I keep pushing him to walk backward until his back hits the door.

I pull away. "I hope so too," I whisper against his lips and see his throat bob. *I did that,* I think to myself.

I step away, and he grabs the door handle to walk into the storm, but before he goes, he grabs my hand again, pulling me to him, kissing me quickly before saying, "I'll be home soon." Then rushes out the door before I can even kiss him back or say a word.

"Not fair," I say, smiling to myself. I walk back to the couch in a dizzy haze of euphoria and plop down next to Shy. She lifts her head to study me, cocking her head to the side.

"I know. I can't believe that just happened either." She blinks a couple of times and then rests her head back down on her paws.

I gather up some of the blankets that Renn must have placed next to the couch earlier. I don't mean to fall asleep, but I do, wrapped up in blankets that smell like him and are as soft and comforting as his kiss.

CHAPTER TWENTY-FOUR

Renn

I meant what I said when I told her she would never have to ask me to kiss her again. But I wanted her to make that decision for our first time, and I knew I'd never be able to deny her if she asked, so when she did . . . I was undone. My selfishness got the better of me again when it came to her. Of course, I knew the possibility of kissing her would be dangerously high if she was going to be in my house, but I wanted it to happen, and I am glad it did, no matter how reckless it was. I was playing with fire, and now the fire that was and is Maven has consumed me. If I had it my way, I would have kissed her weeks ago—on that day we made it to the overlook—when she ran to me and I held her in my arms. Or when we talked under the moonlight that night and she told me about her father. Kissing her was a whirlwind of feelings that I couldn't keep in order. The way she made me come alive at the feeling of her lips against mine, the taste of her skin . . . It felt so right, so easy.

I also didn't lie when I said that she now knows more about me than anyone else in Solitude Ridge, but what she doesn't know is that she actually knows more about me than anyone on this entire planet.

But despite all of that good, there's the lingering fear. No matter what I feel for her, there's the probability that if, or when, she finds out everything, she'll leave . . . The thought of her walking away, hating me, or worst of all, being afraid of me . . . the thought is unbearable.

But then there's a feeling that surprises me. Hope. I dare to let myself think that maybe the universe is telling me that it's time to let go, that it's giving me permission to move on and hold on to this beautiful thing that has entered my life. Maybe it was destined.

I can't help but smile to myself as I drive into town, because even thinking of the universe as a force of good strikes me as ironic.

It'd sort of been an underlying joke within the association that there was some greater force in control of the universe. I never thought much of it, but now that I've met Maven, there has to be something greater at work that led me here to find her.

I hardly notice the glow of the Main Street lights as I pull into town. My mind is a bit foggy, replaying that kiss over and over again, and when she pushed me up against the door . . . the thoughts swirling in my head were nothing if not downright filthy.

There's already a large gathering in front of Val's store as I pull up, a few pickups full of sand bags being unloaded nearby. Sandbags are always readily available, but they usually aren't needed until the end of winter when the snow starts to melt. I'm grateful for the town's preparedness, because there's a heavy amount of flooding toward the end of the street that will start to rise soon if we don't direct the water away quickly. I zip up my rain coat and pull on the hood, getting out of my truck.

Val sees me immediately and calls out to me. "Renn! Thank you so much for coming." She's standing under an umbrella next to one of the trucks being unloaded.

"Hey, Val, you weren't kidding!" I yell over the noise of rain, motioning to all the busy movement as people run back and forth from the trucks. "Where do you need me?"

She beams at me proudly. "Oh, Renn, I can always count on you," she says, taking hold of my arm. "It looks like we should have enough bags to line the street, and we've started to direct the water gathering at the bottom of the street away from the road, but we're going to need to move faster."

It's hard to recognize who all is here with everyone wearing heavy coats and hoods, but I spot Asher and Trey in the group and give them a nod. They wave in return, carrying a couple of bags over their shoulders.

"Alright then." I move toward the trucks, but Val grips my arm again, causing me to pause.

"Did you happen to check up on Maven? I saw her at the coffee shop earlier, and she didn't know about the storm. I figured you talked to her though?"

I cock my head to the side, biting the inside of my cheek, and she smiles wide, seeming to already know my answer. "She's staying at my place, actually, but I have a feeling you knew that," I say, winking.

"I had an inkling, but I just thought I'd ask."

"How is it that you already know everything?" I ask jokingly.

In all seriousness, Val answers, "Oh, please. I saw the way you were around each other from day one. It was just a matter of time. It was always there."

"What was?"

Valery's mischievous grin changes to a subtle smile as she squeezes my arm lightly. "Oh, dear, I think you know. I think you've known for a while now." For the first time ever, I don't have a comeback or lighthearted comment to return. She pats me on the back. "Now hurry up so you can get back home." I don't say anything as she shoos me along.

How strange but comforting it is that I have someone to go back to—that someone is waiting for me. Home. It's as if it's the first time I've ever heard the word because I realize here, standing in the pouring rain, that Maven is home.

Home is waiting for me.

A few hours later, I am thoroughly soaked, every bit of my clothes completely drenched, my fingers so numb, I can't grip anything properly. We're all baffled that it still hasn't snowed. *How much colder can it get?* I think as the night goes on. The large crowd has dwindled, the trucks now empty, and the only people left from the large gathering earlier are Asher, Trey, and myself.

"I don't know about you guys, but I'm pretty sure I will never be warm again," Trey says through chattering teeth. Now that we're no longer hauling heavy bags, the cold has set in more, sinking into our very bones.

This cold is painful, but there are different kinds of cold. My mind flashes back to those long days sitting in the low-functioning ship, floating through space. There's cold, and then there's space-cold, and I would take a rain storm like this over that any day.

"Let's get inside. Val said she would have towels and coffee once we were done," Asher says, and Trey and I follow him without hesitation. Sure enough, towels and hot coffee are waiting for us. I quickly drink my cup and dry off as best I can, anxious to get back to Mave. After a hurried goodbye, I rush to my car with achy limbs and sore hands, trying my best to hold on to the steering wheel. The rain has subsided some, but still falls all the way home.

Pulling up to the cabin, I see the faint hint of light glowing through the windows. I open the door, and Shy lifts her head from her spot on the couch, lying on top of Mave's legs. Maven is sound asleep and doesn't stir as I slowly remove my boots and coat. I walk over to the couch and rub Shy's ears—a silent thank you for keeping Maven company. She sets her head back down on Maven's legs and closes her eyes.

"Good girl," I whisper.

I glance at Maven and notice the blanket she has draped over her is sliding off the couch slightly. I carefully gather it up and place it on top of her and add another quilt on top for good measure, moving it to make sure Shy can breathe.

She doesn't wake, only sighs deeply, her hair draping slightly over the side of her face.

I quietly move to the bathroom and take a quick, scorching shower before heading up to the loft. I secretly hope that she may have woken, but not even Shy follows me to my bed.

I don't want to fall asleep, but this time, it's for an entirely different reason. Nightmares are the last thing on my mind as I lie there, surrounded by the pattering sound of rain, clasping my hands behind my head. Just knowing she's sleeping under the same roof has me on edge, and not in a bad way. My body is alert, but so incredibly sore. I know I will feel it even more tomorrow.

I don't know what finally urges me to close my eyes. Maybe it's the rain or the comfort of knowing Maven is near. But I dream. Real, good dreams. Images of Maven and me sitting at the counter, having breakfast in the morning, taking Shy on a walk through the woods, and that kiss. That kiss was everything if not a promise of what could be. Our bodies were electrified at the first touch and taste of each other.

If only I would have known that the true nightmare would soon become very real, maybe I wouldn't have lost myself so deeply in my dreams of her.

CHAPTER TWENTY-FIVE

Maven

The rain drilling into the roof stirs me from my comfortable slumber. I check the time on my phone, shocked that I've been sleeping for hours. Before falling asleep, the rain seemed to be letting up, but not now. It sounds louder than ever. I must have fallen asleep before Renn got home, because I spy his raincoat and boots near the door. Sitting up, I realize a heavier blanket that wasn't here before lies on top of me, making my cheeks flush knowing he must have draped it over me at some point in the night. I truly wanted to wait up for him.

Just to make sure he's already asleep, I tip-toe up the small flight of stairs to the loft, my weight creaking the wooden slat steps. When I get to the top, the loft is larger than I expected and there are skylights on both sides of the ceiling with the bed sitting underneath. Renn is asleep on his stomach, the sheets stopping just below his waist, leaving his bare back exposed. Meekly, I inch closer, but he doesn't stir. He is soundly at rest, his back slowly rising and falling with deep breaths. I resist the urge to touch him, inching down the steps again to the couch.

Maybe I just wanted to see that he's content with me staying here. I wonder if he will have another nightmare. If he does, I'll be glad I'm here with him. I plump the pillow and lay the blankets over me to settle back in, but then I pause.

What was that sound? I hear it for a second, but it's gone in a flash. I still myself, trying to listen over the heavy beat of the rain, thinking it must have been in my head.

I hold my breath a few more quiet beats until I hear it again. It's muffled by the pounding storm, but I know I hear barking from somewhere outside. I glance around the room for Shy, but she is nowhere in sight.

Why is Shy out in the middle of the night, especially in the pouring rain?

Confused, I peek through the back door's window, turning on the porch light and trying to locate where she is, but it's impossible to see anything clearly through the perpetual downpour. I don't want to disturb Renn in his peaceful sleep, so, reluctantly, I pull on my boots and snag Renn's coat. His coat is long enough to cover most of my legs, my rain boots hitting just below my knees. I grab the lantern that is sitting near the door, then push it open, boots squeaking as I walk across the deck, trying not to fall in the process. It's rained so much that huge puddles have formed, collecting great amounts of the water. Everything is muddy and slick.

"Shy!" I shout into the storm. But there's nothing. My boots splat through the mud toward the tree line, and then I hear her bark again. "Shy!" Still she doesn't come.

I duck into the cover of the trees, grateful to be shielded from the water under heavy thick branches. "Shy? Where are you, girl?" Her frantic barking continues, but I can't decide which direction it's coming from. And then there is a shift in the air, and I get an uneasy feeling in my stomach. Something isn't right. A chill runs up my spine, and a different kind of darkness takes over me.

"Shy?" I whisper, suddenly it becomes difficult to find my voice. A twig snaps from somewhere behind me, and I jump so badly that I almost slip, but catch myself, barely. I stand still for a beat or two, waiting to hear something, anything.

I need to wake up Renn.

I turn around to run back to the house, but before I can take a step, a force slams my head into a nearby tree. Flashes of white spots dance across my vision, and instant throbbing radiates through my skull. I fall face-first onto the soggy, wet ground, unable to catch myself this time. The lantern lands somewhere nearby.

My first thought is that a branch must have fallen from above, but before I can lift my head to get my bearings, a strong grip takes hold of my hair and pulls me to my feet. I scream out in pain, and then a voice hisses into my ear. My body becomes stiff in terror, my balance and senses in vertigo. I can't piece together what's happening in the haze of pain. Is this a dream? The voice continues to say something, but the words mean nothing to me because everything sounds muffled, like something is covering my ears. Shy's barking continues faintly from somewhere. A constant ringing sound in my throbbing head.

Someone holds me and shakes me violently.

It only makes the pain in my head scream, but this time, when I hear the voice, I can decipher it's a male speaking. There's a malevolent tone to the voice, and he's shouting now, pushing me against the tree as he pins my arms behind my back. My face scrapes against the rough bark. The stinging sensation and the hammering in my head make me feel like I'm about to pass out. My vision goes dark, but I need to stay awake. I can't let this man take me and do whatever he is planning, because clearly his intentions are in no way going to be in my favor. I know I'm in grave danger.

The seconds tick on, and no matter what I do, I can't seem to remain present, slowly slipping under, but just as I'm about to fall unconscious, Renn's face clearly comes to my mind. I need to get to Renn . . . somehow . . . My body seems to register this the second I have the thought, and I can almost feel my blood heating up, pumping adrenaline throughout my veins. I see the lantern lying on the ground, giving me enough light to try to focus on my surroundings.

"What do you want?" I muster through a moan. He responds, but I still can't decipher his words as he speaks again, and then it clicks—he's speaking in a different language. "I can't understand you," I say, trying to turn my head so I can see his face, but he pushes me harder into the tree trunk.

My senses keep coming back, bit by bit, fear waking every inch of my body. My fear turns into fuel—the fear of this man, whoever he is. I need to fight my way out of this to stay alive. I know from the sinister tone in his voice that he's going to try to do something terrible to me.

I need to do something now.

I'm still a bit disorientated with pain and shock, but with all the force I can summon inside me, I throw my head back, colliding with something that feels like a nose. The man screams and lets go of my hands. I struggle to find my footing, but before I can manage a few steps, the man grabs my arm and yanks me back as if I were a doll. Instead of restraining me, he steps aside and lets me crash to the ground beside him on my stomach once again.

His mistake.

I peek through blurry vision and see a jagged rock within my reach. I lie still, waiting for him to come closer as I slowly move to wrap my hand around the rock, squeezing it tight, its sharp edges digging into my palm. As soon as I feel him lean down, I spin onto my back and slam the rock into the side of his head. He shouts in agony, and I don't hesitate as I start to run toward the light that I can see vaguely from the porch peeking through the trees. I don't dare turn around, pumping my legs as hard as I can, trying to move fast without falling. The ground is uneven as it is, but the rain makes it almost impossible to stay upright, especially with my heavy boots, but I keep pushing. I keep running. Seconds pass, but it feels like hours—like I'm running in slow motion. But finally, the house comes into view.

"RENN! RENN!" My voice breaks with the effort. I'm struggling to breathe. I try to shout his name again, but my voice is fading. I'm confused and terrified—my screams sound almost inhuman. My lungs burn, my chest blazes, and before I can scream again, the man catches me.

This time, he shoves me to the ground, then flips me over to my back and straddles me, pinning me down at the waist. He now has a knife in hand and holds it against my throat before he leans down, his face just a few inches from mine.

I see his features clearly for the first time in the stream of light coming from the porch. His eyes are dark and full of malice, hooded by thick eyebrows as his lips pull over his teeth, snarling. I've never seen anything so incredibly evil.

I'm going to die. Right here. And God, what will happen to Renn if this man gets to him too?

BANG!

A gunshot rings out. The man snaps his head up to the source, and I follow his gaze.

I find Renn standing there with a gun raised toward the sky. His face is cold and calm, lowering the gun to point it at the man still on top of me. He stares at my attacker, and then begins to speak. I listen intently to his words, but I don't understand what he says. He repeats himself when the man says nothing, and my heart jumps when I realize it.

Renn is speaking in the same language as the intruder. A different kind of chill flows through me, sinking in my chest. Renn speaks again, and the man pulls me to my feet, still holding the knife against my throat while his other arm restrains me against him. With a sideways glance, I watch him stare directly at Renn and smile with such evil delight that it turns my blood cold. I look back to Renn. He still has the gun raised.

"Renn?" I whimper.

He still doesn't look at me, never taking his eyes off the man behind me, like he's a snake and if he glances away he will strike. And I realize, gazing at Renn's face, that he *knows* this man—they know each other.

And whoever this person is, I know he's part of the reason Renn ran away from wherever he came from.

CHAPTER TWENTY-SIX

Renn

There's no one who wants me dead more than Colin Locke. It's been six years since I've seen his face in person, and it's even more sinister when it appears in my nightmares.

It wasn't an anomaly that the transmitter had picked up after all.

How he intercepted the signal, I don't know. But it doesn't matter right now because I have to keep my rage in check; one false move, and Maven or I are dead—possibly both. The sickening pain in my stomach is overwhelming, knowing that he touched her, that he hurt her. But the fury pulsing through my body is mostly to the credit of my own foolishness. This is all happening because of me. I see a fresh cut across his cheek, and even in this horrible situation, I'm proud she did that, but right now he has her in his arms, and I need to get her out of here.

"Well, well, well. Captain Anton, how good to see you again," he hisses, pushing the knife harder against her skin. Maven lets out a wince, and it feels like a punch to my stomach.

"Let. Her. Go," I growl.

"Not a very friendly welcome, Captain. I am disappointed. I thought you'd be glad to see an old comrade after all these years." His voice drips with sarcasm.

"I said let her go, or the next bullet goes through your head."

He shakes his head in disgust. "Goodness, Aldrenn. The man I knew would never resort to such violence. I thought using the dog as bait would have done the trick, but what a surprise when it was her who came instead. And clearly . . ." He pauses for a moment. "I underestimated how much you care for her." He looks down at Maven with a twisted smile. "That changes things. I can't decide what will be more satisfying—killing you, or making you watch as I kill her first." I step forward, and he clicks his tongue. "I don't think so, Captain. I would choose your next move carefully."

"Renn, what's going on?" Maven asks through a trembling voice, and I finally bring myself to look at her directly. The rain has started to let up, so I can see her clearer.

Blood drips down her face, and there's utter confusion and terror in her eyes, making me want to break every bone in Locke's body—to make him suffer. Silently, I'm pleading, begging for her forgiveness, hoping that she can see it in my eyes.

"It's going to be okay," I say slowly in her language.

I should have told her, if only for her protection, to warn her of what could happen. I should have told her *everything*. But I'm a fucking idiot for letting my guard down, daring to imagine that a happy life was possible for me—a life with *her*, and now it will cost me more than I could ever have imagined.

"You know, I've been watching you for a couple of days. I had to make sure I had truly found the great Captain Aldrenn Anton, and I gotta say, you've got some nerve. You honestly thought you'd get to live some comfortable little life? Find yourself a piece of ass and go on your merry way?" I step forward, and he presses the knife into her neck again to stop me. "Does she even know who you really are?"

I want to vomit at the thought of him *watching* us—stalking us. Only one of us is walking out of this, and I will die trying to make sure he takes his last breath, even if I take mine as well. As long as she's safe . . . that's all that matters.

"You certainly haven't changed. You've always loved hearing yourself talk, haven't you, Locke?" He snickers at this. "And you will not say another thing about her. This is between us. Man to man."

His grip on Maven only tightens, and I realize I'm holding my breath. My expression must say it all, because Locke smiles wickedly as he says, "My, my, Aldrenn. I see that your concern for other people hasn't changed in the slightest. That was always your weakness—you care too much. Pathetic, if you ask me. Even the admiral saw that. What a disappointment you were to him."

This time, I laugh in response, because the only thing more satisfying than killing him would be killing the admiral. He gave the order after all.

"Why are you stalling, Locke?" His brow furrows. "But that was always *your* weakness, wasn't it? Only willing to fight those who are weaker than yourself, never up for a *real* challenge. That's why you targeted those planets and people who never stood a chance." Locke's lips pull over his teeth, snarling like a rabid animal. I knew that's what would hit him the hardest; his ego could never handle that I'm a better fighter than him. "Now be a real man. Let her go and let's finish this." His gaze narrows for a moment.

"Put the gun down first," he says through clenched teeth. My eyes dart to Maven, but this time, as I look into the blue abyss, her eyes tell a different story. There's strength; she wants to fight.

That's the Maven I know. A fighter.

The only thing we have to our advantage is that he won't fully understand what we say to each other.

"Maven." She looks at me, her blue eyes full of fury. "Whatever you do, do it fast," I say calmly.

"Renn, what—" she starts to say, but Colin puts a hand over her mouth, still holding the knife against her neck. I see the realization in her eyes of what to do next.

"PUT DOWN THE GUN NOW!" he screams, but then, as we all move in slow motion, she bites down hard on his hand. Colin yelps, and the second he loses his grip, she tries to break free, but I still can't get a clear shot without risking hitting her. She pulls away for a moment only to be tugged back as Locke backhands her so hard across the face that she falls to the ground, unmoving.

Absolute horror is all I feel as I fire the gun, hitting Locke in the shoulder. He stumbles back a few steps, grasping the wound. Before I can fire again, I lose my balance, slipping in the mud, and it costs me dearly as Locke throws the knife still in his hand, striking me in the arm and causing me to drop the gun. Fury numbs the pain as I pull it from my flesh just in time to see Locke charging me. He tackles me, our bodies making a loud splat on the sodden ground.

With the knife still in my hand, I aim to stab him in the chest, only to find that he's wearing body armor underneath. The blade only manages to rip the fabric of his jacket.

He hits it out of my hands, then uses his forearm to press into my throat, blocking my airway. I reach up, digging my fingers into the gunshot wound on his shoulder. He screams but doesn't let up. Then, out of the corner of my eye, I see movement.

Maven.

She picks up the knife and stabs Colin in the back, but because of the armor, it does nothing.

"The gun," I manage to say, choking for air. She looks around, desperately trying to locate it. Locke removes his arm, punching me in the face before he stands to chase after Maven.

A tang of blood coats my tongue, but in seconds, I'm on my feet. Before he can reach her, I shove him down into the mud, except this time, I'm above him, pinning him.

"How has it been for you, Aldrenn? Knowing that they're all dead because of you? She'll be another soul to add to your list of failures," he shouts up at me.

He'll do anything he can to make me suffer, but I intend to do the same. I will make him bleed, so I punch him repeatedly, my fist making contact with his face over and over again.

His attempt to fuel my despair works, so much so that I don't notice the knife now lying close to Locke's hand. He grips it, despite all the mud, and stabs me in the side. The adrenaline still thrums through me to block some of the pain, but I feel it enough that Locke manages to push me off, and I slip again on the muddy ground, landing on my back. The wound in my side stings as I try to get up, and I only manage to rise to my knees to pull the knife out of my flesh once again.

Click.

Locke holds my gun, aiming it at my chest and holding his shoulder with his other hand. Blood flows from his mouth and nose. Maven is standing a few yards away where she has been desperately looking for the gun, but now it's too late. She looks from Locke to me. And I hate myself more than ever, because I'm about to die in front of her. And then what? Will Locke shoot her too?

"Run," I tell her, and she shakes her head. "Maven, run." But she doesn't move.

"Just like I said, Renn, you couldn't save the crew, and you won't save her either," he hisses at me. I turn to Maven to see her blue eyes wide and fearful, and there's nothing I can do to make that fear go away. If I wasn't about to die, that look would kill me enough, knowing that I did this to her. Colin has won.

"Maven," I say, and her lips tremble, the emotion getting caught in my throat. "Forgive me. Please." I bring my attention back to Locke. If he's going to kill me then he'll look me in the eyes as he does it. I won't go down as a coward.

"I believe this is goodbye, Captain, and . . ." I hear a snarl, and Locke turns just in time for Shy to jump on top of him, taking him to the ground.

In a matter of seconds, I'm on my feet, sprinting as Shy latches on to his arm, shaking it violently. The gun lies on the ground a few inches away from his hand. He rolls onto his stomach and tries to reach for it, but I kick it away and then jump on top of him, shoving his face down into a muddy puddle. He gurgles and chokes in his attempts to break free for air, but he can't lift his head above the water while Shy still chews up his arm. He jerks one last time in a final attempt, but my hands shove his face deeper into the mud.

It feels like hours and seconds all at once, but I know the moment Locke is dead. His body goes still as one does only in death. Shy's teeth still sink into his flesh as she yanks at his arm. I'm overwhelmed by what she just did for me. "It's okay, girl. Let go," I say calmly. She obeys and lets it fall with a splat on the soggy ground.

I'm gripping Colin so hard that my fingers are locked up when I try to pry them away. Shy has a cord wrapped around her neck with the end frayed. She must have chewed through it to break free. *Smart girl.* I remove what's left of the cord and toss it aside. I stand, staggering back due to the flaring pain from my side. The rain is just drizzling now, revealing the disturbing scene in front of me. Colin's body face down in a puddle, and Maven falling to her knees, staring at his body with wide, terrified eyes, frozen, with mud and blood covering her. I cautiously approach her. She doesn't move a muscle or look my way, not even as I kneel beside her. Shy trots over and licks her hand, trying to get her attention and to tell her, in her way, that it's over now.

"Mave?" Nothing. She's in shock, and I realize she might not even be able to hear me, but I have to get her inside the house. "Maven. You're okay. It's over. You're safe." Her body rocks slowly to the side, her eyes closing before I catch her, afraid she might faint. I try to brush back her hair to look at the wound on her temple. "Hey, hey, hey. It's okay. I've got you," I say, pulling her into my arms. She lazily lifts her eyes to me. "It's okay. You're okay," I say again, and I don't know if it's unconsciously or not, but she wraps her arms around my neck.

I stand slowly, the wound in my side making me dizzy for a moment, but I manage to hold her legs in one arm with the other around her back. Shy follows me, her eyes on Maven in my arms. The ground is soaked and slick, so I move gingerly but as quickly as I can into the house, easing the door open and then setting her onto the couch.

"Don't move," I tell her, removing my coat and her shoes carefully before wrapping a blanket around her and then quickly moving to get the fire going again. She pulls the blanket around her tightly but still says nothing. Shy whines as she looks at me, clearly aware that I'm injured, probably from the scent of all the blood.

"Stay," I tell her, so she sits beside Maven. The flames begin sparking to life, so I rush upstairs, not caring about the mud and blood I'm trekking over the floor as I retrieve the box beneath my bed, amazed that I haven't passed out from blood loss yet. It must be the adrenaline keeping me upright. I open it quickly and swipe a glob of the healing ointment onto my wound, enough that I can take care of Maven first then reexamine it later. I throw it back into the box to carry it downstairs.

Maven is looking at the flames roaring to life in the fireplace as I set the box down gently, trying not to startle her—pulling the coffee table closer so I can sit in front of her.

"I'm going to check you for any internal injuries, then heal the wound on your head. Is that alright?"

She nods slowly in response.

I place my thumb on the reader, and the lid springs open again. Maven turns slightly, eyeing it with no emotion on her face as I pull out the body scanner first.

"This won't hurt. Just hold still for a moment." The device itself is small, so I hope it won't scare her. Maven doesn't even blink as I scan the device over her, the results quickly read back that she miraculously has no concussion or any other internal physical damage.

She remains unfazed as I pull up the tin, gently moving her damp hair to the side so I can apply the healing ointment to the gash near her temple. "Does that feel better?" She nods again, still looking toward the flames. "I'll get a shower started for you," I say, not expecting a response as I head to the bathroom. I make sure the water isn't too cold or too hot so it doesn't shock her system. Then I lay out clean towels and place her bag on the counter, all the while, Maven still sits in silence. It's unnerving, but I know at some point, the shock will fade, and whatever happens after, I need to be here for her, if only to explain everything.

I take her hand in mine, guiding her toward the bathroom, and once inside, without a word, she robotically begins to remove her clothes.

"I'll be out here whenever you're ready. Take your time."

Then I shut the door softly. I don't want to intrude on her privacy, but I linger near the door for a minute or two, making sure she actually makes it into the shower. Once she does, the pain hits. Like my brain switched the off button as soon as I knew she was okay. I stumble, gripping the wall as the pain in my side overpowers me. I place a hand over it, only to pull it back and see my blood coating my fingers. The ointment I added a few moments ago clearly wasn't enough. It's probably going to take the rest of the salve to heal a wound this deep and severe. Practically collapsing onto the couch, I scoop out a generous amount and apply a thick layer over my side as well as onto the deep cut on my arm. It takes several minutes to feel it working, but it does the job well enough.

I know I'm not handling this situation as best as I can, but I honestly don't know what to do. There's no "standard procedure" for this. For starters, I just killed a man in front of her. If she doesn't already have enough of a reason to be completely freaked out—I don't know what will happen once she knows the whole truth.

I can still hear the shower running, so I walk over to a chair at the small kitchen table and practically fall into it. Shy comes over and rests a head on my knee. "Good girl, Shy. Good girl," I say, rubbing her head for a moment until she walks over to the fire to get warm.

I push the palms of my hands into my eyes. This has been the worst night of my life, and it's only going to get worse. I know the sounds of her screams will haunt me for the rest of eternity. For a moment, she was balancing between life and death, a dangerous game that I forced her into. Maven is my one and only good dream, a light in my life that has given me hope, but now I've pulled her into my nightmares.

I feel like I'm going to shatter. I know what I have to do because there's only one thing I *can* do. Leave. And I need to leave not just this town, but this planet, because I clearly don't have the strength to stay away from her, and I won't let her get hurt again. It's the only way to keep her safe, because the thought of her in danger . . . it isn't going to happen again.

Even now, with Colin dead, there's no way to know what havoc has been conspiring over the last six years. Maybe he was alone, or maybe someone will come looking for him, and that thought makes the fear pulsing through me all-consuming.

After all we've been through, the good and the bad, she deserves to know everything, and after she knows, I'll leave with a promise that she will never have to see me again. I hope that promise will ease her enough to forget about this night, forget about me, and move on.

I go to the kitchen sink to try to wipe off at least some of the blood and mud before I feel too dizzy from blood loss, forcing me to sit at the table. I bury my face in my hands, letting out a shaky breath. If fate is real, then it played me. It brought me here to find her, then ripped it all away. I had one last little piece inside me that was worth saving, and now it will be gone too. This will break me, completely, but I have to leave this place. It has to be done, if only to save the life of the woman I love.

CHAPTER TWENTY-SEVEN

Maven

One moment I'm lying in freezing mud, the next, I'm standing under a stream of hot water raining from the shower head above me. My body locks up for a couple of seconds in fear, going back to that moment when I came to—when I was trying to find the gun but couldn't.

When that man raised that gun and pointed it at Renn's chest, I knew I had failed. It makes me sick to my stomach. Every second mattered in that moment, and I panicked. I take a few deep breaths, inhaling the steam. It calms me enough to realize I'm safe now, but not enough to process it all yet.

Those sights and sounds will live with me forever. I stand under the water for a long while, numb to everything, and gradually wash the mud out of my hair, scrubbing my body, hoping it will erase the horrible events of the night, but it doesn't in the slightest.

When I emerge from the shower, my bag is already here. I don't remember how I ended up in the shower in the first place, let alone grabbing my bag. As

I trace back my steps through the haze, I recall Renn turning the shower on. Standing in front of the mirror, I wipe away the steam sticking to the surface to study my face, grazing my fingers across my forehead where the cut was just moments before. Now, the skin is smooth and unharmed, like it never happened at all. That ointment—the same one he used for my knee on the retreat.

I look unscathed, but inside, my bones ache . . . my soul feels broken. My mind is clouded in a heavy fog as I stare at my reflection, trying to put the events together in my mind, piece by piece, but nothing makes sense, and the confusion grips me tightly. Tears well up in my eyes, but I hold them back. I won't cry—not yet anyway.

I move in slow motion, pulling a pair of leggings and a sweater out of my bag, and once I brush out my damp hair, I nervously reach for the door knob, not fully sure what will be waiting for me on the other side. My hands tremble slightly, but this is Renn, and I still trust him. I don't know if that makes me a fool, but it's him, and he's all I can count on at the moment. I can feel, deep within me, that the next moments are going to change everything we know forever.

Sometimes these life-altering moments come without warning, catching us off guard. Other times it's a reaction deep within, as if our very essence senses a shift in the air. I have now experienced both.

When I tiptoe into the kitchen, I find Renn sitting at the table, elbows resting on top—his hands shielding his face. Shy comes trotting over to me. She's filthy and damp, but seems to be okay. Renn is also still covered in mud, and there's a cakey texture on his skin. Then I notice all the blood. There's some on his hands, his face, and I smell the iron tinge of it in the air. For some reason I think back to that day when my mom bandaged his arm, when I touched his blood washing out the cloth. How strange to think that was only a few months ago. Now both of us have had each other's blood on our hands, but I never would have thought it would ever be for something as horrific as this. I spy the dark red stain on his shirt, but he doesn't seem to be in any pain. He must have healed the wound like the one on my head with the ointment, the moment of him rubbing it gently into my skin strangely comes back. There's a metal box sitting on the table in front of him with the lid open. As I inch closer, he doesn't pull his hands away from his face as I steal a glance at the objects inside, all of them foreign to me.

"Renn?" I say, my voice shaking.

He doesn't move, he's almost too still, as if he's a statue, the mud beginning to dry on his skin like clay. I must have been in the shower longer than I'd realized. Shy walks back over to the hearth and lies down in front of the crackling fire. I watch her and the flames for a moment until I can't take the silence anymore.

"Renn." I will myself to sound steady and say it a bit louder this time.

He looks up, locking his eyes on mine, and what I behold in those pools of green and gray is devastating. It makes my breath hitch.

"Are you okay?" he asks, scanning my face.

I'm not "okay" in the slightest, but I know what he means.

"I'm fine," I say as I take him in fully, his battered but strong body sitting before me.

His shirt is ripped along the collar, he has another small dark stain on his arm, and he has cuts along his cheekbone and eyebrow. He stands, taking a few steps toward me, but keeps his distance, like he can't get too close, and this sudden wall between us troubles me more than I expect.

"Are *you* okay?" I ask softly, and he nods. All I want him to do is hold me in his arms and tell me it was all a terrible misunderstanding, that it will all be alright, but I know from the look in his eyes that it's far from okay.

Without a doubt, I know this has something to do with the mysterious past he's kept secret all these years from everyone in Solitude Ridge. I know a side of Renn that no one else does, yet I still don't know that one thing—the one thing that has such a strong hold on him. The thing that makes him different from anyone I've ever met. I feel the tears forming again.

"I'm so sorry, Maven." He looks down for a moment. "I am so so sorry." His voice is barely above a whisper, and I see the tears he's holding back.

"You saved my life, Renn," I say, looking out the window toward the forest. Even though I can't see it through the darkness, the fear freezes my limbs for a second or two.

He saved me, and there was a moment when I wasn't sure if either one of us would be walking away. I watched him kill someone, but no matter what happened, I hold on to the fact that I'm alive and it's because of him. I almost say, *"You've actually saved my life in more ways than one."*

Flashes of what happened enter my mind. I see Renn, bloody and beaten . . . that man who came to kill him and almost did. The images send a chill throughout my body, but I have to believe there's a reasonable explanation or I might go mad. Maybe I already am.

"So, you knew that man," I say, not a question, and Renn nods in response.

"Renn, what's happening? I don't . . . understand what this all means." I can see the emotion thrumming through him as his throat bobs.

"You won't believe me." His voice is calm.

I wait for him to go on, but when he doesn't, I say, "Well, based on the current situation, I think you have to tell me what the hell is happening anyway."

He stands there a few more beats, looking over my face again. I don't like the way he's looking at me, his eyes full of remorse. "I didn't say I wouldn't tell you, I just didn't think I'd ever have to, because you'll think I'm insane once I do."

I gulp, not sure if it's from fear or nerves. Probably both.

"You don't know that." My voice is practically a whisper. He cocks his head to the side, but instead of a smile spreading across his face like it usually does—like so many times before—it remains unmoved.

"I do, Maven. Because if I were you, and someone told me what I'm about to tell you, I'd run as far away from them as I possibly could." A shiver runs down my spine, and it's not the good kind. I just shake my head at him, not knowing what to say. "I will tell you everything, and you can ask me whatever you want once I'm through. I'll tell you the whole truth, I promise. But before I do, there's something important you need to know first."

He gestures for me to take a seat at the table. I do, and he sits across from me like he thinks we need a barrier between us for the words he's about to speak next. He takes a deep breath, and his eyes darken like he's about to confess his greatest sin. It's agonizing watching all of this play out on his face. He takes another deep breath and holds my gaze.

"The first thing you need to know . . . is that I'm not from this world." He speaks slowly, emphasizing each word.

I inhale sharply. "What do you mean?"

He pinches the bridge of his nose like it's actually paining him to speak, the frustration spreading on his face, not at me, but at himself.

"I mean I wasn't born on this planet, Maven. My home world is a place very much like this one, except that it's more than five billion miles away."

My only thought for a moment or two is that I misheard him. I'm not sure if I should run, scream, or laugh. I'm dreaming, I must be, and for a moment, I pray that I am, that this whole night was just a horrible nightmare. But maybe . . . Could it be true? Renn had shown up in Solitude Ridge one day with no explanation or past. He is always lying low, sharing just enough so people won't ask questions, while at the same time becoming a beloved member of the town. He's always seemed different, but I could never explain why . . . and now, the man who came for us tonight, that man who Renn had killed. He was speaking to him in a language I had never heard before, and they knew each other.

No, this isn't true. I'm still in shock from the attack. My mind is trying to tell me that this is crazy, that Renn is crazy, but my heart tells me something else. I have a million more thoughts and questions running wild in my head.

For a moment, I feel dizzy, so I close my eyes to focus. The disarray of memories of everything he's ever told me, everything that caused me to suspect that he was different. But through it all, I still trust him. This story that Renn is about to unfold for me, I need to know. I need to make sure I hear and understand every word. So I compose myself the best I can, even though my heartbeat is thumping loud in my ears as I speak.

"Who are you, and where did you come from?"

He looks at me with complete absolution in his eyes, leaning forward a bit as he says in a cool, smooth voice, "My name is Aldrenn Anton. I was captain of the starship, Seraphim, and I'm from a planet called Earth."

CHAPTER TWENTY-EIGHT

Six Years Ago

The captain goes through the messages and reports of the day, sitting at the desk in his private quarters on the exploration vessel, the Seraphim. He has this smaller space for more intimate conversations, and a larger office to conduct official business. Most of the ship's interior is bright with shiny surfaces, but his office and personal lodgings are made to his particular taste of dark-walnut walls and leather furniture. It's cozy, which isn't a feeling one typically experiences in space, but being captain has its benefits.

Captain Aldrenn Anton is one of the youngest star captains the Space Exploration Association has seen in the last hundred years, and even at his young age, his reputation precedes him. It wasn't only his natural talent as a pilot that got him noticed at the mere age of twelve, it was also his natural ability to lead. The academy rarely accepts students under the age of fifteen, but they'd made an exception for him based on academic scores, aptitude tests, and the drive he possessed to succeed at such a young age. Not just anyone can be accepted into the Space Academy, and it is even more rare to excel above and beyond. If you can't last in the academy, you won't last in the uncertain and dangerous arena that is space. The single purpose of the Academy is to find the best of the best, because that's what one needs to be to venture into the cosmos and worlds beyond Earth. Aldrenn is one of those special officers who was educated, molded, and trained to the extremes so he could reach his full potential—and he has done just that, and more.

He lost his mother when he was a baby and his father at sixteen. He follows in the footsteps of his father, who was a distinguished captain in his own right. It is strange to think that Aldrenn has been part of the SEA longer than he has not. Maybe that's what makes it easier to go on, to fall back on the life that he is so much more familiar with than those distant memories of when he was a young child being raised by his grandparents. He had persevered through it all, and now, after seven years at the academy, then another six years on various missions, he has made a name for himself. His exploits are nothing if not revered. Now, here he is, captain of his own ship at twenty-five years old.

His crew has reached the one-year mark of their three-year mission, and just like all other Star Exploration voyages, the mission is to explore unmarked space and establish alliances and peace with other human civilizations. Only the best crews are selected for deep space exploration. This is completely uncharted territory in the galaxy, and this crew, under Captain Anton, is no stranger to the challenges of completing such a task.

His agenda for the day is full, having been tasked with putting together a year-end report for his superiors, and just finished his check-in with the paleontologist team. But he still has to check in with the leads of a few more teams before his report is finalized.

Suddenly, there's a knock at the door. "Pardon me, Captain Anton?" says a voice, mockingly, on the other side.

The captain rolls his eyes. He has come to know that voice well over the last ten years. It's the voice of his closest friend, Nathan Hayden. They met during their early years in the academy, and have remained close ever since. Nate is also one of those select, overachieving officers who, like the captain, spent a majority of his life with the SEA.

No matter how much time has passed, hearing Nate call him "Captain Anton" never feels right. Of course, in the company of others, they always put on a good show, and only a few members of the crew know of their brother-like friendship. Nate is one of a handful of others who know him simply as "Renn." While being captain has its many privileges, being addressed as "Captain" or "Sir" day in and day out has become monotonous. He has to admit, he sometimes wonders what it would be like to be just Renn. It's a sort of daydream that he often finds himself wandering through on those long days of moving through the great, infinite plane of space.

"I'm alone, Nate. Come in."

Nate enters the low-lit cabin and immediately flops onto the cushioned leather chair in front of the captain's desk. "Man, did you see the new group of lingos that transferred over yesterday?" he asks happily.

Renn shakes his head, sighing. "Of course you had to be right there to welcome them to the crew." The ship frequently receives transports dropping off or picking up goods. Occasionally, officers also transfer on and off the ship, and linguistic officers are vital.

"It's part of my job! I told them right where to find me if they needed *anything*." He smirks.

"I don't remember seeing anything in the first officer and lead software engineer job description about being part of the welcoming committee."

"Actually, I think it's implied as your second in command, and if their tech for some reason isn't working properly, they know who to come to."

Renn glares at him. Knowing Nate, he'd probably purposefully do something to their tech that would cause them to have to come to him in the ship's technical bay to fix it. Nate is brilliant. He's truly a genius in the tech field, and also a little bit of a troublemaker, but this playboy act is exactly that, an act. Nate has never fully gotten over his first real girlfriend, and as crazy as it was, being only nineteen years old at the time, Renn really thought Nate had found his person. Not that he will ever tell him that. It isn't really worth the trouble, and he is in no position to give relationship advice, having been in exactly zero serious relationships himself. Honestly, he's never had the time. As cliche as it is, he has spent every waking hour for the last thirteen years dedicated to getting to this point in his career. He had the occasional hookup from time to time, and it was usually with women who had no idea who he was. It was always a one time thing, never serious, even when there were times he might have wanted it to be. The only romance in his life at this point is when he has to manage the occasional crew quarrel of who slept with so and so's boyfriend.

Workplace drama is not his favorite aspect of being captain. It only makes him less motivated to date, and besides, how does one date in space anyway? He assumes that he'll meet someone later in life whenever he retires. People in this field usually settle down back on Earth or another allied territory at some point. The job is, in general terms, a lot on a person, and to be realistic, he doesn't feel like he could ask someone to wait for him while he is away for, sometimes, years at a time. He knows from personal experience. His father was away most of his childhood, and he knew somewhere deep inside that his mother would have been proud of the choice he made to become a captain like his father. He always understood that this position is so much more than a job. It is life—sometimes an overbearing and lonely one, and he doesn't want to do that to someone. He doesn't want to leave a wife and family behind.

"So," Aldrenn says, locking his fingers behind his head as he leans back in his chair, "how are things going, by the way? I guess I haven't *officially* checked in with you for the report."

Nate sets his feet on the desk, crossing his legs at the ankle. His uniform is the same style and color—dark blue—as Renn's, the only difference being the ranking pin on his shoulder. The color complements his brown skin well.

"I'm happy to say, with the crew now at two hundred and seventy-four, everything is running smoothly. Would you honestly expect anything else with me in charge?"

Renn rolls his eyes again.

"I'll send you an official report by tomorrow, I promise," Nate adds.

They both sit in silence for a minute or two. It is an aspect of their relationship that Renn has always appreciated. They know when the other needs to talk, but also when being in each other's company is enough. It makes life feel more grounded, something they can always count on. They never feel the need to fill the quiet moments with unnecessary noise.

The captain rises from his chair to gaze out the large window that takes up most of the office wall. "Do you ever find yourself thinking about home?" he unexpectedly asks, staring out into the great beyond of never-ending starlight.

"What do you mean? Like, Earth?" Nate asks, amused.

Renn turns to face him, nodding his head, hinting that he's serious about the question.

Nate removes his feet from the desk, sitting up to answer. "Man, what is home? We spent seven years in the academy and then out here," he says, motioning to the window. "When was the last time you were actually *on* Earth?"

Renn purses his lips in thought. "It's been a long time. I had a captain's council at a nearby station before we headed out a year ago. Never actually made it all the way back, but I wish I would have."

"Why? Is there really anything to go back to?"

"Truthfully, not really. I don't have any family there anymore, so there's no reason to, I guess." He immediately thinks of his grandparents, and even though they passed away years ago, he hopes wherever their souls are now that they are proud of him.

"Me either."

Renn continues to stare out the window, lost in thought.

Nate studies his friend's face for a long beat before he says, "What is it, Renn?"

The captain shrugs.

"You know, it's completely normal to feel a little off after spending such a long time out here. You should go down to the health bay. We have those for more than just accidents and emergencies."

He isn't wrong. It's crucial for every crew member to get a mental health evaluation a couple of times a year. Space can be a very solitary place, it's easy to get lost in your own mind.

"It's not that, but thank you. I swear I feel fine," he says with a heavy sigh. "But maybe ask me again in six months," Renn adds with a reassuring smile, knowing that Nate will most definitely check on his mental state if he needs him to.

"Are you nervous about the admiral coming in the next couple of days?"

Renn shakes his head. Admiral Grey has been a great mentor to Aldrenn throughout his career. He served as his first officer for a couple of years, and he owed a lot of his success in moving up the ranks so quickly to the admiral. He isn't so much nervous as he is stressed. This will be the first time the admiral will see Renn in charge of his own crew, and he wants to make him proud.

"Well, whatever it is that's got you in this mood, you know I'm here."

Before Renn can respond, a tone sounds from the console on his desk.

"Oh, good," he says, sounding dreadful.

"What is it?"

"I'm meeting with Locke in five minutes. That was my reminder, as if I needed reminding. I've been dreading it all day—all week, actually." He lets out a heavy sigh.

"Understandable. I really hate that guy."

"You're telling me. How he ever made his way through the academy without killing someone, or someone killing him, is beyond me."

Nate scoffs. "It's because of his family. That's the only reason. If they weren't so wealthy, and didn't fund so much of the association, I doubt he would've ever been accepted into the academy. Plus, don't forget about all the planets they've generously offered to supply with goods," he says with sarcasm. They aren't strangers to the fact that the Locke's have a long-standing reputation within the association in many ways, good and bad.

Renn nods his head in agreement. "You're not wrong. I'm tired of all the politics. If you ask me, they're starting to intervene too much with the association."

Nate hums in agreement, jumping out of the chair and stretching his arms over his head. "Well, you'll have to tell me how it goes later. I don't want to talk to him if I don't have to."

"I envy you, and I will."

"See you later, Renn," Nate says, letting out a small chuckle before leaving the office and shutting the door behind him.

Alone once again, Renn gazes out the window at the endless universe for a few more seconds before returning to his desk. He runs a hand through his short hair before placing his elbows onto the desk, interlocking his fingers so he can rest his chin on top of them.

No more than thirty seconds later, there's a single knock on the cabin door.

"Come in," Renn calls out, and the visitor steps inside, no urgency in his steps—practically dragging his feet.

Colin Locke's black hair and cold, dark eyes make him appear nothing short of menacing. He's one of those men who thrives on being the alpha. He revels in putting people down because he's stronger; it makes him feel good. There is no question as to why he pursued a career in combat, and there were many times over the years when Renn questioned his tactics. Locke has a reputation, and not a good one as far as Renn is concerned. He's aggressive and brutal. Unfortunately, he carries other characteristics that make him very good for his type of work. He's strong, determined, and skilled in what he does.

It doesn't happen a lot, but not every encounter on these missions are friendly. The main goal of Locke's team is mostly protection for the crew, but Colin and members of his team often find excuses to involve themselves with negotiations on other planets, and they rarely end well. It's why Renn personally requested that Locke was on his crew. It isn't because he likes working with the man, it's to keep an eye on him. And over the past year, Locke has pretty much behaved himself.

"Hello, Lieutenant Locke. Please take a seat." Renn gestures to the chair Nate was sitting in earlier. Locke still says nothing as he strolls over and sits. His uniform is a dark green—Head Lieutenants wear green, while the rest of the crew mostly wear black and gray—and he has a gun strapped to his hip. "First things first, is there anything you want to discuss with me before we dive into your report?"

Locke's emotionless face looks at Renn's, shaking his head once in response. Renn is used to this behavior from Colin; there's a mutual understanding that they don't like each other, so they keep their relationship strictly business.

"Alright then. I looked through your report, and everything looked pretty standard, but I did have one question."

Locke crosses his arms in front of him before letting out a cold, "And?"

Renn makes note of the arrogant tone but goes on like it doesn't bother him. "I saw that you requested an additional ten security officers. Why?"

Locke's eyes narrow, challenging Renn to balk, but he holds his gaze, undeterred. "We are getting further into deep space. I thought it wouldn't hurt to have some extra support in case we encounter something hostile."

Renn leans back in his chair, not surprised in the slightest at the response, but thinks for a moment on how to react without being condescending. "We haven't had any issues this last year."

Locke seems to puff out his chest as he narrows his gaze at his captain. "As you are aware, Captain, you never know what can happen out here."

Another challenge. Renn could tell him "no" and it would be the end of it—his orders are final. But he still has two years working with Locke, and he doesn't want the rest of their time together to be miserable if it doesn't have to be.

"What if we cut it to four?"

Locke clenches his teeth, but to his credit, he holds in the anger no doubt bubbling beneath his skin as he says, "If that's your order then . . . it will do."

Renn smiles wide, trying not to enjoy the reaction. "I'll put in the request today for four more officers. If there isn't anything else, you are dismissed." Before the last word is completely out of his mouth, Locke is already standing, heading for the door. "Aren't you forgetting something, Lieutenant?"

Locke pauses, turning slowly, facing his superior, and it's flat-out painful as he says, "Thank you, Captain." Saluting Renn, his posture is stiff, as if he's fighting with his limbs to give his captain the respect he deserves. Renn nods, and Locke slips out the door.

Renn lets out a long sigh, shaking his head. "Trouble," he says aloud to himself.

Colin Locke is more trouble than he could have realized.

After making the rounds through the ship and spending time on the bridge, Captain Anton eats dinner in the dining hall with some of the crew. He enjoys the downtime he gets with them and likes getting to know them on a more casual level. At times like these, when it's been quite some time since coming across a new planet, relationships are more vital than ever. Instead of feeling uneasy in the overwhelming sense of drifting through space, the crew actually enjoys each other's company; well, most of them. Renn notices as dinner is winding down that he hasn't seen Nate anywhere. It's very unlike him not to make an appearance, especially when most of the crew is gathered together, so he makes a point to send him a message when he returns to his quarters.

The captain stops for a final check-in on the bridge—everything is quiet and normal, so he lazily makes his way to his quarters, saying a few goodnights to the crew members he passes. The lights in his cabin are dim as he enters, evoking a sense of night to ease the transition into sleep. Renn performs his nightly routine of tossing his worn clothes neatly into the bin for laundry, doing a quick workout in his personal gym, taking a shower, brushing his teeth, and ends by sliding into bed with his handheld tablet so he can look over a few more messages and stats before falling asleep.

He types in Nate's name to find where he's currently located on the ship. The crew have their wrist devices for communication that also track their whereabouts. The wrist devices are worn mostly in case of emergency or to ensure they don't leave anyone behind if they ever venture onto a new planet. Nate doesn't come up anywhere on the ship; it isn't alarming, but odd. Just as he's about to message his friend, a beeping tone sounds, indicating that someone is at his door. Again, not unheard of, but odd at this time of the day. Renn makes his way to the door swifty but calmly, then pushes the button to speak to whoever is on the other side.

"Who is it?" he asks softly.

"Renn. Open the door. Quick." Nate's hurried voice comes through the speaker, and Renn doesn't hesitate to push the button to slide the door open. Nate bursts inside and locks the door behind him by pushing a few buttons on the keypad.

"Nate? What is—"

"Shh," Nate whispers, cutting him off. "Not yet. In your office, where it's private."

Renn's eyebrows knit together in concern as he follows Nate into the office they were in earlier that morning. Nate runs a hand over his face, and Renn secures the door behind them. When he turns, he notices that Nate has a sheen of sweat on his forehead, his breathing uneven.

"Nate? What's going on?" Nate doesn't say anything, covering his face with his hands, trying to take deep breaths. "Nate?"

Nate finally looks at Renn, and Renn almost takes a step back out of shock at the fear and panic he sees in his friend's eyes—something he's never seen before in all the years he's known him.

"I found something," Nate says slowly.

Renn carefully studies his friend, trying to get a sense of what he means, and when he can't think of anything he asks, "What did you find?"

Without a word, Nate strides over to the captain's desk. "I'm putting a security block on your computer."

Renn doesn't ask questions. He trusts Nate completely, but why he needs to do this leaves him confused. After rapidly typing away on Renn's touch-screen keyboard, Nate slowly pulls out a small, square, photon drive and sets it on top of the desk where the files can be read easily just from the touch screen-like surface.

"I didn't want to mention this earlier, because I didn't know what it really meant, but I started looking into outgoing messages being sent from the ship. Not just official reports, but personal messages from the crew." Renn cocks his head to the side in disapproval, but is still curious. "I know, but listen. I was just doing my normal check on the systems including the ICM, but I noticed an enigmatic signal." The ICM—Interstellar Communication System—is vital, especially in deep space, so Aldrenn knows routine checks are needed, but looking into messages is something else. Renn gives Nate a wary glance. "I know, I know."

"Nate," Renn says, shaking his head, "do you know how much trouble you could get in? Cyber intrusion, cyberstalking—both are criminal offenses."

Nate offers him a half-hearted smirk. "Oh, come on. It's me you're talking to. Like they could ever trace it back to me." Renn opens his mouth to say something else, but Nate stops him by saying, "Just wait." The look of panic resurfaces in his eyes, forcing Renn to snap his mouth shut. "At first, I found nothing, but then I started seeing a pattern of messages being sent from someone on the Seraphim to a user outside of our system."

Renn leans forward as the messages start popping up on the screen. All the messages seem to be fairly short, one or two sentences at the most, and all appear to be signed by the same person.

"Who are Z and X?" Renn asks quietly.

"I don't know, I couldn't track it down, or at least not yet."

Renn quickly reads over a few of the messages.

Two more sites have been identified. Coordinates will be sent soon. All is well.

- Z

This is good news.

- X

I predict at least five more sites by the end of this cycle.

- **Z**

Proceed with Project Abyssal.
- **X**

"What is Project Abyssal?" Renn asks softly. When Nate doesn't respond he looks at his friend's face and sees nothing short of pure horror. "Nate?"

He still says nothing, but Renn watches him as he pulls a file up onto the screen. "It took me a good four hours to hack it, but . . ." Renn places a hand on his shoulder to steady him. "I have no words, just look for yourself."

Renn pulls up the folder and taps it open with his finger. Images and star maps flash up onto the screen. At first, it doesn't seem like anything concerning, but as he takes a closer look, the realization hits him like a punch to the face.

"Oh my God."

What appears in front of him is absolute destruction and death. Videos and images depict humans on planets across the galaxy being killed or imprisoned in what appears to be hostile takeovers. As Renn scans the maps, he sees certain planets have been marked as targets, and he realizes that many of them are places he and his crew have been this past year. The planets that are being hit in particular are classified as Primitive Planets, meaning that they are home to life forms that have no advanced technology or civilization. They are, in general terms, not to be touched. It's against regulations to disturb the internal development of these planets. They're strictly to be observed and never intervened with. It would be more of an invasion if the association were to try to create a connection with planets such as these, because first and foremost, the mission of the association is to establish peace throughout the galaxy.

"I don't understand. Why would someone do this?" Renn asks. He means it more as a question to himself, and isn't really looking for Nate to answer.

"That's not all I found," Nate says as he pulls up another file.

He taps it, and the documents that flood the screen are familiar—written orders that Renn has seen countless times over the years. He himself has written many orders as a captain. They have the title *Project Abyssal* on the top, a classified tag, and then a command typed below. All the orders are instructions to invade, capture, and detain, with the planet name and coordinates. But what makes Renn step away from the screen in utter disbelief is that every single order is signed by someone named A.T.G.

It can't be, but the first name that pops into Renn's mind is Admiral Thomas Grey. He runs a hand across his face, his mind running wild, his body feels like it will collapse.

"It can't be. There has to be an explanation for this."

Nate says nothing, his eyes still glued to the screen in front of them, but clearly, Nate has come to the same conclusion.

Renn doesn't know how much time has passed when he finally says, "So, you're telling me that Grey and someone on the Seraphim have been working together on, what? Taking over planets?"

Nate nods slowly. "All of the proof is right here."

Renn moves around the desk and sits down, holding his head in his hands. He feels like he's going to be sick. If what they're assuming is true, then not only do they have a traitor on the ship, but he's a high level leader, meaning there are probably others. Something like this couldn't be brought to fruition by two people.

"This is just the surface, from what I can tell. Who knows who else is involved, or how long this has been going on," Nate states simply. When Renn still says nothing after a minute or so, Nate speaks up again. "What are we going to do?"

Renn finally looks up at his friend, and he sees the desperation and fear etched in his deep brown eyes. "This is on me as captain of this crew and a commanding officer. It's my responsibility to do what's right." Nate waits for him to go on. "We can't tell anyone about this. We need to find out who the informant on the ship is first." Nate gives him a knowing look. "I know what you're going to say."

"Renn, it has to be Locke. He is a menace, and not to mention a total asshole, and it can't be a coincidence that Grey is coming here."

"But what if we're wrong? We don't even know for sure if Grey is involved. It's just an assumption."

"A pretty convincing one, if you ask me."

"You're right, but still, if we confront Locke, he won't take it well. Even if it isn't him, he will act out of anger." Renn continues to talk slowly and calmly. "The admiral, on the other hand, may be more understanding if I confront him about it. If it's true, then I need to make sure the safety of the crew will be insured."

Nate stands and moves to sit on the edge of the desk in front of Renn. "But that means you'd be sacrificing yourself." Renn nods. "You don't think they would actually kill you?"

The captain pinches the bridge of his nose. "I don't know what they're capable of. I thought I knew this man. I trusted him with my career, my life, for years, yet I see this in front of me, and now nothing makes sense."

Nate shoots to his feet before pacing the room. "What have I done?" His voice is panicky and uneven.

Renn stands and grabs his friend by the shoulders to stop him. "You did the right thing. Now it's my turn." Nate sighs deeply. "Whatever happens, we are in this together. But my orders are orders. You must do whatever I say. If it means keeping everyone else alive, then that is what needs to be done," Renn says.

Nate gives him a sad smile. He steps away from Renn, straightens, and salutes. "Always, Captain. Always."

Renn feels tears prick at his eyes. Their world has been flipped upside down in a matter of minutes, and yet Nate is still loyal and willing to stand by his side despite the unknown ahead.

"Thank you, Nate."

Nate eases and then pulls his friend into an embrace.

They hold onto each other for a long moment until Renn steps back. "Okay, this is what we're going to do. We still have two days before the admiral arrives. We will proceed as normal." He pauses. "In the meantime, see if you can find anything else about Project Abyssal and who is involved. And don't dare reach out to anyone until we know for sure who we can trust. This is uncharted territory. Until then, say nothing to anyone. If something comes up, call me. No messages until we know more."

"Will do."

They keep their goodbyes brief, then Aldrenn strolls into his bedroom. He doesn't even make it to the bed before he breaks down, falling to his knees, praying that he's doing the right thing and that he, but most importantly his crew, will be alive by the end of it all.

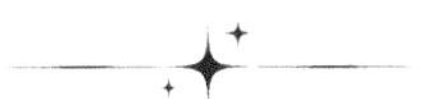

Renn hardly sleeps that night. He finally drifted to sleep for about an hour, but it still felt like minutes. He pulls a fresh uniform out of the closet the next morning, and as he's buttoning the captain's insignia onto his shoulder, the alert of someone hailing him from the bridge rings throughout the room.

"Answer call," he says aloud, and a hologram comes through.

"Good morning, Captain. This is Officer Johnson from the bridge. You are receiving an urgent message from Admiral Grey. He wishes to speak with you immediately."

Renn's heart rate accelerates, but he keeps his voice calm and face neutral, like he isn't at all fearful of what this unexpected call could mean. "Send him through to my personal office please. I will take his call there."

"Very well, Captain," the officer says quickly and then is gone.

Aldrenn can hear his heartbeat thumping in his ears, but he casually makes his way to the office and sits down in the chair with his head held high and posture straight. He taps on the screen, and the admiral's face appears.

"Good Morning, Admiral."

Thomas's face is relaxed as he smiles at Captain Anton. "Morning, Captain. Thank you for taking my call." So far, nothing seems off, maybe this really is all a misunderstanding.

"Of course, sir. I'm looking forward to seeing you in a couple of days."

The admiral's eyes narrow slightly. "That's actually why I'm calling. There's been a change of plans. My officers and I will be arriving at the Seraphim within the hour."

Renn's heart drops in his chest, but he pretends to play dumb. "Oh, very good, sir. I will let the crew know to expect your arrival today."

As Renn looks at the face of the man who has been a mentor to him for many years, he feels a chill shoot down his spine as he now looks back at Renn with a wicked smirk that he's never seen before.

"Come now, Captain Anton, let's stop with the charade. I know you know about Project Abyssal."

For a split second, Renn thinks about acting like he knows nothing, but the strategy doesn't seem to work on the admiral. They know each other too well, or at least Renn thought he did.

"Tell me it's not true, Thomas. Tell me there must be a mistake."

The admiral chuckles darkly. "Oh, Renn, how dare you think you can address me so casually. However, that wasn't your first mistake." He glares at the captain as he goes on. "I had such high hopes for you, but when I realized you thought more with your heart, I knew I couldn't recruit you to the cause."

Renn's blood boils underneath his skin. "And what cause is that exactly? Murdering innocents?"

Thomas shakes his head in disgust. "Even now you can't see it, can you?" Renn says nothing as he clenches his teeth. "The galaxy is only expanding, Captain Anton. Do you really think everyone is going to play along peacefully? It's only a matter of time before one of them decides they want all the control. I'm ensuring that Earth will rule this galaxy. You should be thanking me."

Renn scoffs and then stands. "This is insane. You really think you can rule an entire galaxy through death and destruction—"

The admiral puts up a hand, interrupting him. "Oh, it's not just me, Renn. I think you'll be surprised how many people within our association agree with me, and have from the beginning."

Renn slams a fist on the desk. "Traitor!"

The admiral only smiles wide back at him. "Oh, how wrong you are, my boy. Now, listen carefully to what I am about to explain to you." Renn feels like his skin is on fire, his heart so heavy that it is making it difficult to breathe.

"First of all, I want to know what you did with those files, and I want them back immediately."

It takes Renn about three seconds to know that Nate, in his cleverness, did something with them. What, he isn't sure, but he's proud nonetheless. "I'm sure I don't know what you mean."

"You know, the more you lie, Captain, the more difficult this will be for you and your First Officer. I know he's involved in the disappearance of the files."

Renn huffs out a laugh. "I don't care about what happens to me. My crew is all that matters."

The admiral seamlessly ignores Renn's response as he speaks through clenched teeth. "Locke and his team will be arresting you and Lieutenant Hayden for treason, and upon my arrival, you will both be escorted to my ship"

Nate was right. Locke, of course, is the mystery informant corresponding with someone off the ship. *Damn him.*

"And what about my crew?"

The admiral leans in closer from his side of the hologram. "This crew no longer reports to you. You are no longer captain. If you play along nicely, then I will spare the crew. Do we have an agreement?"

Renn calculates the possibilities in his head of how he can fix this—how he can save everyone and expose the treachery, but he can't see any options that won't result in the death of his crew. It's clear from the images he saw that they are capable of anything.

"Yes, we have an agreement."

"Very good. You will remain where you are and await further instructions."

Renn nods once in response.

"It really didn't have to be this way, Renn. I hope you can live with the choice you've made."

Renn stands, never faltering as he stares the admiral down. "The only mistake I've made, Thomas, is that I trusted you."

"We shall see, won't we."

The admiral's face dissolves as the hologram disappears. Then the tone of an incoming message sounds throughout the entire ship.

"Attention: Crew of the Seraphim. This is Admiral Thomas Grey. I come to you with an announcement that bears some troubling news. Your captain, Aldrenn Anton, and first officer, Nathan Hayden have been found conspiring against the association and have been charged with treason. They will be arrested and detained upon my arrival, and they will be transferred off the Seraphim immediately. You are in no danger as long as you follow orders. Until my arrival, please follow instructions from Lieutenant Locke and his team. This is a direct order from your commanding officer. I apologize for this shocking news. Thank you for your time."

Renn walks over to the window. He can almost feel the panic buzzing throughout the ship. He plays the events of the last twelve hours over and over, still in utter disbelief that this is happening. How many planets has he unknowingly handed over to these monsters? Has he wasted thirteen years of his life to come to this? What kind of a man is he now?

He does the only thing that he can think of that will maybe give some hope, he pulls up a new video to add to his captain's log. He straightens his uniform once more and hits the record button.

"Captain's Log, Earth date five-seven, year twenty-two sixty-four. This is Captain Aldrenn Anton. Whoever sees this message, there is a real possibility that I am dead. Please listen carefully to what I am about to tell you. Classified files were discovered by a member of my crew. These files contain proof of illegal activities happening across the galaxy. Primitive planets are being targeted and taken over by members within the Star Exploration Association. At this time, I do not know who is all involved, but I know these orders have been approved by Admiral Thomas Grey and involve information provided by Lieutenant Colin Locke while he has been under my command. It is my hope that the rest of the traitors will be uncovered and receive judgment for their crimes against humanity. For those of you who were unknowingly involved as I have been, I hope that you will not stand for this treachery. I hope that the integrity of this association is not lost. Godspeed. Anton out."

Aldrenn saves the message and hopes that someone will find it eventually. A sharp rap sounds from the door, and he doesn't have to guess who it is. He grabs a stun gun from the desk drawer, but then sets it down on the desk. It won't do any good to cause a panic, and he will be outnumbered. He walks toward the door and presses the button to open. He is not at all surprised that Locke's face is the first one he sees as it slides open.

"Well, Captain. Are we doing this the easy way or the hard way?"

"You can go to hell," Renn replies flatly.

Locke smiles, pure evil delight flashing in his eyes. "The hard way. Got it." He punches Aldrenn hard in the stomach, and before he hits the ground, members of Locke's team catch him. "Captain Aldrenn Anton, you are under arrest for treason." Renn gasps for air as his arms are placed behind his back and cuffed. "Take him to the bridge," Locke commands, and Renn is dragged down the hall without a word.

Once on the bridge, Renn is forced to his knees. To his left, Nate is already there in the same position, only, his nose drips with blood. There are no other members of the crew on the bridge besides Locke's team.

"Renn, I . . ."

"Shut up!" Locke rages. "You've already said enough." Locke stands in front of them while the rest of his team is behind. "I had safeguards in place in case anyone came snooping around. I should have figured it would be you, Hayden. Did you really think you could uncover all that information and there wouldn't be consequences? You are not the only one with brains in that department."

"I beg to differ," Nate says, followed by Locke's knee colliding with his face. He falls backward, his body in an uncomfortable angle thanks to the cuffs securing his hands.

"The admiral should be here any minute, so don't worry, your suffering won't be long," Locke says, pacing back and forth.

"So, what do you get out of this, Colin? Money? Prestige?" Renn asks. He prepares for a violent blow like Nate, but instead, Locke sqauts down in front of him.

"All of it, actually. Including a few planets all to myself. There's plenty to go around." The dark pits of his eyes are nothing but cold voids of unfeeling as Renn stares back.

"You're sick," Renn says.

Before Locke can respond, an explosion near the entrance to the bridge engulfs the room. Smoke and debris fly through the air, hitting some and scattering the others. Renn and Nate try their best to look around to see what's going on. Guns fire and men fall, then a pair of hands grab Renn and pull him away from the chaos. The smoke fills in his lungs, causing him to cough uncontrollably.

"You'll be fine, sir. Just let us get you to safety." Renn recognizes the voice of Officer Johnson. Once they are finally away from the explosion, the captain gazes around the room to see several members of his crew, including Nate. "Captain, what's going on?" Johnson asks as someone else undoes the cuffs from their hands.

"Did you not hear the announcement from Admiral Grey?" Renn asks, trying to clear his throat the best he can.

"We did, sir," another officer speaks up. He turns to face Officer Kent as she steps forward. "But we knew something wasn't right. Locke instructed us to remain in our cabins, but we saw them take you and Officer Hayden, and we knew we had to do something." The captain doesn't know if he should laugh or cry, but as he looks around at the crew members, he feels an overwhelming sense of pride. "They are contained on the bridge for the moment, but not for long," Officer Kent adds.

Everyone looks at Aldrenn. "Tell us your order, Captain, and it will be done."

Each and every one of them, including Nate, waits for his command.

"I don't know any other way to get out of this alive. If you do what the admiral says, you will be spared." They look at each other.

"But why, sir? What has happened?" a female officer, whose name is Alisha, asks.

They all look at him with trusting eyes. At this point, they are already out of time, so lying to them won't change anything. He tells them the truth as transparently as he can in the short time that they have left. "Lieutenant Hayden and I learned of some illegal activities happening across the galaxy. We confirmed Admiral Grey and Lieutenant Locke are involved, but there are many others." The crew members look at each other wide-eyed then back to him.

As if on cue, the tone indicating a message sounds through the ship one again. "Attention: Crew of the Seraphim. This is Lieutenant Colin Locke. Those of you involved in aiding Captain Anton and Lieutenant Hayden will receive the same fate as they will unless you return them immediately to the bridge. For the rest of the crew, remain where you are and await further orders from Admiral Grey." The message ends, leaving them solemn, a few of them have tears in their eyes. Renn smiles, trying to reassure them, but he knows it won't change what is happening.

"Thank you for your courage. Each of you. All I ask is that you help the rest of the crew remain calm. We don't have much of a choice until we can find out who we can trust."

For a few seconds, no one moves or speaks until Officer Johnson stands up straight and salutes the captain. "It's been an honor, sir."

One by one, they all follow suit, even Nate.

"Thank you." His voice breaks for a moment. "Now, return to your stations."

They file out of the room until it's only Renn and Nate. Renn types on his wrist device to broadcast to the entire ship, then lifts it to his mouth to speak. "Attention: Crew. This is the last time I will be speaking to you as your captain. It has been my honor to serve with you, but in light of the current circumstances, things have changed. I ask you to not panic. This will be my last command. Stay strong. Goodspeed. Anton out." There is a moment of finality after he speaks. He can feel it to his very bones.

"Let's go," Renn says. They walk out into the ship corridors where some crew members are lingering, but Renn pays them no mind, instead facing ahead. It's the only way he can manage to keep his expression neutral. Locke is waiting for them outside the bridge, a new pair of handcuffs in hand.

"The admiral has arrived. Let's move." Locke waits for his team to detain them again before they make their way to the transport vessel taking them to the admiral's ship. No one says a word, but Locke keeps his eyes on Renn, a smirk on his face during the few minutes it takes for them to disembark the transport onto the Zenith—the admiral's ship. Renn knows he's enjoying this, mostly because he finally has what he's always wanted: an advantage over him after being second for so many years in all aspects. They are taken directly to the bridge where the admiral lounges in his chair like it is any other day.

"Ah, there you are, Aldrenn." Renn searches his face for any signs of the man he thought he knew. The last time he saw him in person, he was pinning a captain's pin to his uniform at his induction ceremony. He wouldn't have believed it if he hadn't experienced it first hand. Nate is placed next to him, both forced back onto their knees, holding back grimaces as they practically shove them down. "Now, let's not beat around the bush. Where are the files, Aldrenn? I thought we decided to do this the easy way." Renn feels Nate shift slightly beside him.

"Ensure the crew will not be harmed, and then I'll tell you where the files are."

Nate is looking at him now, but he keeps his eyes on the admiral.

"You are not in the position to make demands. Tell me. Now."

Renn holds his glare, his mind working out what he can do, but Nate interrupts his thoughts. "I have them!" Nate shouts.

Renn turns to him, his face etched in disbelief. Grey nods to Locke, and he pulls Nate onto his feet and begins searching his jacket until he finds the small photon drive.

"Locke, if you would." Colin shoves Nate back to the ground before placing the drive on the admiral's console, and immediately, the files appear. "Very good. Thank you, Lieutenant Hayden. At least one of you has some good sense." Nate gives Renn a quick glance before turning back to the admiral, and Renn doesn't see defeat, but rather a mischievousness in his dark eyes. He has a plan. Renn's anxiousness eases a little, knowing he should have never doubted him.

"Okay, you have what you want. Now let the crew go. Let them return to Earth unharmed." The admiral scans Renn's face for a moment, pursing his lips in thought. Every second that passes makes Renn more unstable.

"Officer Green."

A man stands, bringing his attention fully to the admiral. "Yes, sir?"

Without taking his gaze off Renn, he gives the order. "Set all weapons on the Seraphim. Fire on my command."

"NO!" Renn hurls forward only to be punched in the stomach again, dropping him to the ground. Instead of being dragged back up onto his feet, Locke holds him down, only allowing him to turn his head. The officer doesn't so much as flinch at the order. Neither do any of his crew sitting at their stations. They must all be in on it.

"You son of a bitch!" Nate struggles beside him, seething, trying to break loose. "We gave you what you asked for!" he yells.

"And how do I know you didn't tell anyone else on your crew what you found, hmm?" Grey says as he stands to move closer. "Locke filled me in on your attempted escape. I told you to follow my orders and no one would get hurt."

"They know nothing," Renn begs. It kills him to do it for these monsters, but he will beg if he has to.

"Unfortunately, your life is of very little value to me now, and the same goes for your word," Grey responds.

"Target is locked, Admiral. Ready to fire on your command," Officer Green flatly announces, like they aren't all about to witness the destruction of an association ship and an entire crew. They are supposed to be allies to the galaxy. This is so very wrong. It makes bile rise in Renn's throat. They are helpless—it's going to happen, and he can't stop it.

"Get up." Locke drags him to his feet. "Say goodbye, Captain," he hisses into his ear. Aldrenn could look away or shut his eyes, but he can't bring himself to do it. He wants to watch and remember it all, that this is his fault. Somehow, some way, they will all pay for what they have done.

"Fire."

There is no sound, or if there is, Aldrenn can't hear it as the beams of lasers and missiles hit the Seraphim again and again and again. He feels like he stands there for an eternity, but it must only be a few minutes before the ship is nothing but floating debris scattering through space. If it weren't for the sudden blaring alarms and lights flashing, he isn't sure if he would have been able to look away.

"What's happening?" Grey shouts over the noise. The admiral's crew starts typing frantically on their consoles and screens.

"Sir! There seems to be some kind of virus taking over all our systems," an officer calls out. Renn meets Nate's eyes full of fire and revenge.

"The drive!" Locke exclaims. He lets go of Renn and walks over to the screen where the files were moments before, but now, nothing is there. "They're gone! What the fuck did you do?" Locke screams at Renn, and he isn't sure what happens first, his head colliding with Locke's face, or someone firing a gun, but all at once, utter chaos erupts on the bridge.

He doesn't need to wait for a signal from Nate to understand what is going on. This is their one and only chance to escape. They run toward the doors. Nate has somehow gotten out of his cuffs and picks up a photon gun.

Lasers start blasting for a moment until the admiral screams over the noise. "Don't shoot! We need them alive!" It's all a blur, but somehow, they both end up in the lift, hitting the button to move down. Lights and alarms are still echoing throughout the ship.

"That was genius," Renn says through heavy breaths while Nate releases the cuff still around his wrists, making a loud clang as they fall onto the floor.

"I figured we were dead anyway, so I wasn't going to let them have all the information, but I didn't . . ." Their chests heave in and out from the effort of fleeing and the devastation they just witnessed. "I didn't think he would do that, Renn. I am . . . I am so sorry." His eyes well up, but Renn grabs him roughly by the shoulder.

"Don't you dare say sorry. None of this is on you. This is on me."

Nate gulps down his emotion. "Renn, you can't—"

"Stop." Renn cuts him off. "We don't have time for that right now. We need to get out of here."

"Here, take this." Nate bends down, removing something from his boot, then stands with two small photon drives and hands one to Renn. "I removed all the data from their servers, obviously, and split all the data from the report onto these. I also erased traces of the planets we mapped over this year and placed them in here. We have to split up, and if one of us is caught, then at least they won't get all of the data."

"You're brilliant," Renn says, taking one of the drives and placing it inside his pocket. "This is our responsibility—to make sure this gets to the right people."

Nate nods. "Agreed. But first, we need to get off this ship." The lift slows as the door starts to open, placing them in the engine bay that houses the ship's generators and other mechanical systems. They exit cautiously, Nate has his gun raised. "There should be weapons near the docking bays. If we can make it there, we should be able to get some supplies and find a ship to steal."

"Let's go," is Renn's only response as they make their way through the corridors. They see some crew members running about, but they don't notice them. Clearly, the ship is still in disarray, helping them stay undetected as they gather additional guns and other supplies.

"How much longer do we have until they fix this?" Renn asks, checking around a corner.

"I estimate two more minutes at the most." They turn the last corner, heading toward a set of large blaster doors leading into the docking bay. The moment the door slides open, they are met with blasts.

"Shit!" Nate shouts, lasers shooting toward them. They duck inside the doors, making attempts to fire at the group when they can.

"Damn it. I should have known they would have guessed we would come here," Renn shouts over the noise. Nate pulls out a smoke detonator from his pocket that Renn didn't notice before.

"We only have one shot. We need to get you out of here." Nate adds.

"Hold your fire!" Locke's voice rings out. "Haven't you learned your lesson yet, Aldrenn? You don't stand a chance. Hand over the files!"

Renn holds up a hand, signaling Nate to pause. "You really think the rest of the association is going to stand for this?" he calls out.

"Not everyone will, of course, but we have enough at our disposal to take care of those who don't want to follow. We control so many planets already, and this is only the beginning."

They have to buy more time, so Renn keeps him talking. "And how are you going to explain how the crew of the Seraphim died?"

"A tragic accident."

"You're insane. You won't get away with this," he yells as Nate hands him another detonator. "What about you?" he whispers.

He gives him a smirk. "I've got an idea. Don't worry about me."

Renn gives his friend a worried look.

Nate nods to the drive in Renn's pocket. "The drive also holds a signal that can only be traced by me. Turn it on as much as you can, and I will try to find you. Get far, far away from here, and don't look back."

Aldrenn feels a stabbing in his chest, realizing that this could be the last time he sees his friend. They both could be dead soon, but they aren't going to die without trying.

"Stop fucking around, Aldrenn. Surrender now, or I will kill you both."

"Aren't you supposed to bring us back alive, Locke?" he yells back.

"Accidents happen. Any last words from the famous Captain Aldrenn Anton before he's blown to pieces?"

Renn's finger hovers above the button ready for his touch. "Yeah, just a few." He pauses looking at Nate one last time.

"Ready, Captain?"

Aldrenn nods, and they both push their detonators and throw them into the madness. "I'll see you in Hell."

"RUN!" Nate shouts as they both stand, firing at anyone they see through the smoke. Renn spies the outline of a ship in the fog, running as fast as his legs can carry him. He sees a few people fall from his blasts, but he doesn't stop until his feet hit the metal ramp and he's inside the ship. He doesn't look back to see where Nate has gone, and he doesn't waste a second as he powers up the ship and flies out through the docking tunnel.

Thankfully, his ship's shields are up, because he enters directly into the wreckage of what is left of the Seraphim, and it shatters his heart just as much as the pieces floating around him. He doesn't have a single moment to give his crew the respect they deserve. One year was all he had with them, but it might as well have been a lifetime, and now the beautiful ship, in a blink of an eye, is nothing but broken metal and dust. He closes his eyes before he powers up the thrusters to send him into the vastness of darkness.

Darkness like the state of his own heart.

CHAPTER TWENTY-NINE

Maven

Renn tells me *everything*. He began with a brief background of his career and then went on to explain the series of events that brought him here. He told me how he had come upon Aetherium by pure luck, how he had crashed here, and how he'd blended in over time. I didn't so much as blink or move as I took in his story, word by word. My mind was drowning with so many questions that I couldn't come up for air. I have no idea how long we sat there, but it felt like hours. His voice was steady and calm the entire time, never wavering, even in the most devastating of moments as he told me about his crew—how they had died. All this time, those gray-and-green eyes had truly beheld a storm of his past, raging and billowing, holding him down. Sure, he is good at controlling his demeanor, but his eyes *always* give him away, and I wonder if he knows that but hopes people won't notice.

He also removed all the strange items that were in the box and laid them neatly on the table, explaining each and every one in detail, giving me an example of how they functioned, and their purpose. The ointment was the most fascinating, as I had been curious since that day he used it on the retreat. Renn said that it was more for immediate use, like the gash on my head and the stab wound on his side. It hadn't completely fixed my already healed knee, but there was still a noticeable improvement even weeks after the retreat. I'm sure my eyes were wide the whole time; they certainly felt like they were when he finished.

"That's everything," he says very matter-of-factly, and the room is suddenly unnervingly silent. I look away from him for the first time in hours, rubbing my dry, tired eyes. I don't know where to begin.

"So, you're human, but not the same kind of human as me—as us?" I'm surprised this is the question that falls out of my mouth first. It sounds strange saying it out loud, and Renn looks just as surprised.

"Yes and no. We are genetically the same." He pauses to gauge my reaction. "There's nothing anatomically different about my body in comparison to a man from this world, but my race has no origin to this planet."

I soak in his answer as he waits, already anticipating the next question, and I know he will stick to his word and answer every single one that I have. "How did humans end up on so many planets? Do we all originate from a single place?"

He shakes his head. "No one knows," he says, calmly. "That was part of our mission, so to speak—to find other human worlds and possibly answer the origin of life as we know it. We were an exploration crew." His words send a chill through my body. Such a simple answer to a complicated situation.

"Are you still in danger even with him . . . dead?"

He breathes in deeply before he says, "Honestly, I don't know." I gulp, turning away, trying to think of what to say next as the words sink in. "But I will do everything I can to make sure it never happens again."

I look back to Renn, confused. "What do you mean?"

He stands, running a hand through his hair. "I'll leave and hope that, if there are others tracking me, they will leave this planet alone if I'm no longer here."

Leave? How? The words must appear in my expression because he adds, "I'll find Locke's ship—it must be somewhere nearby. I'll try to make contact with some allies, but I have no idea what's been happening out there for the last six years. I may have to just turn myself in."

"Turn yourself in? But Renn, you're not a criminal," I say before I even have time to contemplate it.

Renn's face is a mixture of shock and frustration. "Maven. Out of everything I told you, you don't see that this is all my fault? That your life, the lives of millions, could be in danger?" He almost yells, but I shake my head, refusing to believe. "Who knows how many people have died because of what I did for years. Years, Maven!" He is shouting now, not out of anger, but disbelief. "Not only did I get my crew killed, I've single-handedly assisted in the murder of thousands of people, maybe more." He turns away from me, running a hand through his hair again.

My heart aches for what he must have been living through all these years, and that he truly believes this, but it couldn't be further from the truth.

"Renn. Is that what you truly believe? That you are responsible for what happened?"

He scoffs, facing me. "That's exactly what I'm saying. I was supposed to be their captain, their leader. I was supposed to be a peacemaker in this galaxy, and all I did was bring about desolation."

I've never heard him speak like this before, with anger in his voice, except towards the man he killed. It catches me off guard, but I don't back down. "I know you didn't do any of that intentionally. You did everything you could to stop it, but you can't control the outcomes that followed. People act of their own accord." I pause as he continues to stare at me, baffled. "I'm so sorry that you had to live through that, Renn. That you've been here, all this time, terrified of what might happen—working through such a great loss alone."

He narrows his gaze at me. "How can you feel sorry for me? I've lied to everyone, pretending to be this man who people can count on. Someone who is good, but that's not the real me. That's what I'm trying to tell you, Mave. I'm bad for you, for this entire planet. You've seen the risk I put you in. It was my mistake to act like everything was fine, it was all a facade." His words feel like bullets hitting me one by one.

"I refuse to believe that it was all an act, Renn. You are a good man, it doesn't matter to me where you came from or what happened," I say as I stand and walk to him, but as I get closer, he takes a few steps backward, distancing himself from me, and that hurts worse than his words.

"Humans from Earth are a different kind of beings. And now I've subjected you to that evil. Yes, we may both be human, but some humans take on a darker face than others." Tears well up in my eyes, but he keeps going. "I'm not the man you think I am. You don't know the real me."

I feel physically ill at this. He can't be serious, but I gaze into his eyes and see that he means every word. Anger builds in me, and I don't hold it back as it explodes.

"How dare you say that to me!" I scream.

He takes a couple more steps, backing away from me, and it only makes my anger burn more and more.

I inhale a shuddered breath before I say, "Don't say things like that to me."

He stays silent while I wait for a response, but he gives none. Nothing.

"You can honestly stand there and tell me that the man I've come to know as my friend, the man who I—" I pause, his gray eyes piercing me, like he's daring me to say it, because we both know what I was about to admit. "Can you honestly say everything that has happened between us doesn't matter now and that I don't know you?"

I don't have any more strength to hold back the tears falling fast from my eyes, yet he still says nothing.

"Did it mean anything to you?"

Renn shuts his eyes tight for a moment then looks back to me with pity, actual pity in his eyes. Again nothing.

"Say something."

Still not a word passes from his lips. I strut up to him and shove him hard in the chest. His strong body hardly moves.

"Say something, Renn!"

He looks at me long and hard, holding back tears that shine in his eyes. "I'm so sorry, Maven." His voice breaks, raw and quiet. The sounds make me hurt in places I didn't know were possible.

"Stop. Saying. That."

He inhales but is still at a loss for words. I stare at him, begging him to say something, to *do* something.

"You came to me, Renn. I let you into my life. And now you're telling me it was for nothing?"

He bites his lip hard and tears his eyes away from mine. "I was trying to be the man I wanted to be, but I can't be him . . . not even for you."

I want to scream.

How could I have been so stupid? How did this happen?

In an instant, that shining light in my heart has vanished, and now I'm nothing but an empty shell standing before him. He took that last bit that my dark heart had left to give and tossed it aside.

"How could you do this to me?" I whisper.

He looks back, a single tear falling from his eyes. "Maven." What used to send warmth throughout my body, hearing him say my name, only burns me.

He takes a step forward, "Maven, I—"

"Stop!" I scream. I inhale a trembling breath. "You're right. I don't know you at all."

Renn reaches out a hand for me, but then his fingers curl into a fist and he lets it fall to his side. I don't look at him as I rush over to the bathroom, grab my bag, and walk past him, not saying a single word or giving him a second glance, not knowing if he watches me as I sling my bag over my shoulder and slam the door, leaving him, and my heart, behind.

The drive home was a haze. I don't remember a single moment of it, or when I went to my bedroom and fell asleep. The only thing my mind seems to remember are Renn's words as they play over and over again in my dreams.

My name is Aldrenn Anton.

I was captain of the starship Seraphim, and I am from a planet called Earth.

You don't know the real me.

I can't be that man, not even for you.

It isn't until the very real nightmare of running through the forest and fighting for my life comes that I'm startled awake.

It wasn't a dream, it had all been real.

I'm still wearing the clothes I had put on at Renn's, and I suddenly feel the urge to rip them off. Anything that reminds me of last night, I want to remove. Once I find my bag, I dig through it to grab my phone. I have two messages waiting for me, one from Tasha and the other from my mom.

Tasha: Mom and I got back into town a few hours ago. Call me when you wake up. Can't wait to hear about EVERYTHING!

Mom: Hope everything went well at Renn's last night. Call me when you get a minute. Love you.

I don't have the energy to try to type a response back. What am I going to tell them? It isn't like I can skip this topic and think they won't ask questions. And the thought of lying about the enormous truth that I now know about Renn already feels overwhelming. I've never felt more alone in my life, but I won't allow it to swallow me whole, not now, not after everything that happened. Even if I can't tell the whole story, if I have to tell them anything, it will be some version of the truth at least, which is that my heart was broken, because at least that part is completely true.

I tap on Tasha's name, and she answers after the first ring. "Maven! I've been dying to hear about last night? Are you still at his house? Did you guys . . . you know?" The excitement in her voice only makes it more difficult to form words. How could things have turned so bad so quickly? "Mave? Are you there?"

I gulp down a sob. "Can you come over?"

"I'm on my way." I hear the rustling of papers and then the jingle of car keys.

"I don't even know what to say, but I just need you right now."

"I'll be there in fifteen minutes."

I hang up the phone and walk into the kitchen to get a glass of water. I take a couple of long gulps, looking out the window above the kitchen sink. It's now the early afternoon and the rain is still falling, but softer now, a haze of fog lingering in the air. The clouds are sinking lower on the mountainside, and then it just happens. I slam the glass into the sink, shattering pieces everywhere.

It would make sense to be angry at Renn, and I am, but I'm more frustrated with myself. Because what doesn't make sense is that he is, in fact, an otherworldly being, but it doesn't bother me. His explanation for what he is doesn't matter to me as much as *who* he is. I believe every single word he spoke when it comes to that part of the story, but he's lying to himself if he truly thinks that whatever it is between us isn't real, even if he denies it, I know it isn't true, especially after everything.

After I raged and screamed, he still reached for me. He thinks he's protecting me from outside forces, but I never realized, all this time, he believed he needed to protect me from himself. And yet I don't care, because the only thing I want is him, even if it makes no sense. The want, the need for him overpowers everything else. But isn't that the way it's always been with Renn? Not fully understanding why I'm drawn to him? He's a man of flesh and blood, but unlike any man I've ever known. It isn't a matter of if I believe him, it's what do I feel for him? I already know the answer the moment the thought comes to me.

I'm in love with him. I'm in love with *Renn*.

But maybe I loved him too quickly. Maybe I fell for him too hard.

However, I can't deny all the things that Renn said—he made me feel things that most people wait their whole life to feel just once, and as crazy as it sounds, it doesn't matter to me if he's from somewhere on the other side of the galaxy.

How strange.

He is a strange sort of beautiful, equal parts foreign to me and familiar all at once. It was what drew me to him from the first time I saw him. My dark shadow of a heart got that part right from the beginning, it recognized that darkness in him, we've both had it branded on us. But what frightens me now is, what's next? I don't want to think about him leaving, but I know he will because he thinks he has to. That serious look in his eyes made that perfectly clear. It made me ache in places I didn't know existed.

I must have been standing at the sink full of shattered glass for more than a few minutes because the next thing I know, I hear Tasha's car coming up the drive. My body is stiff with sadness and soreness, but I walk over to the front door, pull it open, and step out just as she's walking up the porch steps. I can't hold back the sob that escapes me as she moves forward and pulls me into a tight hug.

"Hey, it's okay," she says, running her hand down my hair. I pull away, and she cups my face in her hands. "What happened?"

I should have probably worked out what I was going to say before I called her, because I'm honestly at a loss for words. "I don't . . . I don't know," I say, barely audible in between my sobs.

"Let's get inside, okay?"

I nod, and she places an arm around my shoulder, guiding me through the door.

"It's freezing in here, Mave!"

I don't even notice until she mentions it. "Oh, yeah, maybe the power is back on. I haven't checked."

Tasha doesn't even try to hide the heavy look of concern as she walks over to the kitchen and flips the lightswitch. A soft glow fills the room immediately.

"Do you have any firewood?"

I shake my head.

"Well, let's just turn the heat up, then. I'll grab some more blankets," Tasha says, walking around the room with a skip in her step, like she isn't dealing with the absolute mess that I must appear to be in. She sets up a cozy pile of blankets on the couch, makes me a cup of coffee, and finds a bag of chocolates in the cupboard before she ushers me to sit. "So, do you want to talk about it? Do I need to beat him up?"

I try to muster up a smile to no avail. I gaze down into my mug for a few beats. "It's complicated. He didn't do anything wrong, it's just that . . . he doesn't want me, or anyone for that matter, to truly know him." It's not a lie, even if I am leaving out major details.

Tasha's eyebrows knit together in thought. "Hmm, so he's scared? I didn't think anything scared Renn."

I smile sadly because I don't have the courage to tell her that I am scared too. "Yeah, neither did I, but here we are."

For a while the only sound is the soft pitter-patter of rain on the windows. "What are you going to do now?" she asks.

Tears well up in my eyes again. I'm so sick of crying. "I have no idea." Tasha gives me an empathetic look like she's about to cry too, so I quickly change the subject. "Tell me about your trip. I need a distraction."

She gives me a reassuring smile. I appreciate her willingness to do whatever I need, and I really do want to hear about her time with her mom and family. Thankfully, in typical Tasha fashion, she doesn't leave out a single detail, and by the end of it, I'm ready to go back to bed.

"I'll stay the night if you want," Tash offers as I gather the piles of blankets and chocolate wrappers off the floor.

"I love you, Tash. Yes, that would be great. Thank you."

"Anytime."

I shuffle my way back to the bedroom, my body a little less achy, but I feel mentally spent even though I haven't thought or talked much in the last couple of hours. I'm all too familiar with this kind of tiredness that my mind so easily drags me into, and I fall asleep within minutes of my head hitting the pillow.

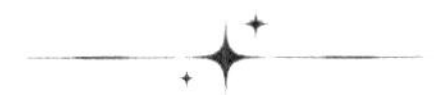

A knock on the bedroom door wakes me the next day. Tasha slowly opens it, seeing me awake, and she walks over and takes a seat next to me on the bed.

"Are you finally awake?" she asks playfully.

I squint my eyes at her as I ask, "What time is it?"

"It's already late afternoon."

I sit up quickly.

"Don't worry. I texted your mom back for you," she says. "I told her you weren't feeling well but that you were fine. I hope that's okay?"

"Of course. Thank you for doing that." I yawn, stretching my arms over my head. "I have no idea what I am going to say to her about Renn." Tash looks down at her hands, pursing her lips. I know that look. "What is it?"

She sighs but finally tells me. "Speaking of Renn. He came by earlier while you were sleeping. Did you know he was planning on leaving?"

"Yes."

Tash shakes her head, clearly confused and frustrated. I know what I have to do, but how Renn will react, I'm not sure; all I know is I am not going to let him leave like this.

"I'm going to go talk to him."

Tash tucks a piece of her dark hair nervously behind her ear. "Are you sure?"

"Yeah. I need to, even if it is just to say goodbye."

Tasha doesn't look at all convinced, but she grasps my hand. "Will you tell me what happened, eventually? I'm not gonna lie, you both are kind of freaking me out."

I scoot closer and wrap my arm around her shoulder. "I know it doesn't make sense, but I will. Someday, I will, I promise." She leans her head against mine. "Thank you for being the greatest friend anyone could ever ask for."

She chuckles softly. "Same." After a moment, she lifts her head and pats me on the leg. "Now, if you are going to say goodbye to Renn, then you better get in the shower before you do."

I grab my pillow and throw it at her, missing her by an inch as she sprints to the door. "Are you saying I smell?"

"Maybe just a little, but your hair has definitely seen better days," she says with a wink.

"Hey!" I throw another pillow at her, but she has already closed the door behind her. I know she isn't wrong about my appearance, so I search the closet to find something to wear, trying to distract myself from thinking that this could be the last time I will ever see Renn.

The last time I may ever see those vibrant green eyes and handsome face. I don't want to think about never hearing his entrancing voice or infectious deep laugh—that smile. It is going to kill me to do it, but I have to see him one last time.

CHAPTER THIRTY

Renn

I stare at the door longer than I care to admit, and it takes all I have left in me to venture back outside to retrieve Locke's body. It's nothing short of horrific, pulling Colin's literal dead weight across the slick ground. I haul it to a spot I deem far enough and check his pockets for anything useful—in which I discover a communication device that will hopefully help me find more info on how he found me and what he's been up to. I bring the rest of the liquid termite and pour it over him. His clothes and flesh dissolve away even more so in the rain; the remnants of his skin and bones soak into the ground, washing away. I hold it in for as long as I can, but I finally vomit behind a tree, taking a good long while before I trek back through slushy mud to the house.

I don't bother to remove my clothes as I step into the shower, tracking in even more mud throughout the house, but I don't have the slightest desire to care. Eventually, I pull my soaked clothes off my body, letting them *splat* onto the floor. I watch the river of blood and mud flow into the drain, slipping away like the terrible night never happened. I don't know how long I stand underneath the shower head, but it's long enough that the water starts to turn cold.

Shy is lying on the bed when I walk up into the loft, whining sadly when she sees me. I rub her ears gently before slipping on some dry clothes, then lie down on top of the bed, letting my legs hang off the side. The exhaustion overpowers all my other senses as I fall asleep quickly, only to be riddled with dreams of Maven's screams echoing through the forest. A new nightmare of torture that makes me wish I would have made Colin's suffering last longer for what he did to her.

When I wake the next morning, my limbs are aching in places I forgot I had muscle, and I don't feel rested in the faintest. Shy, on the other hand, acts like it's any other morning, and I envy her immensely.

I need to leave this place. This beautiful place in the universe that turned into a haven the moment Maven stepped into my life. A painful twinge sparks in my chest. The last twelve hours have been nothing short of chaos, but what I can't get over was how Maven responded to everything. After all the things I confessed to her, after everything she had seen, she was most concerned about me. If I thought I was unworthy of her before, it was an understatement now.

I notice as I sit up that there is actual daylight streaming in through the windows. The storm has finally passed, but I still feel it to some degree raging in my heart. The light is welcomed, but it reveals just how much mud I dragged throughout the house. It also reveals all the blood, which I know is mostly my own, but seeing it in the light of day makes it seem real. I pull up my shirt to check the wound, and it has healed, but the skin is still tender, and I know it will scar. The one on my arm is completely gone.

"Well, this will be quite an exciting day, won't it?" I say to Shy as she jumps off the bed, heading down the stairs like she's done hundreds of times. I want to simply revert back to the way things were just a day ago. But things will never be the same.

Maven has already experienced enough heartache and trauma in her life, and now this mess is piled on top of it. I reluctantly gather up rags, fill a bucket with warm water, and start scrubbing the hardwood floor. After my hands are worn raw, the floors are finally clean. There's one spot near the stairs that is still slightly darker, but what does it matter? It's not like I'm going to be around to see it. I move on to the next task at hand.

While I have Locke's comm device, I'm not so sure if I should try to use it. I worry it may have some kind of tracker that if activated would cause someone else to come looking. But his ship has to be somewhere close, and right now, it's the only way I'll be able to get off this planet. Once I do locate it, it may take me a few days to deactivate the location tracking. My plan is simple enough, but even as I set out to find the vessel, I still feel that pull to her, like I'm a satellite caught in orbit, and the only way to free myself would be to shatter completely, letting pieces of my heart scatter into space.

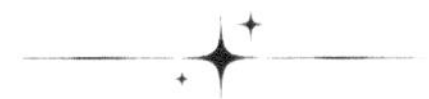

I don't bother checking the time before I make the decision to drive to her house. I found Locke's ship relatively easily. It was well hidden, about three miles into the forest, but Locke and I were both trained at the academy, so I knew what to look for.

The rain has stopped, but it doesn't keep the air from being icy. Even with my jacket and beanie, it's so frigid that I'm surprised there's still no snow. My breath fogs around me as I walk out the door to my motorbike.

I'll get back to Locke's ship eventually. It's in rough shape, and as I looked through his supplies, I found he was low in almost everything—fuel, food. It didn't seem to be a stable conquest. It caused me to wonder if he may have been on a solo mission, giving me a little spark of hope that perhaps his plans were spoiled in my absence. That was the dream, the whole reason I did what I did in the first place. I'm not sure I'm ready to accept that it could've all been for nothing. I climb onto my bike full of dread, second guessing if I should take the truck instead, but this is probably the last time I'll ever be able to ride it.

I always thought that dying in the void of space, starving slowly and alone, had been the lowest moment of my life, but the thought of Maven no longer being a part of it . . . there are no words; it feels just as it had in those dark moments in the abyss. It feels like dying, but I need to see her one last time. I'm already miserable, so why not punish myself more? I don't see a soul as I speed through the dark gray, blacks, and greens of the freshly drenched forest, the roadway shiny and reflective as it whirls past me.

My heart relaxes a bit when I see Tasha's car in the driveway. At least Maven hasn't been here alone. I softly rap on the door and hold my breath, hearing the floorboards creak on the other side.

"Renn!" Tasha's wide eyes tell me enough as she opens the door and steps outside, closing it softly behind her. "Well, you're certainly very brave to show up here." Her face is a mixture of sadness and something else I can't place. I've never seen her look at me the way she is now, but I might call it anger. "She's asleep, by the way. But even if she wasn't, I don't think she's ready to talk to you."

I nod, biting my lip as I stare at my shoes. "Yeah, I wouldn't want to talk to me either if I were in her place right now."

Tasha glares at me—actually glares at me. It shocks me, but I deserve it, so I say nothing. "Renn, what the hell happened?"

I clear my throat. "What did she tell you?"

She narrows her gaze on me. "Not much. Only that you two got into a fight and she still won't tell me anything more. However . . . I *know* it was more than just a fight." Her glare intensifies. "So, are you going to tell me what really happened?"

I'm rendered speechless for a few beats. "It's complicated."

Tasha's eyebrows furrow as she crosses her arms in front of her. "Really?"

I sigh heavily. *This is going so much worse than I thought. I shouldn't have come.* Not only was I losing Maven, but so many friendships. I didn't think it was going to be this hard.

She scoffs. "That's what Maven said too."

"It's not my call. Maven can tell you as much or as little as she wants to when she's ready."

She shakes her head, and there's nothing short of disappointment on her face. "I don't even know what to say. I thought you were going to be good for her." Her words feel like a slap in the face, but I completely deserve them.

"Look, I'm sorry. More sorry than I could ever convey. I just came to say goodbye."

"You're leaving Solitude Ridge?" she says, eyes going wide. I nod slowly. "This will truly break her. You know that, right?"

I want to tell her that this is exactly why I didn't want to get close to Maven in the first place, that she is the only one who could ever truly break *me*, and now my worst fear has come to life. "I never wanted to hurt her, but this is for the best. It's better if she hates me."

Tash shakes her head again, and she gives me a sad smile. "Oh, Renn. Can't you see *why* this is a problem? She doesn't hate you at all. That's why it hurts so much."

And God, I know she speaks the truth. Why couldn't Maven just hate me? Why couldn't she have just ran? There was empathy and kindness in Mave's face where I expected fear and hate. I gulp, tears burning my eyes. I run a hand over my face, blowing out a frustrated sigh.

"Can you just tell her I came by? I'll be gone the day after tomorrow."

She looks down, pursing her lips for a moment. "Yeah. I'll let her know."

"Thank you."

Tash moves toward the door and steps inside. For a moment, I think she isn't going to say anything at all, but she turns back toward me, her eyes now shining with tears.

"Goodbye, Renn."

I part my lips to say something, but she closes the door before I have a chance to say goodbye back.

I swing the ax again and again—sweat trickling down my neck and back, but I welcome the sensation on my skin as the cold air kisses it lightly. Maven will need a good supply for the winter. Plus, I need a distraction to buy me time. In a couple of hours, I will be off this planet. I'll drop off the firewood, then make a last stop at Grant's; I'm hoping he will agree to take Shy. As much as I want to take her with me, there's no way of knowing how her body will react, and then there's the question of if something happens to me, what would happen to her?

It takes years for a human body to acclimate to the changing of atmospheres. It was a big reason The Space Academy accepted students so young, so that we could be adjusted for space travel. Because it's been some time since my last ascent, it may not be pleasant, but I'll adjust eventually.

Just as I'm about to swing the ax down again, something catches in the corner of my eye.

"Hey."

Maven. Her voice is soft. My breath catches in my chest at the sight of her. For a moment, I think maybe I'm imagining it, but she's really standing here in front of me. She has on a dark green sweater that makes her midnight hair look even darker, paired with black leggings and boots. The cold air gives her cheeks a pink hue, and those eyes are as blue as ever. She's a vision, standing against the evergreen trees, and it's killing me. I just want to run to her, pick her up in my arms, and kiss her over and over again.

"Hey," I finally say back, setting the ax down softly against a tree.

She smiles for a second before letting her face go serious again. "Tash told me you stopped by. She's not happy with you, by the way."

I appreciate her trying to make light of the situation; it helps a little.

"Yeah. I don't think I've ever seen Tasha mad before. It was strange."

She smiles faintly then bites her lip for a moment before saying, "I didn't tell her anything."

I exhale deeply, my breath fogging around me as I take a step away from the pile of wood, flexing the stiffness out of my fingers. She watches my every move intently. "I don't want you to feel like you can't tell her anything, or your mom, for that matter."

She crosses her arms in front of her, shrugging. "It's not my secret to tell." Her breath fogs around her too as she speaks.

"I'll be gone soon anyway, so it won't matter." Her body jumps slightly at the harsh words. She gazes at me intensely, eyes blazing. I don't want to say these words, but I have to.

"Then answer me this, Renn." She takes a few steps closer while my feet stay rooted to the ground. "If it doesn't matter . . . why did you come to say goodbye?"

She waits patiently for my response, and I know my answer won't satisfy her no matter how I phrase it. "I had to make sure you were okay before I left."

She scoffs at me in annoyance, clearly seeing right through me like she has since I met her. "So after all that's happened, you still think you need to protect me?" I say nothing as her stare continues to burn into me. "You don't think I'm strong enough to handle this," she adds in a whisper. Her words hammer into me with how untrue her statement is.

"Mave, it's not that. You are strong in ways that most people couldn't comprehend. It's about your life being in danger because of me. There could be more who come for me, and if they know about you, that puts you in danger." Her throat thrums, but she keeps her gaze steady on me; she's not making this any easier. "Do you understand now why I did what I did, why I tried to stay away?" I ask.

She stares at me for a moment, her eyes glassy. "That's the thing, Renn . . . you didn't stay away, you kept coming back." Her voice falters.

I inhale a shaky breath, rubbing a hand over my face, trying to do anything to distract me from the heavy weight in my chest.

"Maybe, in another world, it could have worked, but I have to pay the price for my mistakes, and I won't drag you under with me. You shouldn't suffer because of me," I say.

She sighs deeply, her strong exterior cracking more and more. "Why can't you see I suffer more *without* you? You've been the only thing that's made the pain easier to manage. You made my life mean something more. I had something to look forward to for the first time in years. Don't you think we've both suffered enough?"

Her words resonate in my soul, slowly breaking me down piece by piece. The only problem is, I'm broken for her and by her in more ways than she could ever understand.

"What do you want from me?" I ask, and she doesn't balk at my hard tone.

"I want you to tell me, once and for all, what you really want. No more of what you *think* you should do. Or what is the *right* thing to do. I want to hear what *you* want."

I can see in her eyes that this is it, she means it. If I tell her to go, even if I don't want her to, she will, and then I will never see her again. For some reason, now that I'm faced with that possibility head on, I can't do it anymore.

"Fine. Do you want the truth, Maven?"

She nods, and I see worry furrowing her brow, like she truly doesn't know, and that hurts me more than I expected.

"The truth is, I'm *not* sorry that I let my selfishness get the best of me. When I realized what you meant to me, I knew that you could be used against me, so I stayed away, and I wish I could say that I tried harder to do so, if only to spare you from all this." Her bottom lip trembles. "I've done so much, seen so much in my life, but even after gazing upon countless worlds and wonders in this universe, you have to know that there are no words in this language or my own that could ever describe what you mean to me."

A tear slips from her eye, and she bats it away.

"God help me." My voice breaks before I go on. "Nothing could tear my heart apart more than the thought of you in harm. You could have died, and that is something I know I could *never* live with." My chest is rising and falling with deep breaths, and I realize I'm shouting at her. Not in anger, but because I'm caught up in the passion of it all, and she knows this as she takes a step and then another toward me.

"I don't care about the risk. What happened in the past . . . it wasn't your fault. I know the kind of man that you are. I know you did everything you could for your crew and friends. If that makes me selfish too, then I don't care." She pauses, taking in a shuddered breath. "I accept you because you accepted me—all of me. Even that darkness in me that will always live there, and somehow, I knew you had it inside of you too." I don't move or speak, but I want to touch her so bad that it hurts. She goes on. "I'm here, asking you to stay. Please stay with me, Renn. We will figure it out, whatever comes next."

These sweet words pouring from her mouth fill me more and more, and I know there's no going back for me.

"And what about the other part? You don't care that I'm not from this world? That I'm not a human from this planet?" I ask.

She smiles faintly. "After everything you've done for me, choosing to be my friend, it doesn't matter to me where you come from. Somehow, the universe brought you here, and as crazy as it sounds, that's all I care about," she says softly.

The more she says, the more I fall into that feeling of home. My home. *She* is my home. I lick my lips, taking a step closer.

"I don't know what lies ahead—if someone else will come for me—but it's your choice," I say. She silently looks at me, and I notice her already pink cheeks flush. "I'm yours, completely, but if you don't want this, I swear you will never have to see me again," I add, stepping closer to her until I'm a few inches away.

Tears fall down her cheeks, but they aren't filled with sadness. Instead, she smiles up at me. "I want to be here with you now, tomorrow, always. Whatever the universe grants us. I want to be with you, Renn. Whatever that future looks like, it doesn't matter, because I'm yours too," she says, her blue eyes shining with tears.

I can't help myself from finally closing the last little bit of space between us until my lips are just hovering above hers. I can feel the warmth of her body against mine, her sweet scent feeling my senses as I peer down at her, trying to calm my heart.

"Just promise me one more thing," she says, and I can already taste the satisfying lure of her lips begging to feel mine. "Never let me go."

I place my hands on either side of her face, and she looks at me with such intensity that my breath catches before I can reply.

"Never. I promise."

And then I kiss her.

CHAPTER THIRTY-ONE

Maven

The strength of his lips on mine is beyond anything I've ever felt in a kiss. This isn't like our first kiss, when he was careful and slow. This kiss is all-consuming and wild, taking hold of me completely. He moves his lips to my neck, and his warm breath on my skin makes my head spin in a crazy sort of way. I inhale, smelling the sweat on his skin. I drink it all in, grabbing the front of his jean jacket, pulling him into me until we can't get any closer. His tongue and lips gently slide up and down my throat, and I savor every mark he makes.

He brushes his mouth against my ear, and then his lips are back on mine. His tongue caresses my lips, and I slip my tongue into his mouth in return. He lets out a soft groan, guiding me to walk backward until my back hits the trunk of a tree. I tangle my hands in his hair, and he responds by grabbing my waist and hoisting me to his hips, still pushing me against the tree.

I don't care that the bark scratches my skin, I wrap my legs around him, and then his mouth is back on my neck, breathing me in; he's grazing his teeth across my flesh, his hands on my thighs, his strong fingers digging into me—the things I want those fingers to do to me. I expose more of my neck, urging him to keep going as I tilt my head back and rest it against the bark. I open my eyes to gaze into the branches above us where slivers of sunlight leak through, and I can't help but let my thoughts wander, reflecting on where I am at this moment, and how I got here. This man who owns my heart somehow found me as he was running through worlds—across cosmos—drifting in endless space and beyond. He's here with me, and he's real and good.

He pulls away, breathing hard as he searches my face. A small smile tugs on his lips. The sight of it only fuels my desire for him. I want more.

"Renn. I need you," I whisper.

His eyes dance in understanding of what I'm saying. I need all of him—now. I want to feel his bare skin against mine. I want to know what it feels like to have him claim me completely. I want to hear the sounds he makes as I make love to him. Because that's exactly what I want him to feel—my love. I look back at him, trying to calm my thumping heart, and Renn sets me back down onto the ground. I grab his hand, pulling him along the footpath back to the house. He smiles, taking my command to follow. He squeezes my hand, and his thumb rubs across my knuckles back and forth. Shy lies by the fire, ears up and alert once we step inside. Renn puts a hand up lovingly, reassuring her that we are okay, so she sets her head back on her paws and stays curled up by the fire.

We continue up the stairs to the loft, but once I cross the threshold, I pause as I see the bed. His bed. The sheets that he sleeps in—that smell like him. I've never actually stepped fully into his room before, and it sets my heart racing.

Renn comes up close behind me, moving my hair to the side so he can lean down to whisper in my ear. "Are you sure?" His warm breath sends chills all over my body. I take a deep breath and lean my head back into his hard chest.

"Yes. More than anything. I'm protected, so we're safe."

"I haven't been with anyone in a long time," he says, his hot breath kisses my neck, and I can't help but smile.

"It's okay. I trust you," I say.

He wraps his arms around me and holds me tight against him. I can feel his desire pressing into my back, leaving little to the imagination. It's his silent reply that he wants this as much as I do. My heart jumps wildly at the thought, and the heat rising in my abdomen grows. Dropping his hands to my waist, he spins me around to face him, and just like that night when he came to my cabin, he swiftly picks me up in his arms, carrying me toward the bed.

Except this time, I wrap my arms around his neck and capture his lips with my mouth, sliding my tongue along his bottom lip as he sucks on it, causing me to moan. I use the position to my advantage, taking his face in my hands as I kiss him. I don't have to reach up for him, giving me an angle to kiss him deeper. He responds with his own need, fighting for control as he bites my bottom lip softly. I moan again at the sensation.

"I've been wanting to do that for what feels like years. Every time I saw you bite your lip . . . it drove me insane," he says in his deep, rugged voice as he keeps holding me in his arms. Our kisses become feverish and uncontrolled.

Eventually, he turns to sit down on the edge of the bed, positioning me so I straddle him. He slides his hands under my shirt. His fingertips grazing my skin makes me stop breathing for a second or two. Without hesitation, I pull my shirt over my head while he holds my waist to steady me. Our faces are parallel, and I love being this close so I can see the gray rim around his green eyes as they bore through me, never leaving mine.

"Keep going." His voice is deeper than normal, and it causes the ache between my legs to become more wanting. I leisurely remove the straps of my bra from my shoulders and then reach to unhook the back, letting it fall from me with ease. Renn takes a deep breath, remaining still as I place my hands against his chest, his heart beating fast under my palm. The sensation of the rhythm is reassuring, like I'm checking to be sure he's real.

His hands travel up my waist, then he lifts me, spinning me onto my back. He leans over me, helping me further onto the bed, and with one arm supporting himself, he uses the other to pull his shirt off over his head as he holds himself above me, the taut muscles on his forearms flexing. I run my hand down his arms, feeding my obsession with how they move and feel. His necklace falls from his chest, now lying against mine, right between my breasts, branding me with the heat of his skin. I pull on the pendant forcefully, not breaking it, but enough to pull him down to me. Our tongues roll against each other as I continue to grasp the necklace, the metal digging into my hands like I want the lines imprinted into my skin. Renn's bare chest rubs against mine, and it makes me want to burst out of my skin as I hear his breathing change at the sensation.

I glide my hand over the muscles of his chest and stomach, feeling the new scar on his side, and he hums in satisfaction at my touch. I trail further down, sliding the tips of my fingers ever so slightly beneath the band of his pants. He allows me to drift further as he keeps kissing my mouth and jaw, but then stands as I start to tug them down.

He wastes no time pulling off everything below his waist. I sit up on my forearms, watching, my breath shaky, not from nerves but from the anticipation that I'm about to have this man—that he is about to have *me*—and there is nothing I've ever wanted more. His lean, athletic body before me, bathed in the afternoon sunlight coming through the skylight is something I want carved into my mind forever.

He tugs at the end of my leggings, pulling them down as I help him by lifting my hips. He slides everything off my waist as he eases them down my thighs and legs until they are completely removed. I thought I would feel some shyness at Renn seeing all of me, completely exposed, my insecurities fully on display, but I realize he has already seen me stripped bare and raw, he already knows the most vulnerable parts of me. All I feel in this moment is beautiful, and it's because of the look in his eyes. There's a light in them glowing with such admiration that it makes me believe he's never looked at anyone the way he's looking at me right now.

He looks me up and down, his gaze alone making me shiver. "Maven . . ." his voice quivers, full of passion. I know I will never get used to seeing Renn this way, flooded with emotion. It makes him more attractive than ever. I take his hand, pulling him down to me once again. The feeling of our bodies lying skin to skin for the first time makes me feel whole, like it's the missing piece of myself.

I place my hands on his face, tracing my fingers along his strong jaw, and kiss him at the corner of his mouth.

I purposefully move slowly, touching him lightly, barely brushing my fingers against his skin. I feel him shudder at each touch, and then I kiss him below his ear where I whisper, "Tell me everything."

He pulls away, scanning my face, and then gradually starts to trace his hand down my neck, his thumb tracing the hollow of my throat, mimicking me with that satisfying torture of touching me so lightly, not giving in to our desperate need and losing control. I know we could go there easily, but not this first time together, not yet.

"You are strong," he says, leaning down to kiss the base of my throat. "Passionate." He moves down to my stomach. His tongue, playful on my skin makes me bite my lip, and I see him smile at my reaction. "Brave." He lowers himself further down my body, his hands gripping my hips as he kisses the inside of my thigh while I inhale sharply. I'm burning, every inch of my skin on fire. "You are so beautiful."

The heat of his breath tickles my skin, his mouth close to the place that is begging to be touched, and before I can catch my breath, he kisses his way back up my body. When he reaches my breasts, he cups them in his large hands, squeezing gently, causing my back to arch off the bed with a quiet gasp. He brings his mouth down and sucks softly, his mouth roaming here and there, caressing my breasts and nipples, sending me into ecstasy as his tongue flicks my sensitive flesh. The tenderness of his movements leaves me dazed. I can see the hunger in his bright eyes before his tongue flicks my hardened nipple again. I wonder if we're thinking the same thing, both starved for each other and in disbelief that this is happening. As if catching himself in the heat of the moment, he positions himself above me again so his face is level with mine.

"You saved me," he says, the vibrato of his voice slightly uneven. "You saved me from the torment of my past. You're helping me accept the man I once was, and who I am today. And I would travel this entire galaxy over and over again if it meant I could find you."

I tremble and cup his jaw, making sure his eyes don't leave mine.

"I know you feel the weight of so many lives on your shoulders, that you carry it with you every day. You couldn't save everyone, Renn . . . but you saved me," I whisper. "You saved me from myself." My lips tremble at the words, then he drags his thumb across my lower lip as he looks at me intently.

"Don't do that." His voice is calm and deep. "Don't hate those parts of yourself—that darkness inside you, it's not all of you. There is light, and I see it every time I look at you. All of it together, the darkness and the light, it makes you who you are. *Everything* that makes you Maven is beautiful to me." He pauses. "And *you* are everything to me."

I can't stop the tears from springing to my eyes, and I swallow hard at the words that come to my mind. Those same words I wanted to tell him the day he came to the cabin when I was curled up in bed, hollow and numb. That moment he held me in his arms and let me cry. He didn't try to fix me, he didn't tell me to stop. He let me work through it on my own but never made me feel like I had to do it alone. He freely and openly accepted me for who I was, even in my lowest moments of my life, after all my mistakes and struggles, it was Renn who was there with me—who understood me. I knew it then, and I know it now more than ever. I inhale.

"I love you, Renn," I whisper, my voice unsteady from the overwhelming emotion pulsing through me. He holds my gaze for a moment, and then, with his own tears shining in his eyes, he grins down at me with that smile that holds all of the things that make Renn who he is—a light in my life, my falling star. He wipes away my tears with his thumb and holds my face firmly, making sure I look at him as he speaks in that deep voice that I have come to crave.

"Maven, I love you. I love you. I love you."

Hearing those words pass from his lips leaves me completely undone, and they seem to release something in him too because the next thing I know, he's kissing me, licking me, touching me everywhere. The slow burn of anticipation has vanished, and I can't touch him fast enough. Feel him enough. Show him enough that I love him. I grab his chin, pulling his face back to mine, sucking on his bottom lip hard, then slide my tongue into his mouth. The sounds of his deep, throaty moans alone almost bring me to my climax. I lift my hips off the bed to push myself against him.

"You have no idea what you've done to me," he breathlessly says against my mouth. "How many times I've wanted to tell you everything. How many times I've thought about doing this with you." His voice and control are unraveling more and more by the second, I can't even respond from the sound. He lowers his hand slowly, bringing himself to that part of me that needs him so badly. My body, wet and begging for him. He teases me slightly, pausing, and I lift my hips once more.

"Renn." I don't care if I'm pleading.

Gently, he moves into me, and I let out a sharp gasp of pain and pleasure as I dig my fingers into his back. He pushes into me farther, the ease of our movements becoming more and more consuming with each press into each other, adjusting until we are perfectly aligned. The feeling is pure euphoria. We're both breathing hard and loud, his name continuing to leave my lips as he moves on top of me. I hook my legs around him, holding him closer to me.

"God, Mave," he moans, his forehead resting against mine. We continue to move against each other, and I feel him everywhere—my skin, my blood, my heart as it pounds in my chest. We take our time savoring each touch and sound, an unspoken understanding that we both want the moment to last. Both of us want to revel in this act—an act that is bonding us to each other. I want him to feel that bond in every place our bodies touch, and I want him to touch me everywhere before we are through. He grabs my hands and places them above my head, holding them there as he glances down between us and pauses at the place where he and I are joined. I follow his gaze, and seeing his strong body above me, in me, makes me breathless. He moves his hips in such a fluid motion as I meet him again and again.

I can feel myself on the edge of being completely overcome—that edge that I want to fall over with him and him alone. Something I've never wanted with anyone else and never will again. He can sense that I'm close, and he lets go of my hands to grab my leg, bending it at the knee to angle me so he can go deeper, his fingers digging into my thigh then gliding down my calf, the agony of the pleasure almost too much. I tangle my fingers in his hair as he leans down, kissing between my breasts, the base of my throat, then my ear.

"So perfect," he says before gently biting my ear lobe.

"Renn, I . . ." I can't finish the sentence as I close my eyes tight.

"Maven. Look at me." I open them to see Renn's green eyes full of heat and passion. "I've got you."

I feel a wildness and freedom running through me, and I have to close my eyes again to keep from becoming completely overwhelmed. I know Renn is watching my face with every wave that hits me while I moan his name. He holds me steady against him as I cling to him. He rests his forehead against mine. His grip tightening as he loses himself in me. Renn, who is always unwavering and strong, breaks for me.

He moans something, but it's in his language, and even though I have no idea what he says, I know what the words mean, I can feel it. The sounds that escape his throat are burned into my mind forever.

When we're done, we hang on to each other. The only sound is our breathing, loud and heavy. After some time, Renn scoops me up in his arms again, placing me at the head of the bed. We climb under the covers, lying skin to skin as I cuddle up into his chest. He rests his head on top of mine, running his hand through my long hair over and over so it fans out across my pillow. I look above, watching the afternoon light fade into night. And everything about this perfect moment makes me realize that the internal pull to come back to Solitude Ridge was real, but the reason wasn't at all what I expected. Five years. So much had happened in five years for us both, and yet it feels like Renn had been waiting for me to come home—that he was supposed to find this planet and find me. The events of our lives brought us to this small spot in the universe.

Soon, sleep overcomes me, but I swear before I'm fully asleep, I hear him whisper, "I will never let you go."

CHAPTER THIRTY-TWO

Renn

I could have made love to her all night, but as she lay bare and content in my arms, I wanted to keep her there forever, and there was nothing more perfect than holding her against me. I thought I had experienced sex to its fullest before, but after Maven, nothing could compare. She had taken all my power. The sight of her naked, fingers tracing up and down my skin, that touch I had been so desperately needing from her . . . so much that she could have told me to beg for it and I would have willingly done it without hesitation.

As I fell asleep holding her, before waking the next day with her beside me, I realized it was the first night in a long time I wasn't lost in some nightmare. I swallow down the emotion heavy in my chest as I look down at her face. I know I'll never be able to forget the way she looked at me last night. It was the same face she wore that night on the retreat when she was gazing into the night sky, her intensity as moonlight reflected in her bright-blue eyes. I knew that she saw it in mine too, that my love for her was just as deep and infinite as space. And I thank whatever divine entity it was that brought us together.

She moves slightly beside me. "I was worried for a minute that it was all a dream," she says sleepily, keeping her eyes closed.

"Me too," I say against her hair.

"So?" Her voice is still soft and waking.

"So what?" I ask.

"So, what next?" she asks.

I place my mouth against her ear. "I have a few things in mind."

She pulls away, laughing lightly, and shifts so she can look at me directly, pulling the covers around herself. My gaze lingers on her exposed skin. She notices my stare, blushing, and I love that I can make her blush with just a look, even after last night. "You know what I mean."

I sit up, the covers stopping just below my waist. She looks me over, and damn if I don't feel a jolt of nerves in me. If she keeps doing that, we will never get out of bed. She leans forward, tracing the lines of the muscles on my stomach, and then slightly brushes the scar with her finger tips.

"I'm sure you have a lot more questions," I say, watching her fingers linger there for another second or two.

She nods. "I want to hear more about Earth." It sounds strange hearing her say that word. I haven't heard that name spoken aloud by anyone else for what feels like a lifetime. I rest my elbows on my knees.

"Hmm, where do I even begin?" She watches me, amused, waiting for my reply. "I want to show you something. Stay there."

I jump out of bed and walk over to the dresser, grabbing a clean pair of boxer shorts, taking a mental note of how Maven's eyes watch me the whole time, and I swear I see a flash of disappointment on her face as I cover myself. I kneel beside the bed, dragging out the box from underneath, rummaging around for the atlas. She doesn't say a word as she carefully inspects the device as it comes to life. The projection of stars fill the entire room, and she lets out a quiet gasp. My room is still dim enough with the morning light trickling in. It takes me a moment or two to orient myself studying the star map, walking through the artificial stars and planets until I find what I'm looking for.

"Here is Earth."

She rises from bed, dragging the covers with her, and I try to hide my disapproval. The light reflects off her skin, illuminating her like she is some kind of goddess walking through the constellations. I lightly tap the space and zoom in closer using my forefinger and thumb.

She lets out another gasp of surprise. "It's going to take me a minute to get used to this."

I chuckle in response, tapping the blue-green orb that comes into a larger view. We can see the surface with more detail as it spins slowly

"It looks so much like Aetherium." Her eyes wander over the planet in surprise and awe.

"It's almost identical," I say.

"Almost?"

I nod. "Geographically, there are forests, oceans, and deserts just like here. Even the seasons are similar, but the land masses are, of course, shaped differently, and Earth is much older and more populated."

She continues to tilt her head, observing this foreign world to her, taking in my words.

"This is so strange," she says in a serious tone, unblinking as she continues to take in the artificial Earth before us. "And there's more planets just like this?"

I move closer to her. "Thousands. It would take me years to go over the whole history of just Earth alone, even longer once space travel gets involved," I say as her eyes widen a bit before looking back at me.

"But you'll tell me about it? All of it, right?"

"Of course I will." I capture her hand, squeezing it, reassuring her of my promise that I will tell her everything and anything that she wants to know. I pull her along with me, walking over to the other side of the atlas. "And this is where I'm guessing we are. But it's only a guess," I say, pointing to the blank space of darkness.

"Aetherium isn't on your map?"

"No. Well, technically no. No one else has seen it to record it into the map system as far as I know."

She stares at the nothingness for a beat or two, then looks back to me with tears in her eyes. "It's unbelievable. That you came all this way, that you were alone for so long and then ended up here. What are the chances?" she asks softly, not looking for an answer, just wondering aloud.

Whatever the chances, they are near impossible to say the least.

"I didn't believe in fate, but now, I don't know what else to call it. Whatever guided me here, it brought me to you, and I am grateful for that."

She smiles and traces her fingers on my forearm.

"And I will tell you everything about Earth and this galaxy, my exploits in space, whatever you want to know, but right now . . ." I lean down to whisper into her ear. "I want to feel you around me again. I want to hear you say my name like you did last night. I want you in so many ways."

She whimpers at the words, and it only makes me hungrier for her.

"That is probably the most undignified thing you have ever said," she whispers. "But I loved it."

"Noted," I say, winking.

I make love to her again while the holographic streams of light dance over us, except this time, we don't take the time to memorize each other's bodies. I don't take a moment to pause before taking her to the edge of complete satisfaction, and she knows exactly what she's doing to me when she says my name over and over again like a prayer on her lips. I know I'll never grow tired of the way it sounds, exhilarated to learn all the ways I can get her like this, withering in my arms, spent and completely mine just as much as I am hers.

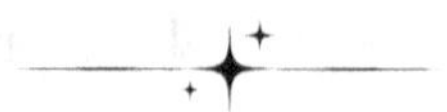

After spending the rest of the morning in bed, Maven eventually deems it time to clean up and become "human again."

"I think I better go into town to see Tasha and Mina," she says, finishing off her second cup of coffee, looking right at home standing in the kitchen.

"I'm assuming you told her about last night?"

She sets down the cup and smirks. "I told her we *made up,* to which she begged for information, but that was all." I give her an amused look. "Why? Are you worried that I'll share details on what kind of lover you are?"

I chuckle lightly. "Not at all, because I know it was nothing short of perfection." She gapes at me, but before she can say a word, I sweep her up into my arms and set her on the counter. She naturally wraps her legs around my waist.

"Don't worry, I won't tell her . . . everything," she says. Her voice is nothing short of seductive, leaning into me as I place my hands on either side of her.

"Good. There are some things that belong to you and only you." I'm taken aback by the sudden tears in her eyes, and she looks down as if she's embarrassed. "What is it?" I ask grabbing her chin lightly to bring her face to mine.

She swallows back the tears. "I'm ecstatic, but also . . . terrified. If that makes any sense," she says, smiling weakly.

I don't hesitate to respond. "I know exactly what you mean, and I'm not expecting you to be fine with the implications of all this, but like I said, there's no going back for me. It's you and me, okay? No matter what."

She grins warmly, her eyes fluttering. "I know, I know. I just don't want this to end, Renn." Her ocean-deep eyes roam into me, making a piece in my heart ache just hearing her saying that aloud.

The truth is, I can't lie and say that everything is going to be okay, no matter how much I wish for it to be true. I still don't know for sure what could happen. The only thing I am sure of is the woman sitting in front of me.

"I love you. I trust you with my heart, and you can trust me with yours. We will take whatever comes our way, together."

She nods, closing her eyes for a moment, and I rest my forehead against hers. "I love you," she whispers softly, and then she crashes her lips into mine, the taste of her against my tongue luring me in for more.

I place my hands on either side of her again, knowing if I touch her body, we will end up back in my bed, but it doesn't stop me from moving my tongue against hers, devouring each sensual stroke.

"I gotta go," she gasps breathlessly against my mouth. I respond by kissing her along her jaw down to her neck. She drops her head back with a smile on her lips. "Renn."

"Yes, Mave?" I say against the pulse of her throat.

"I really have to go."

"Mm-hmm," I hum into her neck. She laughs, pushing me away and quickly jumping down from the counter before I can protest.

"I'll be back in a few hours at most," she says, sliding on her boots and a beanie.

"Take your time. I'll be here when you get home," I say, winking, and then it's that word again that always makes me pause. Home. Not "back" or even "here." I don't know why it suddenly makes me nervous, but then I see her grin turn to a wide smile.

"Yeah, I'll see you when I get home." She pulls open the door and walks out into the cold, bright day. Shy jumps off the couch to watch her go, whining as her car backs away.

"She'll be back, don't worry." The joy that fills me with those words is endless.

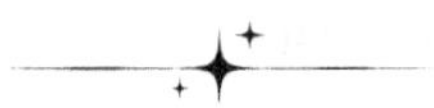

I decide to make use of Maven being in town to do some chores around the cabin. I have the firewood pile to organize, and a couple of things on my motorbike to fix before storing it away for winter. I'll decide what to do about Locke's ship later. It's hidden well enough for now, and soon the snow will most likely bury it until the season changes.

Shy watches me carefully while I work in the garage out back. I need to change the oil, tighten any loose facenters, and tune up anything else that may need it. By the time I'm done, my hands are black, smeared with oil and grime just like a typical day at the shop.

"On to the next," I tell Shy. She rises and follows me. The chopped wood is still scattered everywhere since I became thoroughly detained last night. Gathering up what I can in my arms, I carry a bundle back to the house.

Suddenly, Shy starts barking hysterically. I turn to see her teeth bared and the hair on her back standing on end. She's looking into the woods, warning me, remembering what happened the last time she sensed an unfamiliar scent in the woods. Smart girl, but unease slithers down my spine like a snake, slow and menacing. There's someone else out here. For a moment, I pray it's an animal, but Shy keeps growling in a way I haven't heard before, and I trust her instincts; I'd be a fool not to. But it's too soon to be happening again. Not now, not after what happened between Maven and me. I knew it was a possibility, but I never thought it would be this soon, if ever.

"*Shit,*" I whisper to myself.

I'm not going to be stalked like some helpless prey again, so I rush into the house, grab the gun, and venture back into the woods, hunting for whoever else has come for me. They will meet the same end as Colin. My boots sink slightly into the soggy ground, and Shy stays close to me as I try to navigate through the trees, looking for any signs. For a good ten minutes, I find nothing, but then I spy fresh boot marks—that are not my own—in the mud leading further into the forest.

"Damn it," I say quietly to myself. If Locke weren't already dead, I'd kill him again for leading someone here. I decide to hike up and around, hoping to catch them by surprise by coming from the other direction.

It takes me another fifteen minutes, but I find it, or at least a ship. It's a newer model than Locke's, the sleek, narrow design similar to the ship I stole from the admiral all those years ago. I move swiftly, ducking between trees, pausing and then moving forward until I have a good vantage point. Then I wait. Soon, a tall figure walks down the gangway, turning so their back faces me. They remain standing next to the ship, typing at something on a tablet. The posture and build of the person is clearly male, and he has long, black hair, dreaded back and tied at the nape of his neck. I duck behind a tree, pressing my back into the bark, taking deep, quiet breaths. My hands tremble slightly as I look down at the gun.

Am I about to kill another man? To keep Maven safe, there's no doubt in my mind that I will do anything, so if it has to be done, then so be it. I won't lose her, not like this. I peer around the tree again, and the man walks to the other side of the ship, giving me a window to come up behind him.

"Stay," I whisper to Shy, and she goes still.

The soft ground absorbs the impact of my boots as I sprint until I reach the ship, sliding around the hull until I turn the corner. The stranger still has his back to me. I move quickly and silently.

The moment he senses me, he reaches for the gun holstered at his waist, but it is too late as I set the barrel of the gun on the back of the stranger's head.

"Hands up and turn around . . . slowly," I say in English, assuming he'll understand, especially if he's looking for me. The stranger keeps his hands up as I back away a couple of feet, both my hands on the raised gun. The man begins to turn slowly as I instructed, and the person that I behold as he comes to face me fully almost makes me drop to my knees in utter shock.

CHAPTER THIRTY-THREE

Renn

"Nate?" I lower the gun slowly, not believing who is standing in front of me. He stares back at me, eyes wide and brown like a deer, his mouth slightly gaping.

"Holy shit. It really is you." He says.

Before we can say anything else, we grab onto each other, gripping one another in a tight hug. I pull away, studying his face, feeling the tears stinging my eyes, and find the same tears in his eyes looking back at me. I take in his long hair and the short stubble on his face. He looks different, but it's him. It's Nate.

"How in the hell are you here right now?" I ask, my voice staggering. Nate looks at me with absolute disbelief, and I know I am wearing the same expression.

"I picked up on your signal about six weeks ago, but I wasn't the only one who did."

"Locke," I say flatly, and Nate's eyes go wide.

"He was here?"

I nod in response.

"What happened?"

"He's dead."

Nate's eyes go wide again, but he calmly says, "You killed him."

I nod again. His expression is a mix of shock and awe. "He got here the day before yesterday. He attacked me and a . . . friend."

Nate shakes his head, struggling to find words. "Are you okay?" He looks at the cuts on my eyebrow and cheek.

"I looked much worse yesterday."

"Who is this friend?" he asks quickly, the words muffled together slightly.

I take a deep breath. "She got hurt, but she's okay."

"She?" Nate's eyebrows go so high, I can't help but smile a little bit.

"Yes."

"Does she know?" And I know what he's implying.

"Yes."

He blinks rapidly. "Okay, hold on. Back up. I need to know everything," he says, putting up a hand. The phrase reminds me of how Tasha talks to Maven.

"Same goes for you," I say, laughing, pushing his shoulder to test to see if this is real or a dream. Nate snickers, shaking his head with the same disbelief on his face.

"Is this really happening? Are you really here right now?" he says, grabbing on to my shoulders. I smile wide, and it's all a bit much to put words together. "Renn. You're alive." He says it as if he needs to hear it aloud to believe it.

"I'm alive," I say, smiling. "And so are you. How?"

He smiles back. "How are *you* alive? That's the bigger question. You've been MIA for six years." He steps back a little, scanning me as I do him. He looks older, but well. Age has only enhanced his good looks, which I'm sure he already knows, so I don't feed his ego even now. I must look different to him too. "I like the lumberjack hipster look. Reminds me of when it was back in style like twenty years ago on Earth," he says through a laugh.

I shake my head, blowing my lips. "Hey, don't give me shit about my clothes. I actually really like them," I say, looking down at myself.

"I was kidding. I like it too. It suits you," he says, looking me over again.

"I could say the same for you," I say, looking him over again. He really is standing in front of me right now.

"What can I say? For the first time in, what? Forever? I get to grow my hair out and wear whatever I want. Well, for the most part. I am still technically in the SEA"

"You are?" I ask, feeling the smile fade from my face.

"It's complicated, but let's start with the basics first." I make note of how quickly he wants to change the subject. *That can't be good.*

"How long have you been here?" he says, motioning his hands around us.

"Five years."

Nate's eyes go wide again. "Five years? What exactly have you been doing for the last five years?"

"Let's go inside and I'll explain everything." I whistle for Shy, and she comes bounding down to us. She warmly greets Nate like she's known him all her life.

When I open the door to the cabin, Nate gazes around. "This is yours?"

"It is," I say as I gesture for him to sit at the table.

"I like it," he says, rubbing Shy's ears as she sits besides him.

"So let's just get to it," I say.

"Okay then. Here we go. What exactly happened after . . . that day?" he asks, a little hesitant.

"I did as you said. I ran. Spent a year floating aimlessly in space," I say, looking out the window. "Was on the brink of death, then I came to this place. I've been on Aetherium for five years. I've been living here in Solitude Ridge for four."

"Aetherium?"

I nod.

Nate furrows his brow. "How did you do it? How are you *still* doing it? No one suspects anything?" I scoff lightly at all the questions flying from his mouth, but I don't blame him. "Sorry," he says with a bashful grin. "It just seems like you fit in here. I kind of expected you to be living as a hermit, or worse."

"You can tell just from this?" I say jokingly, motioning to myself and the cabin.

"I'm being serious. You look settled somehow," he says in earnest. It hits me in a way I wasn't expecting.

"What about you?" I ask.

"Oh, I haven't been lying low by any means," he says, chuckling.

I know he doesn't intend for the comment to hurt me, but I'm riddled with guilt.

Yeah, I've been living a good life here, happy and content while God knows what has been happening all this time out there.

And then it slips out, the one thing I've longed to convey to him over all these years. "I'm so sorry, Nate. For everything."

Nate cocks his head to the side, his expression puzzled and sad.

"What are you talking about, Renn?"

Is he really going to make me say it out loud? Spell it out for him with each piece of my broken soul? I guess he is, because he looks at me completely seriously, and he deserves to hear it. I at least owe him that.

I rest my elbows on top of the table, pressing my palms into my eyes. It's almost too painful to say it out loud, but I find the strength to do it because it's Nate.

"For destroying our lives. For the crew. They're dead because of me. Then let's not forget the planets I handed over willingly."

Nate looks down at his hands for a moment smiling sadly. "You would make yourself the villain, wouldn't you?" His joking tone makes me angrier than I want it to.

"What else would you call me when I sacrificed everything—*everyone*—for what I believed?" I try to keep my voice steady, but even after all this time apart, Nate doesn't hesitate to say exactly what he thinks.

"A hero."

I stand abruptly, turning my back to him. "Oh, you've got to be kidding me!" I say, blowing out air.

"First of all, everyone thinks you're dead. Second, you weren't the only one who was deceived, Renn, but you were the only one willing to do something about it. That's why I came to you once I knew the truth. I was too terrified to know what to do, but not you. You took action." I turn to face him, my hands balled up into fists at my side. "And in case you forgot, the crew stood by you until the very end." This time, I don't take a second or two to check myself before my anger gets the best of me.

"Did you think I could forget? I see it every time I close my eyes. I relive it every fucking night!"

Nate remains stoic sitting at the table, acting as if I'm not directing my frustration at him. I take a couple of deep breaths. I'm not angry with Nate, I'm angry with myself because I know he's right.

"I understand. I do, trust me. What I'm trying to say is that you were already admired and respected before any of this happened. They followed you knowing the possibilities, and there is no doubt in my mind that they all would have done it again if they had the choice."

His words sink into me, settling into the parts of me that have been hurting all these years, my shame for what I did, but for some reason, hearing Maven, and now Nate, saying these things makes my mind accept them . . . finally. Nate sees the realization in my eyes as he smiles sadly at me.

"That's why you're the captain. I'm glad I was able to remind you."

I pinch the bridge of my nose, my emotions running too high. I take a deep breath, slightly embarrassed at the stuttering sound I make as I exhale. All this time, I had been so terrified of what Nate thought of me.

I swallow. "You want to know something? I think I've been waiting all these years to hear you say that. First her, now you. How pathetic am I to resort to being this broken?"

Nate perks up a little in his seat. "Not pathetic. Human. It makes you human, Renn."

That hits a chord in me, resonating all the way to my bones.

"Speaking of *her*, are you actually going to tell me who she is?" He gives me an undignified look. I already know where his mind is going, so I flip him off, and he barks out a laugh. "Same Renn it seems. So very protective of his love life."

He's dodging the obvious subject again, and it's not like I don't want to tell him about Maven. I will as soon as I get some answers. The first of them being how we are even having this conversation right now. How did he survive? And what is the state of the SEA?

"Nate, I need to know what's been happening out there," I say, completely serious.

He blows out a breath. "I'm not gonna lie, it wasn't pretty, but everything is back to normal for the most part. Everyone involved was arrested, most of them killed. Unfortunately, Locke slipped through our fingers more than once. That's why I was trailing him."

And even though what he says is good news, the way his voice carries makes me nervous. He gives me a pained look, and I hold my breath for what he's about to say.

"Do you still have the drive? It still has the data?" he asks.

"Yes, and yes."

His shoulders sag a bit relieved, and he clears his throat. "Renn. I need you to come back with me."

I start to shake my head because I know where this is going.

"I need you to come back with me to headquarters on Earth."

Pure panic rises in my chest. I try to speak, but I can't form words. Nate gives me a moment, clearly seeing my distress.

"I can't," I say quietly.

"You have to make things right," he says, his tone sad.

I shake my head fervently. "No."

"But you're still technically captain. You aren't pardoned officially, and people need to hear what happened from your own voice. It carries more weight than others. And I'm not talking about a recorded hologram—they need to see you in person. Renn, you're not just some guy. You're Captain Aldrenn Anton,"

"*Was* Captain Anton, Nate. Was. I think it's safe to say that I'm no longer him, not in the slightest," I say darkly, so much so that Nate actually looks uneasy, like I'm a foreign being that he doesn't recognize anymore. I give him credit as he stares me down, not willing to balk.

"You know you will always be the captain, Renn."

It's so much worse than I ever could have imagined, facing the demons of my past. I've never been afraid to do hard things, but this—this is beyond hard. It's unfathomable.

"I won't do it. I won't leave. I can't leave . . . her." I can't even say her name. It's too painful, like my heart is being ripped from me. Nate is quiet for several seconds.

"What's her name?" he asks, and I know he's not asking to be a smartass this time.

"Maven." I say her name like a confession. "Her name is Maven." Nate blinks a couple of times in thought.

"Maven." He ponders it for a moment. "I like it." Then the realization comes across his face just from me saying her name. It was all he needed to know.

"You're in love with her, aren't you?" His tone is solemn. I turn to face the window, closing my eyes, thinking it will help me say what I need to say out loud.

"I love her more than anything," I whisper. I open my eyes to stare out into the forest. I don't turn to face him, but I hear the chair scrape against the floor, and then he places a hand on my shoulder.

"I'm so sorry, Renn."

And that's all he says, because we both know what I have to do. After all that has happened between Maven and me—our friendship, our love—to be ripped away so quickly, it's the final piece of my heart that wasn't completely destroyed . . . that last bit of my heart that was waiting for her to come into my life only to be lost too soon.

"I just found her," I whisper.

I thought I'd only said it in my mind until Nate says, "I wish there was another way."

I don't know what's worse: that it's only taken mere months to meet and fall in love with Maven, or that we met, only to have our time together cut short. My heart beats faster at the thought of never meeting her, but what's worse? I fell in love with her . . . made love to her only to say goodbye?

Nate stands by me patiently, waiting for me to work through my thoughts.

"You need to finish what you started," he says calmly.

Even after all these years, Nate knows what I need to hear to make me realize what I already know, what I have to do. Even if it's going to kill me to do it, I will do it. For the simple fact that I owe it to my crew. This has to be done right.

"I know," I say softly.

Nate removes his hand from my shoulder, and I run a hand over my face, taking deep breaths.

"So how long do you estimate it will take us to get back to Earth?" I ask.

Nate grimaces before he responds. "If my calculations are correct . . . six months." I swear under my breath. "My ship is small and fast, but we are far, far away, which is why it took so long for anyone to first pick up on your beacon and then get here," he adds.

I bury my face in my hands, trying to calculate the amount of time I could potentially be away, but there's no way of knowing how long I'll need to be on Earth on top of the journey back.

Nate gives me space to process it all, and then finally, I turn to him.

"Tell me everything," I say, and so he does.

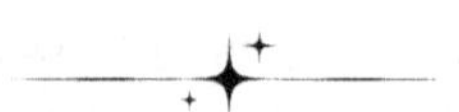

Nate didn't pause for a second as he told me about every moment since the day I had last seen him. We probably sat there for an hour at least. Nate was able to escape by programming the admiral's ship to self-destruct, and by some miracle, no one found him. He gave the crew time to escape, but the chaos was enough of a distraction that no one noticed him jump into an escape shuttle alone. From there, he had to navigate back to Earth but take the "long way" to avoid running to anyone from the admiral's crew, and when he got back to headquarters, he went straight to the highest ranking official he trusted, and then the fire was lit.

The gist of it was that Grey, Locke, and a handful of other higher-ranked officials were in the process of staging a coup to take over the SEA, with the end goal being that they would take over the galaxy.

"Very *Galactic Empire*, right?" he said at one point.

"Are you seriously referring to Star Wars right now?" I asked, unamused, and he just laughed. I didn't need to mention that the movie was almost three hundred years old but, for some strange reason, still beloved by many on Earth.

I found out that the Locke Family, no surprise, were paying off individuals to "quietly" take control of planets with viable resources and little force available to stop them. Then, with the added expertise of members of the SEA, they formed an underground Galactic Conquest. Their knowledge and diplomatic influence helped them gain access to planets all over the galaxy. Add in ground forces, weapons, strategic planning, and a hell of a lot of nerve. They had the moving parts in motion, but fell apart the second Nate found those files.

Admiral Grey wasn't the only higher up officer involved, and after lengthy trials, those who were involved were brought to justice, and the imprisoned planets were set free and promised a lot of resources and assistance to re-build—all to be provided by the association. Some of those involved, like Locke, attempted to escape, so Nate was tasked with tracking them down.

Nate kept speaking as if it was a happy ending for everyone, and I hate that he kept saying things like "because of you" and "thanks to you, this terrible thing wasn't as bad as it could have been." It didn't matter how many times he said it, I still felt that heavy guilt in me. My crew paid the price for the choice I had made.

"They'll want you to make an official statement of the events and"—he purses his lips, hesitating to go on—"to honor you with an award."

"And by *they,* you mean The Council," I say.

"Yes. They want everything straight for the records. You know how the SEA is. They like order."

I run a hand through my hair, scoffing. "That sounds terrible, Nate. No way am I accepting an award. If anything, they should be discharging me with no honors."

Nate shakes his head, blowing a raspberry. "Oh, please."

"Don't they already have enough evidence from my recording and your statement, plus all the records you took? Isn't that enough?"

"Like I said, not when they can confirm it all from the one and only Aldrenn Anton."

I shake my head, unimpressed. "Please stop saying things like that."

"It's the truth, and if you don't come back with me now, someone else will *make* you come back. It's protocol. You know that," he says in a harsh tone.

He isn't wrong; we both know the code well. I'm technically still under the oath of allegiance I swore.

I lean back in my chair, crossing my arms in front of me.

Nate studies me suspiciously. "I see those wheels turning in your head. What are you planning?"

"If I do this, I want negotiations to pardon me from my rank as a captain and from the association altogether." Nate leans forward slightly, listening intently. "And a promise to leave Aetherium alone . . . forever"

Nate blows out a breath and whistles for exaggeration. "That is quite the ask, my friend, but once they know you're alive, honestly, I think they'll give you anything you want." I give him a narrowed look. "Okay, they *probably* will. For you, I would almost say that they would grant you total leniency."

I don't like any of it, but if I have to do it, then I want to make it worth it for Maven and this planet. My presence here doesn't need to involve anyone else. I just need the council to agree once I speak with them and get everything over with officially.

"Look, I'm glad to hear that this planet is in no immediate danger, but if there is a chance I can make this bargain for them, for her, then I'm going to do everything I can to make it so. I can't leave even the slightest risk that someone finds this place in case it ever happens again."

I can see the resolve in Nate's face as he says, "I believe you, and I'll help in any way I can."

I nod in thanks.

Nate stands, stretching his arms over his head. He glances around the room.

"Well the added bonus is that you can tell the council you already took care of Locke. Where *is* he, exactly?"

"About two miles that way," I say, pointing. "At least what I left of him."

Nate is thoroughly stunned, no doubt at my casualness about it. He flops onto the couch, rubbing his eyes. "This is freaking me out a little bit. Everything looks so . . . Earth-like but just slightly off."

I laugh, mostly because nothing feels off to me anymore. When I return to Earth, I wonder if it will feel foreign to me as Aetherium did. The thought causes my skin to crawl, knowing how far Earth is from here and that I will be walking on its surface once again soon.

"How did our lovely friend, Lieutenant Colin Locke, meet his untimely demise?"

I clear my throat and decide to get it all out as quickly as possible. "He kidnapped my dog and lured Maven into the forest." Nate notices my hands going into fits, my knuckles turning white. "He hurt her, almost killed her, but I got there just in time. He almost ended me. But I killed him, then I dragged him deep into the woods, doused him with termite, and it was done."

Nate stares at me for a beat or two. "Oh, is that all? Holy shit, Renn." He shakes his head in disbelief. "All I'll say is that I'm glad the bastard is dead. I don't know how he found your signal, but once he did, I was immediately alerted that someone else had tapped into it. He was already on our radar, and I guess it was a blessing in disguise because he led me to you. He must have been working on that for a long time to have tracked you down."

Perhaps it made me cold-blooded, but killing Colin had little effect on me besides feeling glad that he would never hurt anyone ever again, especially Maven.

"And look at you, a knight in shining armor. If she didn't love you before, she has to now, right?"

I roll my eyes. "It's not like that at all. She is far from a damsel in distress," I say. He smiles, looking pleased. I realize that she will most likely be making her way home soon. "So . . . do you want to meet her?"

Nate smiles wide and nods. "I'd love to."

I pull out my phone to text Maven, asking when she will be home. I tap send as Nate casually adds, "It's too bad I can't get to know her more, but I will take what I can if it means I get to meet the woman who won your heart," he says, swooning dramatically.

Instead of hearing of the sentiment, I only hear the underlying implication that this may be the only time he will get to speak with her.

"Nate, you never mentioned when you were planning on leaving to return to Earth." His face goes sad again, and I know there is more bad news to add to this already strange day.

"Did I not mention that part?"

I ignore the humorous tone to his voice, trying to make light of the situation.

"Nate," I say, urging him to get it out. He turns to me with nothing short of dread in his eyes. "When do we leave?" I ask.

I already know the answer before it leaves his lips.

"Tomorrow."

CHAPTER THIRTY-FOUR

Maven

The moment I open the door, something feels wrong, but I don't see panic in Renn's eyes, rather a mix of concern and worry. And his message, though cryptic, didn't suggest there was anything to be worried about.

"We have another visitor . . ." he starts to say, and my mouth falls open, fear freezing my limbs until he adds, "It's okay, we're safe."

My heart calms slightly, but I'm still worried because Renn also doesn't seem overly happy about whoever this visitor may be. "So, what's wrong then?" I ask, glancing around the cabin as if I can find something out of the ordinary. I'm not sure what I'm looking for, but it all seems normal, nothing out of place.

"I have good news and bad news."

I walk forward to meet him where he stands. "What is it?" I ask, barely above a whisper.

He looks down at me, his eyes sad, so I reach up and cup his cheek. He turns his head so his lips press against my palm, then grabs my other hand, pulling me into him. I wrap my arms around him and he holds me tight, resting his chin on my head. I always thought this gesture was meant to comfort me, but I realize it's just as comforting to him. We mold into one another perfectly every time.

"Tell me the good news first," I say, pressing my ear against his chest, finding the thumping of his heart steady even though he's clearly troubled.

"Well, there's really no other way to say this." The hum as he speaks reverberates in his chest. "Nate is here."

I pull away from his embrace and shake my head, bewildered. I thought Nate was dead.

As if he reads my thoughts, he continues, "He's alive and has been looking for me."

Just when I thought I had a grasp on all this, something else reveals itself.

"Nate's alive." It is not a question, more of a confirmation. He smiles warmly in response. "That's amazing! Where is he now?" I ask, looking around.

"He took Shy for a walk. I asked him to give me a moment to explain everything to you." I see the grievance flash in his green eyes, and it turns my stomach in knots, suddenly remembering that there is more.

"So, what's the bad news?" My voice is not as steady as I hoped. He gulps nervously.

"I'm already breaking my promise to you." My heart sinks in my chest, and the knots in my stomach become tighter. "Nate isn't here just by chance." I stare at him, unblinking, my heart beat becoming louder in my ears as he speaks slowly, "I have to go back with him." I say nothing, nor do I move. "I have to go back to Earth."

If my heart was erratic seconds ago, it might as well have stopped beating now, because all I can think of is the star atlas that he showed me earlier.

Was that only this morning?

All I can picture is the distance that he will have to travel, the literal miles upon miles of dark space that will be between us . . . I can't fathom it.

"Why?" I ask, my voice wavering.

He inhales deeply, his chest rising and falling in deep breaths. "I have to finish what I started," he says, looking back at me. "The association's council, they've been handling everything while I've been away, and now they want me to come back to give an official account of my side of the story." He pauses, shaking his head with annoyance. "And give me recognition for my good works." He scoffs at that last part.

If there's one thing I know about Renn, it's that he doesn't feel pride in what he did. Yes, he saved lives, but also lost many. People who were his family, so to speak. I'm starting to realize that a great deal of people see him for who he truly is, who he's always been, a man of honor with a brave, kind, and loyal heart. Of course he would want to make things right.

"That's not all," he says.

I step back a little. "There's more?" I ask softly, my voice unsteady as I try to process everything.

I watch his throat bob before he speaks again. "I've seen terrible things, Mave. Horrific acts that people like Locke did to humans on other planets, and maybe I'm being overly protective of you, but I won't risk anyone from my planet finding this place, finding you, so …" He turns away from me, rubbing his hands over his face before he goes on. "We can't have contact while I'm gone." His voice shakes, and I can't help the quiet but heavy gasp that escapes me. A couple of tears escape from my eyes. For a moment I think I might fall to my knees, but as I stand here, looking at Renn like this, seeing the pain that he has endured for so long, I know he's right. He needs to close this part of his life completely before moving on. I trust him to make the right call, even if it's killing me. So right now, I need to be brave for him, be strong for him, because he deserves that and more. I step around to stand in front of him and pull his hands away from his face.

"It's okay, Renn." He looks down at me, biting his lip, a painful look in his eyes. I rub his still bruised and battered knuckles. "Alright, it's not okay, but I understand why you need to do this." We stand for a moment just staring at each other.

"God. I don't deserve you," he finally says, then lifts my chin so he can kiss me slow and soft, a thank you searing into my lips. My body instantly feels molten inside. But then another terrifying realization comes to mind.

"We still have time right? Before you have to go?" I ask against his lips.

He doesn't respond. Instead, he kisses me harder, digging his fingers into my hair. I don't notice that he's guiding me to the couch until he pulls me down to straddle him as he sits. His mouth never leaves mine. I pull back, gasping for air, and place a finger against his lips.

"When?"

His chest rises and falls in a quick rhythm, clearly as breathless as I am. I slowly pull my finger away.

"Tomorrow," he says softly as his green eyes shine with tears.

The reality hits me like I'm falling off a cliff. We are, in an instant, on borrowed time. What we have is over before it has truly begun. I can't form words, so instead, I crush my lips back into his, and he kisses just as fiercely back.

His lips travel to my neck as he starts to undo the buttons of my flannel shirt. Once they are free, he shifts me to lie on my back. Our space is limited on the couch, but we don't seem to care. He holds himself above me for a moment, then drops his head down to plant a trail of kisses against my stomach. I run my fingers through his hair, gripping it slightly, urging him to keep going. He moves up my body, and once at my breast, he bites softly through the fabric of my bra. I can't help but buck my hips to push against him, and a deep moan comes from the back of his throat.

I can sense a sort of panic in him, which scares me, but right now, I don't want to care. It's frantic but intoxicating—this need for each other as we try to push away everything that is trying to pull us apart. I wish we could stay in this moment forever and pretend that we are just a normal couple with no worries of other worlds, or pasts riddled with death. But as I look down at Renn's face between my breasts, his tongue coaxing sounds out of me that make him smile against my skin, I don't care about anything, past or future. He is here right now, and that is all that matters.

"I don't want to break my promise to you," he says, looking up at me under his lashes. I tug his shirt, urging him to move until he's right above me.

"You're not," I say. He scans my face, waiting for me to go on. "You have to know that distance would never change that fact that you are mine, right?" I ask. His throat works with emotion, and I reach up to rub my thumb over the hollow of his throat. "Tell me you know that, Renn," I whisper. A single tear drops from his eyes

"I know, and a million miles between us could never change that, because you're mine too," he says, then rests his forehead against mine. I see the resolve on his face, but the worry still lingers in his eyes just as it does mine. It stings a little that he even thought he could disappoint me, especially when it is out of his control.

Just as he's about to press his lips to mine again, Shy's happy barking rings from somewhere outside.

"I'm guessing that's Nate with Shy," I say.

Renn grunts playfully in frustration, pulling himself off of me, then helping me to my feet. He looks down at my open shirt and bites his lip, trying not to smile too big.

Shy barks happily again, closer this time.

"So, are you ready to meet my best friend?"

I glance toward the windows, noticing how strange the sentence sounds.

"Absolutely. Just let me freshen up, and I will be right out." I head toward the bathroom, fumbling with the buttons on my shirt, but he grabs my waist, spinning me back to face him.

"We're finishing this later." His voice is deep and wanting. I press up onto my tiptoes, acting like I'm about to kiss him, but hover just out of reach.

"I hope so," I say, teasing, and pull away, heading back to the bathroom. He squints his eyes at me as if to say *not fair*.

I start to shut the door.

"Maven." The deep tenor of his voice that feels like a spell makes me stop instantly. "I love you."

My heart jumps in my chest. I will never get tired of hearing that from his lips.

"I love you, too."

His gaze travels up and down my body for a second or two, and my cheeks blush instantly—every time.

"I know," he says, winking in a roguish manner. I shake my head, but not without smiling widely.

I close the door, then splash some cold water on my face, smoothing my hair behind my ears. I watch my reflection for a beat or two, a million thoughts running through my mind, trying to let them all catch up so I can make sense of something.

I am about to meet Renn's best friend, who he thought was dead.

They're both from a planet called Earth.

Their crew members were murdered because of what they uncovered.

And on top of all that, I am wildly in love with Renn.

And he loves me back.

"Did I miss anything?" I say to myself. I watch the shock shift into sadness, spreading across my features. I trace my fingers down my throat and chest where Renn's mouth was just moments before. Just thinking about it makes me blush. Then I see tears forming in my eyes, because soon, the sound of his voice, his touch, all of him will be out of reach, and I have no idea how long he will be gone, or if he will come back at all. I wipe away the tears, then take a deep breath. There's still so much to say and do before Renn leaves tomorrow.

Tomorrow.

He's leaving tomorrow, and I'm not sure I can imagine my heart aching more than it does right now.

CHAPTER THIRTY-FIVE

Maven

I'm not sure what I expected when it came to Nate, but the handsome, dark-skinned man I see standing next to Renn when I step outside the cabin is a good surprise. He's incredibly attractive, but in a different way than Renn. Nate is pretty, while Renn is rugged. I can only imagine the damage these two could cause together, breaking hearts left and right from just one look. Shy spies me and runs over, causing Renn and Nate to snap their heads in my direction. Nate gives me a wide-toothed grin, so I smile back.

"Mave." Renn holds out his hand for me to join them. I feel nervous as they both watch me while I make my way over. "Nate, this is Maven. Maven, this is Lieutenant Nathan Hayden."

Nate gives him an irritated look, then rolls his eyes. "Nice to meet you, Maven." It takes me a second to realize that he's speaking my language.

I stammer, trying to respond, but I'm too shocked to put anything together. Nate laughs, loud and hardy, and I turn to Renn, confused. "Wait. What? How?"

Renn laughs then urges him closer. "Let me show you."

Nate obeys then turns his head to the side, folding his ear forward slightly, revealing a small, round device stuck on the back. The translator. The details Renn explained briefly the night of the attack vaguely come to my mind.

"Oh," I say, blushing slightly only for a second or two. "Explain to me how this works again," I say smiling toward Nate, but Renn is the one who speaks.

"The translator deciphers the language it hears, then connects to the part of the brain that is associated with language development and provides neurofeedback so the user can translate the speech. In turn, it helps you learn the language faster. It usually takes a person a good week to really start to understand the language."

"Except for me, right, Captain?" Nate says with obvious pride, and though I can understand what he says, it does sound off somehow.

Renn rolls his eyes. "Nate here is gifted, which really means he's too smart for his own good. He learns things at a much quicker pace."

It takes Nate a couple of extra seconds to decipher what Renn says, the AI translating for him, then he gives him a look somewhere between annoyed and pleased. I like seeing Renn interacting with Nate. I imagine it probably resembles how Tasha and I act around each other—relaxed but comfortable giving each other a hard time when appropriate. I notice Renn keeps watching my face, almost to gauge what I think about Nate, and to be honest, it feels like I know him already.

It must be so strange for Renn to see his worlds colliding almost literally.

"Should we go inside and . . . talk?" I ask, not exactly sure what to do next. This is obviously a first for all of us, and so much has happened in the last day that it is starting to feel overwhelming. We clearly don't know exactly how this will all play out, having never been in a situation like this before.

"Yes," Renn says with an added light in his face as he looks back and forth from Nate to me. We wander back into the house with Shy in tow. "I'll get a fire going," Renn says, hanging his jacket near the door. Nate flops onto the couch.

"So, Maven. You probably don't like me very much right now," he says. I fold my arms in front of me.

"Why do you say that? Because you're taking Renn with you back to Earth?"

His eyes go wide for a moment. "Wow, Renn really did tell you everything then."

"He did," I confirm.

"And you don't care that he's from an entirely different planet?" Renn gives Nate a look that reads *watch it*, but I don't mind. I know Tasha would be doing the same thing if she didn't know the guy I was claiming to be in love with. Especially if he were from a different planet. It feels weird even thinking that, let alone hearing it out loud.

"No. Not at all." He cocks an eyebrow at me, and I can't help but laugh. "Sorry. You just remind me a lot of my friend, Tasha," I say. Renn comes to stand next to me now that the fire is going.

"Nate and Tasha actually have a lot in common. Both talk us into doing things we don't want to. It's kind of annoying, actually," Renn says, then smirks at Nate.

"If you're talking about the time we got lost in that asteroid field, that doesn't count—that was a dare."

Renn rolls his eyes. "He was always getting me into trouble, to say the least."

Nate grabs a pillow to chuck at him. Just then, Renn's phone starts buzzing. He gives me a look, and I laugh lightly.

These damn phones are always interrupting everything, his eyes seem to say.

Renn kisses me quickly on the cheek before making his way over to the door. "It's the shop. This will just take me a minute. Be nice," he says, shrugging his coat on again.

"Which one of us are you talking to?" I ask.

"Both of you. I'll only be gone for a few minutes." Nate does a sort of a half salute, and I give him a reassuring smile as Shy follows him outside and he shuts the door softly behind him.

"I've never seen him like this before," Nate says.

"Yeah, I'm sure it's weird seeing him living such a different way of life." Nate chuckles softly to himself.

"What?" I ask, confused.

"That's not what I meant," he says, smiling. I move to sit next to him on the couch and wait for him to go on. "I mean I've never seen Renn in love."

His words surprise me. I shake my head. "I'm sure that's not true," I say with a sad smile.

"I've known him for a long time, and I may not have seen him for six years, but I've never heard him talk about anyone like this, or act like this around anyone ever. You mean a great deal to him." His voice is kind as he holds my gaze.

"I don't want him to go," I suddenly say, my voice quieter than I mean it to be.

Nate gives me a sad smile. "I know."

"Will he come back?" I ask.

"Nothing is ever a guarantee in space." Nate scans my face like he's trying to decide if I can handle the truth, and he must decide I can because then he says, "And the association might need him to stick around for a while, but it's hard to say. What I do know for sure is that Renn is a loyal man, and once he finishes his duty, he will keep his promise to you."

I don't realize I'm crying until I feel a tear slide down my cheek. I spy a flicker of remorse in Nate's big brown eyes, but then he takes my hand and squeezes it softly.

"I'm trying to be strong for him, but . . ." I say, but can't finish the sentence.

"I'm sorry about everything you've been through. I can understand, to an extent, based on what Renn told me about what happened with Locke. It was brave of you to stay by his side. You are braver than you realize, especially now that you know everything. Renn is lucky to have found you," he says.

I smile at him because his genuineness warms my heart. "I'm sorry about your friends. I can't imagine what that must have been like," I say.

"Thank you, Maven. It was . . . the worst day of my life." He pauses for a moment, clearing his throat. "But I would do it again if given the choice. Renn is still my captain, afterall, but most importantly, he's my best friend."

This time, I squeeze his hand as I say, "I'm glad he has you, and that you'll be with him for whatever comes next."

"I'll take care of him. I promise," he says as he places a hand on top of mine. "Trust me when I say I wish we didn't have to do this, but it's vital, for many reasons."

I nod, feeling the emotion build in my chest. "I know, and I want him to finally have closure. I hope this will help him."

Nate just smiles back at me for a moment. "I can see why he loves you."

I smile, brushing away another tear just as Renn comes through the door with Shy, who runs toward Nate immediately—jumping onto his lap.

"First Maven, now Nate? I really am at the bottom of your list now, aren't I?" Renn says as he dramatically clenches his heart. Then he takes in our faces. "What were you guys talking about?"

Nate and I give each other a knowing look.

"Not much," I say, standing to wrap my arms around Renn's waist, allowing him to tug me in to plant a kiss on my head.

"I don't know about you two, but I'm starving." Renn pulls me with him over to the kitchen. "How about a nice meal, courtesy of Valery's wonderful cooking?" he says, pulling out a container from the fridge that seems to be a stew or soup.

"This should be interesting," Nate says, a bit skeptical.

"It will be delicious. I promise."

After a couple of hours of savoring the delicious soup, which Nate seemed to thoroughly enjoy, and a handful of stories of Nate and Renn's escapades, the afternoon fades away. Renn starts gathering the dishes, and I follow his lead, giving us some space to talk alone in the kitchen.

"I really like Nate," I say, handing him a bowl. He sets it down in the sink then pulls me into him.

"Oh, yeah?" he says, clearly pleased.

"Yeah." He turns to face me. "So speaking of Nate." His eyebrow arches. "Where is he sleeping tonight?" I ask with a whisper.

Renn gives me a wicked smile, and I blush. "That's a good question. Any suggestions?"

He places a hand on the counter next to me, leaning in. I look over my shoulder, and find Nate sitting on the couch with Shy. She seems to be distracting him enough so that he's unaware of the promiscuous position I'm in, because I can think of a handful of things I could do with Renn right now, especially when he's looking at me like this. I swallow heavily.

"I was thinking you and I could stay here, and Nate could stay at my place." He gives me a curious look. "I want to stay here because . . . you're everywhere here, and since you're leaving . . ." I look down. "I just want as much of you as I can get. In any way I can have you. If that makes sense."

He lifts my chin and scans my face, his eyes lingering on my mouth for a second or two longer. "Whatever you want, Mave." Then he leans down as he whispers in my ear, his lips grazing me softly. "But fair warning, I also have a few things in mind for what I want to do." He inhales before going on. "I don't want anyone to see, or hear, what I have in mind, except you and me." The heat in my core flows to every inch of my body.

Almost as if on cue, Nate yells over to us. "I get you guys need some alone time, but can you wait until I'm gone please." I blush, embarrassed, and Renn chuckles.

"Very subtle," he calls over to him, rolling his eyes. "Would you mind staying at Maven's tonight?" he asks as he walks over to the couch.

Nate stands and gives him a bemused look. "I'd sleep outside if it meant I didn't have to sleep on that ship for another night."

Renn nods. "Great."

"Not wasting any time," Nate says, smirking.

"Shut up. But yes, get out, please," Renn says, and I bite my lip to keep from looking too pleased.

"Fine, but I'm taking the dog with me," he says as Shy walks over to sit by his side.

"Looks like her mind is already made up," Renn replies, glaring a little at Shy. He kneels and rubs her head, and his face goes a little sad, like it's just now hitting him that he's leaving her behind too. Just another reason to add to the long list of why this is killing me.

"Take care of Nate, okay? He's new here," he tells her before standing. "Give me a minute and I'll meet you outside." Renn adds to Nate.

"Sure. See you in the morning, Maven."

"See you tomorrow." I watch him and Shy walk out the door, and before I can say or do anything, Renn pulls me into a kiss that is nothing short of heat and passion, instantly turning me into a puddle.

"I'll be right back." He doesn't wait for my response. He jogs toward the door, and his urgency only makes the tingling sensation on my lips travel all the way to my toes. I busy myself by cleaning dishes in the sink and wiping the table down. Just as I finish, Renn returns.

"Everything okay?" I ask.

"Yeah, just had to give him directions to your cabin."

I nod in response.

"So," he says, making his way over to me.

"I hate this," I say, my throat going tight, but I swallow it down.

"Me too," he says, stopping until he's just a few inches away from me. We stare at each other for a few moments, and then I can't wait any longer.

I reach up to whisper into his ear. "Renn. Don't hold anything back."

And so he doesn't.

Renn kisses me hard before sliding his tongue into my mouth. He pulls me up against him, our mouths never leaving each other as he picks me up swiftly, setting me down on top of the counter to pick up where we left off earlier that day.

"Tell me what you need, Maven. Tell me what you want."

I want everything, but I don't know where to begin.

"I want you to do everything you've ever thought of doing. Please." The "please" causes him to smirk.

"It's a long list. I don't know if we'll have enough time." The dark edge to his voice only makes me want it more, even as he reminds me that we only have this one night.

I bite my lip before I respond, "Try."

He drags me to the edge of the counter, sliding my leggings off my hips, then slides a finger inside me, stroking me in a perfect rhythm. My only response is a whimper, and he slides another finger inside. I'm so wet already; his perfect fingers only make me more slick with want.

"Are you serious, Mave?" I love hearing the animalistic gravel to his voice. I only want to hear it more.

"Only for you." I pant. "I've never done this for anyone besides you." It is the truth, my body has never responded this way to anyone else's touch. "If we only have tonight . . . I want to give you everything," I say as he works me and I grasp onto his shoulders, nails digging in his skin.

He quickly sends me over the edge completely, and I scream his name, throwing my head back as his rhythm slows, calming my nerves of pleasure. Before I can catch my breath, he picks me up, and I straddle him from the front as he places his hands on the back of my thighs and carries me to the loft. I bury my face in his neck, inhaling the sweet scent of his skin, a perfect blend of the auto shop and the forest, until he places me on top of the bed.

"That's one thing off the list," he says with a grin, pulling off his shirt, and I follow suit.

Then suddenly, what was a frenzy moments ago, turns into something more intimate and broken. It's the most invigorating and calamitous feeling, knowing that I have this man in front of me right now. But the fact that he will soon be millions of miles away is too much to comprehend. There will never be enough time to get enough of him. It leaves me with the sense of uncontrollable yearning to try to say and do all the things I've dreamt about doing with him. But if we only have this night, I'm not going to waste it. He places a strand of my hair behind my ear as he looks down at me.

"How can something be so perfect and hurt so much at the same time?" he says like he can read my mind.

"I don't want to be sad," I say softly. "I want to enjoy every minute I get with you, it's just . . ."

He slides his finger under my chin, lifting it so I look at him. "I will take you any way. Happy, sad . . . as long as I'm with you, I don't care. We can do, or not do, whatever you want."

My heart feels like it might explode with everything I feel for him. I stand up on tippy toes and kiss him with everything I have to give, brushing my chest against his. He kisses me back, but not with the urgency from moments before. His lips move on me as if they are worshiping. It's the only word I can use to describe it, and I want to do the same for him.

"Lie back," I say, barely above a whisper against his mouth. Renn doesn't question or hesitate as he lies down on the bed in front of me. "Don't move," I command. He licks his bottom lip nervously, and my want for him ignites further. I'll never get used to the fact that I can do things like that to him.

I want to memorize each part of him. The angles of his jaw. The curve of muscles on his forearm. The freckles splaying across his broad shoulders. The way he smells and tastes.

He lifts a hand to touch me.

"Not yet," I say.

If I can't have Renn here with me, then he will be mine forever in my mind.

The tears come quickly, and as they fall, I hate and love each and every drop that runs down my face. I don't even bother to try to wipe them away.

Eventually, Renn can't hold himself back any longer and he kisses me, and as I kiss him back, I can taste the saltiness on his lips. It's satisfying, tasting myself on him. Like I'm truly a part of him now, and they don't stop.

They are tears of sorrow for the things lost.

Tears of joy for the love that we've found.

Tears of longing for what could have been.

Tears for the time we had together and time that will never be.

I let those tears become each and every piece of me that belongs to him. Which is everything.

Because Renn is a light. A fallen star.

And he is mine.

Forever.

CHAPTER THIRTY-SIX

Renn

The taste of Maven's tears are arousing and devastating all at once, and because they belong to her, I want to feel each and every one on my tongue, to savor them so when I'm no longer with her, I can remember. The way she tastes is one thing, but I want the sounds—how she moves and speaks—I want to remember everything.

"Do you mind if I get cleaned up?" she asks as we're both lying naked on the bed after she thoroughly spent me. I nod and take her by the hand, leading her to the bathroom. I turn the water on for her and move to leave, but she pulls me in with her. I don't question it, especially as her breath hitches watching me take a step inside. It makes that need in me come alive again, just knowing she doesn't want to leave my side, even if it's only for a few minutes. We are equally starved and eager to use every moment we have to our advantage. She dips her head back, letting the water run down her head until her hair is completely drenched. Then, carefully, she reaches for the soap and starts to lather it over her skin. I follow her by lathering my body as well, and once we are both clean, I turn to her and waste no time in getting her where I want her.

"Turn around."

She obeys, turning herself so her back faces me. The water skates down her body, little streams mapping her every perfect curve. I bite her neck lightly, and she lays her head on my shoulder.

"Put your hands on the glass," I say.

She does, and I kiss my way down the length of her spine. When I reach the base, I notice for the first time the scars painted against her skin there. They are so small compared to the trauma that encompassed them—the story of her journey of loss and pain. But the scars are part of what makes her the strong, beautiful woman I fell in love with. She's beautiful regardless, but the scars make her even more breathtaking. For a moment, I'm lost in the sight of her, mesmerized by every plane of skin and muscle on her body. I lightly touch her scars the same way she touched mine, with reverence, and she inhales sharply.

She removes a hand from the glass, but I purr in her ear, "Keep. Your. Hands. On. The. Glass. It's my turn."

I feel her take a shaky breath. I could do a lot of things with her in this position, but right now, this is more than sex. Instead, I grab some shampoo and start to gently rub it into her scalp. She hums in pleasure as I rake my fingers over and over through her dark strands. After a few minutes, I pull her away from the glass so she can stand under the water again. She tilts her head back, and I can't control myself. I grab her by the waist, pulling her against me, and kiss the column of her throat. She shivers at my touch and then reaches up to kiss me while the water rains down on us. We stay there a long while as our slick, wet bodies press up against each other.

Eventually, Maven pulls her lips from mine. "I think we're running out of hot water."

I was too busy to notice, but now that she points it out, it's much too cold to stay here. I step out and hand her a towel.

"I'm freezing." Maven's teeth chatter as we exist the bathroom.

I suddenly get a wild idea that I hope she will like. "Wait here."

I grab every blanket, sheet, and pillow I own and drag them down to the fireplace. Then I turn out the lights. She watches me intently with only a towel wrapped around my waist, enjoying every minute of it. She has a glow about her that makes her goddess-like with the fire now the only source of light in the room.

"This is perfect," she says, stepping closer and waiting for me to finish setting up the comfortable pile of blankets and pillows.

"All set," I say once I deem it ready, and she drops the towel and hurriedly covers herself under the blankets. I join her and pull her against me, the scent of her wet hair engulfing me.

"I love this." She turns over onto her back, pulling up the blanket, just covering the top of her breasts. I reach to trace the outlines of her face with my thumb. "So, what else did you have in mind for me tonight, Aldrenn?"

Aldrenn. My name on her lips causes me to stop abruptly, her look of salacious blue blazing through me. "Say that again," I say, my voice low.

Maven smiles wide. "You like hearing your full name?"

"Only from your lips," I say.

She blushes in response, biting her lip before she asks, "What about Captain?"

God, the things this woman does to me.

"Did I say that right?" she asks.

I can't even respond. Instead, I let out a sound that is nothing short of a growl, and she laughs loudly, throwing her head back. I graze my mouth up and down her neck, her throat vibrating as her laugh moves through her. I hold her like that for just a second longer, then she moves so she is on top of me. She pulls back, and her eyes scan my chest while I admire her body, especially her breasts coated in firelight. She's perfect. She slowly lowers herself to me, and I watch as her breasts sway, big and heavy as they skate over my stomach then my chest until they rest against me. I feel like I can't breathe at the pure perfection of it all. Her hair falls over me, shielding my face from the firelight. If there's a heaven, then this is it. I want this forever, right here.

"The night is almost over. We only have this." Her voice is so full of sadness, it nearly breaks me.

"No. No we don't." I kiss her like it's a promise, and that's all I can give her—mark her and ravage her so that she will remember this night forever.

When we are through, I lay her softy on her back and then lie beside her, our hands intertwined as we lie there, listening to our breathing calm until the only sound is the crackling of the fire. We stay like this for several minutes, and for a moment, I think she's fallen asleep.

"Maybe you should stay," she suddenly says. She turns to face me on her side, recognizing the confusion on my face. "Maybe you should stay on Earth."

My heart aches that the thought crossed her mind. I take her face in my hands. "No. That isn't my life anymore."

She scans my face. "It just . . . It sounds like you were born to be a captain, Renn—to lead people. This life seems so below you."

The words ache in my chest. "No. That's not even close to the truth, Mave. Even back then, I think I always knew that this was where I truly belonged. I think I was searching for this place before I even knew it. I will make things right, and then I'm coming back to you. I promise."

She runs her fingers up and down my forearm, then intertwines them with mine, a pained expression furrowing her brow. "You don't know how long it could be, do you?" I'm torn on what to say and do, and when I can't answer, she whispers softly, "Weeks? Months? Please just tell me."

I tuck a strand of her hair behind her ear. "It will be at least a year of travel alone. Six months to get to Earth then six months back. I don't know how long it will take to get things settled once we get there."

She doesn't say anything as I watch her accept the fact that it could be much longer than she initially thought.

"Does that change things for you?"

Her hand tightens around mine. "No, Renn. Never." I watch her azure eyes glaze a bit before she speaks again. "I don't want to think about these things, but what if you can't come back? Nate said it was the plan, but it doesn't mean something else won't happen."

The words stab me over and over, because it is the truth, I just didn't think I would have to say it. I should have known better than to skate over the facts with her.

"Listen to me. If there is one thing I know for sure, it's that, that day—as horrible as it was—brought me here to you, and I'm not letting that slip away, Maven. Even if I die trying, there is nothing that would make me change my mind. I belong here, with you." I take her hand and place it over my heart, then place my hand over hers, feeling the thrumming of her heart in my palm.

"I love you," she whispers. I pause, taking a breath. She still seems to make me nervous, even now.

"Mave, when I look at you I'm home." Her breath is unsteady. "I'm coming back." I say, and her blue eyes glisten as she smiles.

I pull her into me, and she falls asleep not long after. I rest my head against hers as I watch her breathe in and out, her beauty only showcased more in the glow of firelight. The heaviness of sleep never comes for me, but as I hold her against me, watching the night slowly fade, I can't hold the tears in any longer. They fall, one by one, sliding down into her hair. And I know I will never feel completely broken and whole all at the same time ever again.

CHAPTER THIRTY-SEVEN

Maven

A deep layer of snow greets us when we wake the next morning. The first snowfall of the season has finally arrived. It's ironic that it chose today to appear because of what this day means. The next chapter of our story—the blank, unwritten page of unknowns. It frightens me that the words are yet to be written. Will they tell the story of us spending the rest of our lives apart? Or that this is the last time I will ever see him? Instead of adding more chapters, will it simply be the end? Like it never happened? I keep squeezing his hand as tight as I can in these final moments as we trek through the snow to where the ship awaits.

Earlier that morning as he was packing, Renn very sweetly asked me to watch over Shy and his cabin. I had already planned to stay at Renn's for however long he was away, so when I said I would, he said, "Good. Because it's your home too."

We hike through the bright landscape for a long while. I expect my knee to flare up again, but it never does. An old habit I guess. A wide open field of blinding white comes into view, and nestled near the edge of the treeline is the ship. I'm surprised to find that it looks like a great bird with its wings tucked in, made up of a sleek, metal surface of black and dark gray.

"I'll get her ready for departure," Nate says, looking over at us.

"I guess this is goodbye," I say to him.

Nate walks toward me and wraps me in a tight hug. "Goodbye, Maven. I'm so glad I got to meet you."

I turn my head to whisper into his ear. "Take care of him." I feel him nod, and I let go, stepping back beside Renn. "Goodbye, Nate."

He smiles at me one last time and then turns to Renn. "We should be ready in a few minutes."

Renn gives him a single nod, and we watch him enter the ship through the ramp that appeared under one of the wings. The second Nate is out of sight, Renn takes my face in his hands, and they feel like icicles. I don't care—my face is already freezing—but the second his lips meet mine, I feel instantly warm. We hold nothing back as our kiss becomes feverish and consuming with every stroke of his tongue against mine. I kiss him harder, trying to put everything I feel for him into this last kiss, because I could never say enough words or formulate the right goodbye to make it feel like the right thing, to make it feel like enough.

The only thing I know without a doubt is that this man loves me. This incredible specimen of a person. He has loved me at my worst times and he sees me for who I am, and he still loves me, even the darkest parts of me. And I love the darkest parts of him just as strongly. We both have been broken, but somehow, our broken pieces fill each other, making us whole, together. We found each other, and for the first time in my life, I'm grateful for all the bad that brought me such good.

He pulls away slightly, keeping his hands on me. "Do you want to know the moment I fell in love with you?"

My lips tremble, our breath fogging around us. It's almost painful to look at him because he's too perfect. His green eyes shimmer with love, and the stubble on his jaw is the perfect length, just long enough that I feel it when it grazes against me, but it's still soft. His perfect lips are so close to mine as he speaks.

"The moment you made it to the lookout on the retreat."

I hold back a sob, looking down because it's all too much.

He lifts my face to look back at him, stroking my cheek with his thumb. "I had never seen anything so beautiful. It was right then and there that I knew I loved you."

I'm going to die. It's too much. He's making it so much harder, but I don't want him to stop. If this is dying, then so be it.

"You were mesmerizing. So strong and brave. I wanted you so badly, and I can't believe that you chose to love me back."

I start to cry, unable to speak.

"Keep this," he says, unzipping his coat to remove the necklace from around his neck, placing it over my head. I take the pendant in my hand, rubbing my thumb over the sun, moon, and star embossed into the metal. "Don't forget how far you've come. Keep going." I look up to him. "I'll catch up to you soon," he says with a wink.

I place my hand over the pendant now lying against my chest—lying against my heart. "I love you, Renn," I say, and he inhales deeply.

"You are my sun, and even if I'm millions of miles away, my mind will always be centered around you." His breath is unsteady. "I love you . . . more than anything."

And I know that this is it, this is the last time I will hear his voice until he returns—*if* he returns. I pray he will. I wrap my arms around him, holding on to him as tightly as I can, and he squeezes me back just as hard. Clinging to each other like it's our last breath. I feel him inhale in my scent, and I do the same, letting it engulf me wholly—the freshness of rain and dark woodiness of the forest. Then he pulls away and takes my face in his hands as his eyes roam over every feature.

He starts to cry, tears trickling down his face, and I can't bear to look at him like this. I reach up to him just as he leans down for one last kiss. The tears on his cheeks mix with mine. He kisses me softly as I fade into him, and just when it feels like it's too much, he rips himself away, quickly turns, and doesn't look back, not once.

I let my arms fall slowly to my sides, watching him until he disappears inside the ship. The ship starts to hum, and I spot Nate in the window where he motions for me to stand back. I move until I'm several yards away, and then, gracefully, the ship rises from the ground, hovering for a moment. Then the great, birdlike wings start to unfold before it almost floats upwards. I watch as it reaches higher and higher, then, as if it is perfectly planned, the first rays of the sun erupt over the peaks, making it impossible to see anything as I look upwards. I try to shield my eyes, but once I am able to focus enough to search the sky, the ship is nowhere to be seen.

I close my eyes for a moment, the light reflecting off the snow making it unbearably bright and blinding. When I finally open my eyes again, there's nothing besides the sound of my own breathing. The snow always makes everything so quiet and calm, I almost scream just to break the silence, but instead, I look up to the sky one last time and tell myself that whatever happens, I know he wants to come back.

If that's all I'm left with, it was worth it all, just knowing that, in the end, he was mine and I was his—completely.

CHAPTER THIRTY-EIGHT

Maven

"*Maven. You're still sleeping as I record this, and I know my time is limited. Last night, before Nate left to stay at your place, he gave me a photon drive containing all my captain's logs from the year I was on the Seraphim.*

"*These logs were mandatory for me to record, as it is for all captains in the SEA. They were required, not only to have records of our missions for histori-an documentation, but to hold us accountable for our actions as captains. Most importantly they are an outlet for self-reflection, stress management, and, as the association likes to word it, 'a personal legacy' for generations to come. If you put on the translator that I left behind for you, you will be able to watch and understand my words.*

"*Since I can't be with you on Aetherium, I hope these logs help you to know that even if I'm on the other side of the galaxy, I'm still here with you. These should help you get to know the man I was, and who I became.*

"I want to keep my promise to tell you everything, so in the meantime, I hope these will suffice until I come back to you.

"Just know that, wherever I am, I am always thinking of you. I love you. Always."

When I walked into Renn's bedroom after returning home, I saw the phone-shaped device lying on top of his bed, and thought he left something behind. But when I saw the note on top, I knew it was something else entirely.

"Maven, tap the screen three times," it read, and I didn't question following his written instructions. When his face appeared on the screen, it took everything in me not to burst into tears again, but when he started to speak, it broke me. I watched it over and over again.

After several minutes of tapping and navigating, I feel like I have a handle on how it works. I discover many files, each with a date and time listed in chronological order, and all I have to do is tap on whatever day I want to watch and it will appear on the screen.

I find the translator sitting on the nightstand and place it behind my ear. I start with day one, and when Renn's face comes up on the screen, I smile at how young he looks. He still looks young now, but this was years ago. I can see the excitement in his beautiful green eyes as he starts to explain that the crew has successfully begun their three-year mission. His hair is shorter, and his face is clean shaven. It takes me a moment to adjust to the translator, but it actually works. I can understand everything he says perfectly. A couple of times, I have to pause and go back a few seconds, but I'm getting the hang of it.

"We've been preparing for this mission for months, and now that it's actually happening, I couldn't be more honored to be captain of this fine crew. I know we will do great things out in uncharted space. For many of the crew, this will be their first mission in deep space, and I can sense the elation throughout the ship. I share in their enthusiasm, but I know I must discipline myself and remind them that we all have sworn an oath, and that we must carry out our duties day in and out for this mission to be successful.

"Based on our calculations, we should be arriving in uncharted territory in a couple of weeks, and then from there, the true mission begins. It is my greatest hope that we will be successful in our quest into the unknown. Anton out."

I spent a couple of days hiding out at Renn's place, but I knew I would have to start explaining why Renn was no longer in Solitude Ridge. It took careful wording and delivery to explain where he had gone and why.

I landed on a simple, straightforward approach.

"Renn had an emergency with a distant relative far away."

Not everyone was totally convinced right away, especially Tasha. She asked me question after question. She kept her eye on me, lovingly, and was wary that something else was going on. And I couldn't blame her. It was odd, and there have been so many times I wanted to tell her the truth, but I worry she will officially confirm me as insane. So I decide to wait until Renn returns; we will figure out a way to tell her together.

"Has he called? Do you at least get to see him virtually?" she asked when I first told her Renn was gone.

"Of course I do," I said. It technically wasn't a lie. I still hear his voice and see his face every day. She just doesn't know the context. And I stuck to that story even as the weeks went by, and eventually, she let it go.

It doesn't take long to learn just how amazing Renn is as a captain. Not that I am surprised in the slightest. But hearing him explain his days on the Seraphim makes it seem much more real. He always speaks of members of the crew with respect and has a genuine care for their well-being. He takes his job seriously, but he knows when to have fun too.

I didn't know what to expect from the other logs, and wondered if they would all be straightforward and professional like the first message, but I find that there is a variety based on what happened that day or just Renn's mood in general. I can tell the days when he's more relaxed, and times when he's concerned about something. Sometimes, the log for the day is two minutes, sometimes an hour. And it's exciting, feeling like I'm really there with him on his journey. On the days when they go weeks without coming upon a new planet, Renn talks more about himself and his thoughts. I come to understand why that self-reflection aspect is important. Those logs are my favorite because I get to see him a little undone from his professionalism as captain. But no matter what's happening, they all begin the same way. He states the day of the mission, the date, and his name.

"Captain's Log. Day seventy-seven. Earth date two-five, year twenty-two sixty-four. Captain Aldrenn Anton.

"Today would have been my mother's fiftieth birthday. I can't help but wonder if she has somehow been beside me all my life, or if, because I'm closer to the heavens—so to speak—I feel closer to her in retrospect. Maybe it's just space travel playing with my mind, but I sometimes feel like she's near, guiding me somehow. I wonder if that happens for some of us on these missions. Because everything around us is celestial, we feel some kind of connection to it deep in our souls. Maybe our souls themselves are celestial and that's why we're pulled to explore and learn more about this galaxy."

Then there are some entries that actually make me laugh out loud.

"Captain's Log. Day two hundred and eight. Earth date three-two, year twenty-two sixty-four. Captain Aldrenn Anton.

"It's officially been sixty-two days since our last contact with an inhabitable planet. I can sense the cabin fever settling in more and more with the crew, but we are doing what we can to make life feel a little more grounded. Lieutenant Hayden suggested we start a three-on-three basketball tournament. We have the court in the exercise bay, but I worry with all the pent up energy, it may end in more fights than comradery, but he is adamant we try, so we will see what happens . . ."

"Captain's Log. Day two hundred and nine. Earth date three-three, year twenty-two sixty-four. Caption Aldrenn Anton.

"Lieutenant Hayden punched Lieutenant Locke in the face during the first game. So no more basketball."

I have no idea what basketball is, but obviously it's sports related. I'm glad to hear Nate's name whenever he's brought up and am not surprised at all that whenever Colin is mentioned, it's never a good thing.

There are countless experiences that I would consider near-death. Nate told me a few stories when he was here, but now, watching the logs, I see it was a pretty normal thing for them to experience. Renn, of course, always calmly explains the situation every time.

"A couple of officers were conducting routine inspections on the outside of the ship, and somehow, their tether disconnected. I assisted in the rescue."

"The ship came close to a solar flare that came upon us unexpectedly, but the Engineering team assured me that the Seraphim is unharmed and functioning properly."

I have a few favorites. One of them is a very short message, but it's one of a handful of videos where Renn is strictly Renn. Not at all Captain Aldrenn Anton.

"I was due for my mental health check-in, and after speaking with the ship's psychologist, Dr. Jacobs, she asked that I spend the next week doing three things for myself that are not related to my position as captain. She advised me that I need to remember to take care of myself first, and if I do that, I will be a better captain as a result. So here we go.

"Number one: I'm going to watch a favorite movie that I haven't watched in years.

"Number two: I made a request with the mechanics team to include me on their next project, whether it be repairs or just routine checks on equipment and vehicles. I miss those days at the academy when I was working more with my hands.

"Number three: Lieutenant Hayden and I are going to watch an actual live sporting event. What we are going to watch, I don't know, but we are going to make it happen."

The last log is the hardest to watch—his last message as captain before everything fell apart. Even amidst all the heartbreak and betrayal, Renn is stoic and brave as he records it, and my heart aches for him. I want so badly to reach out and kiss him, tell him everything will be okay.

All of his entries confirm all the things I already knew about him—like his loyal, good heart. His bravery. It's all been magnified by a hundred after hearing him talk through all his adventures. But I also learn so much, like his hope that he will someday see his family who have passed on again, or that he has an internal drive to constantly prove himself. But something I didn't expect to find was his unconscious desire to find somewhere to call home, to find that place where he could be grounded.

He has an adventurous spirit—you'd have to in order to want to travel into the unknown—but with Renn, it is like he was looking for something else out there in the galaxy. My mind flashes back to our last night together, when we lay beside each other in the firelight.

"Even back then, I think I always knew that this was where I truly belonged. I think I was searching for this place before I even knew it. I will make things right, and then I'm coming back to you. I promise."

It's all true. He was right.

All along, the universe was leading him home, leading him to me.

CHAPTER THIRTY-NINE

Maven

FOURTEEN MONTHS LATER

Bright pink hues paint the sky. It snowed again last night, leaving the ground under a new frost-covered blanket. It's mornings like these that make me miss him more than usual. What I wouldn't give to be standing here with him beside me. I worry about what his morning looks like wherever he is. Is it as beautiful as this one? Is he safe? Is he alive? These are the questions that run through my mind on a daily basis. I've learned to live with the memories of him and pray that they're not all he is now—someone who *was*. That bright light in my heart, never to be seen or felt again. I refuse to believe it. On those nights I've spent looking through my telescope, I often find myself wishing that the stars mapping across the galaxy could carry my voice to him to tell him I'm thinking of him.

But Renn isn't the only one I think of, especially on those perfect, stargazing evenings. I can feel my dad, and I wonder what he would think about all this.

I can almost picture my dad's reaction if I told him my boyfriend was an intergalactic space traveler. He would probably be more excited than anything, and maybe that is why it was easier for me to accept the truth of who Renn is. My dad had made me curious about the unknowns of the universe, instead of afraid. I think we both felt, somewhere inside us, that there was more out there; it just turned out to be more than we could have ever imagined.

Shy whines by the front door, waiting for me to finish up my cup of coffee.

"Alright. One minute and then we will go play fetch."

I rinse out the cup and place it into the sink before heading upstairs to put on warmer clothes. I pull off my oversized shirt, and Renn's necklace gets tangled in my hair. I twist it free from my long strands, then rub my thumb over it a few times before letting it fall against my skin where it has remained every day since Renn went away.

My phone starts to ring from where it's lying on the bed. I look to see a picture of Tasha and me light up the screen. It's a picture of us on the latest retreat. I went with Tasha again this year. At first, it was the last thing I wanted to do without Renn—there are too many memories of our love beginning in those woods—but then I thought of what Renn would have said if I told him I didn't want to go. *Keep going. I'll catch up to you soon.* I can hear his rugged voice so clear in my mind, the taste of him lingering on my mouth.

"Hey, Tash," I say, answering the phone.

"Hey. What are you up to today?" she asks in a bright, happy tone.

"Nothing much. What about you?"

"I thought it would be nice if you came with us to dinner tonight." Her voice sounds hopeful. I want to say no, especially with the fresh layer of snow that is no doubt also coating the roads, but I haven't seen her in a few days. Which is a long time for us. Even after all these months, I still haven't told her the truth about Renn. I hate keeping things from her, but it never felt like the right time to share with her that my Earth boyfriend was back on his home planet, and that he may or may not come back.

Shy barks loudly, making me jump. Clearly, her patience is up.

"You know what, Tash? That sounds great," I say enthusiastically.

"Great! Meet you at The Blue Bird at seven?"

"Perfect. See you then."

Ending the call, I rush downstairs to pull on my winter hiking boots. My phone pings with a message from my mom.

Mom: *Getting excited to see you in a couple of weeks for your birthday! And for you to officially meet Ethan.*

Ethan is my mom's boyfriend. Still feels weird to think about, but he is actually a really nice guy. He lost his wife in a similar circumstance and has a couple of kids. I'm happy for my mom, and to be honest, Ethan coming into her life helped a lot with my mom not asking too many questions about Renn. I told her, and everyone else for that matter, the same thing I told Tasha.

I text back quickly, although Shy grows more impatient as she jumps up, trying to lick my face.

Me: *Me too! Going into town tonight for dinner with Mina and Tash. I'll call you when I get home.*

Mom: *Sounds good. Love you!*

Me: *Love you too!*

I stuff my phone into my pocket. "Alright, alright. Let's go," I tell Shy. She practically breaks down the door before I can pull it open. No matter the weather, she always wants to play, and I amuse her by following her wherever she wants to go. She knows the woods just as well as I do. Better, probably.

We play our game of fetch, me throwing the ball for her so she can dig through the deep snow to find it—walking further into the woods as I keep throwing the ball through the trees, watching her prance through the snow, happily wagging her tail and coming up with white fluff on her face when she digs through snow banks. Again and again, she joyfully comes back. The snow absorbs all of the sounds except for Shy's panting and the sound of the snow packed underneath my boots. So when it suddenly goes deathly quiet, I pause. I wait a moment for Shy to come back, thinking it must be taking her a little bit longer to find the ball, but she doesn't come. The memory of the night Locke came for Renn comes to mind.

"Shy? Come, Shy!" Nothing but dead silence returns my call. "Come on, girl!" Just as I'm about to panic, I hear her barking somewhere up ahead. "Damn dog," I say under my breath. I run as best I can through the drifts as I follow her barking. Pretty soon, I come up on a bend of rocks and trees. Shy's barking seems to be coming from the other side, so I sprint over, and as I round the corner, the first thing I see is Shy's tail wagging wildly, but when I see why, I almost drop to my knees.

He's crouched down, petting Shy's ears and trying to stay upright as her excitement almost pushes him to the ground. My body is frozen in total shock, but then he looks up at me. When our eyes lock, I can't breathe or move.

He slowly stands.

He's wearing a black jacket and jeans. His hair is longer, but his face is clean-shaven. And then he smiles. I don't know who moves first, but all at once, we are running to each other. I don't get too far through the snow, but when we reach each other, I practically throw myself at him and he catches me, spinning me like the day I ran to him at the lookout. The sobs that escape me are uncontrollable, but then, suddenly I'm laughing, and a deep rich laugh erupts from him too. Shy barks happily next to us, jumping and begging for attention, but Renn keeps holding me, my arms still wrapped around his neck. I feel his chest as he breathes deeply in and out against me, and it finally convinces me that this isn't a dream, this is really happening. I finally loosen my grip, and he sets me back down onto the snow.

It's Renn. He's back.

I'm almost nervous to look up into green gray eyes, but when I see them, I can't keep myself from kissing him.

Our lips move effortlessly together, and when his fingers dig into my hair, I can't help the soft gasp that escapes my mouth, and I feel Renn smile against my lips. He breaks our kiss, but not before he bites my lip playfully. His breathing is shaky, and I think he trembles slightly as I smile up at him and place my hand on his jaw.

His eyes shine with tears, and then, finally, that deep voice, the one I've only been able to hear in the recordings or in my dreams, fills my ears as he speaks, barely above a whisper.

"I'm home."

THE END

ACKNOWLEDGMENTS

This book has been over ten years in the making—or at least the idea was born ten years ago—and now here it is as an actual book. Somehow, many late nights, a handful of emotional breakdowns and consuming copious amounts of chocolate and Dr. Pepper brought about Maven and Renn's story and it turned into so much more than I could have ever imagined.

I was very fortunate to have so many people supporting me in writing this book.

First and foremost I want to thank my husband, Austin. I started writing this book right just as we began an extensive home addition/remodel. It was probably the worst timing ever, but we did it! He was always there to support me on those hard days when I wanted to give up, and he would practically push me out the door to go to Barnes and Noble to write just so I could have a change of scenery and inspiration. Austin, thank you for being the best husband, father, and friend. Renn's goodness was inspired so much from who you are and I am so grateful I get to spend forever with you.

To my parents, there has never been a time in my life where I haven't felt your love and support. You always taught me to be non-judgmental and to be kind, while also teaching me to stand up for what I believe is right, even when it may not be the popular opinion. I love you so much and I would not be the woman I am today without you both.

To my grandma, thank you for distilling in me a love of books. I can see us as clear as day when you read Harry Potter to me. It's truly a shame not everyone gets a grandma like you.

To my brother, I love that we are as close as ever as adults and that we love so many of the same things. I've always felt an obligation to be a big sister you could look up to, so I hope I am.

To the rest of my family: Sadie, Juno, Vickie, Lacia, Chase, Quynton, Brayden, and my son, Maverick, I love you. Thank you for all your support and love, especially throughout this process.

To my editors Cait and Rachel: Cait, this book may have never happened without you. You gave me validation that I had a story to tell and that it was worth something. Thank you for taking a chance on me and your patience as I worked through the construction of this story. You are an inspiring woman and I can't thank you enough. Rachel, you reading and editing my book was one of the best experiences in this whole journey. I felt like we clicked from day one and your love for this story gave me life at a time when I was worried that all this hard work was for nothing. I love you.

To my beta readers, I can't thank you enough for taking the time to read my debut novel. Your reactions and suggestions took this book to the next level. I valued your input immensely.

Last but not least I want to thank YOU, the reader. Thank you, thank you, thank you. I hope you enjoyed Maven and Renn's journey of overcoming the darkness inside them by finding the light in each other. And most importantly, I hope you have come to know that no matter where you come from, no matter how unworthy you may feel, you deserve to be seen and loved. Forgive yourself and find the light.

ABOUT THE AUTHOR

Shandy Mandarino is an avid reader, Dr. Pepper addict, and mom. Shandy's dream of being an author started around the same time she fell in love with reading—when she was a child. She has a Bachelor's Degree from the University of Utah and was born and raised in Utah where she still lives with her husband and son. If she's not writing or reading you can find her spending time with family, playing games, or baking.